WHERE IS
WHAT IS ITS SECRET?
WHO HOLDS THE TRUTH?

"Careens at a breathless pace from dark crypts to exotic sunlit shores. Full of historical mystery, rife with intrigue and suspense...a tour de force."
—James Rollins,
New York Times bestselling
author of *Black Order*

continued . . .

"Rich with historical and archaeological detail, this well-constructed debut . . . celebrates the power of legend while delivering an engrossing mystery that skips nimbly between continents and cultures. . . . This intricate and absorbing thriller augurs well for Hartley's career."

—*Publishers Weekly*

"Absolutely spellbinding . . . Compulsively readable . . . the terrible beauty of ancient Greece collides with the merciless obsessions of the twentieth century."

—Eloisa James, *New York Times* bestselling author

"*The Mask of Atreus* is the perfect debut—a high-octane thriller crammed full of long-buried secrets, treacherous betrayals, jaw-dropping twists, and a healthy dash of romance. Deborah Miller is an engaging, sympathetic heroine, who you can't help but root for. Move over Michael Crichton—A. J. Hartley is right at your heels."

—J. A. Konrath, author of
Whiskey Sour and *Bloody Mary*

"Reminiscent of the best Dan Brown intrigues."

—*The Charlotte Observer*

"Intriguing. A labyrinth of history and mystery."

—Steve Berry,
New York Times bestselling author of
The Templar Legacy

"I find *The Mask of Atreus* engaging because it's a rare accomplishment: a genuinely thrilling thriller that's also intelligent and brilliantly written. They said it couldn't be done." —Phillip DePoy, author of The Fever Devilin Mysteries

"Terrific . . . A. J. Hartley provides a fabulous whodunit made fresh by its deep historical and archaeological base and an endearing heroine." —*Midwest Book Review*

ON THE
FIFTH DAY

A. J. Hartley

BERKLEY BOOKS, NEW YORK

THE BERKLEY PUBLISHING GROUP
Published by the Penguin Group
Penguin Group (USA) Inc.
375 Hudson Street, New York, New York 10014, USA
Penguin Group (Canada), 90 Eglinton Avenue East, Suite 700, Toronto, Ontario M4P 2Y3, Canada
(a division of Pearson Penguin Canada Inc.)
Penguin Books Ltd., 80 Strand, London WC2R 0RL, England
Penguin Group Ireland, 25 St. Stephen's Green, Dublin 2, Ireland (a division of Penguin Books Ltd.)
Penguin Group (Australia), 250 Camberwell Road, Camberwell, Victoria 3124, Australia
(a division of Pearson Australia Group Pty. Ltd.)
Penguin Books India Pvt. Ltd., 11 Community Centre, Panchsheel Park, New Delhi—110 017, India
Penguin Group (NZ), 67 Apollo Drive, Rosedale, North Shore 0745, Auckland, New Zealand
(a division of Pearson New Zealand Ltd.)
Penguin Books (South Africa) (Pty.) Ltd., 24 Sturdee Avenue, Rosebank, Johannesburg 2196,
South Africa

Penguin Books Ltd., Registered Offices: 80 Strand, London WC2R 0RL, England

Unless otherwise noted, all scripture references are taken from the King James Version of the Bible.

This is a work of fiction. Names, characters, places, and incidents either are the product of the author's imagination or are used fictitiously, and any resemblance to actual persons, living or dead, business establishments, events, or locales is entirely coincidental. The publisher does not have any control over and does not assume any responsibility for author or third-party websites or their content.

ON THE FIFTH DAY

A Berkley Book / published by arrangement with the author

PRINTING HISTORY
Berkley edition / July 2007

Copyright © 2007 by A. J. Hartley.
Cover and stepback art by axb group.
Cover design by Rita Frangie.
Interior text design by Stacy Irwin.

ISBN: 978-0-425-21628-6

BERKLEY®
Berkley Books are published by The Berkley Publishing Group,
a division of Penguin Group (USA) Inc.,
375 Hudson Street, New York, New York 10014.
BERKLEY® is a registered trademark of Penguin Group (USA) Inc.
The "B" design is a trademark belonging to Penguin Group (USA) Inc.

PRINTED IN THE UNITED STATES OF AMERICA

10 9 8 7 6 5 4 3 2 1

To Finie,
ever graceful and unbowed.

PROLOGUE: THE WRATH OF GOD

He would have to go back to the village soon. He had been swimming for almost an hour, and though it had been little more than languid floating about, he was getting tired. The moon was up, and while he had gotten used to the darkness of both sky and sea, he couldn't help an occasional shudder that could not be blamed on the warm oil-like water. The sea was extraordinarily calm, the waves unwinding onto the shore so softly that he barely heard them over the sound of his own breathing and the slow, rolling splash of his breaststroke. He would have to go back to the village, and tomorrow he would have to go home. Whatever he had sought in these tropical islands, he hadn't found it.

Except that that wasn't entirely true. He hadn't found what he had been looking for, but he had, perhaps, found something else in the silent tranquility of the sea these past three nights. He was going to have to abandon his search—his quest, he thought of it, always with mixed emotions—but his time on the island might make that a little easier, might stay the nagging, driving impetus to bring him back here, or drive him somewhere else.

But where else was there to go? If it wasn't here, maybe it wasn't anywhere.

It wasn't a thought he had permitted himself to consider before, and he smiled to himself, rolling onto his back and staring up at the stars, clustered in their millions in ways he had never been able to see in the States. Given time, he thought, he could probably count them . . .

He allowed himself to drift on the current, feeling the water chill beneath him as the beach shelved fast away, kicking suddenly, propelling himself out to the thin outcrop of rock that tapered into the sea like the tail of some great volcanic lizard. He remembered the hope—no, the conviction—he had felt surging through him when he first saw that jagged spit of stone: surely it would be here.

But there had been nothing, and his meager resources were long exhausted.

Normally the bay would be dotted by the lanterns of simple fishing boats, but tonight he was alone as he had been for the previous two evenings, made king of the sea by the locals' blend of commonsense science and a whiff of superstition. He could swim here for another week and have the horizon to himself. But what would be the point . . . ?

He felt the movement in the water beneath him like a sixth sense. For a second he thought something had touched him, but it hadn't been that. Something had glided past him. Something big.

His unease about the dark, the stories of sharks and stranger creatures heard in half-translated snatches from the villagers, all came rushing over him in a second. He righted himself, treading water vigorously, getting his bearings, figuring out which way would get him most quickly to land. He struck out for the rocks.

He had swum a few yards before the initial panic subsided. He could see nothing in the water around him, no sign of anything moving, no sign that there ever had been. He breathed, stilled himself, and laughed once into the blackness overhead. His imagination—always overactive, as his superiors were fond of pointing out—was playing tricks on him. He swung around and took two gentle strokes toward the beach, wondering vaguely how far out of his depth he was. He pointed his toes, held his breath, closed his eyes, and thrust himself down as far as he could go, his arms up over his head.

He hit something solid about two feet below him, but it wasn't rock, and it wasn't sand. It shifted when he made contact, but only slightly. It was big and hard and almost suspended motionless beneath him in the deep black water.

Shark?

No. Sharks swim. They move constantly. They have to or

they drown. This . . . whatever it was, was just hanging there in the water, as if it were chained to the bottom.

All his panic returned and he shot up from the water gasping for air as if he had been under for minutes. As soon as he broke the surface he started to swim, harder than ever, turning for the beach and the village beyond.

He struck out as far as he could reach, pushing the water with his hands and pulling back so hard that he lifted chest and shoulders out of the water with each surging stroke.

Maybe he should have made for the rocks. The beach was farther and there would be no hurried dragging himself up onto land: This way he would have to swim the whole way, then stagger with agonizing slowness through yards of waist-deep water . . .

So he swam, knowing he was already losing energy, that he couldn't possibly sustain this sprint for the shore, that if something was swimming there with him it would be faster than he could ever be. But as each second went by without teeth tearing at him from underneath, he took another breath and kicked forward once more.

The moon lit the beach a soft blue-white, distant and surreal now that the idyllic tropical scene had shifted into this curiously nightmarish register. It seemed impossibly far away, but whatever he had touched did not lunge, did not bite, did not appear to follow, and he kept going, flailing blindly now, all grace gone from his stroke. He had left his composure out there in the open water, and now there was only panic and the desperate will to live . . .

It felt like minutes but it could have been only seconds before his foot hit the sandy bottom. He tried to run, but the water was chest deep, and with something like despair he returned to swimming, almost crying out with the frustration of it all. Then his knee touched the seafloor and he straightened up, leaping forward with great lumbering strides, each time expecting something snapping at his heels. Then sand, the night air on his body, and he was out, staggering drunkenly up the pale beach, laughing at his escape, finally permitting the idea that there was really nothing out there at all, that he had imagined the whole thing. His brain teemed with possibilities: a fallen palm tree, the sunken hull of a small boat, a crippled marker buoy . . .

It was only then that he turned. He wasn't sure why but he didn't like the sense of the sea at his back.

It was quickly clear why.

For a second he just stared, unable to believe what he was seeing, and then, with a dull dread mixed with a strange exhilaration, he began to run toward the distant thatch of the village.

He had been right. All the time. He had been right.

He was shouting now, fear and excitement merged as he ran from the beach, calling to the firefly lights of the village.

Now he would be able to tell them. All of them. Now they would see and the world would change.

He was thinking this, still running in his rapturous terror, as he reached the first bamboo hut, and it was still there in his head as that hut, and every other hut in the village was suddenly sucked upward in a great white flash that lifted him and every sleeping soul high into the air and then scattered them with an unspeakable violence. The sound came a half second later, a vast cannon shot that shook the very air, turning into a low dragging roar.

When it finally subsided, when the waves lapping at the shore ceased to boil, when silence once more descended on the blackened beach and the once fertile land above it, the village and everyone in it had ceased to exist.

PART I

MY BROTHER'S KEEPER

Out of the depths I cry to you, O Lord,
Lord, hear my voice.
O let your ears be attentive to the voice of my pleading.
If you, O Lord, should mark our guilt,
Lord, who would survive? . . .
Because with the Lord there is mercy and fullness of redemption.

—Psalm 130:1–4,
The Liturgy of the Hours, Psalter (Grail)
version (London: Collins, 1963).

CHAPTER 1

Thomas Knight had his desk cleared out in five minutes. He had never kept much that was personal there anyway. He separated out his own books—a complete Shakespeare, an overly selective sampling of the Romantics, some Austen, Dickens, and the Stephen King and J. K. Rowling with which he lured the kids to reading—and tossed them in a sagging cardboard box which wouldn't close.

At least there was no one he had to break the news to, he thought. *Not now.*

For the same reason that there's now no job?

Not entirely, he answered himself. *That was a totally different set of screwups.*

Thomas grinned bleakly, got his arms under the box, and walked the interminable length of corridor that took him past the gym and the faculty lounge, eventually dumping him out in the parking lot and unemployment. He said his farewells to Frank Samuels, the impossibly ancient janitor who was smoking by the Dumpster, laughing loudly and shaking Samuels's hand with a tad too much vigor in case anyone was watching. Then he walked to his car through the snow, whistling tunelessly as if it were just another day, as if he hadn't a care in the world—both of which were true, he reminded himself, if not helpfully so. At least the media had gone.

On the way home he picked up a liter of cheap scotch in a plastic bottle at Toni's on Old Orchard and wished the clerk good night.

"Same to you, Mr. Knight," said the clerk, simulating the manner of someone who hadn't seen him for weeks, and might go longer before seeing him again.

Thomas picked up a pizza for dinner at Carmen's and drove home through the deepening twilight of Evanston's heavily wooded streets, his outrage sliding further into a familiar sense of stupidity and failure. He went running to get it all out of his head.

He ran badly—even when he had been in the best shape of his life—and he hated every step, lumbering along the treacherous sidewalks like a sloth on skates. Running bored him and always had, though he usually got the payoff of feeling vaguely virtuous. This time he couldn't shake the day, the memory of which lumbered after him like a lost wolfhound.

His firing had been coming for a long time. Peter, the high school principal (Thomas thought of him as a cartoon squirrel: Peter the Principal) had given him chance after chance, and he had blown each one like a man carefully dynamiting bridges behind him. Maybe Peter wasn't the only cartoon character in the scenario.

He wheezed his way home; showered; ate the pizza, which was by far the best part of the last twelve hours; and started on the whiskey. By eight o'clock he had drunk almost a quarter of it, a dangerous amount. He drank from good crystal, two rocks per glass, and he sipped rather than throwing it back, but did so steadily, with barely a pause between mouthfuls or, for that matter, between glasses. The glass had been part of a wedding present, he thought, considering it, like some appraiser on *Antiques Roadshow* speculating about some lost era.

At ten o'clock he stumbled into the bathroom, collected every pill he could find, and dumped them all into another whisky tumbler, which he set on the coffee table beside his leather armchair. The mundane—white and brown and red and yellow—were mixed with the exotic—translucent, iridescent caplets of neon blue and green. They were mainly ibuprofen and aspirin, but some were of more obscure purpose which he had long forgotten. Cold medicine? Laxatives?

"Oh, this is going to be fun," he said aloud.

For several minutes he just sat there and looked at the glass, musing: no wrestling with eternal verities, no despair, no angst-ridden consideration of what yet might be. The decision, he thought, would be driven by a whim, like choosing which coat to wear in uncertain weather.

That's not really good enough, is it? And besides, it's bound to look like a response to losing your job. Worse, it will look like a "gesture."

"God," he said, "not that. Anything but that."

He picked up the glass of pills and rattled it, putting it down slowly but with conviction. No cheap melodrama for him, not tonight anyway, even if he had no conceivable reason to get up in the morning.

At that he began to laugh quietly to himself. Then he set his teeth, splashed water on his face at the kitchen sink, and tipped the pills into the garbage disposal. Only after the machine's deafening crunch had turned into the familiar whine that said the contents had been ground to nothing and flushed away did he think that he would probably want some of them in the morning.

He stayed in the house all the next day reading distractedly from *Paradise Lost* because he found the rhythm of the lines familiar, even comforting. He had no time for Milton's God these days—or anyone else's for that matter—but rereading the poem took him back to his high school years, removed the sense of accumulated failure. The following day he watched a pair of bad movies on TV and went out to a steakhouse, returning home to drink because it was cheaper and less humiliating than sitting alone in a bar. And he ran, of course, punishing his body for the inadequacies of what Peter the Principal called his "character."

He was thirty-seven, though he felt older, a large, rangy man with untidy limbs and a ponderous way of moving. His ex-wife had called him by every animal name she could think of, sometimes affectionately, particularly those clumsy, undramatic zoo beasts that most people skipped to get to the big cats: bulls and camels, water buffalos and rhinos.

And mules, he thought. *Don't forget mules.*

Because it wasn't just about his body and how he used it. It was also his temperament. There was nothing mulish about his mind. Kumi had been fond of saying he was too clever for his own good, in fact. But he had a stubborn streak, a dull-edged defiance that could turn belligerent if sufficiently goaded, and, if he was going to be really honest about it, a distinctly mulish insensitivity where other people's priorities were concerned.

Not surprisingly, perhaps, he had lived by himself for the last six years, long enough to be almost used to it. In that six years he had woken up alone every single morning so that it had come to feel quite normal, and not because he had never had the opportunity to take someone to bed with him. All drunken melodrama aside, he told himself, he was comfortable alone.

Which is handy, because no one can put up with you for long . . .

Another of those bleak, self-deprecating smiles that were becoming his habitual expression.

The house was dark and cold and it occurred to him that he should start economizing as far as heating the place was concerned, so he stacked a couple of logs on the fire and poured himself another shot of the Cluny, which he warmed in his hands till the vapors made his nostrils tingle. His mind was still replaying the interview with which his career had ended.

"When you first came here," the principal had said, "we thought we'd hit the jackpot. The kids loved you. The parents loved you. The school board, hell, even the media loved you. Your students were acing tests and winning scholarships and starting their own reading and writing clubs. *Their own clubs!* It was amazing. You were always opinionated, but you were also principled, hardworking, and—frankly—the best teacher I'd ever seen."

Thomas nodded, smiling softly, remembering as if it had all happened to someone else. Of course, that was not how the conversation had concluded.

"But five years or so ago," Peter had continued, "it all started falling apart. All of it. Now . . . I don't know. It's not your damned causes or your bluster, Thomas. You complain about all these . . . these *issues,* but at bottom I'm not convinced you really care about any of them."

Thomas sat there as he had sat in front of the principal, still no nearer an answer. In the end he had said, "I don't know how to fix it. It's who I am, I guess. It's what I do."

To which Peter had replied with a finality that was the day's only real surprise:

"Not anymore, Thomas. Not here."

And so it had ended.

When the phone rang Thomas was barely conscious and his first response was to ignore it.

Probably Peter, calling to explain the pressure he was under, hoping that Thomas wouldn't hold it against him. Peter the Principal was not, after all, a bad guy.

No sir. Peter's an upstanding citizen, a prince among men.

Thomas moved to the phone slowly and stood for a second looking at it, thinking of nothing, feeling only a blankness and a dull exhaustion. He picked it up to stop its ringing and, he supposed, to bring about some kind of closure. If he left it to the machine he'd have to listen to Peter's earnest apologies here in the dark and then again when he inevitably called back and Thomas could dodge him no longer.

"Yes," he said.

"Could I speak to Thomas Knight, please?"

It was a man, but not Peter, and the voice was oddly formal. The press?

"You could," he said, "but he's currently engaged with a bottle of whisky. I'm surprised he's still newsworthy. I mean, it's been a good ten minutes since he was fired." A Hamletic exaggeration, he thought, dignifying what was obviously a pretty sophomoric jibe. "Or is this the human interest follow-up?"

There was a fractional pause. The voice when it returned was careful, even grave.

"I'm sorry? I'm looking for Thomas Knight, brother to Father Edward Knight."

And then the room began to spin a little, his elder brother's name jarring him with its unfamiliarity.

"Speaking," he said again, needlessly adding, "this is Ed Knight's brother."

"My name is Father Frank Harmon. I'm the provincial superior for the Society of Jesus here in Chicago."

Thomas nodded and then forced himself to say, "Yeah?" There was a hint of something sardonic, an old bitterness that he couldn't quite suppress when dealing with officials of the Catholic church, a bitterness that surfaced even through the dread he felt gathering like fog.

"I'm afraid I have some bad news for you," said the voice.

CHAPTER 2

The taxi seats were hard and cold, but his ancient Volvo, after two days of sitting idle in the snow, had refused to show any sign of life. Watching from the backseat as Oak Park's grid-plan streets unfolded around him, the driver beyond the Perspex screen making Hindi chitchat into his radio, it felt to Thomas a little like he had been arrested. There were still a couple of inches of snow on the ground, but the potholed roads and driveways were clear so that the overall impression was one of a job only half done. The single-family homes spread on, their little differences somehow reinforcing their uniformity. The rectory, if that was the word, was different in form, but not in kind.

It was attached to a dilapidated brick church, smaller than Thomas remembered and badly in need of maintenance; the roof was patched, the walls stained and crumbling, the blue gloss trim peeling and rotten. ST. ANTHONY'S PARISH CHURCH said the sign, its gilt lettering cracking. Thomas would bet good money that the place was only a quarter full on Sundays and a good deal less than that the rest of the week. It was a church like the one he had grown up attending, a building that was somehow fading, part of a bygone world. Not old enough to be quaint, not grand enough to inspire awe, a building constructed on the expectation of plenty, now obscure, its foothold in relevance slipping further by the day . . .

Give it a rest.

Thomas shrugged the mood off, set down the empty suitcase he had brought to collect Ed's things, and pushed the doorbell. It rang, a thin, monotonous jangle in the distance. Then nothing but the cold wind. Thomas hugged his jacket to himself ruefully. He considered the discolored white Honda on the drive. It was old enough to still have those square angles, and the body work was half eaten away by the Chicago cold and—probably worse—the salt they put on the road.

The door opened and a man appeared, one hand clutching a half-eaten sandwich. He was perhaps fifty, thin, balding and chewing. He gestured with the sandwich and stepped aside, allowing Thomas in. As the door banged shut behind them, the biting wind abated, but the hallway was not significantly warmer. It was also dark and smelled of damp and mildew.

"Cup of tea?" said the man, through his sandwich, walking quickly along the corridor.

"Er . . . sure," said Thomas. He entered the thin man's slipstream and hurried after him, catching the thick tang of peanut butter in his wake.

"Cold one today, huh?" said the man as they emerged in a stark and faded kitchen.

"It'll get worse before it gets better," said Thomas.

"I'll give you something for now and see if I can call a shelter," said the other, rooting through an uneven stack of papers. The room seemed to double as kitchen and office, both inadequate. "But they get pretty short on beds this time of year," he said, not looking up.

"I'm sorry," said Thomas, "my name is Thomas Knight."

"Jim," said the other, looking up and giving him a nod. He sounded Irish or maybe Scottish. He continued to thumb through the papers, scattering the ones he decided were of no use, his eyes tightly focused.

"Ed Knight was my brother," said Thomas.

It took perhaps half a second, and then the man who had called himself Jim froze midshuffle, straightened slowly, and gave a long, vocalized sigh, part realization, part self-deprecation.

"Right," he said. "Sorry. I thought . . ."

"You thought I was homeless," said Thomas, finding—to his surprise—that he was smiling.

"It's the suitcase," said Jim, nodding to Thomas's battered luggage. "And the force of habit."

"It's no problem," said Thomas, thinking that in other circumstances, he might have taken the other man for homeless too. "Better icebreaker than most. And you are . . . ?"

"Jim," said Jim. "Sorry, I thought I said."

"You did," said Thomas. "I mean, you're the housekeeper or the gardener or . . . ?"

"Have you *seen* the garden? There's no bloody gardener here, I'll tell you that. No. I'm the parish priest. Father Jim Gornall. Pleased to meet you. Your brother was sent by the Js to help out here. He was a good man."

A good man. He didn't emphasize *good,* as if he were making a statement on Ed's piety or moral standing. He said it as a soldier would of a fallen comrade.

Thomas hesitated a fraction too long, processing the idea that this disheveled and ungainly Irishman was a priest, and Jim shrugged without embarrassment or indignation. He didn't care, and Thomas immediately warmed to him.

"You still want tea?" said Jim.

"That would be great."

"More force of habit," said the Irishman. "When in need of warmth, welcome, or consolation, tea is generally the first line of attack."

"Unless you can get to the whisky first."

"Exactly," said the priest with a sudden grin that lit his

whole face. "The obligatory Catholic vice. You fancy a small one?"

"Bit early for me," said Thomas, adding almost apologetically as the lie struck him and registered, "not today."

"Fair enough," said the priest. "Then tea it is."

They drank from heavy mugs, chipped but clean, on either side of an inadequate electric heater that was turned to its lowest setting.

"Completely bloody useless," said the priest, "but if I turn it up any higher it blows every light in the building."

Thomas grinned.

"So what's a genuine Irish priest doing in Chicago?"

"Priest shortage," said the priest. "I fancied coming to America, so I applied to seminary here rather than at home. That was a long time ago. I think of myself as a kind of missionary," he said, grinning again.

"Don't you think America has enough religion?" said Thomas, his gaze level.

"That's why they need a missionary," said Jim.

"I don't think I follow," said Thomas.

"Forget it," said the other, shrugging it off. "Private joke. You look familiar. Have we met before?"

"I don't think so. People say I look like Ed."

"Maybe that's it. So when do you want to start going through Ed's stuff?" said the priest. "It won't take long. There isn't much."

"What about . . . wherever he died?" said Thomas. "They didn't tell me. They said he was overseas, but they didn't say where." He paused, and the silence seemed long and loaded. "I suppose I should have asked," he added lamely.

The priest made a face.

"He wouldn't have had much with him," he said. "Nothing beyond a suitcase or two. His worldly goods, such as they are, are here, and whatever you don't claim will go to the order."

"So what was he doing?" said Thomas. "He wasn't a missionary, right?"

"No," said Jim. "Unlike me. He had been based here for a few months. I'm a diocesan priest. He was a Jesuit—a member of the Society of Jesus. He was sort of on loan to me here for a while, helping me out. When things calmed down, he went on retreat. I expected him back for a little while, but he would probably have been moved again by the end of the year. There was talk of him teaching at Loyola."

Thomas nodded, but there was something in the priest's manner he found careful, even evasive despite his breezy manner. He was intellectually agile, somehow, this priest, and if his scattered and disheveled appearance wasn't actually an act, it was certainly misleading.

"So. Ed's stuff," said Thomas. "I just take what I want and toss the rest away?" It seemed wrong, disrespectful.

"You're not so much an inheritor as an executor, as I understand it," said the priest. "The Js take a vow of poverty, so he doesn't really own property as you or I do. They are going to send a lawyer round to help out. Technically everything belongs to the order, though I'm sure they will respect your wishes if there are personal things you want to keep."

"I shouldn't think there will be," said Thomas, more brusque than he had meant to be. The priest nodded and Thomas looked away. He didn't want to get into a conversation about why he had so utterly lost touch with his only brother.

"Then it will be a short visit," said the priest, sipping his tea and watching Thomas over the rim of his mug. "But you can stay the night, if you like."

"That won't be necessary," said Thomas. "I live locally."

"What's 'necessary'?" Jim shrugged. "I could use the company."

Thomas thought quickly. It was not as if he had anything to rush home to, and odd though it seemed, there was suddenly something appealing about being in his brother's space, in what had been his life, if only for a moment.

"Okay," he said. "Thanks."

"You can take Ed's room," said the priest. "Top of the stairs on the left. Illinois game tonight. You a basketball fan?"

"Not really."

"Perfect," said Jim. "Me neither. We can get a pizza, a couple of beers and watch freakishly tall people running around for no good reason."

The sheer ordinariness of the generosity took Thomas off guard, so it was a moment before his pleasure and gratitude could make its way into his face and voice.

"That would be great," he said. "Can I go on up?"

"Sure. I'll leave you to it, if you don't mind," said the priest. "I have a spiritual direction meeting."

Thomas laughed. "Sounds like something I could use," he said as he made for the stairs, avoiding the priest's gaze.

CHAPTER 3

Ed's was a sad little room. The minimal furniture was cheap, old, and stained with years of use. Apart from a meager selection of clothes there were only books, papers, an overstuffed manila folder bound with rubber bands, an ancient transistor radio, and a couple of shoeboxes of oddments, all stacked haphazardly on a set of shelves made of planks and cinder blocks. The place looked less like the home of a priest than it did a dorm room that had been hurriedly vacated. A crucifix hung on the wall, but the place was otherwise unadorned except for an Amnesty International calendar. As Jim had said, there was nothing here, certainly nothing of value. Thomas's trip—save the pizza and basketball part—was likely to be done within the hour. If he'd known, he wouldn't have bothered coming. Now he had to kill time before the lawyer arrived with the paperwork.

He sat on the bed. The mattress was thin and uneven, the springs pressing insistently through.

God, what a place.

It felt empty, joyless: not unlike his own house, Thomas thought wryly. This was what Ed had chosen, what he had dedicated himself to, sacrificing God-alone-knew-what for this blank little cell with its cheap crucifix for company. Thomas had found a certain comfort in calling Ed's life an escape, a way of dodging the soul-killing business of everyday life, but sitting here now he had to admit that if his brother had thought in those terms he had been sadly deluded. But Thomas suspected that his brother had known exactly what he was getting himself into and, perhaps more tellingly, what he wasn't.

Thomas picked up one of the boxes and emptied it carefully onto the bed. Most of what spilled out looked like junk (a ticket stub from a Cubs game, a few faded and unframed photographs, a dusty cassette tape, some weird little silver trinket shaped like a fish, a stub of pencil), but it all felt saved somehow, hoarded as if it had all once been special, meaningful. The thought depressed him.

He flipped one of the photographs over and his breath caught. His own face looked up at him from the paper, a smiling, confident face Thomas had searched for in the mirror for the last six years. Next to Thomas was his brother in full clerical array—vestments, collar, the works—but somehow still looking like his brother as he had been when he taught him how to read a curveball or showed him the best comic books. And beside Ed was Kumi, her long black hair up and knotted in a suitably Japanese arrangement, the white of her wedding dress almost too bright for the camera to capture. They were all beaming, glowing with happiness, standing in the weedy garden only yards from where he now sat. Thomas closed his eyes, permitting himself to remember her as he so rarely did, suddenly feeling her absence as he had done when she first left.

The picture was almost ten years old, but she'd been gone for more than half of that. It struck Thomas that his wedding day had been the beginning of the end of his relationship with his brother. They had always been a little different, but that day, the sheer rightness of it—in spite of everything that had followed—had been their last moment of harmony. The next time he'd seen Ed, things were already unraveling. The three of them would never be caught smiling like that together again.

When the doorbell rang the first time, he ignored it, but when it rang twice more it occurred to him that he might be the only one in the building. Then he remembered the lawyer who was coming to meet with him about what was laughably referred to as his brother's "estate." He moved swiftly down the narrow hall and rickety staircase, only pausing for a second to wonder what he would do if it was a homeless person as Jim had assumed him to be, or someone with some pressing spiritual crisis. He opened the door and gasped as the cold wind struck him forcibly in the face.

The man outside had taken a few steps back as if to look up to the windows for signs of life. He looked at Thomas for a second without moving, one hand holding a black attaché case, the other thrust deep into his pocket.

"You Knight?" he said.

"Yes," said Thomas, a little taken aback by the man's brusque manner. "Come in."

"Parks," he said.

"I'm sorry?"

"Parks," he repeated. "Ben Parks."

He stepped past Thomas without extending a hand. He was maybe thirty, thin-faced with curly hair, a goatee, and hard eyes that didn't meet Thomas's when he spoke. The coat he wore looked old and a size or two too large. He didn't look like a lawyer.

Thomas led him back into the spartan kitchen.

"Do you want to go straight to his room or what?"

The look on the lawyer's face was reminiscent of Jim's when he had realized that Thomas wasn't looking for a handout.

"His room?"

"I'm sorry," said Thomas. "You are the lawyer come to see about Ed's stuff, right?"

"Ed?"

"Ed Knight, my brother. The priest who died."

There was another split second of uncertainty and the man's eyes tightened. For a moment he was silent, and then his demeanor changed, lightened so that he looked like a different person entirely.

"Oh, you're his *brother.* I'm so sorry. I've never actually met Father Knight and I didn't know him by his first name. I assumed you were a priest."

Thomas laughed at that.

"No," he said. "My brother got the spiritual gene. Or the Catholic gene. Something. Me, it skipped. So," he said, moving quickly in case his confession had made the lawyer uncomfortable, and because it was bravado and not really true at all, "you want to look over his room?"

"Sure," said the lawyer. "That would be great."

Thomas led the way.

"Been in town long?" said Parks.

"I live here. Well, Evanston," he said, adding for no particular reason, "the cheap end. I came as soon as I heard. I figured I'd need to be here a few days, but Ed seems to have owned so little—unless you know something about assets I don't—that that might not be necessary. And no doubt Mother Church will make sure everything is in order."

"Right," said the lawyer.

Thomas opened the door to the miserable little bedroom.

"Chateau Knight," he said.

The lawyer stood in the doorway and looked carefully around without moving, as if he were afraid of disturbing a crime scene.

"I don't think there's much I'm going to want," said Thomas. "Unless he turns out to have had some offshore account worth millions, I think the order will get the lot."

"Do you know much about your brother's life, any assets we might not immediately find?"

"The car outside is his, I think," said Thomas, "though it's only worth a few hundred bucks at most. Maybe it belongs to the parish or the Jesuits. He probably had a suitcase or two with him. I don't know."

"Anything else?"

"Look," said Thomas, "we weren't what you'd call close. Didn't really see eye to eye on a lot of stuff."

"I see. I'm sorry."

"I'm not looking for sympathy. I'm just saying that if you talk to people here, people he worked with, I mean, you'll find out a hell of a lot more about him than you will if you ask me. I didn't know anything about him."

He was angry and ashamed to say it, but there it was. It was the truth.

"Where did he die?"

"I'm sorry?" said Thomas.

"You said he had a case or two with him. He was on vacation somewhere?"

"Kind of," said Thomas, glancing out of the window, "I don't really know."

"And you don't know where?" Parks sounded faintly incredulous, even irritated.

"No," said Thomas, weary and with a swelling sense of failure and humiliation. "Overseas somewhere. I'm sorry. Does it matter?"

The lawyer hesitated for a second, his eyes uncertain, and then the smile snapped back on, reassuring and dismissive.

"I shouldn't think so," he said.

"Do you mind if I just leave you to it?" said Thomas. "I'm just going to get in the way."

"Sure," said the lawyer. "If I need you, I'll holler."

Gratefully, Thomas descended.

Thomas sat at the kitchen table for twenty minutes, staring at his chipped mug, wishing there were something to fill the silence, wishing he could go home. There was, after all, nothing for him here. It was as he had expected. If this was closure it was amorphous and deeply unsatisfying, though what else he could have hoped for he really didn't know. Abruptly he got up, snatched a pen from inside his jacket, and fished for something to write on in his pockets. He spread a creased napkin onto the tabletop and scribbled quickly:

"Jim. Gone home. Barring anything surprising, see that Ed's stuff goes to the people and causes he cared for. Neither include me, and you are a better judge of what he would have wanted. Sorry about the game. Thanks, TK."

He looked at the note. It would do. It felt a little cheap, a little easy, but this was not the time to be his brother's keeper. He hadn't been so for the last six years; why pretend otherwise now?

He was on his way to the front door when he heard it open and men's voices drifted through to him from the windswept street: Jim, and someone else. Thomas grabbed the note and stuffed it quickly into his pocket as the priest entered the kitchen.

"All right, Thomas?" said Jim. "This is Father Bill Morretti. We met on the street."

The other man was sixty and stooped, but his eyes were bright and shrewd.

"I'm very sorry for your loss," he said, extending his hand.

"Thank you," said Thomas.

"Do you want to get started right away?" said Jim, looking expectantly from Thomas to the other man, who was shrugging out of a heavy, old-fashioned overcoat.

"Started with what?" said Thomas.

"I'm sorry," said Jim, grinning at his absentmindedness. "This is the lawyer who has come to go through your brother's possessions with you."

For a second Thomas just stood there.

"If you're the lawyer," he said, at last, "who's upstairs?"

CHAPTER 4

Thomas was the first to move, but even so he was halfway up
the stairs before he hit his stride, driven by a vague outrage he
couldn't explain. Jim followed, the lawyer a slow third at his
back. At his brother's bedroom door, Thomas twisted the handle as he crashed his shoulder against the timber, but the door
did not give. For a second he thought he could hear movement
on the other side, and then he was slamming repeatedly against
it with all his weight and strength, suddenly angry.

"Thomas, wait!" said Jim, grasping his arm. "He could be
armed. He could be . . ."

But Thomas wasn't listening. He gritted his teeth and
rammed the door again. Distantly through the noise of his ef-
forts Thomas heard Jim tell the lawyer to go and call the police,
and then the jamb splintered and the door shuddered open.

The room was deserted, the window open. He blundered in
with Jim at his heels, grabbed the window frame and looked
out, but could see no sign of tracks in the snow.

It all happened in a second: movement behind him, a
muffled crunch, and a groan as Jim slipped to the floor.
Parks—if that was his name—had been behind the door
waiting for them. With Jim down, he now took a menacing
step toward Thomas.

"Hold it," said Thomas, raising one hand defensively, "what
do you want?"

But the other man said nothing. He raised his right arm and
Thomas saw that the fist was large and clublike, as if he were
wearing an absurdly large glove or had wrapped something
heavy around his hand.

Thomas backed up against the window, feeling the ledge
against the backs of his thighs. He raised his fists and splayed
his legs, waiting for the other man to come at him. Jim was
still down and silent.

Parks now showed his other hand and Thomas felt his heart skip with panic that was as much alarm at the strangeness of the thing as it was fear for his own safety. The man was holding what could only be described as a sword, short—only eighteen inches or so—the blade leaf-shaped, sweeping to a point long and lethal-looking. It was the weapon of a psychopath or a cultist. Thomas faltered, unsure which way to go.

"We don't have to do this," he said, his voice unsteady.

"Au contraire," said the other with a grim smile. He took a step forward and swung the sword in a broad arc toward Thomas's face.

Thomas reacted instinctively, ducking back, swatting at the blade with his left hand as he closed to punch wildly with his right. He felt the stinging *thwack* of the sword's cold steel against his splayed palm, a pain so sharp and sudden that it was a moment before he could be sure that he had caught the flat of the blade and not its edge. Parks pivoted his shoulder toward him, dodging his punch, and that was when he brought his right hand crashing down on the side of Thomas's head. It was no glove, no fabric wrapped around his fist. It was as hard and unyielding as iron, and it sent Thomas to the floor as if his legs had been cut from under him. For a second he saw only blackness, and while he knew he was falling he could do nothing to prevent it.

He barely made a sound as he crumpled to the carpet, and though he didn't completely lose consciousness he was, for a few moments, so completely disoriented that he could not move at all. He sensed Parks only vaguely as he clambered over Thomas's stricken body, knowing only that he had gotten out the window to freedom long before Thomas was in any shape to do anything about it.

Even when he felt fully alert Thomas stayed where he was, gingerly testing with his hand the back of his head where he had been hit, and only then hunching himself into a cautious squat. A few feet away, Jim groaned.

"That went well," said Thomas.

"What the hell was that thing?"

"The sword?"

"Sword? What sword?" said Jim. "I didn't see a sword."

"I think you were already down for the count by then," said Thomas, resting his weight against the wall and sitting flat on the floor.

"You didn't do so well yourself, Rocky," said Jim. "Hellfire, what did he hit me with?"

"Same thing he hit me with," said Thomas. "It was like a glove made of metal. Something between a gauntlet and the world's biggest knuckle duster. You okay?"

"I think so. You?"

Thomas rose slowly, nodding only when he was completely upright and didn't find the floor swimming back up at him.

"That thing could have cracked my skull," he said. "I prefer not to think what he could have done with the sword."

Jim was running his fingers over his left temple. There was a thin trail of blood where the blow had broken the skin, but the cut was nothing to the lump that was already rising.

" 'Wait,' I said," he intoned. " 'He could be armed,' I said. But no. In the red corner we have Thomas Knight, all the way from Idiot's Landing."

"Thanks," said Thomas. "Sorry."

He turned and looked out the window to where footprints in the snow on the porch roof ended in a confused scraping at the edge. He leaned out to look down the street, but the impostor was nowhere in sight. He couldn't even make sense of where the footprints led.

Goddamn it.

He wasn't sure why he was so furious, and as he stood there leaning out into the cold the rage seemed to blow off him so that he felt only stupidly ineffectual and hard done by. He cursed under his breath and turned back to Jim, who was now perching gingerly on the bed, still cradling his temple. The lawyer had appeared in the doorway.

"Everything okay?" he said.

Thomas shot him a baleful look.

"Brilliant," said Jim, sardonically upbeat.

"He was looking for something," said Thomas, sitting beside him on the edge of the bed and taking in the carnage that had been visited upon the room: its papers scattered, its books strewn about, the meager remnants of his brother's life hurled around with no remorse or respect . . .

"He asked me if I was *Knight*," he said, thinking it through, trying to remember. "I assumed he meant me, but I think he meant my brother. He said his name was Parks, and I assumed he was the lawyer, but I think . . . I'm not sure. He didn't know Ed personally, but I think he came specifically to see him. I think," he added, troubled by the realization, "that he didn't know my brother was dead."

Jim frowned.

"I don't know what to do with that," he said, massaging his head.

"Neither do I," said Thomas.

"Is anything missing?" asked Jim, picking up one of the books and considering it.

"I have no idea," said Thomas. "There wasn't much to steal except for papers, and if some of those are gone, I'd never know."

He stooped, righted an overturned box, and saw the wedding picture lying there, bent slightly now.

"Wait," he said. "Something *is* missing. A little silver fish. You know the one I mean?"

Jim shook his head.

"The police are sending someone over," said the lawyer. "They said we should touch nothing."

"He asked me where Ed died," said Thomas, half to himself. "I told him I didn't know. I felt bad about it . . . that I didn't know, I mean. I think he really wanted to know. I'm not sure why, but . . ."

"I don't know where he was," said Jim. "Far East somewhere. He had been in Italy, then went to Japan, but I don't think he died there."

"Japan?" said Thomas, all the old mixed feelings flooding

back as they did when anyone mentioned Japan. It was a bit like being hit again, though it turned into a cold numbness edged with apprehension. It was like waking up and knowing that something terrible had happened the day before but being unable to remember what it was. "What was he doing in Japan?"

"No idea," said Jim. "We could call the order. The Jesuits, I mean."

Thomas looked at him, and then nodded, which made his head ring again with pain.

CHAPTER 5

"He said his name was Parks," said Thomas, for the second time in as many minutes.

"And this silver fish thing is all you're sure is missing?"

The cop who had introduced himself as Officer Campbell looked bored, as if he had been sent on a wild-goose chase. Now that the initial outrage had subsided, Thomas couldn't really blame him.

"Yes," he said. "I didn't really get chance to look at the papers before he arrived . . ."

"You think it was valuable?"

"Probably not. I suppose it depends what it was made of. If it was silver it might be worth a couple of hundred bucks."

"Could you describe the fish, sir?" said the cop, blowing out a sigh and scribbling on a pad with a black pen.

"Three or four inches long, kind of funny shaped, detailed scales . . . I don't know what else."

"Funny shaped?" said Campbell.

"Crudely modeled, I guess. Fat tail. Big, clumsy-looking fins."

"And it was just a model fish, not, you know, a container or something? Did it open up?"

"I don't know."

"You think it was, like, symbolic or something? You know, him being a priest and all."

"Symbolic?" said Thomas. "How do you mean?"

"You know, like those metal fishes folks have on their cars. *Jesus fish.*"

The policeman sketched an outline on his pad, a single line looping back on itself to form a leaf-shaped body and open tail. Thomas considered it. It reminded him of a Möbius strip or part of a double helix.

"I don't know," said Thomas, honestly. "I hadn't thought of that. This looked different from those. More realistic."

"We'll keep an eye on the local pawnshops," said the cop. "And he had a sword? Like, you know, Robin Hood or one of those guys in *Lord of the Rings?* Like a *sword* sword?"

"A short sword, yes," said Thomas. "Like a Roman legionary's sword, if that means anything to you."

"Nope," said Campbell. "And he hit you with that?"

"No, with this clublike glove thing he was wearing. Metal. Weighed a ton."

"Weird," said the cop.

"I thought so," said Thomas, expecting a bit more.

"Was there anything else?" said Campbell. "He have a horse or anything?"

"No," said Thomas, smiling in spite of himself.

"You sure?"

"I think I would have noticed, it being upstairs and all."

"Still," said the cop. "Look on the bright side. If he'd been serious—I mean, if he'd been a real hood, you know?—he would have shot you. You just got whacked with a glove, see? Bright side."

"I'm ecstatic about the whole episode," said Thomas.

"Okay," said the cop, grinning and putting his pad away. "If you see him again, you call us. Otherwise, I'll ask around, but . . ."

He shrugged.

"I shouldn't hold my breath," said Thomas.

"Not unless you got gills someplace."

"Thanks," said Thomas, matching the policeman's smile. "You've been of invaluable assistance."

"All in a day's work, sir."

On the way out they met Jim coming in with a box of files. Thomas turned to introduce him.

"Jim, this is Officer Campbell," he said.

Jim nodded peremptorily and glanced away, but the policeman's gaze was steady, and his former wryness had evaporated.

"Hello again, Father," said Campbell.

"You two know each other?" said Thomas. Jim was still looking anywhere but at the cop.

"Oh, we go way back," said Campbell. "Ain't that right, Father?"

Jim didn't reply and the cop left without another word.

CHAPTER 6

The man they called the Seal-breaker hung up the phone and considered it for a long moment.

It was supposed to be over. It was all supposed to have died with the priest, but however much War had tried to make his report sound casual, the relaying of a formality, he hadn't been able to conceal the trace of unease in his voice.

The priest had a brother.

They had known that before. Of course, they had. It just hadn't seemed important till now.

And may not be still, he thought. And if it became important, if this brother to the hapless priest became a threat, the Seal-breaker would move, and fast.

He had stalled with the priest, assuming the problem would just rinse out over time, but the man had been persistent and stubborn. He would not wait for his brother to become a threat.

Before the man could even rise to the level of irritant or distraction, the Seal-breaker would swat him like the gnat he was.

It wasn't as if he didn't have the resources, he thought, with the whisper of a smile. He had the reach, the finances, the sheer power to achieve all manner of things. He also had the will, and that was what would really terrify his enemies, or would if they ever knew who he was. The Seal-breaker himself was impossible to see. He could shake the hand of his most loathed adversary and they would not know him. And when it came time for action, the Seal-breaker would be a world away while his operatives struck.

His horsemen, he called them, all four poised to do his bidding, ready to release whatever private apocalypse the Seal-breaker thought appropriate. He had handpicked each of them for their special talents.

War, his general, a skilled soldier who could deploy his own assault team in any terrain.

Pestilence, his spy, who spread disease with dissimulation and lies.

Famine, his private horror show, a man who sowed terror wherever he walked.

Death, his wild card, and the measure of his near-limitless power.

What could he not do with such cavalry at his command?

It wouldn't come to that, he thought. But if it did, there would be no hesitation this time. For now he would merely alert them, but if he had to unleash all four of them, he would.

The Seal-breaker considered the two solitary words he had written down during his conversation with War:

Thomas Knight.

He looked at the name of the man who was now blundering aimlessly around the detritus of his brother's life, and the Seal-breaker, as he dialed the first of the horsemen, felt almost sorry for him.

CHAPTER 7

Thomas sat by the tiny hearth in the tiny living room listening to the oily-voiced secretary of the Jesuit house, his patience wearing thin.

"We're so sorry for your loss. Father Knight was a valued and respected . . ."

"What happened to him?" said Thomas. He didn't want to hear about his brother's life right now. It would complicate his already conflicted feelings too much.

"Well, we don't know, exactly," said the voice, picking its words carefully.

"What the hell does that mean?" said Thomas. He said it quietly, but he could tell the priest on the other end took offense.

"Just what it says," said the secretary. "We were notified of your brother's death by the American embassy in Manila, but we don't know why he was there or what he was doing."

"Manila?" said Thomas. Jim turned to look at him, his expression quizzical. "In the Philippines?"

"That's right."

"I thought he was in Japan," said Thomas, feeling his familiar reluctance to even say the word rising like gall in his throat.

"So did we," said the secretary, and Thomas thought he could hear something in his voice. Awkwardness? Embarrassment? "And indeed he was, for a while. But it seems he left and went to the Philippines, which is where he died."

"How did he die?"

"Some kind of traffic accident, we think," said the priest.

"You think?"

"Again," said the priest with careful patience, "I don't have all the details. You'd have to go to the foreign office for those, or the Philippine embassy directly."

"Right," he said. "Thanks."

He hung up before the priest could shower Ed with more postmortem accolades about piety and orthodoxy.

"Why do I get the feeling I'm not being told the whole story?" he said. He was looking at the phone, but as soon as he had spoken he turned his gaze on Jim. The priest looked down. "How did you know the cop?"

"Oh, you know," Jim said with a dismissive wave. "Small neighborhood. Similar lines of work, in a way."

"He didn't seem to like you that much."

"Sometimes the people they want to lock up are the ones people like me and Ed are trying to . . . what's the word?"

"Save?"

"Protect. Nurture," said Jim. "That kind of thing. Kids, mainly."

Thomas nodded, still feeling evaded.

"You said he was in Italy before Japan?" he said.

"A retreat house in Naples," said Jim. "He was back for a few days before heading over to Japan. Look."

He took a postcard that was propped up on the mantel and blew the dust off. It showed a collage of statues and mosaics from some ancient site, superimposed on a picture of a conical mountain and deep blue sky: Pompeii, according to the back. Ed's looping handwriting was scrawled on the back in blue ink: "*De Profundis!*" it said. "Cheers, Ed."

"*De Profundis?*" said Thomas, studying the mosaic, the way it made images out of meaningless fragments.

"Psalm 130 and an old Catholic prayer," said Jim. " 'Out of the depths.' It's a statement of faith in the face of despair. 'Out of the depths I cry to you, O Lord, Lord, hear my voice. O let your ears be attentive to the voice of my pleading. If you, O Lord, should mark our guilt, Lord, who would survive? . . . Because with the Lord there is mercy and fullness of redemption.' "

"Seems an odd sort of thing to write on a card," said Thomas.

"I took it as a joke," said Jim. "The voice of despair coming from this beautiful, fascinating place."

"Compared to here," said Thomas.

"He was in his element," Jim agreed, grinning.

The doorbell rang.

"Excuse me," said Jim. "I'd better get that."

As the priest left the room, Thomas put his hand in his pocket and found the note he had written earlier. He drew it out, read it once, and then crumpled it and dropped it in the trash can by the door. He wouldn't be leaving just yet.

He was still standing there when Jim reentered the room. There was something in his face, a hunted, anxious quality that hadn't been there before.

"What's up?" said Thomas. "Who is it?"

"It's for you," said Jim, and his voice was unnaturally low, almost a whisper.

"For me? Who is it?" Thomas repeated.

The question was answered by two men in dark suits who entered the room behind Jim. One brandished a badge in a flip wallet.

"Mr. Thomas Knight?" he said.

Thomas nodded, absorbing something very like panic from Jim.

"We're from the Department of Homeland Security. We'd like to ask you some questions about your brother."

CHAPTER 8

It was turning into a very strange day. Emotionally, Thomas had run the gamut from the dull shock of his brother's death, through the strangeness of dealing with the residue of his life, to the fury and humiliation of the battle with the man who had called himself Parks. Now he was even more baffled, even more defensive and outraged, but he was also scared.

"You don't fool with terrorism," said Jim after they had gone. "Not anymore."

He was right. One day in the not too distant past this might have been the subject of a thousand sardonic cracks about the absurdity of what he had been asked by these men, but not now, not with the country flinching every time someone left a bag unattended. Thomas muttered his irritation and exasperation at the craziness of it all, but inside he was badly alarmed.

They were both in their fifties, sober suited and careful. One of them, a guy with narrow eyes who introduced himself as Kaplan, seemed tense, always looking around, a coiled spring physically and mentally. The other did most of the talking. His name was Matthew Palfrey, and he smiled all the time, as if to reassure, though the result managed to be the opposite. Maybe that was the idea.

They had asked him about his brother's "sympathies," and whether his religious sensibility had ever led him to connect with religious leaders from outside Catholicism. They asked him if Ed had known friends or associates of Arab descent, and if he had a copy of the Qur'an in his bedroom. They asked if he had access to large sums of money or had ever had any weapons training, a question so thoroughly wrong that in any other circumstance Thomas would have howled with laughter. They asked how much Thomas knew of his brother's whereabouts over the last six months and whether he had letters or e-mails from him, whether Ed had suffered what they called "a crisis of faith." Thomas recalled the scribbled *De Profundis!* on the postcard with its overtones of despair, but he shook his head.

Then, very politely, always calling him *sir* in that formal way some officials have that somehow reinforces the impression that they are in control, they started on him. He had, they observed, a history of "dissident opinions" and "counterculture beliefs." Had he ever been approached by people who avowed violent solutions to the issues close to his heart? Had he ever been to the Middle East? Did he maintain connections with people who had?

The whole encounter had been surreal, and a couple of times Thomas had wanted—again—to laugh, but there was another part of him that wanted to curl up until they went away, though whether that was because he was afraid for himself, or for what his brother might have been involved in, he couldn't say.

Except that there was no way that Ed was involved with terrorists. No way at all.

Did he really know that? Did he know anything substantial about his brother over the last half-dozen years?

The only time he did actually laugh was when they rose to leave and he, mustering a defiance he didn't feel, demanded what had prompted this absurd line of questioning.

"I'm sorry, sir," said Kaplan. "That's classified."

And even then Thomas's laugh didn't ring quite true, because if the world had strayed into the realm of such TV clichés, he really should be afraid.

"How did my brother die?" he demanded.

"That is still being investigated."

"So you are going to tell me nothing?" he said.

"We're not at liberty to go into details at this time," said Palfrey, the one with the open, smiling face.

"Would I find out more if I hopped a flight to Manila?"

He was being flippant, testing their boundaries, though he also knew that he had no job, so a trip to the Philippines was only unlikely, not impossible. He thought there was a fractional hesitation before the other one spoke.

"They won't let you into the country," said Palfrey. Thomas stared at him.

"And if they did," said the other, without a hint of emotion, "we'd pick you up the moment you got back."

"And, sir," said Palfrey, "I advise you to discuss this matter with nobody. The investigation is ongoing."

What exactly was being investigated—or who—they didn't say.

CHAPTER 9

Thomas spent a half hour on the phone to the State Department and another ten minutes trying, without success, to reach the American ambassador in Manila. He learned nothing from either call. His brother had died in the Philippines, but how he had died or what he had been doing there in the first place, no one was saying. Whether they knew or not, he couldn't begin to guess, and though it might be normal when dealing with bereaved relatives, he sensed their wariness. He felt his irritation mounting as he was shuttled from one uninformative receptionist to another, but he also knew instinctively that his customary bluster would get him nowhere. He was being stonewalled by people who wouldn't be intimidated by anything he had to say. In the end, he thanked them wearily and slid the receiver back into the cradle.

"Nothing?" said Jim.

Thomas shook his head.

"I don't get it," he said. "I'm being dodged."

"I don't suppose you know any powerful politicians, ambassadors, officials in the State Department, things like that?"

Thomas turned so quickly and with a stare so level and baleful that Jim's face fell.

"What?" said the priest. "I just meant . . ."

"I know," said Thomas, regrouping fast. "Forget it. I thought you were . . ."

He shrugged and, registering the look of startled alarm on the priest's face, smiled.

"My wife, or rather my ex-wife, works for the State Department," he said, a little embarrassed. "She's not high up or anything and we don't talk so . . ."

Jim relaxed visibly.

"You don't want to call her over this?"

"No," said Thomas. He wasn't smiling now, and Jim knew better than to push the point.

"What about Devlin?" said Jim.

"Who?"

"Devlin," said Jim as if it should be obvious. "Senator Zacharias Devlin; your brother knew him."

"Senator Devlin?" said Thomas, incredulous. "The family-values, school-prayer Republican? Ed knew him?"

"Met with him at least a few times."

"You don't sound impressed."

"You think I should be?"

"You're a priest," said Thomas, the smile returning.

"So?"

"Nothing," he said, "I just figured you religious types would have more in common with a guy like that."

Jim gave him a steady look. "You seem to have me confused with Pat Robertson," he said.

"My mistake," said Thomas, shrugging.

"You don't much like priests, do you?" said Jim.

"Not as a rule," said Thomas, bristling.

"Present company excepted, of course," said Jim.

"Of course."

The two men looked hard at each other, and for a moment the situation could have turned unpleasant.

"Tough day," said Jim. "For both of us."

He wasn't talking about the aftermath of Ed's death so much as the fact of it, and Thomas, who didn't want to appear hostile on this, just nodded and sighed and wondered why he couldn't simply grieve for his brother as a regular person would.

"I'm ready for a drink," said Jim. "You?"

"Sure, what the hell," said Thomas.

The priest pulled a bottle of Bushmills out of a kitchen cupboard and poured two generous measures into the bottoms of a pair of chipped mugs.

"We're low on crystal," he said, proffering one of the cups. "I'd like to blame the Jesuits' vow of poverty, but we diocesans will take whatever we're given. We're just not given much these days."

"Oh, for the good old days of the Holy Roman Empire," said Thomas, "when charity meant . . ."

"Giving us your money," Jim completed for him, grinning. "Now look at us. I've known Carmelites with better gear."

Thomas smirked and sipped the Irish. It was warm and smoky: familiar as childhood and as conflicting.

"It's good," he said, as if he'd never tasted it before.

"Let's see how badly the Illini are doing," said Jim, jabbing the remote toward the boxy TV.

"So how did Ed know Devlin?" Thomas said, deflecting his own thoughts.

"Not sure," said Jim, scowling at the game. "Met with him right after he got back from Italy. But that wasn't the first time."

"When did he come back?"

"Two months or so ago. The Js use a retreat house in Naples and he went out for a couple of weeks after he'd been helping out here. He was working on a book on early Christian symbology. No idea what interest Devlin might have had in him."

"Did you know Ed before he came to work here?"

"Not well. We'd met a couple of times at conferences and diocesan functions, but it's amazing how separate priests can be, especially when one is of the lowly diocesan clergy like yours truly, and one is of the exalted ranks of the papal stormtroopers."

Papal stormtroopers. It was an old joke, one that Thomas remembered Ed using in the days when they still talked. It wasn't that funny and hadn't been accurate for decades. The Jesuits didn't just take a vow of poverty. They also took a vow of obedience to the pope. Thomas supposed that had once meant something, but times change, and lately the Jesuits' famously leftist intellectualism and social activism had stirred the impatience of the Vatican.

"You sure we've never met?" said Jim. "There's something about your face . . ."

"Don't think so," said Thomas.

"Maybe you've been on the telly," said Jim, grinning.

Thomas waited for the memory to catch, saw it in the priest's face, and opted to head it off.

"Actually, yes," he said. "I'm a high school teacher. *Was*. I made the grave error of telling a parent what I really thought about how he had raised his lying, cheating, plagiarizing, bullying thug of a son, something of which the school board took a dim view, doubly so since said parent worked for the local Fox affiliate. Not my finest hour."

Jim smiled, shrugged, and raised his glass.

"Here's to going out in style," he said. Thomas drank.

The third quarter ended, and as the bright-orange-shirted Illinois players trooped off the court looking beaten, the TV kicked into commercials.

"So this is how you spend your time?" said Thomas.

He hadn't meant it to sound so snide. He sounded like that a lot lately, hearing it after it was too late to take it back. Jim just raised his eyebrows.

"When I'm not doing the masses," he said, "the sick visits, the pastoral meetings, the young-adult discussions, the hospital calls, the endless parish meetings, coordinating . . ." he ticked them off on his fingers, "the drug and alcohol counseling sessions, the community food bank, the baptism classes, the single-mom dinners, a dozen different support groups, deaconate training, funerals, community outreach. Then there are the real problems, like people who can't pay their rent and get tossed out into a Chicago winter . . ." he said, the anger in his voice building, though Thomas felt sure it wasn't directed at him. "It's not all sitting around saying the rosary."

"Or watching basketball," said Thomas, apologetic.

"A game I find tedious and baffling," Jim added. "In fact, it's a penance to watch it."

"And a kindness," said Thomas, raising his glass to him. "Which is appreciated."

Jim shrugged to show there were no hard feelings.

"You liked Ed," said Thomas.

"Kindred spirit," said Jim. "And not just because he was a

priest. He was more of a reader than me, but he didn't mind spending the afternoon washing pans at the soup kitchen. It's always nice to meet a priest whose liberation theology doesn't stay in the bookcase."

Thomas nodded and smiled.

"You think I should speak to the senator?" he said.

"Wouldn't hurt to try, I guess," said Jim.

Another silence.

"So," said Jim, eyes on the TV, "what happened? Between you and Ed, I mean. You didn't just drift apart. You looked happy enough together in those wedding pictures."

There were so many ways he could answer that, many of them things he had said before to others, many of them dodges or feints intended to wrong-foot the defense. But Thomas was tired and he probably would never see this lonely priest again after today.

"He ended my marriage," he said.

CHAPTER 10

Thomas sat in the reception room of Senator Zach Devlin's South Dearborn Street office and looked at his hands. He felt overawed by the place with its immaculate carpets, well-made furniture, and framed, official photographs of Devlin looking comfortable and imposing. Once he would have been delighted at the prospect of meeting with someone from the staff of a Republican senator, and would have gone in feeling confident and wittily aggressive, his pet subjects lining up in his head like paratroopers ready to jump.

I was wondering, Senator, how you could begin to defend a policy—and I'm using the word in its loosest sense—so clearly asinine . . .

Not lately, and certainly not today. Today he was antsy and

nervous, and once already in the last ten minutes he had considered getting up and taking the elevator back down from the heady thirty-ninth floor and into Chicago's cold and blustery streets.

He had expected when he first called the senator's local office to be dodged as he had when he had called Manila or—at best—to be given an address to write to, a phone number to reach some Washington flunky. What had happened was that he had been put on hold, then invited to make his pitch to a secretary, and then put on hold again, for longer this time. But just as he was ready to dismiss the whole venture and hang up, the secretary came back on the line and told him to come downtown this afternoon. She had sounded slightly surprised, impressed even. Thomas had put the phone down with something like elation, but that faded as the hours wore on, and now that he was actually here he felt close to panic.

The receptionist, a young blond girl with a bright, perky smile, answered her phone, said "Yes" twice and "Certainly" once, and then hung up and looked at Thomas.

"Mr. Hayes will see you now," she said.

"Mr. Hayes?" said Thomas, getting slowly to his feet. It wasn't a real question, more an opportunity to steady himself.

"The senator's private secretary and chief of staff," she said, showing him to a paneled door.

"Right," Thomas muttered, taken aback. "Thanks."

Rod Hayes was about Thomas's age, though his cropped hair was starting to show a brush of silver about the temples. He wore black horn-rimmed glasses that could have made him look studious but looked instead as if they'd been lent to him to somehow balance his hearty athleticism. He was broad of chest and shoulder, and his sleek dark suit did nothing to hide a body that was well exercised and taut. His eyes, as they turned to Thomas, were gray, intelligent, and a little guarded. But that was understandable. If Homeland Security thought Thomas a dissident of the very-small-pond variety, it was at least possible that Hayes knew he was in the company of the political enemy.

The smile he dredged up didn't try too hard and thus seemed real enough.

"Mr. Knight," he said, crossing from the window and extending a strong, tanned hand, "I'm glad you could drop by. Please, have a seat."

Thomas shuffled to the proffered chair and sat cautiously.

"We were sorry to hear of your loss," he said. "Father Knight was a good friend of the senator's and an important ally."

"Really?" said Thomas.

"Oh yes," said Hayes, choosing to treat the question as sincere rather than snide, which was, for once, the way Thomas had meant it. He knew nothing of his brother's recent activities, and though the Ed he had known had been more than a Democrat, that Ed had disappeared off Thomas's radar long before he had actually died.

"We weren't that close," said Thomas, opting to get that into the open right away, "but I know he was a man of principle."

"Absolutely."

"Well that's kind of why I wanted to speak to you," said Thomas. The office with its clean lines and gleaming window, this athletic and successful young conservative, and the subject of their conversation all made him uncomfortable and anxious to be gone.

"I don't seem to be able to find out much about what my brother was doing when he died, and it seems like I'm running into some kind of national security investigation. I don't imagine you or the senator can tell me much or do much to . . . er . . . call them off, but I was wondering . . . since the senator knew him . . ."

He gave up. He should have rehearsed this speech beforehand. *Call them off?* He sounded as if he were asking for some kind of favor. Worse, he sounded guilty.

"National security?" said Hayes, giving him a hard look.

Thomas deflated further. He had hoped someone here would be able to tell him something right away. They obviously knew no more than he did.

He told Hayes about the trouble he had had getting information about his brother's death and about his interview with the DHS. Hayes's confusion seemed to deepen, but he said nothing, letting Thomas pick his uneasy way through his story. When he got to the part about the intruder who had brandished a sword, Hayes shifted and the muscles around his eyes tightened. He nodded slowly when Thomas stopped talking, took a pen from his jacket pocket, and began scribbling on a blotter, muttering occasional questions without looking up.

"They came when?"

"Do you know who you spoke to in Manila?"

"Some kind of road accident?"

Each time Thomas bobbed his head and answered, feeling as he had as a child, kneeling in the curtained confessional.

"Okay," said Hayes, after a moment's pause in which he seemed to decide the matter was exhausted, "leave your contact information with the secretary and we'll see what we can come up with. Obviously if it is a matter of national security there won't be much we can do, but . . ."

He stopped, staring over Thomas's head to the door.

"It isn't," said a man's voice from behind him. Thomas turned to see Senator Devlin himself standing in the open doorway. He was a big man, still powerful in spite of his sixty-some years. His hair was thick and white, his eyebrows bushy, his eyes blue and a little wild.

Hayes got to his feet, clearly surprised.

"Senator," he said, "this is . . ."

"Thomas Knight," said the senator. "Yes, I know. The girl outside has a tongue in her head."

He walked in with long rolling strides as if he'd just gotten off a horse, moving through the room as if he were pushing aside waist-high underbrush: a man used to taking a direct route to wherever he wanted to go.

"Ed Knight was no terrorist," he snorted over his shoulder as he heaved his briefcase onto Hayes's desk with a thud. "Somebody screwed up."

"Don't you think we should turn this over to Homeland Security or the CIA . . . ?" Hayes began, suddenly sounding a little plaintive and overawed by the unexpected appearance of his boss.

"No, I damned well don't," said the senator, with a steely glare at his chief of staff. "I knew Ed Knight, and his death is a great loss to this community. That those Washington numbskulls would desecrate his memory by turning him into some kind of leftist paramilitary because he happened to die in the wrong place is worse than insulting. It's incompetent and stupid and . . ." he sought for a suitable term, "blasphemous."

Hayes opened his mouth to speak but said nothing. His eyes darted to Thomas, who was getting slowly to his feet feeling as if he'd strayed into a family quarrel.

"Don't argue, Hayes," he said, raising a hand with absolute authority. He filled the room like a general astride the turret of his tank.

"Mr. Knight," said the senator, turning those bright, intense eyes on Thomas, "you have my word as an American that we'll clear your brother's name and get these idiots back to doing their job properly."

Thomas found himself smiling, inexplicably, swelling a little with something like pride, knowing even as he did so that the feeling was absurd and unreliable. But he thanked the senator anyway, unable to stop himself from feeling privileged to be in his presence, awed by the scale of the man even as he knew they agreed on almost nothing.

"Sit," he said. "We'll have a drink. Senate's not in session, right? Must be, or I'd be back in D.C. resisting the impulse to take a swing at the esteemed senator from Massachusetts."

He grinned wolfishly.

"You can fill me in on your story," he said.

Thomas did so. The senator, like Hayes, said nothing, but watched him carefully, snorting and scowling at the right moments, giving his secretary the nod as Thomas drew to a close.

Hayes ducked out of the room.

"A good man," he nodded to Hayes's back as the door shut

behind him. "Conservative with a small *c,* perhaps, and what I call a trust-fund Republican with a tendency to be a little holier-than-thou, but I'll make a fighter of him yet."

"Whereas you are conservative with a capital *C*?" said Thomas, mustering a little of his familiar archness.

"There isn't a letter big enough," said the senator, and the grin broadened till it split his colossal face and showed his bright, even teeth. "You're not, I take it?"

"No," said Thomas.

"Well, that's too bad. But I respect your right to believe whatever dumbass liberal crap you like. Hell, I'll fight to the death anyone who says otherwise. That's a hell of a story you have there, Mr. Knight. This guy who thumped you: you think he was searching for something?"

"I do," said Thomas, "but I've no idea what."

The senator frowned so that his forehead tightened by two inches, and nodded.

"Hayes! HAYES!" he roared suddenly. "Where did you go, Kentucky?"

Hayes reappeared at the door with a tray carrying three tumblers of Waterford crystal, two rocks and two fingers of Makers Mark in each.

"Bourbon okay?" said the senator, thrusting the glass into Thomas's hand.

"Sure," said Thomas, wondering what would happen if he said no.

"To your brother," he said, raising his glass a fraction. "A good man and a good priest. And that's coming from a hellfire Southern Baptist: spiritually speaking, of course."

He knocked the whisky back in one and banged the glass down on the mirror-polished mahogany desk. Hayes raised his glass for the toast, such as it was, but he didn't actually drink.

"So did Rod here give you anything useful to go on, or did he fob you off with a bunch of bureaucratic doublespeak?"

Thomas smiled a little and his eyes met those of Hayes, who returned the smile with what looked like familiar patience.

"Oh, he was very helpful, thanks," said Thomas, "and told me to leave my contact information in case . . ."

"Bureaucratic crap," snapped Devlin, glowering at his chief of staff, who was nursing his untouched drink with his feet together like a maitre d' poised to sweep away their empty soup bowls. "I don't know what the hell is going on over there—in Manila, I mean, though I guess I mean in Washington too—but I'll find out and you'll hear from me. In the meantime, do nothing that would arouse anyone's suspicion. Leave the detective work to the authorities. And to me."

"Thank you, Senator," said Thomas, tasting his drink. "Do you mind my asking how the two of you met up in the first place? My brother and you, I mean."

Devlin seemed to hesitate for a moment as if trying to remember, but Thomas thought Hayes shot him a quick look, and he wondered if something passed between them. A warning? A caution? Something. Whatever it was, it reminded him that for all the senator's bluff camaraderie, the man was a career politician. Such men didn't get where they were by always speaking their mind, even if he had mastered the illusion of doing exactly that.

"He approached me about a year ago," he said, his head cocked thoughtfully on one side. "He had ideas for a kind of faith-based organization: interdenominational, you understand. Local community leaders working together to address the causes of social problems in the city at the grassroots level. I liked the idea. I liked him, the way he thought. Smart, you know, but not too smart: concrete, not abstract. I can't be doing with a bunch of theory and high-concept nonsense that never puts bread on anyone's table . . ."

"Or lets them work for that bread themselves," said Thomas, arch again.

Devlin nodded emphatically, shrugging off the irony.

"God helps those who help themselves," he said.

"And you stayed in touch?" said Thomas, avoiding the argument. "He saw you again after he got back from Italy."

There it was again: that momentary hesitation on Devlin's

part and the watchful tension that seemed to bind Hayes for a moment.

"Yes," said the senator. "I wanted him involved on a local school board. He had the experience. Would have been good for the job. But he was committed to parish work and the book he was writing. Couldn't spare the time. I was disappointed, of course, but I respected his position."

"And afterward? Did you speak again before he went to the Philippines?"

"Is there something you are driving at, Mr. Knight?" said the senator with that same wolfish grin. "I'm starting to feel like I'm being interrogated."

"I'm just curious," said Thomas, pulling back. "Trying to fill in the blanks. We weren't close, as I said, and . . . Well, I guess I'm just trying to find out what he was doing out there in the first place."

The senator perched on the edge of the desk and leaned forward, looming over Thomas, and giving him a cool and studying gaze.

"You're afraid that there might be something to this terrorist talk," he said. "You are feeling guilty for losing touch with your brother and you are anxious that he really might have strayed from the path, become a traitor to his country."

Thomas said nothing, not absolutely sure what he thought of this pronouncement, but wilting a little under the senator's level stare. Devlin spoke the next words with slow precision.

"Put. It. Out. Of. Your. Mind."

Thomas nodded.

"Your brother was no terrorist. This will all blow over. Remember Ed for what he was, not for what a few misguided bureaucrats think he might have been. Everyone is afraid these days: scared of their own shadows. They see terrorists and their sympathizers everywhere. Ed wasn't one of them. You know that."

Thomas nodded, wondering if he shared the senator's conviction. They shared so little else.

CHAPTER 11

Thomas missed the city. As a younger man he had spent a lot of time there, but with home and work keeping him to the tamer environs of Evanston he came downtown rarely now. He liked Chicago's erratic, gray vastness, its bare trees and the wind rippling in over the lake. He headed down to the shore, thinking about Ed and wondering what he would do with his life when all this blew over. He was at Lincoln Park Zoo before he realized it, and since the place looked quiet and was still—amazingly—free, he went in as he had done so many times with Ed when they were boys.

It wasn't so much quiet as deserted. It was late afternoon and very cold, but he found strolling around by himself, considering the animals hardy enough to venture out, strangely satisfying. He was usually conflicted about zoos, drawn to the beauty and magnificence of the animals while still feeling something like pity for the creatures themselves, however much he told himself that such places served all manner of positive functions. Today he felt only a kind of peace and the fleeting ghosts of memory.

He saw just one family, a thin-faced man and his wife who drummed on the glass of the gorilla house to the delight of their screaming kids. Thomas nearly objected, but he didn't have the energy, and the gorillas just watched blankly, waiting for the humans to leave.

He walked through the Kovler big-cat house, watching the snow leopards stalking back and forth, and then went back outside into the cold where the lions lounged on snow-patched rocks, separated from him by a low fence and a steep, empty moat. They had always finished up here as kids, he and Ed, going from enclosure to enclosure and arguing amiably which was cooler, the lynx or the serval, in the same way that they had debated outfielders or wide receivers. The lions looked as lions always seem to look, casually haughty and indifferent, lazily tolerating people like him who came to gape at them, secure in the knowledge that they were the lords of their turf, however limited it might be. Even enclosed like this, even in the Chicago winter with the gray towers of the city on one side and the grayer waters of Lake Michigan on the other, they brought a little piece of the savannah with them and ruled it.

You have to respect that, thought Thomas, suddenly feeling the absence of his brother as he had not done all day.

He was watching one of the lionesses snoring and scratching herself absently, and didn't sense the presence of the man until he was standing right beside him. He was dressed in a heavy thermal jacket, gloves, and a knitted hat that covered most of his face.

Thomas instinctively started to move away. The man was too close, too conveniently bundled up against the cold, and suddenly he had an arm against Thomas's back, bracing him against the fence.

Thomas tried to shrug it off, but the guy—he was white, but Thomas could say nothing beyond that—took his left wrist and wrenched it high up his spine, a single swift movement that was over before he could flex against it. Thomas assumed he would go for his wallet—and given the way things had gone over the last couple of days, he was content to let that go—but he made no such move. Then the guy's knee stabbed upward into Thomas's groin and he doubled up.

"Leave it alone," hissed his attacker, his mouth against Thomas's ear.

For a second the words meant nothing and Thomas, overcome by a wholly unexpected fury, came surging up out of the near-crouch he was in, and struck out with his right fist.

He caught the man squarely on the side of his head, blindsiding him. For a second or less, Thomas thought the other man might run. But the punch had only made him angry, and his head snapped back around toward Thomas with a snarl so that the eyes beneath the woolen hat flashed an icy blue, which made Thomas step back, his momentary fury turning quickly into panic. He raised both fists to protect his face from whatever onslaught was about to come, and the error almost killed him.

There was no sudden rain of blows. Instead the attacker stepped in close and grabbed Thomas under his raised arms in a sudden and unsettling bear hug. Then he was lifting and pushing, and Thomas felt his whole weight rise up the fence and wedge briefly against the rail. For a moment he saw those furious eyes and the deserted zoo spread out behind his attacker, and then he kicked and the muffled face registered first pain, then a wild determination.

Suddenly Thomas was tipping back, over the metal rail and the chain-link fence. His head and upper body teetered in space, and then he was falling backward, turning.

He clawed at the fence as he fell, but his fingers scrabbled at nothing, and then he was rolling heavily in the air, bouncing off the concrete lip and tumbling twenty feet down into the dry moat. His mind moved twice as fast as his hands so that he had time to watch them grasping at nothing, powerless to do anything about it, with time enough to sense the coming impact with terror and fury. The sky fell away and he dropped like a stone.

CHAPTER 12

He landed in the thin underbrush at the bottom, crashing onto the frozen, compacted earth and a single fallen tree limb. His left leg took the worst of it, absorbing the whole weight of his body so that it buckled unnaturally beneath him. The breath was driven from him, and as he sprawled on his back the pain flashed through him like heat so that he saw whiteness bright as lightning, and then nothing.

When he opened his eyes it took him a second to remember

where he was. He didn't know how long he had been lying there. The thin remnant of snow hadn't been thick enough to muffle his fall, let alone cushion it. The ribs on the right side of his back and the base of his spine smoldered, and when he tried to move, his left leg from the knee down sang with an agony so intense that he almost blacked out again.

Keep still. Wait.

He opened his eyes again. No one was around. No sign of his attacker or other visitors who might have glimpsed his fall. There was only sky, the steep rock of the moat walls, and the dead, twisted tree limb that had been blown into the trench months ago where it had lain ever since, waiting for him to land on it.

"Help!" he managed. It was a thin cry and set him coughing. He groaned and closed his eyes again, opening them with relief at the sound of movement above.

Somebody saw me fall in, he thought. *Thank God.*

But when he opened his eyes he saw no one at the rail. Then a pebble skipped down the rock wall of the trench and, realizing it had come from the other side, his eyes moved slowly up to the top. The great tawny head of the lioness looked down at him.

Oh God.

The animal leaned out and put one massive paw on the edge, testing her foothold as she strained to get a better view. She was only about twelve feet above him, almost directly above. He could see the splay of her paws, part of the pads beneath.

If she drops on you . . .

She had amber eyes and a great pale muzzle. Her mouth opened, part exercise, part yawn, and Thomas saw that she could probably wrap her jaws around his entire head. Her teeth were great yellow chisels. She flicked one ear, then lowered her head, her eyes still bright and focused.

Keep still.

For a second Thomas remembered the cocktail of pills he had considered taking not so many days ago, how languidly he had decided not to swill them all down. Now he lay here, badly bruised at the very least, maybe broken, with a four-hundred-pound cat staring at him, and the irony of how badly he wanted to live through the next few moments struck him so forcefully that he actually laughed.

The lion's ears pricked and her neck and shoulders flexed. Thomas stifled the chuckle and kept still. It took him a moment to realize that the dull rumble that he heard, a sound like the distant turning of a large engine, was actually coming from the animal's throat. He tried to ignore the pain, keep absolutely still, and once more avoid the temptation to laugh.

Getting eaten by a lion, he thought, *might be absurd, but it's not actually funny.*

Not if you're the one being eaten, no.

Well, at least you'll make the news.

Not good enough, I'm afraid. I have to get out of here.

Slowly, excruciatingly slowly and with his battered body crying with outrage, Thomas began to roll into a crouch. For a moment this meant taking his eyes off the lion, a terrifying prospect that left him straining with his ears for sounds of the animal's descent. She could be on him in two bounds, he guessed, and would probably not suffer at all from the drop, particularly if she could land on something soft.

Something like you, you mean.

Oh, that's helpful, he responded to his own inner voice. *Scare yourself stupid.*

She might not be able to get back up unassisted, but he doubted lions' minds worked like that, so he just had to hope that the beast felt neither especially threatened by his presence, or hungry. Wincing at the pain, he turned to the far side of the trench and considered the rock wall.

It was definitely climbable, though whether he had the strength to do it was another matter altogether. He couldn't put weight on his left leg for more than a second before the pain became blinding. He checked the lion. She was watching him from the top, her head weaving slowly from side to side, her eyes somehow never leaving him. The truth of the situation hit him with the clarity of a lightning bolt. She was gauging the distance to pounce.

Lying where he was, he was no better than meat. She growled and her tail lashed, so that even before the sinews of her forelegs began to stretch, he knew she was coming.

Thomas had not doubted that she could get down the rock wall, but the ease with which she did so was still staggering. She leaped down in one easy, almost lazy motion, her massive paws absorbing the impact of her drop so that she barely troubled the thin dusting of snow that had escaped the watery sun. She landed ten feet away and paused, her yellow eyes fixed on his, her mouth lolling slightly.

Down here with him she looked bigger than ever. Careful not to take his eyes off hers, Thomas groped behind him for the broken branch he had landed on, fingers splayed wildly as they scoured the icy ground. When he found it, he rose quickly, agonizingly, and took two steps backward the moment he was even close to vertical, shrugging out of his coat as he did so. The lion seemed to be leaning forward, like a man on a slowing bus countering inertia. When it stopped entirely, he'd fall forward. For the lion, Thomas knew, the inertia was all in her mind. When she thought the time was right, she'd come.

And if she does, you die. It's that simple.

For a second he thought about brandishing the branch as a weapon, but that would be a futile gesture. If she surged forward now he could be armed with a rocket launcher and she'd still kill him. It was all about her decision.

She gazed unblinking, and he stared back as his hands fiddled with the branch and his heavy coat. When he was ready, he took a fractional breath, stood as tall as he could, and roared at the top of his lungs, hoisting his jacket on the branch high above his head like a war standard.

It was a desperate, absurd noise, a great whooping yell like some woad-painted berserker hurling himself at the locked shields of a hundred Roman legionnaries. The moment he ran out of air, he sucked in another breath and repeated the same cry, high and long as loud as he could manage.

The great cat faltered, and her eyes flashed up to the top of his ludicrous scarecrow staff where his coat flapped. In a second or two, Thomas had doubled his height, and the lion was—if not actually scared—surprised, even uncertain. He was bigger, and certainly noisier, than she had expected. Ignoring the shooting pain in his leg, he flailed his arms and rehearsed his barbaric yawp one more time.

Thomas could see her body contract, her head withdraw a fraction, her eyes flash around as she considered her options, and the fractional hint that he might yet snatch victory from the jaws of defeat—a phrase which had never seemed so delightfully apposite—filled his shouting with a determined vigor. In seconds she was backing away.

The moment she did, Thomas turned his back on her, reached as high as he could up the molded concrete sides, and launched himself up, fingers scrabbling for handholds in the stone. The cement was pinkish and shaped to look like eroded rock strata. There was just enough purchase for him and not quite enough for the cat. Sparing his left leg as best he could, he dragged his weight up a couple of feet at a time until he could reach the fence.

He knew that he shouldn't have taken his eyes off the lion, but he was too elated. When he did glance back, it was just in time to see her change her mind. She rushed the moat wall and threw herself up at him, snarling and slashing with one immense paw. Thomas snatched his leg out of her reach, fought not to lose his grip, and grabbed at the rail above him as the lion fell back to earth. Before she could lunge again, he was clambering over the rail, chuckling again to himself, relief making him slightly hysterical.

He was barely out when he caught sight of a large black woman in uniform moving swiftly in his direction from over by the carousel.

"What the *hell* do you think you're doing?" she roared.

She was closing fast, her eyes wide and furious, giving off almost as much raw menace as the lioness.

Thomas considered quickly, raised an apologetic hand, and started limping away toward the seal pool and the exit as quickly as he could manage. He looked down into the moat as he beat his retreat, and the lioness stared back, watching imperiously as he stumbled off, his eyes scanning Stockton Drive for a cab.

"Dead?" asked the Seal-breaker.

"No," said the voice on the phone. War's voice. "Shaken up, bruised. He may have to see a doctor, but he'll live."

"Probably as well," said the Seal-breaker. "But scared, yes?"

"Count on it."

"Scared enough?"

War's voice stalled, and the Seal-breaker pounced on the hesitation.

"That's what I thought," he said.

"He'll drop it," said War. "He's a *high school teacher*. He didn't even like his brother. He'll drop it."

"Perhaps," said the Seal-breaker. "But in case he doesn't, I want you close, particularly if he starts sniffing around."

"There's nothing for him to find here."

"I don't mean here," said the Seal-breaker, irritation flickering suddenly and then dying away again like dry lightning. "I'm sending Pestilence back to Naples. Just in case."

"There's no way Knight will go to Italy," said War. "Why would he?"

"I said 'just in case,'" said the Seal-breaker carefully. "For now, watch and wait. Dealing with him here—if it comes to that—is likely to be messy anyway. Who knows," he said with a smile as momentary as his anger had been, "maybe a European trip is just what Mr. Knight needs. The world is, after all, a very dangerous place."

CHAPTER 13

It was almost dark by the time Thomas got back to the rectory, and the rain had turned to sleet. Finding no lights on in the house and no sign of life, he inched his way up the stairs to Ed's room and sat on the bed. He was pretty sure he had sprained both knee and ankle in his fall, but he didn't think he had broken anything. He'd be black and blue in the morning but, on the whole, he had been lucky.

Not often you end the day relieved not to have been eaten, is it?

He grinned to himself.

"Leave it alone," his attacker had said.

His grin faded. There had been no attempt at robbery, no gleeful laughing at a lethal but well-executed prank. *Leave it alone.* Someone was trying to scare him away from poking into Ed's death.

Well, they'd succeeded in scaring him. Just not enough to stop him.

Mule, said Kumi's voice in his head. *Ox.*

The room was still untidy from the rifling of Parks, the thief who had taken what the beat cop had called the Jesus fish. Could the same man have subsequently tossed him to the lions? He had no way of knowing for sure, but he didn't think so. The thief had seemed impetuous, reckless even, something that his odd weapons seemed to reinforce. The guy at the zoo had been a professional, all his movements economical, and his strength prodigious. The guy had picked him up and thrown him as if he were no more than a child. Men like that carried automatic pistols, not swords.

"Devlin?" he mused aloud.

He got to his feet, restless, suddenly anxious to get out of this room and its oppressive silence. He wanted to find Jim and tell him about his afternoon with the senator, the lion, and the man who had thrown him to her, but on descending saw no sign that he was home. The rest of the house was still dark, so he wandered down to the one part of the building he hadn't seen, away from the front door and kitchen, past stained wooden cabinets through a musty-smelling corridor lit by a bare, low-wattage bulb. There was one door on the left, which was locked, and another at the end of the corridor. He tried it, and as it opened he stepped into his past.

It was a sacristy, where the priests dressed for mass, where they stored their vestments and the accoutrements of the liturgy. It smelled of incense and candle wax, and it was gloomy and wooden floored, like the sacristy where he had been an altar boy thirty years before. As a rule, Thomas didn't like dark, enclosed places, but this was different: familiar. At the far end were a pair of double doors into the church, and through them came a faint murmuring: Jim, saying mass, doubtless to a huddle of lonely seniors who had nothing better to do on a cold March night.

For the first time Thomas felt the loss of his brother wholly without rancor. This could have been where they horsed around in their cassocks before mass, messing about with the candles, arguing over who got to be the cross bearer and who had to be the acolyte. Ed always got the cross. He was two years older than Thomas, which made him taller, so Thomas would be paired with one of the shorter boys and together they would carry the heavy brass candlesticks on either side of Ed, who walked slightly ahead of the procession. The smell brought it all back to him, as if it were yesterday: the dead matches, the exotic fragrance of the incense so alien to the rest of their working-class world, and for a moment he thought he could turn and see his brother, ten or twelve years old, pulling the white surplice over his head and mimicking Father Wells's nasal singsong: *"In the name of the Father, and of the Son . . ."*

Tears started to his eyes, not because his brother was dead, but because Ed and this place announced so clearly how very much he had lost since those days, that so much had gone of life and left him with so little. It wasn't just Ed that had gone, it was also his parents, several friends, and, of course, his ex-wife, and though she was very much alive, her absence from his life seemed to speak loudest of isolation and failure. Thomas stood still in the gathering darkness, only thinking to wipe the tears away when brought back to himself by the once-familiar rumble of the congregation saying in broken unison, "We believe in one God, the Father Almighty, Creator of heaven and earth, of all that is seen and unseen . . ."

The mass he had listened to through the closed doors had been over for two hours. He had shared a dinner of frozen chicken pot pies with oven fries and baked beans with Jim at the kitchen table and had watched the local news while Jim made a round of phone calls and tapped out e-mails on a droning, yellowed PC: "parish admin stuff," he said. Jim had listened aghast to Thomas's account of the incident at the zoo, speculating that Devlin had arranged the whole thing.

"Maybe," said Thomas, pleased by the priest's ambivalence about the senator, even by the way he seemed to be taking Thomas's side. "But Devlin didn't even try to warn me off."

"He didn't need to! He had some goon ready to kill you!"

"Not really," Thomas admitted, sipping his Bushmills. "I think he came to warn me off. I, sort of, fought back, and he lost his temper. I could have been killed, but I don't think he really intended . . ."

"That's about the dumbest argument I've ever heard," said Jim.

"So you think I should go to the police?"

Jim faltered.

"Well," he said. "I don't know. *The police* . . ."

"You don't trust them?"

"Cops are too fond of rule books," said the priest.

"Isn't the Bible . . . ?"

"No," said Jim, abruptly.

"Anyway," Thomas said, "reporting it will achieve nothing beyond making me look like an idiot."

"That's what you're afraid of?" said Jim, his good humor returning as quickly as it had gone. "Looking stupid?"

"Well," said Thomas, "it *is* humiliating to have to talk about how . . ."

"Right," said Jim dryly. "I can see that. If I had been thrown down a trench to be eaten by lions I know that what would really bother me was how *embarrassing* it all was. I mean, what does one *wear* for such an event . . . ?"

"I'm not kidding, Jim," said Thomas. "The guy told me to leave things alone. If I'm going to keep poking into Ed's death, I need to be discreet about it. Sitting in a squad car and chatting to some well-meaning cop who can do absolutely nothing to help will achieve nothing, and may give whoever is watching me a reason to put me out of the picture for good. It's not worth the risk."

"And I thought *I* was paranoid," said Jim.

"When someone tries to make you into whatever lions have when they can't get zebra, you're allowed a little paranoia."

"Point taken, Daniel," said Jim, managing a smile.

In the lion's den.

"Funny."

"I thought so."

"I keep coming back to what Ed was doing in Italy," said Thomas.

"Research and a bit of downtime," said Jim. "But I got the impression he spent a lot of time away from the retreat house. They called here once asking if he had left early."

The phone rang in the kitchen. Thomas checked his watch and raised his eyebrows. It was after ten. Jim, used to being called—and called out—at all hours, just sighed and lumbered into the other room. Thomas closed his eyes and settled back. He was ready for bed. It had been a long, strange day, like the one before it, and he didn't know what to do next. He wondered why he was still in the presbytery and if he was ready to go back to his empty house.

Better be. You'll be spending a lot of time there for the next few months.

The prospect of no job, no income, nothing to do with his time depressed and wearied him still further. He turned and noticed that Jim had left the computer on, the screen showing the parish website. One of the thumbnail images of the community was the very picture of Thomas's wedding that currently lay on the floor of Ed's room. That Ed would have used that picture, particularly after they lost touch, surprised him, and he stared at it, wondering what had been going on in his brother's life before he died.

"It's for you."

Jim was standing in the doorway holding the portable phone.

"Here," said Jim. "I'll see if I can turn up that contact address in Italy."

Thomas took the phone from him frowning.

"This is Thomas Knight," he said.

"Hello, Tom."

It was probably only a couple of seconds, but he felt that he had been standing there for at least a minute in stunned silence.

"Tom, you there?"

No one else called him that. No one ever had.

"Kumi?"

He didn't need to ask, hadn't really meant to. It had just come out, hoarse, distant, like the echoes of the past he had heard in the sacristy. The hairs on his arms were bristling and his heart had started to race.

"Hi, Tom."

"Hi. It's been a while."

"Five years, yes."

She said it without resentment, perhaps a little sadly. It was he, after all, who had refused to talk to her anymore.

"I called you at home, but I guess you still don't check your messages, so I thought I'd try to reach you here."

"Right," he said. He just couldn't find words. Jim had just walked back in brandishing a slip of paper, but his smile died when he saw Thomas's face, as if he thought he might be having a stroke. Maybe he was.

"Listen, I just wanted to say how sorry I was about Ed," she said.

"Right," he said again. "Thanks."

"I know things hadn't been good between you lately, but . . . well, it's just terrible. I wish I could do something."

"Thanks. I know. It's okay." Then, as an afterthought, "Wait. How did you know?"

She seemed to hesitate.

"I had a call from DHS," she said.

"Oh," said Thomas, unsure of what to do with this.

"So," she said, moving things along. "You doing okay?"

"Not bad, you know."

"Work okay?"

"Fine," he lied. "You know, the usual."

"Right."

"You? Work, I mean."

"Oh yes. All work and no play. I was thinking of you in the office the other day," she said. Her voice was light now, almost frivolous. It sounded forced, ghostwritten.

"Yes?" he managed.

"Yes. I was thinking back to when we went to Arizona with Ed, and we went on that hike. That was great, wasn't it? I think back about that a lot. Remember, when we came down that dried-up creek bed? And Ed was there, and we were all laughing . . ."

"Kumi," he interjected, "you okay?"

She ignored him, her voice a little shrill now, high and fast as if she were auditioning for a sitcom.

"And the three of us were staying in that little hotel and it was just the best time and . . . And Ed kept talking about that time he went to Italy. Remember? I keep thinking about that hike up the creek bed. Remember that? Going back to the river source—and Ed said it was just like that place he went to and . . . Anyway. Listen, I'm sorry. I'm rambling. I'm calling from work so I shouldn't stay on. I just wanted to wish you all the best and say how sorry I was. Okay?"

"Kumi," he repeated, more carefully, more seriously, "are you okay?"

"I'm fine. *Really*. It's you I'm concerned about, Tom."

"Wait," he said.

"I'm sorry, Tom. I really have to go. We'll talk again, okay? Bye."

"Kumi . . ."

"Bye, Tom."

The line went dead.

Thomas stood there in the dimly lit room, staring at the phone.

"You all right, Thomas?" said Jim.

"I don't think so," said Thomas. The hairs on his arms were still bristling, and he felt very cold. "I think things are worse than I thought. Far worse."

CHAPTER 14

"It was your wife," said Jim, recapping, clarifying.

"Ex-wife," said Thomas, looking around the room. Maybe he should take his brother's papers.

"Ex-wife," said Jim, "who you haven't spoken to since the divorce."

"We're not divorced," said Thomas. "She wouldn't. Catholic, you see," he added bitterly. "Didn't want to be cut off from the Church, but couldn't stand being on the same continent as me. So, at my brother's advice, she went back to where we met and stayed there."

"Where you met?"

"Japan." Just saying the word pained him.

"But she's not Japanese?"

"Born in Boston," said Thomas. "Second generation."

"So she called to offer her condolences . . ."

"That's not why she called," said Thomas. "Not really. She called to warn me."

"By talking about a trip you took to Arizona with her and your brother? I don't get it."

"We never laughed in Arizona," said Thomas, darkly. "We never hiked. We sat in the hotel room and screamed at each other for five days straight and then we went home and she packed her case and left. It was supposed to pull us back together but it drove us apart."

"You didn't hike up a creek bed?"

"I did," said Thomas. "She didn't. I stormed out and trekked up some damn mountain. Anyway, I was climbing over a boulder—too furious to pay attention to what I was doing—and I fell and broke my ankle. It took me all night to get back to the car, by which time I was nearly dead from exhaustion and heatstroke. Kumi, assuming I'd abandoned her, had taken a cab to the airport, so she never even heard about it till a week later, by which time we were too angry at each other. It was the perfect end to the trip from hell."

"What about Ed? Couldn't he help?"

"He might have been able to," said Thomas, snapping the case shut and turning to face Jim. "But he wasn't there."

Jim stared at him.

"What?"

"We might not have been the perfect couple," said Thomas, "but when we took a trip to try and fix our ruptured marriage, we didn't take my brother along for the ride. Especially since he was part of the reason it was ruptured."

"If she was trying to warn you of something, why wouldn't she just say it right out?" said Jim.

"Because she's scared."

"Of what?"

"I have no idea, but she's not scared for herself, she's scared for me. I asked her and she said so. *'It's you I'm concerned about.'* It was the only thing she said that sounded like her. That and the stuff about going back to the source."

"Which means what?"

"Where this all started, I guess," said Thomas.

"Which is where?"

"Ed said it was just like that place he went to," Thomas recited, reaching out to Jim.

For a second the priest stood there bemused, and then Thomas took his right hand and opened it. The slip of paper with the address lay on the priest's palm.

"Thomas," he said, "that's crazy."

"I don't know what else to do," said Thomas. "I don't know what's going on. My ex-wife thinks I'm in danger, and given my episode at the zoo, I'd say she was right. My brother is dead and no one will tell me why or how. The whole situation is crazy, and the only thing I know for sure is that it started here. Italy. That's what she's telling me. Start there."

He held up the slip of paper that his late brother had dictated over a crackling phone to the priest in front of him two months ago.

"I had little in common with my brother," he said, "and I have no interest in what he believed, but I have to find out what happened to him. I owe him that much. I'm going to Naples."

PART II

THE FOUR HORSEMEN

And I saw when the Lamb opened one of the seals, and I heard, as it were the noise of thunder, one of the four beasts saying, Come and see.

And I saw, and behold a white horse: and he that sat on him had a bow; and a crown was given unto him: and he went forth conquering, and to conquer.

And when he had opened the second seal, I heard the second beast say, Come and see.

And there went out another horse *that was* red: and *power* was given to him that sat thereon to take peace from the earth, and that they should kill one another: and there was given unto him a great sword.

And when he had opened the third seal, I heard the third beast say, Come and see. And I beheld, and lo a black horse; and he that sat on him had a pair of balances in his hand.

And I heard a voice in the midst of the four beasts say, A measure of wheat for a penny, and three measures of barley for a penny; and *see* thou hurt not the oil and the wine.

And when he had opened the fourth seal, I heard the voice of the fourth beast say, Come and see.

And I looked, and behold a pale horse: and his name that sat on him was Death, and Hell followed with him. And power was given unto them over the fourth part of the earth, to kill with sword, and with hunger, and with death, and with the beasts of the earth.

—Revelation 6:1–8

CHAPTER 15

Pestilence sat alone and unnoticed on a wrought-iron chair, sipping espresso, watching a handful of ragged boys pursuing a soccer ball up and down a washing-hung alley across the piazza. There was no one else in the tiny Neapolitan café and nowhere to put them were they to arrive. From time to time someone would drop by and chat with the owner behind the tall bar, though such visits seemed as much social as professional and the American saw no money changing hands. Someone sped by on a scooter, and Pestilence watched the sun setting behind the once-elegant apartments with their eighteenth-century façades, now dirty, the lower stories plastered with election posters and daubed with the graffiti that covered the city. In the middle of the square the traffic honked and jostled around some forgotten equestrian statue, so that anyone not listening with special concentration would not have heard the cell phone when it rang.

Pestilence heard, and did not need to check to see who was calling. Only the Seal-breaker had this number.

"Yes?"

"Expect the target within the hour," said the Seal-breaker without preamble. "He will make for Santa Maria delle Grazie. You should expect him there."

"I'm already in position," Pestilence said, smiling.

The rider on the white horse, the first of the four horsemen of the apocalypse called forth by the Seal-breaker in the book of Revelation, had been the subject of many interpretations over the years, though the figure was probably rooted in the Parthians, whose mounted archers terrorized first-century Rome. One of their preferred tactics was to gallop away in apparent retreat, only to turn in their saddles and greet their pursuers with a hail of arrows: a Parthian—or as it came to be known in English—*parting* shot. The deadly duplicity of the strategy fed Bible readers who favored less historical and more allegorical readings of the book's curious symbology. For them the whiteness of the horse combined with the treacherous use of the bow suggested deception and falsity of a particularly lethal kind. Pestilence, or this modern, coffee-sipping, version of him, liked that. What was the use of murderous malice if you could see it coming a mile away?

That last thought raised an awkward possibility.

"Are the others here?" said Pestilence.

"You don't need to know that."

"We could get in each other's way," said Pestilence with a flush of irritation.

There was a momentary silence on the other end of the line, and Pestilence became still.

Shouldn't have asked. He'll know what you really mean.

"There will be other agents in the field," said the Seal-breaker.

Pestilence took a breath. A taxi blared unnaturally close.

"Famine?"

"Already there," said the Seal-breaker.

Pestilence's eyes closed for a moment and one hand clenched. There was no point saying anything else. And what could be said? How could anyone give words to the kind of creeping terror another human being generated without seeming weak or irrational?

"OK," said Pestilence. "Just keep him out of my way."

The phone went dead, and Pestilence drained the last smear of coffee with a gesture that looked determined, in spite of the way the cup tinkled uneasily in the saucer.

At almost the same instant, Thomas Knight walked into the piazza. He was squinting at the sun, laboring with his bag, and generally oozing the air of baffled anxiety that clings to tourists the world over. His clothes marked him out as different, as American, so that he was conspicuous and out of place long before he paused to consider the map in his guidebook. He looked as if he might be limping slightly.

Pestilence smiled and turned away from him, setting down the tiny espresso cup with a hand that was now quite steady.

CHAPTER 16

Thomas had emerged from the taxi rattled and slightly nause-ated. The traffic had been relentless and moved seemingly at random and at high speeds over the ancient cobbled streets. Twice he thought they would hit pedestrians who stepped out in front of them, and they did actually tap the mirrors of a passing van whose driver responded with a volley on his horn, but no reduction in speed. Unable to make sense of the taxi driver's Italian, he had held out a fistful of notes and the man had taken ten euros without further comment, before turning the battered turquoise Fiat back onto the street.

Thomas dragged his luggage behind him and squinted at the road names etched into the sides of the corner buildings, turned a couple of times, and finally located the appropriate side street. There, where the sun was less insistent and the traffic roar more muted, he found a great arched door squeezed in between a bakery and a café/bar. The door was a good twenty feet high, covered with ancient green paint and studded with nails, black with age. He tried the bell, which was set into the mouth of a bronze lion head, and waited.

This was the church of Santa Maria delle Grazie and, more particularly, the retreat house where Thomas's brother had spent some of the last weeks of his life. Thomas, who spoke no Italian beyond a few phrases he had picked out of his guide-book on the plane, shifted from foot to foot uneasily. The next few moments—assuming someone answered the door—were bound to be uncomfortable.

A small door within the larger one cracked and opened, like the portal in a dream, and a young man stepped out. He was dressed in a black cassock, his hair was neatly trimmed, and he looked frankly at Thomas through rimless oval glasses for a moment. Thomas began muttering in apologetic English, but before he had said anything of substance a strange change

came over the young man. His eyes widened and he took a
half step backward, his mouth open but no sound coming out.
He looked confused, maybe even scared.

Thomas's apologies accelerated.

"I'm so sorry to just show up," he said. "I don't speak Italian. I hope this isn't a bad time. I'm Thomas Knight. My brother
Ed stayed here last year. He was a priest from America."

"You are his brother," said the priest, the uncertainty melting
away as quickly as it had come. "Yes. I can see. Come inside."

Thomas followed him in to a dark, barrel-vaulted hallway
that was several degrees cooler than the street and, beyond it,
a sunlit courtyard shaded green by orange trees on which the
fruit—still small and pale—hung improbably. As the door behind him clicked into place, the street noise faded and they
could have been in some country villa.

"I am Padre Giovanni," said the young man. He offered a
strong, olive-skinned hand and Thomas shook it once, smiling.

"I would have warned you I was coming," Thomas began
again, "but it was a spur-of-the-moment kind of thing."

The Italian looked unsure of the phrase, and Thomas
waved it away as unimportant.

"You are looking for somewhere to stay?" said the priest.
"I think we have a room available for a few days, then we will
be full with *Franciscana*. Nuns from Assisi."

"A couple of days would be fine," said Thomas, glad that
he would not have to venture out into the city traffic again in
search of a home for the night. His leg hurt from the fall at the
zoo, and he was exhausted. He might sleep for a couple of
hours before going out for dinner, then he would figure out
what exactly it was he was trying to achieve on this trip, other
than not being in Chicago for health reasons.

"I think also that your brother left some boxes," said the
priest, leading him across the courtyard to a flight of stone
steps.

Thomas became quite still.

"Perhaps you would like to see them," said the priest.

It was like stepping through a rain shower, and it washed all his tiredness away.

"Yes," said Thomas. "Right away, if you don't mind."

The room he was assigned contained a bedstead, an ancient chest of drawers, a desk with a single chair, and a plain wooden crucifix on the white plastered brick. He paced the terra-cotta tile in his bare feet, feeling their coolness, and then slipped on a pair of sandals and headed back the way he had come. Father Giovanni was waiting for him at the bottom of the stairs with a heavy iron key in his hand.

"This way," he said.

They walked past a large communal dining room and the open door of a kitchen that smelled heavily of baking bread and rosemary, making small talk about the flight, the temperature back home, and when meals were served. There had been no mention of money thus far.

At the foot of another staircase the priest greeted a passing nun in a brown habit, then showed him into a storage room heaped with crates and boxes.

"Those two belonged to Eduardo," he said. "I did not know him well but I think he was . . ." he paused to find the word, "interesting." He smiled at the memory and then left the room, closing the door behind him.

Thomas stood there for a moment and then pulled one of the boxes toward him and flipped the cardboard flaps open. Inside were books, some in English, some in Italian, a few in other languages including French and Latin. Most of those he could read looked like works of theology, biblical exegesis, church history and archaeology. Some seemed more scientifically inflected and there were several by or about someone called Teilhard de Chardin. But it was the papers and journals that caught Thomas's eye. He reached in and removed a slim notebook. Inside were lists and scribbled, halting notes in his brother's familiar scrawl. The first page was headed "Pompeii."

Thomas smiled distantly at his brother's studiousness, then looked up as the sound of raised voices drifted down the hallway outside. Two men, one loud and angry, and getting closer.

Without a thought, Thomas shoved the journal into the inside of his jacket just as the door blew open and a man stumbled in, shouting, his face red with fury and his eyes fixed on Thomas. Behind him, rushing to catch up, looking alarmed and hesitant, was Father Giovanni.

The first man—also a priest, it seemed from his clothes—was perhaps sixty, a big, broad-shouldered man with a voice like thunder. He stabbed at Thomas's chest with his index finger, the stream of Italian invective unbroken. Thomas raised his hands, fingers spread.

"He says you have to go," said the young priest. "He says this place is only for religious. You cannot stay."

"Why?" said Thomas. "What did I do?"

Another rapid exchange in Italian. The old priest's temperature seemed to be going up by the second.

Thomas lowered his hands and looked sidelong at Father Giovanni, who shrugged small and slow.

"I told him who you were," he said, "but he said this is church property till the order says otherwise."

"Father Eduardo was my brother . . ." Thomas began, attempting a more conciliatory tone.

"You go!" roared the other suddenly. "Now."

And then there was silence, save for the furious priest's labored breathing. His eyes remained fixed on Thomas and his nostrils flared like a bull poised to charge.

"These are my brother's things," said Thomas with a composure he didn't feel. "I have a right to look at them."

The old priest snarled a few words in Italian out of the corner of his mouth, and Father Giovanni's discomfort increased still further. Thomas caught the word *Polizia*.

"He is telling me to call the police," said the young priest.

"Yeah, I got that."

"I'm sorry."

"And I cannot stay here tonight?"

"There is a hotel around the corner," said the young man, clearly embarrassed. "The Executive. I am sorry."

Thomas looked back at the other priest, but the blind rage had not abated one iota.

CHAPTER 17

The Executive was a stone's throw from the retreat house, on the corners of Via del Cerriglio and Sanfelice in the heart of the old city and less than a mile from the castle and harbor. Had it been a longer walk, Thomas—suffering the combination of a sprained knee and a rising indignation about how he had just been treated—would have been too distracted to find it. But he checked in to the renovated convent building without incident and within moments found himself standing on a third-floor balcony overlooking the crazed traffic in the street below and wondering how he would ever sleep through the noise.

He tossed his wrinkled jacket on the bed and plucked the notebook from its inside pocket.

It was thinner than he would have liked, and the back half was empty. The notes were arranged by location: Pompeii, Herculaneum, Castellammare di Stabia, Paestum, and Velia. The only one that meant anything to Thomas—and not much at that—was Pompeii, the ancient Roman town destroyed by the eruption of Vesuvius in AD 79.

Each section seemed to be a list of locations, Pompeii being the longest at fifteen closely written pages, then Herculaneum. The lists seemed to be places within the site, many of them sounding like private residences (*the house of the dancing fawn, the house of the Vettii, the house of the wooden partition*), though others were temples and public buildings. Paestum featured a single, lengthy entry, added to in different-colored inks and scribbled pencil. The other two bore the same inscription: "No visible evidence."

Of what?

His first response was a sense of deflation. Ed may well have been poking around ancient Roman sites for his book on early Christian symbols, but that didn't seem terribly promising as a link to terrorism, the Far East, or anything else that might have somehow gotten him killed.

He gazed down at the street to where a young Asian man was tentatively edging through the constant stream of little cars and scooters, and suddenly felt tired beyond the capacity to think. He closed the glass door to the balcony, electronically lowered the outer screen—nicely cutting out most of the street noise—shed his clothes, and flopped heavily onto the bed. In seconds he was asleep.

He woke an hour later, still tired but somehow sure he couldn't get back to sleep. He showered, put on shorts and a T-shirt, and went down to the tiny lobby, where the concierge took his key.

"How long does it take to get to Pompeii?" he asked.

"Maybe one half hour. By train, yes?"

"I guess. Can I get a cab to the station?"

The concierge picked up the phone and barked orders in Italian.

"Five minutes," he said, eyeing Thomas's shorts skeptically. "When you get to the station, look for the Circumvesuviana line. And watch your wallet."

The station was dirty, chaotic, and packed with people, including huddles of uniformed policemen with dogs. No one seemed to pay them any attention, so this was, Thomas surmised, a routine presence. Buying a ticket proved complicated, requiring him to go to a different area of the building and then follow a grimy subway down to the track. He carried only a small digital camera that he had borrowed from Jim in Chicago, and Ed's notebook, which he studied as the train pulled out into the sun.

After the second stop, a band of musicians boarded and launched into an effusive song accompanied by accordion, tambourine, and—improbably—double bass. Most of the passengers ignored them, but Thomas dropped a couple of euros into their hat as they moved to the next coach. Afterward he wondered whether he should be spending his money rather more carefully. It was not as if he had an income anymore.

The train's passengers were about a quarter tourists, some of them Americans. There was one group sitting close by who were pale and large, and oddly dressed in pastels and baseball caps. They talked loudly to each other, clutched their cameras, and puzzled over the foreign currency as if it were written in Sanskrit. It was as if they were playing tourists in a movie.

Of course, there might be others on the train who blend in so well you don't notice them.

Thomas considered the people around him and thought it unlikely, though he couldn't put his finger on exactly what marked out the Italians as so clearly Italian. Tanned skin, dark eyes, and manes of black hair dominated but were by no means the rule. It was something in the way they dressed, the way they carried themselves that made them so conspicuously different, an elegant nonchalance that made even the most ordinary of faces strikingly intriguing. The only one who might be American was a woman in the brown habit of the nun he had seen at the retreat house.

Thomas looked out over the Tyrrhenian Sea to his right as the track traced down the coast with its fishing boats and black lava beaches. There were two Ercolano stops, one of which would probably take him to the ancient town of Herculaneum, should this blind search seem worth pursuing elsewhere. At the moment, with no idea what he was looking for and deeply skeptical that there was anything valuable to be found, Thomas thought that unlikely. He had a vague sense of mission that served only to make him anxious and uncertain, but to all intents and purposes, he was no different from the tourists. The idea depressed him.

But it was only after the train left him at the Pompeii station and he got his first glimpse of the site that the enormity of his problem truly registered. This was no huddle of stone fragments dotted with statues, no cluster of columns on an acre or two of patchy mosaic. The place was huge. It was, in fact, a town, vast and breathtaking, its streets radiating out for what seemed like miles in all directions.

What the hell am I supposed to do now?

He began by buying a glossy guidebook and spending ten long minutes under the shade of a palm tree studying a map of the remains, marking every site he could find listed in Ed's notebook.

"It's a bit daunting, isn't it?" said a voice.

Thomas looked up, shading his eyes against the light. It was the nun from the train.

"It is a bit, yes," he said, getting to his feet. "We're here, right?" he said, prodding the map with one finger.

"No," said the nun. "We're at the Marine Gate, here."

"Christ," muttered Thomas, hastily adding, "sorry. No offense."

"None taken. I realize that for most people such words don't really mean what they say."

"No," said Thomas, relaxing a little. "You're right."

She smiled back. She was perhaps thirty, maybe a little more, though it was hard to tell with the habit and headdress that revealed only her face and hands. She wore a silver crucifix around her neck, a white rope belt around her waist, and heavy, buckled sandals on her feet. If she was Italian, her English was flawless.

"I didn't mean to interrupt you," she said, smiling and taking a step backward as if ready to leave. "I just thought you were looking lost. You seem slightly familiar too, but I expect I'm thinking of someone else."

"Probably," said Thomas. "I just arrived from the States. Chicago."

The nun frowned and shook her head.

"I'm from Wisconsin," she said. "Here for a retreat."

He could just about hear it now that she said it, that slightly Nordic inflection and the flat, open vowels of the upper Midwest.

"Wait a minute," said Thomas, the light going on. "Are you a Franciscan?"

"What gave it away?" said the nun, with a comic glance at the floor-length habit.

"You're at the retreat house in Naples? Santa Maria . . . something."

"Delle Grazie!" the nun completed, her smile broadening. "That's right. I saw you there, didn't I?"

"Briefly," said Thomas.

"Are you a priest?"

"God, no," said Thomas. "Again, no offense. I was just . . . visiting. I'm staying at the hotel around the corner."

"I'd say it was a coincidence, but since this is the major tourist attraction in the area, I guess it's not that surprising," said the nun. "I've been here since Wednesday but I was so jet-lagged at first that I haven't seen much yet. My retreat doesn't start for another few days so I thought I'd better get some sight-seeing in. I came here yesterday for a few hours, but it was just too much to process. I figure you really need a week to see the place properly."

"A week?" echoed Thomas, crestfallen. "I thought I'd get it covered today."

"Well, you've only got a couple of hours left today," said the nun. "The site closes at six. Was there something special you wanted to see this afternoon?"

"Not really," said Thomas. "I hadn't expected it to be so . . . *enormous.*"

"Best to do it in bits," she said. "I was going to look at the theaters today. Join me if you like."

Thomas glanced at the map and chose one of the places he had circled at random, glad he didn't have to produce Ed's notebook.

"I was hoping to visit the Temple of Isis," he said.

"Perfect," she said. "That's right next to them. Shall we?"

"I'm Thomas, by the way," he said, as he followed her into a stone-flagged tunnel that climbed up into the ancient town.

"Sister Roberta," said the nun. "I'm glad to have someone to talk to. My Italian is patchy at best, so it's been a pretty quiet couple of days."

"I would have thought you'd be good at silence," said Thomas, grinning.

"We're not Trappists," laughed the nun.

They climbed the Via della Marina toward the Roman forum, passing the Temple of Apollo on the left. Thomas was amazed. Few of the structures had roofs, but he'd seen early-twentieth-century buildings that had decayed more completely than these two thousand year old remains. The streets were bustling with tourists, most in large guided groups, so that he wondered how different the place would have been the year the mountain—looming in the distance over the brick columns of the Temple of Jupiter—had blown its wooded top, showering the area in a killing rain of lava and rock and suffocating ash.

"They didn't know it was a volcano," said Sister Roberta, distantly, following his gaze to the broken summit of Vesuvius. "A few scientifically minded folks had made connections to other known volcanoes like Etna, and there were more concerns after the earthquakes of AD 62, but the ordinary people had no idea at all. One day they were just living their lives in a fairly average Roman town, and the next . . . Everything gone. Everyone dead."

Thomas nodded, thinking of Ed.

"Funny, isn't it," she said. "It should be sad. Should make you think about mortality and such. But it's just so amazing that you can't get past the awe. It's like a movie set abandoned in the desert, but it's all real: a museum that people lived in!"

She looked thoughtful for a moment and then her face lit up.

"Let me show you something," she said, suddenly girlish in her excitement. "It's a bit out of our way at the other end of the forum, but you really have to see it to see what I mean."

She led him quickly across the great expanse of the

forum—once the city's marketplace and formal piazza—edged with white columns, and skirted the Temple of Jupiter, pointing out features she noted as she walked. Thomas smiled at the way her enthusiasm transcended the harshness of her attire.

"That was the Temple of Vespasian," she said. "And that there was the public Lararium, a kind of shrine to household gods, I think. There's a carved marble relief somewhere that shows the citizens making sacrifices to the gods after the earthquake here. The Macellum was the food market proper. You can imagine the townsfolk coming here to buy bread and fish . . ."

She was as good as a guide.

She led him through a brick arch and onto the Via di Mercurio, its great flagstones rutted with years of cart traffic before the eruption, and stood proudly pointing at the entryway of a building generally known as the House of Tragic Poet.

"There," she said. "See? They were just regular people. It's like they just stepped out for a while, except that they've all been dead for two thousand years."

What she was pointing at was a large floor mosaic in the entryway to the house, made mainly of tiny black and white squares, each only a half inch or so across. They depicted a large chained hound with a red collar, its teeth bared. Set into the mosaic beneath the beast, were the words *Cave Canem*.

"What does it mean?" said Thomas.

"Beware of the dog," she said. "See?"

And he saw.

CHAPTER 18

They meandered along the streets with their stepping-stones and their rope ties for animals, peering into once-grand villas with rectangular pools for collecting rainwater in the center of peristyled atriums. Some of the plaster walls still bore the original deep crimson paint ornamented with cupids and vines and stylized animals. They filed through the cool bathhouses with their hot rooms, cold pools, and dressing rooms; watched lizards skittering through the thermopolia where the ancient Pompeians bought wine from great clay amphora set into stone counters by the street; and marveled at the fragments of political graffiti daubed on the walls.

And they talked. The nun was surprisingly good company, and Thomas felt comfortable, perhaps because of the strangeness of the place and the fact that it all seemed so far from the States and the circumstances that had brought him here. He told her that his brother had been a priest and about his recent death, though he left any sense of mystery out of the account and made it sound as if his presence in Italy now were more pilgrimage than investigation, which was not far from the truth. He didn't know what he expected to find here, though it pleased some part of him to retread his brother's footsteps. Maybe that was all he could hope to get from the visit.

"And he was interested in archaeology?" asked Roberta.

"I guess so," said Thomas. "He was writing a book on early Christian symbols, I think, but I'm not sure why he'd be here."

"Oh, but there is some very exciting evidence of a Christian settlement here," said the nun, her face lighting up again. "Think of that! Less than fifty years after the death of Our Lord, there were already people gathering to worship Him here."

It had never occurred to Thomas that there would be a Christian presence here as early as AD 79, and he said so.

"There's a house," she answered, "though it's not open to the public, that has an engraving on the wall. It's what they call a magic square. There are five Latin words arranged in rows one on top of the other and they read the same horizontally as vertically."

"What does it say?"

"It's not what the words say that is important," she said. "It's a kind of an anagram. You rearrange the letters like this."

She squatted on the dusty ground of the triangular forum, shaded by trees and, picking up a stick, scratched into the ground:

Thomas considered it. He had enough church Latin to recognize the two key words she had arranged in the cross: *Pater Noster.* Our Father.

"It forms the first words of the Lord's Prayer," said the nun, leaving a pair of Os and As to add the Greek alpha and omega, the Beginning and End, referring to Jesus. "It's how the early Christians secretly announced their faith to each other."

Thomas wasn't sure. He was skeptical of literary codes, the reduction of complex and ambiguous meanings to simple and secret meanings. It was a strategy some of his students had found appealing and he had done his best to disabuse them of it: "Literature is complex and plural in its meanings," he always said. But there was no denying that religions, especially persecuted religions, used secret symbols that were intended to have a "correct" reading. Maybe this was indeed what had so interested his brother. For all Roberta's enthusiasm, he found the idea a little disappointing.

They walked through to the theaters. Thomas had expected something like the Coliseum, but its humbler Pompeian equivalent was nestled just within the walls in the far northwestern corner of the town. They certainly wouldn't make it that far before the site closed. The two theaters they saw were remarkable and clearly still usable structures, one broad and grand, seating perhaps five thousand, the other not even a quarter that size. Thomas climbed to the top of the stone seats and sat there for five long minutes, taking in the view down to the marble-flagged stage area and outward over the city. He liked the intimacy of the place and the fact that most of the tourist groups never made it this far, particularly this late in the day. But the more he sat there, the more the thought recurred that he didn't know what he was looking for, and that it might be best to think of this trip as a kind of farewell to his brother.

By the time he had rejoined Sister Roberta, it was time to leave.

"You'll have to come back to see the Temple of Isis," she said, leading him back round through the triangular forum. "Sorry."

"That's okay," he said. "I have no particular plans for the next few days. I can come back."

But in his heart, he doubted that he would, and he saw in her eyes that she suspected as much.

The shops out front sold the usual tourist stuff: postcards, plaster replicas of statuary, Priapus bottle openers, guidebooks, and local handicrafts. One place marked itself out from the rest with a selection of replica weapons from ancient Rome, including gladiatorial equipment. In the center of the display was a familiar *gladius*, or short sword, and a mailed glove called a *cestus*.

So Parks was here, he thought, *and picked up some souvenirs with which to terrorize Chicago . . .*

Roberta had to return to the retreat house, so Thomas dined alone at a little restaurant a stone's throw from the harbor: mussels, linguine with anchovy pesto, and a carafe of a light, fruity red. Midway through the wine he considered going for a run, but his leg had begun aching again after all the walking in Pompeii. He abandoned the idea and immediately felt better. He had an ice cream dessert called a *tartuffo* to celebrate, and ended the evening with a shot of grappa.

Back at the Executive he had been in his room several minutes before he noticed that things were not precisely as he had left them. A pouch on his bag that he had left unzipped had been carefully closed. The arrangement of tickets and luggage tags and the stub of his boarding card—things about which he was neurotically organized—had been reversed. He wanted to put this down to the maid, but he knew the room wouldn't be cleaned till he had spent a night there. That someone had gone through his room, and with care, made one thing clear: whatever trouble he had encountered in Chicago had followed him across the Atlantic.

CHAPTER 19

Thomas woke with a new energy, some of which came from anger. He didn't like being spied on and poked at, he didn't like the way he had been turned away by the old priest at the retreat house, and he was sick of not knowing what was going on.

He told the concierge, a middle-aged man whose face suggested a constant boredom touched with impatience, that someone had been in his room.

"That is not possible, sir," the Italian said with a dismissive shake of his head. "The keys are all kept here."

The keys were large and metal with heavy brass fobs trimmed with burgundy cord. They sat in a set of wooden cubbyholes above the concierge's desk.

"But if you had to step out for a second, anyone entering the hotel could take a key."

"Then they would be caught on the camera," said the concierge, as if this proved his point.

"Maybe we should take a look at it."

"Was something stolen from your room, sir?"

"No, but that hardly seems the point."

"I would say, respectfully, of course," said the concierge, "that it is entirely the point."

"May I speak to the manager?"

The concierge sighed in muted exasperation.

"I will look at the tape this afternoon," he said. "If anyone took the key, I will let you know."

Thomas nodded his agreement and then said, "Can you make a phone call for me to Sister Roberta at Santa Maria delle Grazie, please?"

"The place around the corner?"

"Yes."

Another sigh and a slightly disbelieving glance out the glass doors into the street, as if looking for the reason that this tiresome American couldn't walk the fifty yards to the retreat house instead of having him phone them.

Sister Roberta seemed surprised to hear from him.

"Listen," said Thomas. "I need to come and look at my brother's things, but I don't want to get thrown out on my ear."

He explained quickly what had happened last time, and the concierge listened unapologetically, raising his eyebrows at the absurd scrapes his guests got into.

"If Father Giovanni will let you in, that shouldn't be a problem," said the nun, a little unsure of herself. "Monsignor

Pietro has gone to say mass at his parish church, so I guess the coast is clear."

Thomas thanked her, feeling a little guilty for testing the conscience of someone he knew so slenderly, even if he thought there was no cause for moral anxiety.

She met him at the front door with Father Giovanni. The young priest seemed unsurprised and untroubled by Thomas's return, and led him back down to the storage room with the smallest of nods.

"Padre Pietro is unnecessarily strict," he said with a shrug. "And old. Old men can be . . . what is the word in English?"

"Difficult?" suggested Roberta.

"Stubborn?" said Thomas.

"Stubborn," agreed the priest. "Like a donkey, yes."

He twisted the wrought-iron handle of the door and showed them in.

Thomas knew immediately that the boxes had been tampered with. The books were all there, but there was no sign of the handwritten pages and journals.

"Some of it's missing," he said.

"Could anything have been moved for safekeeping?" said Sister Roberta to Giovanni. Thomas thought this less hopeful than naïve, and he felt a flush of irritation.

"Where might Father Pietro have put them?" he asked, pointedly.

"Now Thomas," cautioned Roberta, "we don't know . . ."

"Father?" Thomas cut in.

"I suppose he could have taken them to his room, but I cannot search there."

"How about if I do that?" said Thomas, still grim.

"I'm afraid I could not permit it," said the priest.

"Where is his room?" demanded Thomas. "Upstairs, right?"

"Please, sir," said the priest. "Thomas. I have tried to be of assistance, but this is going too far."

Thomas kept walking. At the top of the stairs he did a quick assessment and marched up another flight to a third story that overlooked the courtyard on the inside. The doors up here were numbered: guest rooms. He strode past them as Giovanni and Roberta hurried to keep up, each urging a caution he didn't feel capable of. On the far side he found two doors marked with the priests' names. As he put his hand on the handle there was a split second when Father Giovanni seemed to be contemplating some more drastic action. The two men's eyes met and the moment was broken only when Thomas clicked the latch.

"Unlocked," he said.

"Padre Pietro has, I am sure, nothing to hide."

"We'll see."

Sister Roberta's face had fallen.

"I will take nothing that doesn't belong to my family," said Thomas, and pushed the door open.

The room was small and surprisingly bare, even for a priest's room. There was a bed, a desk, a dresser, a cross on the wall. It looked no different from the guest rooms.

"This is it?" said Thomas, knowing already he would find nothing here. "This is all he has?"

"He does not always stay here," said Giovanni. "He looks after a small parish in another part of the city. Sometimes he stays there."

Thomas peered under the bed, opened a drawer of undershirts. Nothing. Then he saw the fireplace.

It was a small hearth probably designed for coal. Now it was heaped with the blackened remains of paper.

"Kind of warm for a fire," said Thomas, "wouldn't you say?"

But he felt no triumph, only a hollowing dismay.

"When will Father Pietro be back?" said Thomas.

"I do not know," said the priest.

"Would you tell me where he is?"

"He was going to his church and he said he had to go . . . somewhere else."

The priest's hesitation, and a certain hunted look in his eyes, caught Thomas's attention.

"Where?"

"A place called the Fontanelle," said Giovanni.

There it was again: a palpable discomfort, as if saying the word upset him.

"Could I find him there?"

The priest laughed, a short, unconvincing bark.

"No, you couldn't get in."

"Why not?"

"It is not open to the public. Fortunately."

"Fortunately?"

"Father Pietro will be back this afternoon," said the priest, a hint of pink rising into his sallow cheeks. "If you wish to speak to him, I suggest you do it then. I don't see what you can expect him to say, but . . . okay."

"What's the Fontanelle?" said Thomas. "I got a guidebook, but there's no reference to it, even though there are almost a hundred pages on Naples."

He was sitting at a small pizzeria a couple of blocks from the harried and unsettling railway station with Sister Roberta. He had a *quattro formaggio* pizza unlike anything he'd ever had in the States—rich with cream and a sharp, salty blue cheese—and was washing it down with some nameless red wine from a glass jug.

"I've never heard of it," she said. "Why are you interested?"

"Father Giovanni seemed uncomfortable talking about it," Thomas shrugged. "That intrigues me. And anything involving Father Pietro seems worth further scrutiny."

She frowned, apparently not too happy with his assessment of the old priest.

"You don't know for sure that those ashes were your brother's papers," she said, sipping mineral water.

"True," said Thomas. "But I'd like to know why he didn't want me looking at them in the first place, even if he didn't go on to burn the lot."

"Priests can be protective of their own," she said. "The monsignor is a deeply spiritual man. He gave a homily on the Immaculate Conception shortly after I arrived. I didn't understand most of it, of course—my Italian is not good enough—but it was a beautiful sermon, full of devotion and piety. At the end he was close to tears at the thought of Our Lord being conceived without sin, then entering this dreadful world . . ."

Thomas shook his head irritably.

"What?" said Roberta.

"I just don't get it. Any of it."

"The business with the notebooks or . . . ?"

"Priests. Nuns. Religion," said Thomas, his exasperation finally getting the better of him. "Come on. We're going to miss our train."

CHAPTER 20

Father Pietro was kneeling in the front pew of the chapel concluding his Angelus prayer to himself, his lips whispering the familiar words, his mind trying—without much success—to focus on their content. As soon as the prayer was finished, he sat down.

"Perdonami, o' signore."

Sorry, Lord, he thought. *I'm distracted. Again.*

It had been this way for a while, and he wasn't the only one to feel it. Giovanni had shed what little closeness the two of them had shared when the young priest first arrived, had become distant. Pietro couldn't blame him. He knew they all thought he was secretive, paranoid, emotionally erratic, and, more generally, just strange, all of which had intensified since Eduardo left. Word that the American priest was dead had hit Pietro like a stroke, immobilizing him, plunging him into a black mood that had lasted for days and dogged his every step still.

And then there were the rumors, always tied somehow to the Fontanelle. Pietro didn't believe them, of course, and put the reports of a strange nocturnal prowler down to a combination of his own antisocial behavior and the overactive imagination of novices who confused a retreat with a species of summer camp. But the rumors had started when Eduardo was visiting from the States, and they had ended when he left. Now Eduardo's brother was poking around, and they were starting again.

Pietro had said nothing to anybody, but only yesterday a young Benedictine monk from Rome had reported waking in the night convinced there was somebody—or something—in his room. Pietro probably wouldn't have given it too much thought, except for the fact that the monk had reported the same sound that a young Dominican had reported in the last days of Eduardo's stay: a long, rasping breath that turned into a guttural snarl, like the growl of a large cat.

But it hadn't been a cat. Because unless the monk had imagined the whole thing, what had been in his room was unlike anyone who had been seen in the retreat house by day, unlike anything the Benedictine or the Dominican had ever seen in their lives. Something so unsettling they couldn't put it into words . . .

Forget it. It's just night terrors and people who want a little attention. God knows there's enough of that in the religious orders.

But this morning, shortly after sunup, he had unlocked the chapel for matins and found . . . what? He assumed it had been a dog, maybe one he'd seen from time to time in the streets outside, though it was impossible to be sure in its present condition. It had taken him an hour to clean it all up, and the sweet rankness of the blood still hung in the air. It must have taken the killer almost as long to do what he—assuming it was a man—had done to the animal. Pietro hoped to God the beast was dead before the worst of it started.

He would have to speak to Giovanni about it, he supposed. Eventually.

And how much would you tell?

Pietro knew that Giovanni—a levelheaded, serious-minded man—did not like the Fontanelle. It hung between them constantly like a sickness too painful to be discussed, so that the young priest only ever heard of it in the dark whisperings of those who had never been. Giovanni had probably hoped that with the church's relinquishing of the Fontanelle to the city, and the city's plans to one day reopen the place to the public, Pietro would leave it alone. But the opposite had happened. He couldn't help himself. He had spent, if anything, more time there than ever, skulking back at all hours feeling shifty and defensive.

And guilty.

Catholics always feel guilty. It comes with the territory.

But there are those who merely feel responsible for sin, and those who earn it. Isn't that right, Monsignor?

Please Jesus, he thought, let it not be his fault. Let him not be the one who . . .

Waked it?

Yes, please God, not that.

Yes, Monsignor, pray. But don't pray for what you may have done already. Pray not for what is past. Pray for what might still happen. What has already started.

CHAPTER 21

Steve Devon looked up from his laptop screen, where a jittery piece of low-resolution home video was playing in a two-inch window. Then he threw his head back and laughed with delight.

"Yeah!" he said into the cell phone. "I'm looking at it right now. Man, you hit the daylights out of it!"

"I just *saw* it, you know?" said his son. "Like the pros say when they talk about seeing the ball real well. I could just see it all the way from the mound to the plate. Soon as it left his hand I could see it. Is that crazy or what?"

"Sometimes it just goes that way, I guess," said Steve, still beaming, as he hit the replay button on the RealPlayer. "I'm so proud of you, Mark. A month ago you'd never have hit that ball. Now look at you! Your stance is great, your focus. Everything. Pow! Look at that thing go. The pitcher looks like they canceled Christmas."

"I felt kinda bad for him," said Mark.

"He'll have his day," said Steve. "This one was yours. You done good, kid."

"Thanks, Dad."

"Put your mother on, will ya?"

"Sure. Love you, Dad."

"Love you too, Mark. And Mark?"

"Yeah?"

"Enjoy it. You earned it."

"Thanks, Dad."

There was a click and some mumbled voices in the background, and then a woman's voice came on.

"Is that awesome or what?"

"Pretty cool," said Steve. "Thanks for sending it."

"I'm sorry you didn't get to see it. It would be the one game you miss."

"He'll hit more next time."

"We miss you," she said, pleased but tender.

"Likewise," he answered. "Hey, I was thinking. You want to book us a week at the condo? Just the three of us."

"That's a great idea. When do you think this will all be done?"

"I should be home within the week. The end of the month at the latest . . ."

The phone in his other pocket buzzed softly.

"Hold on," he said. "That's the office. I'll call you right back."

"Okay," she said. "Love you."

He hung up, took out the other phone, and tapped the receive key.

"This is War," he said.

"I have your weapons contact lined up," said the Seal-breaker. "What do you need?"

"Heckler and Koch Mark 23 Special Operations Pistol. And a five-shot Taurus 415 revolver with an ankle holster."

"Is that all? You don't want your team?"

The rider of the red horse grinned.

"If I can't do this job by myself, you should consider replacing me."

As soon as the Seal-breaker hung up, War tapped the send button on the other phone.

"Hey, honey, it's me again. Yeah, so about this trip to the beach . . ."

CHAPTER 22

Herculaneum was different from Pompeii. For one thing, it was much smaller and most of the remains were residential, not the grand temples and official buildings of its more famous sister in disaster. The size of the place had less to do with the scale of the original town than it did with the positioning of the present one: the site went right into the edge of the modern city. Without relocating large numbers of people, the excavators just couldn't go any farther.

Herculaneum had perished in the same eruption as Pompeii, but had been buried not by ash and falling stone but by a river of volcanic mud that had swamped the city, producing quite different conditions in terms of preservation, even carbonizing wooden furniture.

The place had been excavated pretty much at random after

a local cavalry officer digging a well chanced on part of the theater in 1709. Under Charles III, the arbitrariness of the digging continued, teams tunneling in at random, taking what they could find for their private collections, donating to local museums or spiriting stuff away. Buildings were uncovered, but there was little scientific or systematic about the excavations for more than two hundred years.

The remains sat well below the level of the modern city that had been built on top of it, in some cases almost forty yards below, and entering the site meant a long descent down a ramp. Thomas immediately noticed that the streets were narrower than those in Pompeii, the houses more complete, many with intact second stories. He recalled the lines from Keats's "Ode on a Grecian Urn" about the abandoned city:

> *And, little town, thy streets for evermore*
> *Will silent be; and not a soul, to tell*
> *Why thou art desolate, can e'er return.*

True enough.

Sister Roberta had agreed to meet him back at the entrance in two hours. Since his crack about not understanding nuns and religion she had barely spoken to him, so the decision to see the ruins separately had come as a relief. He wasn't sure whether she was offended or just unsure of what he thought of her, but he would have to apologize and go into more of his personal history than he wanted if he was to smooth things over. He sighed at the prospect, wondering why he cared. He barely knew the woman, after all.

Still, for all your isolated-maverick routine, it was nice to have someone to talk to. Someone who didn't judge you, or didn't do so out loud.

On the train he had been struck by a strange idea. It had occurred to him that Pietro might think him unworthy of his brother, which was why he had burned Ed's papers. The possibility angered him even though he thought it might not be so wide of the mark. There was no question that what Ed had shared with Jim, Giovanni, and Pietro spoke more to who he was than did any contact he had had with Thomas in recent years.

Was that why he was on this blind quest? To prove he loved his brother as much as did his brother priests?

He blinked, stared at the map, and tried to get a sense of where everything was. Ed had listed several locations, under-lining some. One—the House of the Bicentenary—had been set apart in a box drawn with red pen and marked with a single question mark. It seemed like a good place to start.

It was about as far from the entrance as he could get, right back in the shadow of the modern city, but Thomas walked quickly, pausing only to check where he was, looking at what he could see from the street: stone-flagged roads with raised sidewalks, houses with ornate doorways and second-floor bal-conies, the now-familiar *thermopolia* with their jars set in the counters.

The House of the Bicentenary was one of the better pre-served two-story structures and he found it with no difficulty at all, but it was completely locked up, all windows and doors shuttered with padlocked panels of steel mesh.

Thomas peered in. He could see paintings on the walls, a deep skylit atrium some way back in the house, and a flight of treacherous-looking stairs. There was scaffolding all over the place, but it was too dim inside to see anything noteworthy.

He flagged down a guide at the corner of the street, a short, officious-looking woman wearing huge sunglasses that made her look like a mantis.

"I'm sorry," he said. "Can I ask a question?"

She considered him for a moment, knowing he wasn't part of her group.

"One," she said.

"The House of the Bicentenary . . . ?"

"It's that way," she said, pointing.

"I know," he said. "I saw it but . . ."

"It's closed."

"Why?"

"I said, *one question*," she remarked, turning away. "It's having work done on it."

"Excavation work?"

"No," she said, turning back at him and glowering through those dinner-plate shades of hers, but she was back in guide mode and talking primarily to her group. "If you look around you, you will notice that there is work going on all over the site to consolidate the existing remains, reinforcing walls that are sagging, bracing arches and lintels that might collapse. Conservation of the *existing* remains," she spelled out as if she were dealing with an idiot child, "*not* excavation. Maintaining the site is an expensive and time-consuming project. We are fortunate to be supported by a grant from the Packard Foundation. Now, if you don't mind . . ."

She turned away again.

"Thank you," he said.

She waved a hand behind her in acknowledgment and dismissal.

Thomas stood there, listening to the sound of machinery to the south. He walked down Decumanus Maximus and turned right onto Cardo V, another street of astonishingly well-preserved house fronts. Inside a cordoned section of crumbling brickwork and scaffolding a group of men were mixing concrete and taking measurements. Between him and them was a table with clipboards, folders, and tools. The workers hadn't seen him yet.

Thomas stepped out into the street. A few yards away was a large notice board explaining the reconstruction work being done by the Packard Foundation. Thomas stowed his camera and map and marched back into the work zone with an air of someone who knew what he was doing. As he walked in, he picked up a clipboard and a yellow hard hat.

"Excuse me?" he said over the drone of the concrete mixer. The workers looked from him to each other. They were all

Italians. One of them, a shirtless young man in dungarees with a deep and complete tan, stood up, his eyes neutral.

"You speak English?"

The man nodded.

"I need to get into the House of the Bicentenary," said Thomas, as if this were the most normal thing in the world.

The Italian shook his head. "It is not safe."

"I just need a quick look to check something," said Thomas. The words were vague, and he instantly regretted them, but the young man—he was probably a graduate student—didn't seem unduly concerned. "It will take two minutes. Less."

"You work here?" he said.

"I'm visiting from the foundation. They didn't tell you I was coming?"

The other shook his head and his eyes narrowed a little.

"You are excavator? Archaeologist?" he said.

"No," said Thomas, smiling. "I'm from administration . . ." he began, then waved away the rest of the sentence as if it were all tiresome and pompous. "I'm the money," he concluded with a jokey, self-deprecating shrug.

The young archaeologist smiled.

"Hold on," he said. "I'll see if I can get you in."

The young archaeologist walked slightly ahead, his gait easy, the bunch of ancient keys he had retrieved from somewhere dangling carelessly from his left hand, his long, brown, muscular arms swinging as he walked. Thomas stared straight ahead and said nothing. He doubted he was about to make some great discovery, but he felt a thrill of anticipation at his minor deception.

At the house, the archaeologist opened a juddering gate and brought him inside, snapping the padlock back in place as soon as he did so.

"I come with you," he said. "Touch nothing and be careful where you walk."

Thomas nodded and followed him into the dimly lit house.

"This the Tuscan atrium," he said, gesturing to a spacious chamber with a low roof.

He paused, as if waiting for his guest to take the lead, so Thomas walked purposefully into another room and consulted his clipboard in a businesslike way. The floor inside was a different-colored marble and there were extraordinarily detailed paintings on the walls. He considered a delicate fresco in russet and sea green of cupids playing some kind of oversized lyre, scribbling random numbers on his pad for the benefit of his guide before going quickly into the next room, and the next.

There was a garden surrounded by porticoes and a large hall, all bespeaking the opulence of the place and its impressiveness as an archaeological find, but why his brother had marked it out for special study, Thomas still had no idea.

"Can we go upstairs?" said Thomas, trying to make it less a real question than a directive.

"We can go up the ladders, but the floors are not safe to walk on."

He pointed to one of the rickety wooden stepladders and Thomas began to climb. The upper story was divided into two sections. Thomas paused, peered into the deep shadows, and saw immediately what had interested his brother.

Against one wall was a charred wooden cabinet, its doors open. Above it, in a square of unusually pale plaster, was a dark shadow, an outline, as if it marked where something had been mounted on the wall, something sufficiently precious to the owner of the house that it had been pulled from the plaster as the deluge of volcanic mud bore down on the town. It was shaped—quite unmistakably—like a crucifix.

The cross was tall, the horizontal beam short and high. It would have been at home in every Catholic church Thomas had ever been in, except that this one had been put up no more than forty-five years after the death of Christ.

CHAPTER 23

Thomas drifted down Cardo IV toward the exit lost in thought. If his brother had been doing some work on early Christian presence in Pompeii and Herculaneum, what could he possibly have done or discovered that could put him into danger? The cross in that upper room seemed perfectly orthodox, as did the Our Father inscription—if that was what it was—in the Pompeii "magic square." It was interesting stuff, perhaps, for church historians and the like, but it couldn't have been news to any of them. He wandered in a desultory fashion from house to house, through *thermopolia* and bathhouses with their mosaics of sea divinities and strange-looking fish.

Outside he stopped for a second, looking to see if he could catch sight of Sister Roberta. His dealings with the House of the Bicentenary had sapped most of his enthusiasm for being alone. Roberta's brown habit would stand out a mile even among the huddles of milling tourists and busloads of local schoolkids. He was scanning the street ahead when a man stepped out of a building only a few meters in front of him. He was studying a book as he walked, and his eyes were lowered, but there was something about the curly hair and the goatee . . .

Parks!

The man who had raided Ed's room in Chicago, the man who had escaped from Thomas and Jim by brandishing a sword . . .

Thomas stepped hurriedly into the nearest doorway.

Part of him wanted to confront the man, chase him down among all these people where he could do nothing except talk. But as soon as the idea occurred to him, he knew it would yield nothing and would blow what seemed to be the only advantage Thomas had yet achieved. He looked back out into the street. Parks was still there, considering his book, a long nylon bag slung over his shoulder, a bag large enough to hold a weapon.

Another reason to keep your distance.

Thomas ducked back into the house and, for extra security, stepped into the next room, where there was a dazzling, shrine-like wall mosaic of Neptune and Aphrodite in vivid blues and greens. When he looked back out into the street, Parks was moving away from him purposefully. Thomas followed, staying close to the doorways, poised to duck into what slim shadows the high sunlight afforded.

This could be no coincidence. Parks was following him, or—like Thomas—was recreating Ed's footsteps.

At the Decumanus Inferior, which bisected the excavated portion of the town, Ben Parks—or whatever his real name was—took a left. Thomas, still keeping a good thirty yards behind, picked up his pace. The other man paused in the street and rotated the book in his hands. He was following a map.

So he doesn't know the site any better than you do.

Then he was moving again. They were getting close to the southeastern limit of the excavations. Above, Thomas could see the ramp down which he had entered the site. Parks moved through some rambling and dilapidated ruins braced with scaffolding, a move that put him on the very edge of the dig. Thomas stole a glance at his map.

Where the hell is he going?

When he looked up, Parks was gone.

Thomas hurried to where he had last seen him. To his left was what his map called the Palaestra, a large open space with a colonnade down the northwest side and a ceremonial space with a marble table that could have been an altar. Directly ahead lay the rock wall of the dig itself with the houses of the modern town sitting high above, and behind him was a sharply declining jumble of excavations. There was no sign of Parks.

Thomas cursed and moved forward, scanning wildly all around. According to the map, he was standing just to the left of something that—now that he looked at it—made a large cross on the ground plan in clear but dotted lines. Thomas

glanced around him, expecting to see some large structure he
had missed, but there was only the stone cliff that rose up to
the entry ramp. He checked the map again. According to the
scale, the cross-shaped building should be huge: fifty or sixty
yards long.

So where is it?

He walked a little farther, wondering why the cross was
marked in dotted lines. Did that mean it was only a foundation, that it belonged—perhaps—to an earlier settlement?
Maybe, but that didn't help with where Parks had gone.

Then he saw it. Ahead and to his right was a dark, rectangular doorway into the cliff, braced with what looked like
concrete supports on either side.

He moved cautiously toward it. The town here was largely
unvisited by tourists and was curiously silent, which was probably why he suddenly felt so vulnerable. He could leave now.
Just walk away and wait for Parks to reemerge in some more
populous place.

In truth, Thomas had never liked dark, enclosed places
where you couldn't see who was sharing the shadows with
you. After a while he always started to feel as if there might
not be enough air . . .

No.

Ed had marked this place in his notes and now Parks was
snooping around it as well. He had to see what was inside.

There was no sign of Parks within.

It was larger than he had feared it would be, and it was cool
and dark: a cave, effectively, though Thomas doubted it had
always been such. The rock above him was the mottled gray
tuff produced as the lava mud cooled. In AD 79, this place had
been open to the air like the streets outside. But unlike the
streets and houses, this part could not be cleared because of
what sat on top of it, so the excavators had tunneled in at the
ancient ground level, fashioning a cave out of what had been a
sunny expanse.

But an expanse of what?

It was hard to say. There was no artificial lighting. The tunnel moved into the cliff, the rock ceiling rising into an irregular dome, and there, in the center, was a roped-off square of black-and-white mosaic several yards across. There was a strange bronze sculpture, perhaps a fountain, now green, its features hard to determine in the dim light, though it seemed to be serpentine and many-headed. The mosaic was gray with dust, though Thomas could make out a large anchor, a man apparently diving into water, and a strange fish with oversized front fins.

He squinted at the cross-shaped outline on the map. Could it have been a swimming pool?

And then Thomas heard footsteps on the gravelly earth behind him. Someone was coming in through the tunnel.

He spun around.

It was Parks.

Thomas moved quickly deeper into the cave, knowing that there was only one entrance. He was trapped in the dark.

CHAPTER 24

Parks stopped just inside the cave and slipped the long nylon bag off his shoulder. He didn't speak, didn't act as if he knew anyone was in there with him.

Thomas could see little more than a silhouette, the only light coming from the tunnel entrance behind the other man, but he knew that as Parks's eyes adjusted to the dark, his chances of remaining unseen would fade to nothing. The place just wasn't that big. He could try to bolt past him, trusting to surprise, but there was no way he could slip by unnoticed, and with his sprained knee he could hardly trust to speed. He could confront him, he supposed . . .

*Play the action hero? You're a high school English teacher.
Or you were . . .*

He had to get out.

He tried to recall everything he had heard about the city,
the eruption, the subsequent excavations: anything that might
give him an option other than crouching here in the darkness,
waiting for Parks to see him. If the other man hadn't been so
focused on whatever he was getting out of his bag, he would
already have done so.

Thomas began to move, inching carefully to his right, hugging the cave wall. The Bourbon excavators had moved almost at random around the ancient city, dropping tunnels and
trenches, pillaging the place for statuary and other artifacts for
their private collections. Maybe there was more than one way
into the cave they had hewn out of the tuff once they had
found the great cross-shaped structure in the earth. He took
another excruciatingly silent step, his fingertips tracing the
smooth contours of the rock at his back, groping for an alcove,
a recess of some kind in which he could hide. Thomas heard a
distinctive metallic *swish*. Parks was setting up a piece of
equipment.

A tripod?

A moment later he heard the faint rising whine of a flash
unit charging, and a jolt of panic went through him. He had
only seconds of invisibility left.

He moved with reckless haste across the cave wall, still
pushing back against the rock, his breath held, sweat beading
on his brow despite the chill of the cavern. And suddenly, just as
the flash was about to fire, there was empty space behind him.

Thomas shrank into it as the cavern suddenly flared in the
camera's blue-white brilliance, the shadows leaping and vanishing in a second. Had he been seen? He waited through the
agonizing clunk of the camera's shutter, then the drone of its
power wind, and then, as Parks shot off another picture, Thomas
took a second step back into the darkness of the alcove.

But it wasn't an alcove at all, as was clear when he turned
into it and found he could move still farther in. It was a tunnel,

albeit only about waist high, one the excavators had made two hundred fifty years earlier. He would have to crawl, and he would have to be absolutely silent since every sound would echo back into the cave, but he might be able to get out: assuming there was enough air, assuming the walls didn't close in on him till he felt like screaming.

Of course, if Parks heard, he would have Thomas like a trapped rat . . .

Better make sure he doesn't hear then, he thought.

With agonizing slowness, Thomas started to crawl.

The flash fired again, and though he knew he wasn't visible from the tripod, the light bounced alarmingly around the tunnel. If Parks was to vary his positioning by only a few feet, he would see Thomas the moment he depressed the shutter release.

The stone was cold and hard on his knees, but smoother than he had feared. Ten feet farther on the tunnel bent slightly, and the darkness softened. If he could keep his head—and his luck—for a few more seconds, he might see daylight. He might get out.

Just before the bend in the passage the roof lifted and he was able to sit up for a second, take some of the weight off his aching knees, but as he did so he felt something brush against the back of his head. Something soft. He reached up instinctively, and felt the weight of something in his hair. Something that moved as he tried to unsettle it. His fingers passed quickly over fur and a cool, elastic substance like skin, but edged with a tiny hooklike claw.

A bat.

He flinched involuntarily, trying to shrug the thing off, banged his head against the rock in the process, and gave a grunt of pain and revulsion, stifled a second too late. He heard rapid movement in the cavern behind him. Parks was moving to see who was in there with him.

Thomas abandoned caution and scrambled forward, scraping his forehead on the tuff as the rock ceiling lowered again. But then there was light that brightened to an almost unbearable

whiteness and in two surges forward that left his right knee
bloody, he was out and running clumsily back into the ancient
town as if worse things than bats were in pursuit.

"What happened to you?" asked Sister Roberta, taking in his
scraped and dusty appearance. She said it with surprise and a
concern that cut away any coldness she might have felt about
the way they had parted.

"Can we just get out of here?" said Thomas. He was red-
faced, sweaty, and badly rattled.

"I had no idea you found ancient sites so exciting," she
muttered as they climbed through the streets up to the railway
station.

"What's that, nun humor?" said Thomas.

She grinned. "You can tell me about your adventure on the
train," she said.

He didn't, of course. He made up some story about falling
off one of the elevated sidewalks onto the cobbles, and she
made sympathetic noises while his mind wandered back to
what he had seen, each image—the ghost line of the crucifix,
the underground swimming pool, Parks himself—all feeling
like fragments of mosaic, small and hard in his hands, waiting
for him to lay them out, to make sense of them. But all he saw
was randomness and confusion.

CHAPTER 25

That evening, Thomas popped open a beer in his room and
called St. Anthony's rectory in Chicago. Jim sounded genuinely pleased to hear from him, but his tone quickly became
anxious.

"They are looking for you," he said.

"Who?"

"Not sure. Homeland Security for sure," said Jim, "though I also got a call from Senator Devlin's office. Both want you to call them."

"They're probably worried I'm getting too much sun," said Thomas. It was funny the way he slid back into a comfortable familiarity with this priest he barely knew. It was like talking to Ed in the old days, before everything between them soured.

"They sounded sort of urgent," said Jim. "Like something had come up. The DHS guy was one of the ones who came here: Kaplan, his name was. Said to call him directly."

"But I haven't been charged with anything right?" said Thomas. "And it's still a free country."

Jim agreed, but grudgingly, and Thomas wondered if the priest was suffering in his place.

"You doing okay?" said Thomas.

"Sure. I'm used to dealing with stuff by myself."

"Got to say," said Thomas, opting for bluster as a way of lightening the mood. "I don't know how you do it. Being a priest, I mean. Must be kind of lonely."

"Oh, it's like a lot of things," Jim said. "You have good days, when you feel involved, productive, part of everything, you know? Other days . . . all I can hear is Paul McCartney singing about Father McKenzie writing the words of the sermon that no one will hear. You know the one? *'Darning his socks in the night when there's nobody there.'* That's life, I guess. It's only really lonely when it feels pointless."

Thomas said nothing, unsettled by the priest's sudden confidence. He had never said so much when they had been together. Why now? Was it just that the phone made some things easier, or living in the hollow where Ed had been or . . . something else?

"Well," said Thomas. "At least you have your faith."

It was impossible to say it without sounding condescending, and he was about to take the remark back when Jim said, "Most of the time, yes."

Thomas felt out of his depth.

"You okay?" he said, again.

"There's a Baptist church on the other side of town," said Jim. "It has one of those signs outside that you can switch the letters around so you post different messages each week. A couple of months ago it said *Doubt is the opposite of faith.*" He said it slowly, letting the words of the quotation ring like separate bells.

"And?"

"I guess I think the opposite," said Jim. "That if you have one without the other, it doesn't mean anything."

"Tough way to live," said Thomas.

"Sometimes," said Jim, "but better than the alternatives."

"It will be okay, Jim," Thomas said, directing the conversation back to where they started. "It's just some bureaucratic screwup. It will blow over."

"I guess," said Jim. "Oh, and you had another call."

"Yes?"

"Your wife."

"Ex."

"Right."

"What did she say?"

"Nothing," said Jim. "Just asked if you were here, then asked if you were going to Japan."

"Why would I go to Japan?"

"No idea. She sounded relieved when I said you weren't."

"I'll bet," said Thomas.

Thomas massaged his knee. It hurt less than it had when he left Chicago, and his exertions in Herculaneum seemed to have caused no ill effects. A little gentle exercise would probably do him good, so long as it didn't involve tangling with people who wanted to kill him.

Odd, he thought, the way his almost suicidal apathy had been so completely eclipsed by his desire to unravel what had happened to Ed. He felt energized, driven, even though the investigation itself seemed slow and indirect at best, as if he were meandering along unmapped country roads looking for a freeway. Was it for Ed, or did he just need to know the truth? Both, probably. His bullish tendencies had been awoken, given something specific to charge at after years of seeing red everywhere. Yes, that was it. He had spent half a decade pounding around his paddock looking to gore anything he could reach, usually managing only to injure himself.

But this was different. What had happened to Ed was something he could discover, a truth he might be able to bring to light. What that truth would finally mean to him he could not begin to guess and preferred not to consider. He would go running, something he knew no doctor would have endorsed, because he knew the pain in his knee would dwarf his other concerns.

"Mr. Knight," said the concierge.

Thomas, wheezing from his run and halfway to the elevator, turned.

"Something to show you," said the man at the desk. He crooked his finger and got up, proffering his seat. "You watch. I'll get you a drink. Beer? Wine?"

"Beer's good," said Thomas. His knee hurt, but not as much as he had feared, and he felt as if he had worked out some of the stiffness pounding through Naples's crowded, dusty, and sweltering streets. He would see how it felt in the morning, but right now he needed a long draught of something very cold.

He sat at the lobby desk and looked at the six-inch video monitor under the counter. A thirty-second snatch of tape was playing in a continuous loop. It was fuzzy, monochrome, and discontinuous, but what it showed was unmistakable: a man in dark glasses carrying a satchel, taking a key from the storage unit behind the desk, checking over his shoulder as he did so, and making for the elevator. Then the same man returning, replacing the key, and leaving the building as another guest came in. The two incidents had taken place in the middle of the day, twenty minutes apart.

At first, Thomas could see nothing beyond the proof that someone had indeed been in his room, but as the sequence wound through a fourth time he developed a hunch.

He's Japanese.

He watched again, trying to home in on why he thought so. The man's face was indistinct and the shades gave little away, though it was *possible* that he was Asian.

He watched it again, and two things struck him. First, there was the man's gait. You couldn't see much when he was close to the counter, but as he walked up to the elevator there was a curious shuffling to the way he walked, a dragging of his feet.

At the school where Thomas had taught in Japan, everyone took off their shoes as they entered the main office building and put on plastic slippers stored in a bin by the door. The slippers virtually demanded that you dragged your feet to keep them on. He recalled the way his students trod down the backs of their own shoes even outside, something necessitating a certain shuffling movement his wilder kids seemed to equate with cool.

He looked back at the video monitor. There was a momentary pause as the other guest came in. Thomas watched it again and saw that minute and surely involuntary bob of the head . . .

A reflex and rudimentary bow. He'd know it anywhere. The guy was Japanese.

Thomas felt a rush of doubt touched with an old anxiety. He didn't know why a link to Japan made the break-in feel worse, but it did.

"Your beer," said the concierge, handing Thomas a chilled bottle of Peroni featuring the Italian World Cup team from 2006. "You want I call *polizia?*"

Thomas shook his head. With nothing missing the police would do nothing.

"Just keep your eyes open in case this guy shows up again," he said. "And thanks."

He turned toward the elevators, beer in hand, and then stopped.

"One other thing," he said.

The concierge looked up from his copy of *Il Mattino*.

"What's the Fontanelle?"

The concierge, normally urbane to the point of carelessness, seemed to hesitate.

"It's closed," he said, at last, his voice low, his gaze level and guarded. "You can't go there."

"What is it?" said Thomas, his curiosity mixed with an unaccountable dread.

"A bad place. Forget about it."

"And no one can go there?" said Thomas.

"Only the dead."

CHAPTER 26

Thomas breakfasted on the Executive's roof terrace. It was nine o'clock and there was only one other diner, an athletic-looking American in a suit who chatted to the Hawaiian-shirted waiter in unabashed English. The waiter did a lot of nodding and smiling but didn't seem to be getting much of it.

Thomas considered the buffet table's selection of prepackaged breads, crackers, and spreads—mainly jams, Nutella, and cheese triangles.

"You need to come earlier for the good stuff," said the American. "Even then, it ain't eggs and bacon. Coffee's good, though."

On cue the waiter materialized.

"Cappuccino, espresso?" he said.

"Cappuccino," said Thomas. *"Grazie."*

"Prego," said the waiter, ducking back into the recessed work station in the curl of the spiral staircase down to the rooms.

"Italians don't do breakfast, apparently," the American volunteered. "Weird. All their other food kicks ass. Breakfast is like a tea party thrown by an eight-year-old girl. Go figure."

Thomas smiled and helped himself to juice and a plastic-wrapped piece of plum cake.

"You here on business?" said the American.

"Vacation," said Thomas.

"Lucky man," said the other. "Brad Iverson," he said, offering a strong hand. "Computers. Not sales though, so you can relax."

"Thomas Knight," said Thomas, biting back a weary reluctance to make small talk. "English teacher."

"Whoa," said Brad. "I'll have to watch my grammar."

"I wouldn't worry about it," said Thomas.

"You look familiar. You been here before?"

Thomas shook his head.

"My third time in six months," said Brad. "Still haven't seen a damn thing in Naples that would make me want to come here on vacation. Guess you have your reasons."

"Guess so," said Thomas.

"I'm not into culture, history, stuff like that. Snoozer. You weren't here back in January?"

"No," said Thomas, patiently. "My first time."

"Huh," said Brad. "You remind me of someone . . . There was a guy I met a couple of times in a little restaurant down toward the harbor: The Trattoria Medina. A priest. Could have been your brother."

He said it lightly, a mere figure of speech, but it stopped Thomas cold.

"Could have been," he said. "My brother actually was here then."

"You're kidding?"

"No," said Thomas. "What did you talk about?"

"Oh, you know," said Iverson, "the usual BS, right?"

"Right," said Thomas, disappointed, not sure what he had hoped for.

"One time he was with this Japanese guy," he said.

Thomas sat up.

"Japanese?" he said. "You're sure?"

"Yeah, why?"

"I used to live out there," said Thomas, as if it were mere coincidence.

"Hey," said Iverson, looking at his watch. "I've gotta haul. I'm around a few more days. Maybe we can get a cold one sometime. Americans abroad, right?"

"Right," said Thomas again, as the other man slapped him on the shoulder and moved out.

Was he likely to learn anything useful from Brad? It seemed unlikely, but he had so few avenues open to him he would have to pursue it. The fact that Ed might have been connected to someone in Japan was certainly worth pursuing. In the meantime, he had another meeting to arrange. To do so, he would first have to win over his informant and he wouldn't do that by being bullheaded, by broadcasting every skeptical thought he had, every irritation he felt. He would have to be subtle.

From miles away and years before, he thought he heard his ex-wife laughing.

CHAPTER 27

"Do you know what Ed was writing about?" said Thomas.

Father Giovanni shrugged and took the smallest sip of his espresso. He had agreed to this little chat reluctantly but seemed hopeful that it would curb Thomas's stalking of the monsignor. Privately Thomas thought that unlikely, but if that was what the priest needed to believe before he would talk to him, so be it.

"Early Christian symbols."

"Like what?"

"The cross."

"Is there much to say about that?"

"I asked him the same thing," said Giovanni, grinning.

"And he said?"

"He said, 'Don't you think it strange that the universal symbol of Christianity is the image of its failure: the humiliation and execution of its leader?' "

Thomas said nothing. Giovanni had spoken the phrase verbatim, as if he'd replayed his brother's words a thousand times in his head since.

"I mean," said the priest, in his own voice, "if someone started a religion now, but they were executed, could you imagine that person's followers wearing symbols of the electric chair or the hangman's rope?"

"I guess not," said Thomas, grudgingly.

"But," said Giovanni, raising one finger and smiling, "the cross is the symbol because the life of Christ is finally about his death, taking on the sins of the world for the salvation of others."

"So Jesus was a suicide," said Thomas.

Again, he hadn't really meant to say it. An image of pills in a whisky tumbler had popped into his head and the words had slipped out unbidden. Giovanni looked surprised, but he answered evenly:

"Suicide is self-important. Self-sacrifice is the opposite."

"Okay," said Thomas. "But I don't see why Ed cared. So far as I can tell he was a priest for the present. Social justice, liberation theology: these were the things he lived for. What do they have to do with the theology of the crucifixion?"

"Everything," said Giovanni. " 'Greater love has no man than this, that he lay down his life for his friends.' That's what the cross is about, and it's what liberation theology is about: giving up what you have so that those who have nothing might have more. The personal and spiritual is part of the social and political. That is the message of the Gospel."

"Here endeth the lesson," said Thomas, suppressing the sneer too late.

"Tell me," said the priest, "are you an atheist from conviction or on principle?"

Thomas smiled a little at Giovanni's polite but firm retaliation.

"Is there a difference?"

"Of course," said Giovanni. "One doesn't believe in God, the other refuses to."

"On principle?"

"Because of what he associates with religion, yes."

"Then I'm an atheist from conviction," said Thomas. "I see no reason to believe in God. That what gets done in the name of religion is largely ignorant, judgmental, and destructive merely reinforces my conviction."

Giovanni's eyes held his, and though he said nothing, Thomas looked down and took a sip of his coffee. The other man didn't believe him.

Maybe he's right not to.

"I'm not my brother," he said, simply. That at least was true.

"No," said Giovanni.

"Meaning?"

"Nothing," said Giovanni, his eyes still unblinking on Thomas's.

"Did you consider yourself a friend of Ed's?"

"Yes," said the priest. "We didn't correspond after he left Italy, but yes. I thought I would see him again this year. He was planning to come back. I was sorry when I heard he had died."

"Did they tell you how or where he died?"

"No," said Giovanni, his face suddenly darkening. "Is there something . . . ? I do not know the word in English. Something not right?"

"Something sinister about the circumstances of his death? I'm not sure. I think there might be."

"I had no idea."

"Can you think of anything that Ed was doing here or writing about that could have put him in danger?"

"Danger from whom?"

"I don't know. Anybody."

"I did not see him the day he left," said Giovanni. "I was sick and in the hospital when he flew. I did not even know where he had gone. He left me a card."

"Do you still have it?"

The priest smiled and reached inside his jacket.

"I thought you might want to see it," he said.

It was a postcard with views of Herculaneum and was written in English. It said, "Father G. When you get this I'll be gone, I'm afraid. $\stackrel{\rho}{\mathbb{R}}$ ian symbol-wise, I might have hit the mother lode (should that be *father lode*??!!), but it's pointing outside Italy now and I have to follow. Will send details later. Get well soon! E."

"That symbol," said Thomas considering the $\stackrel{\rho}{\mathbb{R}}$. "It's familiar but . . ."

"It means Christian," said the priest. "He's using the Greek chi rho letters that the early Church used to signify Christ."

"What does he mean by 'the mother lode' symbol-wise?"

"I don't know," said Giovanni. "I assumed he meant something to do with the cross, since that is the primary Christian symbol. But I couldn't say."

"And he had just come from Herculaneum?"

"He was going between all the ancient sites," said Giovanni, "Herculaneum, Pompeii, Paestum, the archaeological museum here in Naples. Every day he was at one or the other. Came home late, often excited, tired. But he kept most of his ideas to himself. Or," he added, "he did not tell me."

"Did he confide in anyone else?"

Giovanni shrugged and said nothing. Thomas gave him a hard look.

"Did he talk to Pietro?" he asked.

"Some," said the priest, grudgingly. "He and the monsignor talked. I don't know what they talked about."

"Were they working together?"

Giovanni's face shifted in a smile that did not reach his eyes.

"Oh no. I think they did not get along. At least where Eduardo's work was concerned."

"They argued?"

"Yes. Violently sometimes. Why, I don't know."

"So Pietro was glad when he left?"

Giovanni seemed to think long about this, and his answer was uncertain and edged with something that might have been sadness.

"I think he was relieved," he said. "But he was very upset to hear of your brother's death. Now he seems . . . *different*."

"Different how?" said Thomas, pressing.

"I don't know. Angry. Sad. Worried? Yes, I think so."

"But you've no idea what Ed could have done or said to unsettle him like this?"

"Padre Pietro is old," said Giovanni, struggling to put the thoughts into words. "His ideas, I mean."

"He's a pre–Vatican Two Catholic," Thomas nodded.

"Not just that," he said. "Some of his ideas are not just old Catholic. Some of them have never been orthodox, never been—how you say it?—*mainstream*. He doesn't talk to me about his beliefs because we don't agree. Some of his ideas I do not understand."

Thomas was intrigued, as much by the young priest's increasingly halting and anxious manner as by what he was being told.

"For example?" he said. "What does Pietro believe that you don't?"

"He believes very strongly in the . . . *mediation* of the dead. Any dead."

"Intercession?"

"Yes. In the old Church people prayed through saints, yes? They thought in terms of rank, class . . ."

"Hierarchy?" prompted Thomas.

"Yes. So they did not speak to God directly. They went

through Saint Paul or the Virgin Mary or other more modern saints: people who had died who would intercede for them before the Lord. It gave them a personal link to God, a face they knew. It still goes on, of course, but it is less central to the Church. Some people think—as Luther thought—that the saints become . . ."

"An end and not a means?"

"Precisely. People are praying *to* the saint, not *through* him."

"And Pietro still holds with this?"

"This is not uncommon. But about one hundred years ago, in Naples, a particular kind of *intercession* grew around the dead in a particular place."

"The Fontanelle?" said Thomas, unable to stifle a cold thrill that moved down his back like a trickle of ice water.

"The Fontanelle," said Giovanni, with a sigh. "Pietro took me once, six or seven years ago. I have never been back. I do not wish to go back."

"What is it?"

"Originally the place was a kind of—what is the word? Where you take stone from the ground?"

"Quarry?"

"Yes," said the priest, smiling at the term. "Quarry. It is many caves and passages below the city made by the extraction of the stone for building. Naples is very old, you see, and very restricted in size. Here," he said, laying one hand on the table, "is the city. On this side are the mountains and on this side is the sea. So, as time passed—and the city goes back many thousands of years—the new town was built on top of the old town. Land was used again. It is not like Rome, which spread out so all its ancient monuments were left intact at the center. Naples builds on itself, so all the old places are underground. Since land is so valuable in the city, places of burial also get reused after time has passed.

"Long ago," Giovanni continued, "there were great sicknesses that came through Italy killing almost everyone."

"Bubonic plague," said Thomas. "The Black Death."

"Exactly. There were too many bodies to bury. Nowhere to put them. Most of them were the poor who could not afford to leave the city, and when they died their bodies were put together without names. Hundreds of thousands of dead people. Eventually, they were moved to the Fontanelle."

"How were they buried if the Fontanelle was a stone quarry?"

Giovanni smiled bleakly, as if Thomas had hit the nail on the head.

"They were not. They were piled together. Just bones. Heaps of them. Filling the place."

Thomas swallowed and tried not to look uncomfortable, but the idea of these dark corridors filled with dead people was the stuff of his nightmares.

"In time, people began to treat the bones like saints," Giovanni went on. "They cleaned and polished the bones. They took them flowers and candles. They adopted them. They prayed to them."

Giovanni shrugged and smiled at the simplicity of it, but he was clearly troubled.

"The place attracts strange people. Some say the Mafia meet there. There are other kinds of legends too."

"Like?"

"Folk tales," said Giovanni. "There is one about a captain. I don't know it properly."

Thomas nodded encouragingly.

"It is mere foolishness," said Giovanni.

"Go on," said Thomas, smiling.

The priest sat back and looked away for a moment, then sipped his coffee and said, "Okay. A young woman wanted to get married. She tried to find a husband in the usual ways, but without success. So she went to the Fontanelle and chose a head."

"A skull?"

"Yes, a *skull*. She cleaned it, polished it till it was so bright and smooth that no dust or dirt would stick to it, and she asked it to help. One week later, she met a man and in a few months, they got married. At the wedding there was one man in the crowd she did not recognize: a tall, handsome man dressed like an army captain. He began to whisper to her. Her new husband, seeing this, was overcome with jealousy. He hit the stranger in the face very hard. At once, the handsome captain vanished, and the husband died of fright. When the young woman returned to the Fontanelle, she found that her polished skull now had a black eye!"

Thomas smiled.

"There are many such stories," said Giovanni with a dismissive gesture. "Some funny. Some scary. Some concern particular bones, like that one. There was a skeleton of a baby that some local people particularly liked. When work was going on to rebuild the Fontanelle, they said they would attack the laborers if they did not find that skeleton."

"Did they find it?"

"They said so," said Giovanni with a noncommittal shrug. "But you see? The place attracts the *superstitious*. It is full of dark stories, strange feelings. I wish the place had never existed."

"And Pietro?"

"The Fontanelle was connected to a particular church. When Pietro was ordained, he became the priest of that church. But then, about thirty years ago, the bishops said this should not go on any more, that it was superstition. They closed the Fontanelle, separated it from the church, and now no one can go there."

"No one?"

Giovanni framed that uncomfortable shrug and smile again, and his meaning was clear: Pietro still went there, for reasons he could not begin to fathom.

CHAPTER 28

The message light was blinking on his phone back at the Executive. Jim had called from Chicago. Thomas checked the time, counted back seven hours, and dialed.

"Jim," he said. "It's Thomas."

"I was right," said Jim, without preamble. "When I said the DHS guy was behaving as if something had happened. It had. I saw it on the news tonight."

"What?"

"At dawn this morning DHS agents working with CIA and FBI counterterrorist investigators found a cache of weapons in the basement of a single-family Chicago-area house," said Jim, sounding like he was reading from a newspaper. "AK-47 assault rifles. Sacks of fertilizer and other products that could be used in bomb making."

"So?" said Thomas. "What does that have to do with Ed?"

"It's not about Ed," said Jim. "It's about you."

"How so?" said Thomas.

"The raid took place at 1247 Sycamore in Evanston," said Jim. "Thomas, it was *your* house."

"I'm being set up," said Thomas into the phone. "I spoke to Father Jim Gornall back at St. Anthony's and he told me about the raid on my house."

It had taken him ten minutes to get through to Senator Devlin's office. He was now talking to Rod Hayes, the senator's chief of staff, explaining what he had heard and what he was doing in Italy. The young man listened without interruption and then said, "I'm going to pass this over to the senator. I just don't have the authority to start poking around."

"Thank you," said Thomas.

"He's in a meeting right now," said Hayes, "but I'll get him to call you in about . . . three hours."

"Okay," said Thomas, feeling sweaty and uncomfortable. "Thanks."

"And Mr. Knight?" said Hayes.

"Yes?"

"Try not to worry about it. The senator is a powerful man."

"Yes. I know."

"How's Father Jim holding up?"

The shift caught Thomas slightly off guard.

"Okay, I think," he said. "Why?"

"Nothing," said Hayes. "Tougher job than most, I would imagine. And he's had a rough six months, what with that eviction case and all."

"Eviction case?"

"You hadn't heard," said Hayes, sounding suddenly less assured. "I'm sorry. My mistake. He probably doesn't like to discuss it. Please, forget I mentioned it."

Thomas went to the National Archaeological Museum to take his mind off things, making the journey on foot in an attempt to work some of the stiffness out of his legs. Waking the morning after his last run convinced him that he should be getting more exercise. So he walked through the bustling streets of Naples, passed a broad square where some kind of political rally was taking place, and skirted a row of cardboard shanties where homeless men slept.

The museum was too big for him to process, and his exclusive focus on pieces from Pompeii and Herculaneum didn't significantly reduce the scale of the collection. He studied the painted panels taken from the Temple of Isis with their Egyptian motifs and assortment of strange sea creatures, many with the forequarters of horses or crocodiles and the tails of fish. Then there were the extraordinary and vivid mosaics from various Pompeian houses, and an overwhelming collection of statuary, and then he gave up. He had a coffee in the museum's courtyard garden and returned to the hotel, constantly checking his watch to make sure he didn't miss the senator's call. After trying to make sense of all these ancient artistic fragments, he was hoping that the senator might have more clear and direct information for him.

CHAPTER 29

Sister Agnes, of the Woodchester convent of the Poor Clares in England, who had been traveling constantly for almost thirty-six hours, thought that they would never reach the Naples retreat house. When they did, they were almost two hours late and had time only for a light dinner, taken in silence as the Mother Abbess read to them from Augustine, before unpacking their few belongings. They came from various chapters in Europe and a couple from America, though the majority were direct from Assisi, so that the recreational period between dinner and the bell for evening prayer at seven-fifteen was filled with the bubbling conversation of the newly acquainted.

They had been introduced to the chaplains of the retreat house: Monsignor Pietro, who seemed both strange and severe, and a sweet, soft-spoken priest called Father Giovanni, who had excused himself to work on tomorrow's sermon. After evening prayer came the Great Silence from seven-thirty, and the tasks of the day would be completed by nine-thirty. They would all be in bed with the lights out in another hour, and would rise for morning prayer at five-thirty.

It wasn't an easy life, particularly in this day and age, when such things were under perpetual assault by the materialism and skepticism of the outside world, thought Sister Agnes, but it had a rhythmic simplicity and purity of focus that suited her temperamentally. She had chosen to spend the last moments of the day in the silent chapel before returning to her room, because her Italian was so poor, and because the other English speakers were Americans and thus almost as foreign in speech and culture as the Italians. Or so she feared. Agnes was, she knew, a timid girl, always had been, and she avoided newness and exoticism so acutely that it could get in the way of the plain Christian charity to which she daily dedicated herself. Indeed, this very trip had been the Mother Abbess's idea, a thinly disguised treat designed to strip her of some of her fearfulness and closeness.

It was ironic, she thought, that a nun could be considered too cloistered, but she knew that she was difficult to work with and that though the Poor Clare sisters spent much time in private devotion, they also needed to be able to work together. Tomorrow she would introduce herself to the Americans. Surely they would have enough in common to put her at her ease.

The chapel was blissfully cool after the heat outside. She missed England's gentler climes and was glad that she would be home for Easter week, but this too was part of her Lenten penance to be offered up in memory of Christ's wounds. She felt as she always felt in church: small and insignificant in ways she found oddly comforting. She slid the rosary beads between her fingers, opting to say one decade before bed. The sorrowful mysteries would be her focus, as they always were.

The first rustle of movement behind her she ignored, assuming another sister had joined her, but when it came again, accompanied by a sibilant hiss that she took to be whispered speech, she turned, indignant that the Silence should be so troubled. But no one was in the chapel but her, and the unfamiliarity of the place contrived to make her uneasy, even fearful, something she had never once experienced in the house of the Lord before.

She completed her decade of the rosary, conscious that she had rushed the final Glory Be, promising silently to return and do two decades before bed tomorrow, conscious that her hands were slightly unsteady as she moved along the pew and into her genuflection. She gave one last look at the tabernacle light, took strength from it and its reminder of the Lord's presence, and left, the door booming hollowly behind her.

The chapel opened onto a vaulted corridor with peeling paint and no lamps, so that with the church door closed the only light filtered through from the courtyard ahead, and that palely. She moved quickly toward it, listening.

Her imagination was playing tricks on her, she thought. She was tired and unsettled by the foreignness of the place; that was all.

Then it came again, that hiss that was almost a snarl. Her eyes grew wide as saucers, the hair on her arms prickled, and her feet somehow lost their sense of purpose. She stopped quite still.

"Who's there?" she said to the dark, stone hallway. There was no sound in reply, not until she was ready to take another step, and then it was only the faintest scraping, like the sound a large insect might make over a hard surface, the sound—perhaps—of long fingernails on stone . . .

She whirled suddenly, looking back to the chapel door. The darkness was almost complete, but something pale crouched there, something still and hairless. It might have been some discarded gargoyle left to sit behind the door, except that the eyes were bright as glass.

She stood rooted to the spot, tears starting to her eyes, incapable of looking away.

And then it moved, and she ran screaming as if the hosts of hell were at her heels.

CHAPTER 30

"I don't believe it," said Devlin over the phone.

"Thank you, Senator," said Thomas.

"This isn't just a leap of faith, Thomas," said Devlin. "Your brother was a good man, but I couldn't vouch for you in a matter like this with nothing else to go on."

"So why do you believe me?"

"It's too convenient. No terrorist in his right mind would leave this stuff lying around while he went on vacation. It makes no sense."

"That's not exactly hard evidence, sir," said Thomas.

"Did they tell you that they found copies of the Qur'an and downloads of hard-line religious writings?"

"No, sir."

"You read Arabic, Thomas?"

"No, sir."

"That's what I figured."

"Again, sir, that's not exactly evidence . . ."

"It's not just me," said Devlin. "Even the DHS guys are skeptical. Some of them, at least. The ones who aren't too used to jumping at shadows that they start pumping hollow points through everything that moves. See, there's all this printed stuff in Arabic: books, pamphlets, computer printouts. Stuff that could have come from anywhere. But there isn't a scrap of Arabic *handwriting* in the place. The books are all new, the weapons barely handled, the bomb-making stuff missing crucial hardware that would suggest a Middle Eastern source. It smells like a shell game to me."

"So what do I do?"

"Nothing," said Devlin. "Stay where you are. If you think you can learn something about Ed, do so. Let them examine the stuff they've found and see if they produce anything more than circumstantial evidence."

"Right," said Thomas. "Thank you, Senator."

"Just understand, Thomas, that if they do find your prints all over those guns, I will hang you out to dry and do my damnedest to ensure they throw the biggest and heaviest of books at you. We clear on that?"

"Yes, sir," said Thomas. "It won't come to that."

He hung up, hoping to God that was true.

CHAPTER 31

Thomas spent half the next day reading the guidebooks he had bought, and then browsing online at a tiny cybercafé a couple of blocks from the hotel, where he paid eighty cents for half an hour on the web. He learned a lot, but what loomed largest was that the early Christian presence in the cities destroyed by Vesuvius was well known, as was the *Pater Noster* acrostic and the shadow crucifix in the House of the Bicentenary. Most of the online material was of a decidedly Christian bent, often possessing a slightly shrill jubilance about the way that the archaeological evidence was seen to prove the historicity of the biblical account of the early Church. One site that made much of the Herculaneum cross specifically targeted the Jehovah's Witnesses, who said that Jesus died not on a cross but on a kind of stake; others were less specific but often seemed informed by a zeal and a defensiveness that made Thomas wary.

He called Sister Roberta.

"I was planning to go to Paestum," he said. "Feel like joining me?"

"Confined here today," she said, apparently unhappy about it. "Sort of an emergency orientation. One of the English nuns got spooked in the night."

"Spooked?" said Thomas. "By what?"

"Probably nothing. A shadow. Her imagination. One of her sisters suggested the girl was looking for an excuse to go back home."

"Is she okay?"

"Of course," said Sister Roberta with a touch of impatience. "There's nothing wrong with her."

"You sure you won't join me in Paestum?"

"It's a long way," she said. "You have to take the train down to Salerno. I won't have the time today. I was thinking of going up Vesuvius this afternoon. There's supposed to be a wonderful view, and it would be nice to get up to the crater, see the grand villain of all this archaeology up close and personal."

"Another day, perhaps," said Thomas. Vesuvius seemed like something to visit when he was done with all this other stuff. Or when it was done with him.

Thomas went to Paestum alone, expecting it to be another well-preserved Roman town, another victim of the eruption, but, from what he could gather from his guidebook, it was quite a different kind of place. It had been a Greek settlement, founded about six hundred years before the birth of Christ, but—like Naples—it had been occupied by the Samnites and the Romans. It was well south of Pompeii and Herculaneum, on the bay of Salerno, and beyond the reach of Vesuvius's destructive power. In fact, the city had been inhabited all the way into the medieval period, though in consistent decline, and at some point in the eighth or ninth century AD, the population— decimated by malaria and Saracen raids—had just moved away, abandoning the ancient city to weeds and marsh.

It didn't sound especially promising, and Thomas, having walked the high-hedged lane from the railway station, was therefore astonished to see three massive Doric temples rising up from the flat expanse of the old town. In form, completeness, and simplicity they outshone anything he'd seen in Italy and, indeed, anywhere else. Their massive columns of golden stone supported monumental friezes. All that was missing were the roofs and whatever colored plaster had once covered the rock.

For a long moment, Thomas just gazed at them, awestruck. The sheer scale of the temples, coupled with a windswept antiquity that was absent from the newly unearthed remains he had seen elsewhere, bespoke an almost mythic majesty. At Herculaneum he had been struck by a sense of ordinariness, by the idea that the town had been inhabited by people like himself, a place that had died in living memory, leaving clues to what that life had been writ large on its walls. This was quite different. This was history on an epic scale, full of power and dignity: a history that leaned toward legend.

This was, he knew, a projection of his own, something any serious historian or archaeologist would dismiss as romantic hokum, but he felt it nonetheless, and stood astonished and humbled that he had never even heard of the place before. Where he was supposed to start looking for what had rendered the remains so interesting to his dead brother—how this piece of the mosaic might be turned to fit what he already had—was a different problem entirely.

The other sites had a convenient and unique historical specificity. They illumined a single year, even a single moment when the sky had rained ash and fire. This place, by contrast, had evolved over centuries until the human fabric that held it together had finally melted away. While he knew nothing about Roman art, he could at least be sure that whatever he saw in Pompeii came from AD 79 or was, at least, still in use then. Here he could make no such assumptions. Any stone fragment he saw could be part of a thousand years of continual life on the same site. If he found things Ed had thought were interesting, he wouldn't have the first idea how to make sense of their history.

He wasn't alone. As a little reading demonstrated, archaeologists had disagreed for two hundred fifty years about what the various structures were, to which Greek gods the temples were dedicated, and, in the case of one building, whether it was a temple at all. It was generally called the Temple of Hera, queen of the Olympian gods (the Greek equivalent of the Roman Juno), but in the older guidebooks it was still referred to as the Basilica.

Thomas sighed, considered his brother's scribblings, and oriented himself. He was close to the northernmost side of the site, beside the Temple of Ceres (the Roman Demeter), which may have also been dedicated to Athena; gazing south across the forum to the temples of Poseidon (Neptune) or Apollo and Hera (Juno) some seven or eight thousand yards away. It was all very confusing. Ed's notes referenced "the tombs of the divers," though they did not appear on his guidebook map at all. He frowned, mounted what had once been some kind of table or podium, climbed three massive but eroded steps, and gazed out across the flat expanse of the site.

In the middle distance a hoopoe alighted in the grass and flexed its black-and-white plume. Thomas watched as it took flight again, swooping pink as it soared in undulating waves, tail and wings flashing against the violet of the mountains beyond. It settled again close to the half-excavated amphitheater he had passed on his way in, where a man with binoculars was turned toward him. As soon as Thomas's gaze fell on him, the man lowered the binoculars and turned away, but not before Thomas had glimpsed something of his face under heavy sunglasses. Before he had shuffled busily away, Thomas was already convinced that he had seen the Japanese man before, crossing the street outside the Executive and then again on videotape . . .

As before, his first response was anger. He had fled Chicago, he had been stymied by Monsignor Pietro, he had dodged Parks in Herculaneum like a hunted animal, and he was done running. At least out here in the sunlight and open spaces, where tourists milled in clusters like grazing cattle, he would not be chased off. If nothing else, he thought, as he climbed down from the stone pedestal and began to walk briskly toward the amphitheater, he had the element of surprise on his side.

Thomas broke into his wildebeest run. As soon as he had gotten down from the stone platform he had lost sight of the Japanese man with the binoculars. Now all he could do was make for the spot he had last seen him as quickly as possible. He put his head down and blew like a charging bull, feeling the heat, wishing for the cold air of a Chicago spring.

A hundred yards or so to his left, tourists bought postcards at the stores and restaurants that lined the access road on the other side of a tall fenced embankment. To his right were the low, sprawling remains of ancient walls, dotted occasionally by a column or a solitary pine tree. There weren't the crowds he had seen in Pompeii, and for all the brightness and openness of the place, it was easy to be alone here. A flicker of unease shot through him like a spasm of pain, but he shrugged it off and picked up the pace.

The entrance into the amphitheater was a great stone arch—almost a tunnel—in a wall some fifteen feet high. Thomas broke in at a flat-out sprint, mainly because he didn't like lingering in its shadow. The amphitheater lay before him, a shallow semicircle of grass and dusty earth surrounded by tiered stone ranks of seats, the whole cut short by the embankment on which sat the road above. There was no sign of anybody there.

Thomas turned back to the entry arch slowly. And then the man who had been crouching in the high alcove beside it leaped down at him like a pouncing jaguar.

CHAPTER 32

Thomas took the full force of the attack, crumpling to the arena floor under the weight of his assailant. For a moment he seemed incapable of thought or action, and then his old rage was back and he was punching and kneeing as the other man thrashed to get loose.

Until a week ago, Thomas hadn't thrown a punch in anger since high school, but it all came back—the adrenaline, the panic, the blood in his eyes—only worse, because they were men and he knew, instinctively and certainly, that his attacker might be able to kill him, might try to do so . . .

The Japanese man was small and wiry but he was strong. He was also quick. His fists jabbed twice. Thomas felt his windpipe crunch, and for a moment he couldn't breathe and thought he would throw up. He rolled to his knees as his attacker broke away. But he could not let it end like this.

With a surge of will, Thomas roared after him, sprawling and grabbing his ankle. He twisted and the man came down hard, unable to break his fall. As Thomas clambered on top of him, the other clawed at his face, reaching for his eyes. Thomas twisted his head back as far as he could, slammed his hand across the other's Adam's apple, and squeezed. The fingers still dug into his cheeks, and he felt the blood run. With his free hand he grabbed a handful of the sandy dirt and palmed it into the other's open mouth. As he tried to spit it out, Thomas closed his hand over the man's lips and pressed down as hard as he could.

Immediately the smaller man began to writhe and wriggle like a fish. For perhaps ten seconds he squirmed and flailed and then the wordless fury turned desperate, pleading, and his body went limp in surrender.

Thomas withdrew his hand and sat back, letting him twist his head and retch the grit out, heaving himself onto all fours as he spat into the earth.

Thomas, by comparison, was merely winded and bloody.

"Why are you following me?" he said, getting to his feet.

The man gargled and sputtered in Japanese.

"What?"

"Eigo ga hanashimassen," he said.

"Like hell you don't speak English," said Thomas, his anger flaring again. He took a step toward the man, who flinched away, still incapable of standing.

He spat once more, and then seemed to calm.

"I knew your brother," he said, his English flawless, almost unaccented. "My name is Satoh."

"Go on."

"We had a deal. He didn't keep his part."

"What kind of deal?"

"He acquired something for me and then refused to hand it over."

Thomas squinted at him doubtfully. The Japanese man turned and sat heavily in the dust.

"What did he acquire?" said Thomas.

"Information."

"About what? You'd better start picking up the pace with these answers or I'm going to lose my temper."

Satoh grinned slightly. His lower lip was bleeding heavily.

"You ever heard of the Herculaneum cross, Mr. Knight?" he said.

"Yes. I've seen it."

The other man's smile broadened as he shook his head.

"No," he said. "You've seen the imprint on the wall of a house where the cross once hung. I'm talking about the cross itself."

"There is no cross," said Thomas.

"Not till about three months ago, no," said the other. His breathing was stabilizing now. In fact, it seemed that he was starting to enjoy himself. "A lawyer in Ercolano who lived about half a mile from the excavations was digging a swimming pool in his garden. He found a Roman road and part of a human skeleton. Without notifying anybody, he dug around it till the whole body was cut free of the rock. Clutched to the rib cage was a silver crucifix perfectly matching the shadow on the wall in the House of the Bicentenary."

Thomas stared at him.

"Nonsense," he said. "It would be in a museum. Its picture would be in every guidebook, on every website . . ."

"Not if the man who found it died shortly after confiding in a young American priest who was researching examples of early Christian symbols."

Thomas stood there, staring in silence. The Asian man's smile broadened still further. Its amusement was bitter.

"That's right, Thomas," said Satoh. "Your brother took it into safekeeping for 'research purposes.' Wanted to document it, study it, write about the little fish emblem in the center of the cross. But after he'd had it for a few days, he had a better idea."

"Sell it?" said Thomas. He was trying to sound sarcastic, disbelieving, but the words sounded hollow, only a hair's breadth from despair.

"Do you have any idea what that would be worth?" said

Satoh. "The world's first extant crucifix. Think of it. Think
how much collectors would pay just to get a look at it. To own
it? He could name his price. Tens of millions? More? Someone would pay. And I was the one to make sure it all went according to plan."

"I don't believe a word of it," Thomas said.

"You don't sound so sure."

"My brother wouldn't have done anything like that," said
Thomas, daring him to contradict a statement that was less
about real conviction than it was about holding on to a version
of the past.

"What would you know about it?" the Japanese guy fired
back. "You barely knew him. I knew him as well as you did.
Better."

Afterward Thomas would think back on this and know he
had been baited. At the time, the confusion and frustration coalesced into the anger that made him ball his fists and take two
lunging strides toward where the smaller man sat.

Satoh timed his move perfectly. As Thomas got close he
rolled to his left, pivoting on one hand as he sprang to his feet,
the energy of the leap revolving him sharply. By the time he
had completed the spin, his right foot was high enough to
meet Thomas squarely on the jaw.

The impact stopped Thomas's forward progress cold. His
head snapped back so sharply that he thought his neck might
break. He was unconscious before he hit the ground.

CHAPTER 33

Thomas woke with the sun hot on his face, his jaw aching as if
he'd had a root canal, and a gaggle of tourists staring at him as
if they had stumbled on the last bit of combat to be staged at
the Paestum amphitheater. There was no sign of Satoh.

He brushed off the offers of assistance and made for the exit, humbled and confused, sure only that he understood even less of what his brother had been involved in now than he had an hour before.

He didn't believe it. How could he? Satoh was a liar who had spied on him, broken into his room, and—when caught out—had spun the first tale that had come to mind. Even the fight had been fraudulent, leading to that final sucker punch—or whatever the kick equivalent was called. Thomas rubbed his jaw. No. He wouldn't believe it. It all felt wrong.

But a part of him also knew that the parts that felt wrong weren't the right parts. The yarn about the Herculaneum cross had not been made up on the spur of the moment. It was too good. It fitted the facts too well. What felt most wrong, if he was going to be honest with himself, was the way he'd gotten the guy to talk at all. The end of the fight had shown that Satoh had some real skill as a martial artist. That Thomas's clumsy sparring had managed to beat him into a submission forcing Satoh to sing for his supper now seemed suspicious at best.

Could this business about the Herculaneum cross be more disinformation, a smear campaign like the suggestions of ties to terrorism intended to make Thomas stop asking questions? If so it wasn't going to work. That wasn't loyalty or love for his brother. It was his accustomed defiance and need to know the truth that had surfaced at numerous uncomfortable moments in his career, particularly when he thought he was being snowed.

His ticket to the site also gave him admission to the attendant museum, and he drifted in, as much to get rid of the dirt and blood as to see whatever might be on display. He found a restroom and washed thoroughly, frowning at his torn cheek and the gash above his eye in the mirror. There was no way he was going to be able to make himself look like a regular tourist. He pushed at the wound with his fingers and winced, stopping only when two men speaking what sounded like Dutch came in and regarded him with unmistakable concern. He left hurriedly.

The collection and the manner of its exhibition were surprisingly impressive. The place was air-conditioned and cool, the artifacts nicely spaced in display cabinets of blond wood and elegant wall mountings: stone metope reliefs of Hercules, a bronze head of Zeus found in a local river, ancient pots, terra-cotta statues, a pair of extraordinary bronze vases from the strange triangular *heroon* he had seen outside. The shrine apparently dated from the sixth century BC and archaeologists had been forced to cut away part of its sealed roof to get in. They found six bronze jars of honey that was, some said, still edible.

Impressive though the collection was, it was only when he reached a room at the back that the urgency of his visit came back to him. There were five stone slabs, all painted with scenes of young men reclining on couches, playing pipes, and engaging in some kind of game that seemed to involve drinking and throwing cups of wine. The men wore wreaths of plaited leaves around their heads but were otherwise naked, at least to the waist, below which they were draped with sheets or rugs. The youths were mostly grouped in couples and one pair was touching each other in ways that seemed to Thomas undeniably amorous or sensual, but then the ancient Greeks attached none of the Christian world's stigma to such things.

The panels made up the four sides of a long stone box: a tomb, painted on the inside. The lid of the sarcophagus showed a naked man—presumably the deceased—arcing down through empty space into blue water overhung by stylized trees.

The tombs of the divers.

Thomas stared, then riffled through his guidebook. The tomb dated from the fifth century BC and was unique. The diver image, said the guidebook, was a metaphor for the soul's transition from life into death and the world beyond.

Thomas gazed at it, arrested by the energy and gracefulness of the image.

Is this what Ed felt in that final second: a freeing plummet

into a new, life-giving element that washed away the accumu-
lated dust of life?

He would like to think so, but death still seemed to him a
blankness, a wall: an end, not a transition. Ed had not swum
into cooling waters, or climbed ashore in some Elysian field
any more than he had ascended to join the heavenly choir. He
was merely gone, and Thomas—after yet another strange day
traipsing around ancient places that had been home to rank
upon rank of the dead—was no nearer to knowing why.

He looked back at Ed's notes.

"Where's the other?" he asked an elderly curator who had
looked up to reprimand someone for taking a flash photograph.

"Other?" he said, peering quizzically at Thomas's face,
where a cut above his eye had reopened.

"Tombs of the divers," said Thomas, reading aloud from
the journal. "More than one. Where are the others."

"No others," said the man, slightly offended. "Only this
one. Only this in the world."

Thomas opened his guidebook to the map of the site.

"Where was it found? I couldn't see it outside."

"Not in the town," he responded, as if he were talking to
some kind of mental defective. "In *necropolis.*" And the curator stabbed his finger at the edge of the map beyond the walls.
Then he looked up and pointed north. Thomas did not wait to
hear any more.

As he walked along the road that skirted the site, looking
for the Porta Aurea—the golden gate in the old city walls—
Thomas began to feel his scuffle with Satoh starting to tell.
Apart from the cuts, his right hip was beginning to throb
where he had fallen on it, and his left side ached with each
deep breath: bruised ribs?

Should take your mind off your sprained knee.

He was walking in the direction of the modern town, he
thought, but this was no urban site like Pompeii and Herculaneum; beyond the walls there were only fields, derelict barns,

and colossal thistles as tall as elephant grass. He kept going, feeling the increasing strain on his rib cage as he labored, feeling the sweat on his neck as he hiked along the shadeless and deserted road, increasingly doubtful of any sense of purpose. The heat stood in a dense haze over the vivid greens and yellows of the fields, and even the birds had vanished, so that the only signs of life were the dry rattlings of stalks as the ubiquitous lizards skittered for cover at his approach.

Then, before he saw the weavings of stone in the ragged grass, he saw a distant lean-to and a bright array of gleaming metal and vivid orange tape: part of a dig. He cut sharply off the road and headed straight through the brush. In seconds he caught sight of a tall, angular man in shorts and a wide-brimmed hat stooping to consider something on the ground.

The man had his back to Thomas, who was able to approach unseen, getting a few seconds to prepare his opening remark. He stepped over the orange tape and down into a brushed-out rectangle of dusty earth in which stones were set like the base of a wall.

"Excuse me, sir," he said. "Do you speak English?"

The man leaped to his feet, turned, and swept the hat from his head in a single fluid motion. Except that it wasn't a man. It was a woman, unusually tall and broad, but sinewy-slender, with dark hair that now fell about her shoulders in rumpled waves. Her green eyes were lit with fury.

"What do you think you're doing? Get out of that square!"

"I'm sorry," said Thomas, his composure lost, as he glanced stupidly at his feet. "Right." He started to step forward.

She's American.

"Not that way, you idiot," she roared. "Back the way you came."

Then she stared at him, her eyes narrow against more than the sun, as if she couldn't see him properly or as if he reminded her of someone.

"I thought . . . ," said Thomas again, bridling a little. "I'm sorry, *who* are you?"

"Who am *I?*" she snapped, her eyes wide at his audacity. "I'm Deborah Miller, I'm in charge of this site, and I want you out of it."

CHAPTER 34

"Yes, I knew your brother," she said. "Not well. But I'm sorry to hear he is dead."

Her anger had evaporated almost as quickly as it had come, dispersed the moment Thomas told her who he was.

"He came to the site about a week after the find," she said. "He was baffled at first."

"What find?" said Thomas.

"The second diver tomb," she said. "I assumed you knew."

Thomas smiled ruefully and shook his head. So his brother's pluralized "tombs" was right after all. He thought as much. Ed didn't make mistakes like that.

"For a week or so he kept coming around here," she said. "He didn't talk much, which I was glad of, to be frank, especially with his being a priest and all. I don't have much experience with priests. Anyway, the last time I saw him he was excited, scribbling constantly in a notebook and beaming like an eight-year-old who's just won a year's supply of ice cream. Then he disappeared."

Her eyes were sad, not full of tears or anything so melodramatic, but sad nonetheless, and Thomas decided to trust her.

"So there's a second diver tomb," he remarked, half to himself. "I'm amazed it's not common knowledge, at least around here, given the pride of place given to the original."

"Original is right," she said. "This one won't get the same press because it's later. Much. Good news for me."

"Why?"

"The place would be crawling with archaeologists. Some local university would be given control of the dig or it would simply be commandeered by the Italian government. The original tomb dates from about 500 BC. This is early medieval, more than a thousand years later. Come on, I'll show you."

She got up, and Thomas was again struck by her gangling height. Not that she was graceless. Far from it. She moved with a surprising economy if not actually elegance, like a giraffe, he thought, knowing immediately that to say anything of the sort would likely get him in serious trouble. This was a woman who didn't take a lot of crap from anybody.

"So," he said, "if you don't mind me asking, why are you running the dig? You're from . . . ?"

"Atlanta," she said, "currently."

She had no trace of a southern accent.

"I'm here because I persuaded the Greek government to help support a little expedition to what was once a Greek site. The Italians don't mind so long as nothing leaves the country and I don't destroy anything precious in the process. They send an inspector every week or so to see if I found the Lighthouse of Alexandria. Otherwise they leave me alone."

"The Lighthouse of . . . what?"

"Sorry," she said, and her habitual sternness flicked into a smile. "Archaeological humor. The Pharos lighthouse was one of the seven wonders of the ancient world. It's nowhere near here."

"I see," said Thomas, watching her with interest. She was in her midthirties, he supposed. Peter the Principal would have called her an "odd duck." He found himself liking her.

"I'm a museum curator," she said. "Sounds grander than it is. Anyway, I wanted a little break, get a little fieldwork under my belt. And I had done a sort of favor for the Greek government, so they helped land me this. Impressive, isn't it?" she said, dryly, gazing out over the deserted tangle of weeds and shallow trenches. "Once in a while I get a little help from some local students, but for the most part it's just me. Which is okay."

He believed her.

A kindred spirit, perhaps. Would rather be by herself.

"This is it."

They had arrived at a ramshackle construction made of transparent sheet plastic and old scaffolding, a tent of sorts, just under six feet high and half as much again in length. She stooped and showed him through a flap in the plastic.

The air inside was hot and slightly sweet-smelling, moist like mown grass, but the light was filtered and Thomas felt his face relax as his eyes adjusted. The find was clearly of the same basic construction as the earlier Greek tomb: five stone slabs, all currently draped with transparent sheeting. She revealed each one with tremendous care and the hint of a smile that softened her features still further.

Thomas caught his breath. In place of the lounging drinkers of the Greek tomb, the two longer side panels showed what were clearly crosses. The shorter end panels showed a stylized fish with prominent front fins and oddly well-defined teeth. The final slab, the lid, was what made the connection to the other tomb explicit. It was almost exactly the same image: the naked diver slicing through space into water. The only differences were that the cross and fish motifs appeared here too, in the corners of the painting's border, and that the water toward which the diver was plummeting was a deep crimson.

CHAPTER 35

"Why is the water red?" he said, staring at the painting.

"The sixty-four-thousand-dollar question," she said. "Your brother asked the same thing."

"And?"

"It's a Christian tomb," she said, studying the images again as if seeing them for the first time, considering them with a meticulous reverence, "about seventh century AD. The Christian cross and fish symbols have been worked into the older imagery of death. I'm not an expert on Christian theology, but I'd say that if the water in the original diver tomb represents passage into death, then what we're seeing here is a kind of resurrection: the diver—the dead man—about to be cleansed . . ."

"By the blood of the Lamb," Thomas concluded for her.

"Right. The blood of Christ that is consecrated in the mass, the blood shed for sinners on Calvary: these are the means of salvation. It's a typically Christian reusing of centuries-old iconography for its own purposes. Your brother loved it."

"Why?"

"Because the gap between the original Greek tomb and this one was more than a thousand years. The culture and religious climate had changed radically. But even though the people had turned their backs on paganism, the way they understood and expressed themselves as Christians was still informed by folk memory and custom from their pagan period. This is a Christian burial, but the religious images are derived from people who worshipped Apollo and Poseidon a thousand years earlier, people who lived a few hundred yards back that way."

"Is that normal?" said Thomas. He knew in general that Christianity, like most successful religions, had often absorbed as much as it had replaced, but he had never seen so strikingly specific an example.

"Did you see the terra-cotta statues of Hera in the archaeological museum?" asked Deborah.

"I think so. I didn't pay them too much attention."

"There are dozens from this site and others in the area. The local form shows the queen of the gods holding a pomegranate, which is, presumably, a fertility symbol because of all the seeds, right?"

"So?"

"So, if you drive down the road to Capaccio and check out the local Catholic church there, guess what the Virgin Mary there is holding?"

"A pomegranate?"

"Bingo. The Madonna of Granato of Capaccio. I think it's pretty cool, but some people . . . not so much."

"Why?"

"The usual," she said. "People want their religion to be unique, self-contained, uninformed by things like culture, social structure, and politics. If they admit that any part of that religion is shaped by people and the times they lived in, then they have to deal with the idea that it didn't spring whole from the mind of God. Some people find that idea troubling."

"Not you?"

"Not me."

"What about Ed?"

"Didn't seem to, no," she said, seeming to really think about it. "It was part of why I let him nose around."

"Not everyone gets that privilege, I take it."

She frowned. "The site was discovered by accident and I didn't get here till a few weeks later, by which time there had been unofficial digging."

"Looting?"

"I'm not sure," she said. "The human remains had rotted to nothing. This area was frequently inundated by marsh, and moisture plays havoc with bones. We can tell from soil samples that the body decayed here, but there's nothing left of it."

"But you think there may have been other things in the tomb?" he asked. "Things that were stolen?"

"Hard to say," she said, brooding. "If stuff was taken it happened before anyone official got a look at the place. Nothing is clearly missing. But it seems odd to me. The other medieval tombs around here tend to contain grave goods: armor, weapons, jewelry, vases and such, buried with the dead person. This one . . . nothing."

"And people have been snooping around since you took over?"

"It's a good thing you look like Father Ed," she said. "I'm getting real tired of it."

"A Japanese guy, for instance."

"You know him?" she said, quick, even suspicious.

Thomas gestured to the cut above his eye.

"We met today," he said.

"He's been by here several times, mostly by night when there was no one around, taking pictures, asking questions—nothing specific—avoiding me, generally. After he showed up the first time I told him where to get off, which seemed to irk him." She grinned at the recollection. "I couldn't figure out his interest in the tomb. He also asked why the water was red and about the other symbols."

"Did he discuss a cross found in Herculaneum?" asked Thomas. He was trying to be cautious, but he instinctively trusted this lanky, cantankerous woman and he needed to get her response to what Satoh had told him.

"The shadow-cross from the House of the Bicentenary? No, why?"

"Do you think it possible that the crucifix that left that impression on the wall could have been found?"

"No," she said, taking a slug from her water bottle.

Thomas raised his eyebrows.

"You sound pretty sure," he said.

"I am," she replied. "The 'crucifix' that left that impression could not be found because it wasn't a crucifix that made the mark. Simple as that."

"How can you be so sure? I've seen the mark. It certainly looks like a cross."

"I know," she said, unruffled. "But lots of things can leave cross-shaped marks. It could have been nothing more than a shelf bracket."

"But lots of people believe it was a Christian cross," Thomas began, "I've read half a dozen accounts of it . . ."

"Online?"

"Yes," said Thomas, wilting a little at the amusement in her eyes.

"Next time you have a free moment on the Internet, try typing 'faked moon landing' into the search engine of your choice," she said. "You'll be amazed at the number of sites that will come up. And if you're still laughing, try typing 'faked Holocaust.'"

Her smile was less broad now, more knowing.

"Okay," said Thomas, "so there's a lot of crap on the Web, much of it posted by wackos and people with an agenda . . ."

"And the incredibly badly informed who think they have the whole story because they want to believe it," she said. "Look in respectable, musty, academic books published by reputable presses and you'll see that while it is quite possible that there were Christians in Herculaneum, they almost certainly weren't using crucifixes in their worship and wouldn't for about another three hundred years."

"What about the magic square in Pompeii?"

"What about it? That same square pops up all over the Roman Empire. It's a word puzzle, and doesn't clearly have any mystical significance, let alone a Christian one. Yes, it can spell out *Pater Noster*—if you leave out a few letters—but it can spell out a bunch of things, mostly gibberish. There's nothing cruciform about the layout of the square. Turning it into a cross requires a real leap of faith. Again, people want to find a clear and unchanging version of their own religion, so they do. That doesn't mean it's there."

Thomas felt at sea, not just because he felt as if he'd been exposed as gullible, but because the sands beneath his sense of Ed's death—which had always been inconstant—seemed now to be washing away, leaving him standing on nothing at all. It was as if she'd given his mosaic a kick and what little of the image he had managed to piece together had been scattered.

"But isn't that argument about there not being any early crosses a self-fulfilling prophecy?" he said. "I mean, if each one is dismissed because it's too early . . . ?"

"I suppose," she conceded. "But the cross starts cropping up all over the Roman Empire *after* Constantine makes Christianity 'official,' but that's not till the fourth century. If the cross *was* used as a symbol before then, it's an aberration. The fish is much more consistent with early Christianity. The theology of redemption took centuries to mature. It's only after the belief that Jesus came to the world *in order* to die and redeem it that the cross becomes the center of Christianity. That just isn't where the religion was in AD 79."

Thomas had sat silently on a tree stump above the excavated squares of earth. From here he could look back toward the ancient town and glimpse the tops of the stone temples that glowed amber in the early evening light. He didn't know what to say.

"Did this Japanese guy say anything to you about what this crucifix was supposed to look like?" Deborah asked.

"Silver," Thomas answered. "Marked with the sign of the fish."

She frowned.

"I suppose it's not completely impossible," she said. "If you accept the idea that first-century Christians used crosses—which I don't. Pompeii did have some fine silver, and the fish symbol makes sense as part of the design."

"But you don't buy it," said Thomas.

"Sorry," she said. "If it's any consolation, I doubt Ed would have bought it either. He knew this stuff better than I do."

Thomas scowled.

"I should be heading back before I miss the last train," he said, not entirely sure when the last train was. He had been here much longer than he had intended and it would be dark soon.

"Hang on," she said, "I'll walk back with you. I like to walk through the site at this time, after the tourists have left. No offense."

"Am I a tourist? I thought I was a detective."

They walked in companionable silence through the darkening fields, and Thomas considered how odd it was that he should have spent so much of the last few days with women he didn't know. Not including his former students—whom he didn't consider adults in spite of the politically correct

literature passed along to him by the social studies teacher—
he had probably spoken more to Deborah and Sister Roberta
than to any woman in weeks. Maybe longer. He wondered
why, wondered also if he found either of them attractive. They
both were, in different ways, but the idea had not occurred to
him till now.

It never does, does it? Not since . . .

Enough of that.

"How long will you be in Italy?" he said.

"A week," she answered.

They had reached the edge of the old town and the remains,
now largely sapped of color by the fading light, looked
hunched and ragged, save where the temples loomed like cliffs
in the shadows. They reentered the site. It was closed by now,
but the gate stood open and no one was on duty to turn them
away or demand tickets. In fact, no one was around at all.

"I'm ready to go home," she said. "The trip has been a
blast: an educational blast, but still . . . I'm not a field archaeologist. I'd rather be cataloging and arranging displays: gives
me more control. Sifting through dirt in the vague hope that
you may find . . ."

Thomas's eye had been caught by something inside the
roped-off Temple of Ceres, a curiously pale shape against the
dark mass of a column. He slowed, staring, wondering why
he felt a tightening in his gut, a cold dread that made him
want to turn away, to run, before his eyes—or his brain—
could make sense of the shape.

"What is that?" he said, very quietly. "It looks like . . ."

He faltered.

"Like a man," said Deborah. The sense of dread had passed
to her too. The darkness seemed to be falling fast around them
now and there was no sound anywhere in the deserted remains.

"We should get out of here," said Thomas. Since Ed's
death he had been in danger several times, but he had never
felt like this, never been so chilled, so desperate to be elsewhere. He felt cold. He felt the dull panic of dreams when you

know something terrible is coming but you don't know how to derail the story or wake up.

In a moment, he thought, *you'll see, and you'll wish you had never come. You'll wish . . .*

"Oh my God," Deborah whispered. They were at the rope now, under the deeper shade cast by the massive temple. "It *is* a man."

And then she was racing forward, clambering over the rope and up the great stone steps, and Thomas was following, drawn magnetically toward it even as he wanted to look away. But by then Deborah had stopped running, had in fact grown quite still, her hands clapped over her mouth to keep the screams in, and Thomas could see the pale flesh, could just about make sense of the blood-streaked corpse tied to the column, tied, it seemed, by its own entrails.

CHAPTER 36

For a long moment they just stood there, paralyzed in their horror. Then Thomas retched hard into the grass, staggering away from the temple to the pillar where he had stood earlier that day, where he had first seen the flash of binoculars . . .

He forced himself to turn back toward the body, managed even to take two steps toward it: just enough to be sure.

"It's Satoh," he whispered into the dark.

"Yes," said Deborah quietly. She sounded eerily calm, shocked out of any real feeling.

"Whoever did this," Thomas began, "may . . ."

"Still be here," she concluded in the same drab monotone. "Yes."

"We need to go. Get help."

"Help?" she said, turning to him with real curiosity.

The question caught Thomas like a slap in the face. There

was no help to be gotten, not for the man trussed up with his belly opened so that everything below the ribs was a slick, black hollow . . .

Don't think about it. Go.

He started to walk, taking her hand as he did so. The gesture seemed to bring her around. He felt her body tauten, her mind snap on, and suddenly she was in control of herself again.

"I know the people at the restaurant on the corner," she said. "Everyone else who works here lives in town. We'll get them to call the police."

She pulled forward and he ran a couple of steps to keep up. They were still holding hands, like the survivors of a shipwreck afraid of being swept apart. The gate to the road was back the way they had come. Deborah moved resolutely and they surged over the uneven grass. Getting the body behind them was both a relief and the source of a less specific anxiety, and Thomas risked a look back into the deepening twilight of the dead city, stumbling as Deborah stopped without warning.

"What?" he said.

"Look," she whispered, something of the robotic lifelessness in her voice again. "Look. The gate."

Thomas looked. The gate through which they had entered the site only moments before had been closed.

"We can get over it," said Thomas.

"Maybe. But who closed it?"

Her point stung him like a spider bite.

"You think he's still in here with us?"

He? What man could do that . . . ?

Deborah shrugged cautiously, her face pale, eyes flashing around.

"I fought Satoh earlier today," said Thomas, "and the guy could look after himself. I don't want to tangle with whoever . . ."

He nodded quickly back toward the temple with its butcher-bird trophy strung up on the column, but managed not to look at it.

"You think he's waiting for us?" she whispered.

"I think he wanted us to see Satoh," said Thomas, thinking it through. "I think he wants us to be afraid."

Deborah's glance at him was almost sardonic. *Then he's doing pretty well,* she didn't say. Thomas looked around the expanse of the hulking ruins. It was dark now, and the killer could be anywhere; every broken wall, every weathered and fractured column, every irregular mound of stone and vegetation could be a hiding place or the man himself.

You keep thinking man. It could be a woman. It could be several people working together.

He didn't think so. He was just old-fashioned enough to find it hard to imagine a woman doing that, and had just enough faith in humanity to doubt that a group of people could do this, working together, discussing it . . .

Worse things have been done by groups, by communities, by whole complicit nations.

Maybe. But this felt like the handiwork of an individual. Some single, twisted consciousness was behind this, he thought. Someone had enjoyed it.

"There are two ways out," said Deborah. "There, and up between the Temple of Apollo and the Asklepeion. Which do you want to use?"

"This one," he said. "The other means going all the way through the site. There are too many places for him to hide in there."

"But the body is here. The gate was closed here only moments ago," said Deborah. "He must be at this end."

"By the time we worked our way through the ruins he could be waiting for us at the other end. And the road is higher than the site, so he'd be able to see us all the way."

He didn't say that the prospect of returning into that maze of stone in the dark was too terrifying to seriously consider.

Deborah looked hard at him, thinking.

"Okay," she said, letting go of his hand as if just realizing he was holding it. "What are you doing?"

Thomas had stooped to the ground. When he stood up again he held a chunk of rock in one hand.

"In case . . . ," he began.

She nodded quickly, as if she didn't want him to complete the sentence.

Together, cautiously, they began to walk toward the gate. That was when they heard it: a guttural, rasping hiss behind them, unnaturally loud in the night. It was the sound a large cat might make, sucking air through bared fangs.

Thomas spun around, looking madly for the source of the noise, his right hand clutching the rock hard, raising it to shoulder height.

Over there at the base of the temple, only yards from the mutilated body of Satoh, was a pale figure, crouching batlike on the stone. He was quite still, and at this distance Thomas could see little of him save for the hairless head, the wide open mouth, and the splayed limbs that clung to the rock like some hellish gargoyle. He was skeletally thin and seemingly naked, and he was staring at them with a focused malice that froze Thomas's blood.

Deborah began to walk toward the gate, but for a second Thomas's legs didn't move at all and he could only stare, paralyzed by horror as the figure began very slowly to crawl toward them on thin spidery limbs, hissing as he came. Then Deborah was dragging him backward and he broke into a staggering run after her.

CHAPTER 37

"What was that thing?" said Thomas.

He hadn't asked the question aloud in the three hours they had been talking to the police, but now that the interview was over he finally voiced it.

"That thing?" said Deborah. "It was a man, Thomas."

"It didn't look like a man," he said. "It didn't move like a man."

"There are no alternatives," she said with finality. "And it did look like a man. A strange one, perhaps, but we could have guessed that from what he had just done."

He wasn't sure if she was as convinced as she was making out, but he knew she was right.

They had reached the restaurant-store on the corner without any sign of the killer, who—it seemed—had been content to scare them off. They had summoned the skeptical, middle-aged widow who lived there and she had called the police, Thomas grateful that Deborah's Italian was considerably better than his.

"Homicidal lunatic" and "vampire" don't exactly make the Berlitz guide.

He didn't know why the word *vampire* had popped into his head. He didn't believe in such things, of course, and didn't for a moment think that that was what had killed Satoh. It was just the paleness of the killer, the crablike way he had scuttled over the rocks like Nosferatu . . .

By the time their interview was over, the police had erected some kind of protective tent over part of the Temple of Ceres, and the entire site was bathed in the blue-white light of a dozen halogen work lamps. The entire environment seemed surreal, dreamlike. The police had not, thank God, asked him to look again at the body or, indeed, to venture back into the site.

They had been interviewed separately, but once they'd been released, he and Deborah had compared notes. Thomas was particularly relieved to find that neither of them had held anything back, so their stories agreed. Even their answers to the key question, casually floated by the chain-smoking translator in the museum where the police had set up their temporary operations base, had been frank: "Did you know the deceased?"

Thomas had known that any discrepancies between his story and Deborah's would get them into deep water fast. So he had told them: about Satoh searching his room at the Executive; about the struggle in the site earlier in the day; about the supposed link to Ed, whose death had first led him to Italy. The translator had gone over each point several times, clarifying, responding to rapid questions from the investigating officer, the three men regarding each other cautiously, circling, almost, as if spoiling for a fight.

Camoranesi was a heavyset man with a thick black mustache and sad, heavy-lidded eyes. Like the translator, the policeman smoked constantly and spoke in a low, gravelly voice like someone who knew so much of the world's nastier side that he was numb to it, almost bored. By contrast the translator, a young man barely more than college age, seemed as rattled as Thomas, and though the greenish tinge left his face in the course of their long conversation, the jitteriness never went away.

They didn't like what he had to say. It complicated a messy situation further, and he knew it. They would have to liaise with the Americans, maybe with Interpol, and if Thomas was reading Camoranesi correctly, they thought it was irrelevant. They were dealing with some psycho, they thought. It had nothing to do with Thomas's rambling and arbitrary crusade.

Thomas couldn't blame them. By the end of the interview, he too felt that Satoh's death was most likely a coincidence. He had, perhaps, been spying on Thomas, maybe on Deborah too, but that had not been connected to his death. He had been in the wrong place at the wrong time, and had fallen afoul of a maniac. It could happen, he supposed uneasily, anywhere.

The police didn't say any of this directly. They copied his passport—which he had been carrying with him since the break-in at the hotel—and asked for names and contact numbers here and in the United States. He gave them Jim in the States, and Father Giovanni at the retreat house in Naples. The policeman raised his eyebrows at the fact that both were priests, and the strangeness of it struck Thomas too. They asked for his fingerprints, and Thomas gave them without complaint. He had nothing to hide.

He'd had no more than ten minutes to speak to Deborah, and he didn't really know what to say anyway. After rehashing what she had told the police, she offered her number and he took it, doubtful they would ever speak to each other again, wondering how they could possibly chat about history and culture when all that held them together was soaked with the evening's horrors.

After their halfhearted farewell, he was invited to a police car and driven to the local station. He waited there for twenty-two minutes alone in a dingy room whose window was so high it may have served as a cell, before being put into another police car and taken back to the Executive in Naples.

It was two in the morning. He got the desk clerk to open the bar long enough for him to take a couple of beers to his room, drinking them in a series of long gulps the moment he got inside. He undressed quickly and got into bed, hoping against hope that he was too tired to dream.

CHAPTER 38

The Seal-breaker considered the display on his cell phone and answered it on the third ring.

"Yes?"

"This is Pestilence. We have a problem."

"I'm aware of the situation."

"What the hell were you thinking? I could have told you this would happen."

The Seal-breaker stared out the window. He had expected this response from Pestilence. War was always in his corner. Death did as he was told and Famine was . . . well, who knew what went on his head? But Pestilence was always second-guessing, prying, challenging. It was, he supposed, inevitable

with hired—if expensive—labor, but it was tiresome nonetheless.

"The project is moving according to plan," he said. "If necessary you will liaise with War."

"And if I decide to eliminate that loose cannon once and
for all?"

"That's not your decision."

"That's not what I asked," said Pestilence.

"It's all the answer you need."

After Pestilence had hung up, the Seal-breaker considered
his options. Knight had been left alive thus far because it had
seemed more useful or less risky to let him run aimlessly
around like a headless chicken. But if he was picking up a
scent, he could quickly become a liability. Ever the prag-
matist, the Seal-breaker wanted no more corpses than were
strictly necessary, but the death of Thomas Knight might soon
be inevitable. It was also a matter of serving the greater good.

The phone was still in his hand. He dialed, composing the
instructions he would give War as he did so.

CHAPTER 39

"Rough night?" said Brad Iverson over his *Wall Street Journal*
as Thomas arrived for the last ten minutes of the breakfast
buffet.

"Slept badly," said Thomas.

"Apparently," said Brad, playing the genial guy's guy.
Jockular, Thomas called it. "I hope she was worth it," said
Brad, and laughed once, head flung back.

Thomas gave a wan smile but he didn't feel like playing
along.

"What's on the itinerary for today then, Tourist Thomas?"

154   A. J. Hartley

"Not sure yet," said Thomas, almost to himself. "Back to Pompeii, I think."

"Dude! Once wasn't enough? What do you see in these piles of rocks?"

"Not enough, apparently," said Thomas.

He went to the retreat house not caring whether Pietro, Giovanni, or Roberta answered the door. He would want to speak to all of them today anyway. For once the great doors were open to admit a small delivery truck.

"Supplies for the *Fransiscana*," said Giovanni, somewhat wearily, waving him in. "The rest arrive tomorrow."

"I hear you had a bit of a scare with one of them," said Thomas.

Giovanni shrugged.

"Probably nothing," he said, though Thomas doubted that he really believed that.

Pietro would be gone all day, but after hearing how Thomas had spent his evening, Giovanni said he would make sure the old monsignor sat down with Thomas before the day was out for a long overdue chat.

"Mind if you and I talk now?" asked Thomas.

Giovanni checked his watch.

"Okay," he said. "One hour. But not here. This place is getting . . ." He gave up looking for the word and raised his hands almost to the sides of his head: noisy, frustrating, crazy.

They walked up to the junction with Via Medina, weaved their cautious way across the street, and strolled down toward the sea, passing the long row of elegant eighteenth-century façades, now blackened and tagged with graffiti. They passed a cluster of little restaurants, their roadside patios closed up till lunchtime; circled an imposing fountain featuring statues of vaguely nautical mythology; and then, quite suddenly, were presented with an imposing and well-maintained fortress, the Castello Nuovo.

"I came here with your brother," said Giovanni. "I'd never been before. He showed me around."

"I guess when you live in a place you don't always see what visitors get so excited about," said Thomas.

"Right," said the priest. "The castle is typical Napoli: lots of layers. Under the earth there are Greek remains, then Roman. The building is thirteenth century but it was restored in the fifteenth century and again later. Now the city council meets here. Ed liked the . . . what is the word?"

"History?"

"Yes," he said, tilting his head onto one side to say *not exactly.* "More like *continuity,* yes?"

"Yes."

They entered the castle over a broad wooden bridge and through a floridly carved archway, flanked by columns and surmounted by a frieze with horses and a chariot. The archway was almost as high as the two massive, dark towers that flanked it, and led them to a stone-flagged courtyard. Thomas stood there, absorbing the age—the continuity—of the place, while Giovanni purchased a couple of tickets in what had been the gate house.

"You told me about Ed's interest in symbols," said Thomas, when the priest returned. "Can you recall any particular focus?"

"I don't know much about his work," said Giovanni, "but I remember him collecting images of the fish from the catacombs in Rome and other earlier Christian art."

"The fish symbol? Like those things you see on people's cars?"

Giovanni shrugged and motioned them up a long straight flight of steps.

"It was an early Christian symbol," he said. "A very simple design. Some people think it began as a word you make up from the first letters of other words."

"An acronym?"

"Yes," said Giovanni, "but I think it was also a kind of

code. The language of the early church was Greek, and their word for fish was *ikthus*. Your brother showed me this. Wait."

They had emerged in one of the sea-facing towers in which a circular room was laid out with formal pews: a parliament building or a courthouse. The vaulted ceiling was perhaps sixty feet high, webbed by arcing stone braces. Giovanni pulled a paper napkin from his pocket, leaned against the edge of a wooden desk, and jotted with a black ballpoint:

*I I*esous: *Jesus*
*K K*ristos: *Christ*
*Θ TH*eou: *God's*
*Ÿ U*ios: *Son*
*Σ S*oter: *Savior*

Thomas considered the words as Giovanni traced his finger down their initial letters.

"See?" he said. "*Ikthus*. Fish, but also Jesus Christ, son of God and savior. The word was used so that the persecuted Christians could recognize each other. When they met, one would draw a line like this."

He sketched a curved line, like a stylized wave.

"And the other would complete the image."

He added the bottom half of the curve, joining the line at the left end to form the fish's head, crossing it at the right to form the tail.

"And this is a very old image?" said Thomas.

"Maybe one of the oldest. Ed said it was a common symbol in other religions too, but the early Church claimed it. The New Testament is full of stories that use the fish."

"*I will make you fishers of men,*" Thomas said.

"And the feeding of five thousand people," said Giovanni. "Eduardo said that the fish was an 'archetypal fertility symbol' also," he concluded, smiling at his memory of the phrase.

They walked for a while in silence until they found themselves in a long room facing the sea whose floor was made of thick glass. Beneath it they could see the building's lower level: the remains of storerooms, dungeons, passages, and graves, some containing skeletons.

"They say the foundation is full of tunnels dating back to the earliest days of the building," said Giovanni. "Some may connect to the sea. There is a legend that prisoners left in the dungeons would scream in the night. When the guards went to check the next day, they had vanished from their cells. After several years, soldiers went through all the tunnels and found a crocodile that had escaped from a visiting boat from Egypt and had been living in the passages down there. They killed and stuffed the crocodile and hung it over the gateway. Only a legend, but Eduardo liked this story."

Again he smiled, wistful this time.

"I should get back," he sighed. "You have to go to Pompeii, and I have nuns to deal with."

Thomas nodded.

Symbols, he thought. *Crosses and fish. Could these be at the heart of Ed's death? How?*

"It's all so . . . inadequate," he said aloud. "There's something I'm missing."

Giovanni said nothing and Thomas wondered again if Ed's friends were withholding information, to protect his memory, or to protect themselves. If so, from what? From whom?

CHAPTER 40

Back at the retreat house, Roberta was hovering.

"You are heading back to Pompeii today?" she asked. It was a prelude to a request to join him, and Thomas found his heart sinking a little. He had enjoyed her company well enough, but he was ready to be alone, to think.

"Yes," he said, trying to be amiable. "Surely you've seen enough of that place?"

"Better than hanging around here," she said. "And these are my last days of freedom before the retreat proper starts. Mind if I tag along?"

Put like that, of course, with that slightly desperate hope in her eyes, what was he supposed to say?

"I'll wait here for you."

She had barely left his side when Giovanni stuck his head over the courtyard rail and shouted down to him.

"The police just called. They are on their way over to speak to you."

Thomas's first instinct was to leave, but that made no sense, so he forced himself to sit.

Camoranesi arrived with a uniformed driver and the still-nervous translator almost immediately. He had called, he explained, from the Executive.

"What can I do for you?" Thomas said.

Camoranesi drew a small cloth bundle from his pocket and began to unfold the fabric.

"Have you seen this before?" said the translator, his eyes on the investigator. "It was found in the dead man's clothes."

It was the silver fish that Parks had stolen from Ed's room in Chicago. Thomas picked it up, felt its weight and coolness, and then told them.

For a long moment nobody spoke, and then Roberta was blundering in, asking if Thomas was ready to go, and Camoranesi was wrapping up and pocketing the fish without another word. As they stood up, the policeman muttered a few words in Italian and then turned and began walking away.

"He wants you to contact him before you check out of the hotel," said the translator.

"Am I a suspect?" said Thomas.

The translator looked embarrassed.

"I don't know," he said, and Thomas believed him. But in the cold pit of his stomach, he was sure that he was.

CHAPTER 41

Roberta talked constantly, first on the crowded number two bus that collected them from outside the tobacconist's across the street from the Executive, then on the Circumvesuviana platform, then on the train, and finally in the hot and shadeless site itself. She talked about Italy and Italians, Italian food, the Italian language and how she wished she understood more of it. She discussed her nervousness about the upcoming retreat. She offered various reflections on Thomas's horrific night, the imminence of mortality ("it can come any time: the trick is to be ready") and the necessary spiritual preparedness for death. She talked about the wonders of archaeology and history, and how being confronted by the past changed one's sense of the present. In short she said much of what she had said before, and while it had formerly sounded like thought, it now sounded like something she'd read. While she was listening in on a guided tour in the forum, Thomas ducked back toward the Temple of Apollo and waited till she had given up scanning the faces around for him, and wandered off alone.

Thomas felt a little bad for ditching Roberta, but it was what he had planned to do from the outset. He hadn't seen the magic square firsthand, and knew it was in a house that wasn't open to the public. The plan that was forming in his head on the train was that he would find a place to hide, maybe in the amphitheater, which was well-removed from the most frequented parts of the site, and wait the day out. When the site closed, he would locate the house of Paquius Proculus, break in, and see what the square might have to show.

In the meantime, Thomas made for all the places Ed had listed, places he had largely missed in his last visit: the bathhouses with their sea-creature mosaics, and—most important—the Temple of Isis, which he had somehow walked past twice last time without noticing. All the while he tried to process what he knew, about Ed's research, Parks, how Satoh wound up with the little silver fish, the tale of the Herculaneum cross, and, most insistently, the circumstances of Satoh's death. The rambling chaos of his thoughts was mirrored by the sites he looked at: fragmented mosaics; half-intact structures of crumbling brick, stone, and tile; nameless houses stretching down empty streets. There was no order, no sequence; nothing was making any sense. He stood in the Temple of Isis and saw only pieces of a puzzle he could not hope to solve. What had his brother seen here that was so important? What had this place been? What function had this column and that altar served? Why was an Egyptian god being worshipped in a first-century Roman town anyway?

The last question was new and gave him pause. Rome had had territories in North Africa. He recalled Cleopatra's links to Julius Caesar and Mark Antony from Shakespeare. So the cult of Isis had been imported, absorbed into the Roman pantheon as foreign cultures were absorbed into the empire, as Christianity would be absorbed and made official three centuries later?

He considered the remains of the temple. It was laid out as a square courtyard surrounded by a walkway lined with columns, and with steps up to the shrine in the center. Several large stone blocks were arranged around the open space, though whether they were statue bases or altars he wasn't sure. In one corner of the square was a blockish building covered in white plaster. Thomas checked his guidebook. This was the purgatorium, a building containing a subterranean, vaulted room that once held water from the Nile: holy water.

He approached the pale structure, his gaze sliding over it, already frustrated and a little bored. Then he shaded his eyes, caught by a familiar image, and looked again. A little over head height was a plaster frieze of fish. Strange ones, with oversized fins at the front and, in some cases, triangular teeth like alligators.

Fish again.

His mind flashed quickly over the other sites he had seen that day, and the ones Ed's notes had pointed to elsewhere, and the image of the fish suddenly seemed to be what he had been seeing constantly since he arrived. He had seen it in the mosaics of the bathhouses and the underground swimming pool in Herculaneum, in the Christian tomb of the diver with the red water in Paestum, in the silver votive stolen by Parks and found on Satoh's corpse, in locations all over Pompeii, and most clearly, here in a Greco-Roman temple to an Egyptian god.

Thomas felt his pulse starting to race. Was this it? And if so, what could it possibly mean?

He stared at the plaster reliefs of the curious fish, with their bulbous snouts, wriggling tails, the toothed jaws, and those massive forefins that looked like . . .

Like legs.

It was an Egyptian cult, and one of the beasts most clearly linked to Egypt was the crocodile. Could these odd images be representations of those animals made by Italians who'd never seen one? But he'd seen the paintings from the temple in the museum in Naples and they had been full of detailed Egyptian divinities with jackal heads and motifs that came from real knowledge of Egypt. He'd also seen plenty of representations of fish from all over Pompeii and Herculaneum, many of them not only lifelike but recognizable. But then there had been the others, the weird ones with the large fins that looked like legs. They hadn't all come from Egypt. They'd come from here, had probably been local images grafted onto the imported Isis cult as Hera's pomegranate had been grafted onto the Virgin Mary.

So the legged-fish symbol was local and was old, and—as the Paestum tomb demonstrated—had been adapted for Christian use. Giovanni had said that the fish in its familiar form had plenty of symbolic resonance for Christians, but the legged fish would surely have even more. A legged fish could cross between land and water, could—now that he thought of it— echo Christ's own walking on water as the terrified apostles cowered in their boat on the sea of Galilee. If the earlier Paestum tomb used the symbol of the diver as an image suggesting the passage into death, wouldn't the Christian use of a *legged* fish suggest a kind of transcendence, moving through death and beyond it: the ability to live in both elements?

What had Ed's note to Giovanni said?

"*Ʒian symbol-wise, I might have hit the mother lode (should that be father lode??!!), but it's pointing outside Italy now and I have to follow.*"

Was the legged fish the mother lode symbol of early Christianity? The supreme icon of Christ's triumph over death? If so, why didn't it become part of the mainstream iconography of the church, and where had Ed followed it next? And how could such a quest have gotten Ed—and Satoh—killed? He had no idea, but he felt it in his veins, a humming energy. He was on to something at last.

CHAPTER 42

Thomas found Roberta waiting at the Marine Gate. The magic square was, he decided, a moot point. Ed hadn't been interested in crosses and probably didn't believe that they were Christian symbols as early as AD 79. If there was truth to Satoh's story about the Herculaneum cross, the key was surely the fact that the cross was marked by the image of a "strange fish." That would certainly have piqued Ed's curiosity.

"So now what?" said Roberta as they rode back.

He had given her the gist of his ideas in a muted and unspecific way as a way of salving his conscience for abandoning her. She was probably lonely, as so many religious seemed to be, doubly so here.

"I have to talk to Pietro," said Thomas. "No evasions, no

hostility, no excuses. If he doesn't tell me what I need to know, I'll give his name to the police."

"You think he was connected to the death of that Japanese man?"

"No," he said. "But I do think he was implicated in a larger puzzle centering on my brother."

"He's doing sick visits this afternoon," she said. "He won't be back till six. Let's take a break for an hour or so, think it all through, then go and talk to him."

For a long moment Thomas considered her pale round face and serious eyes. He probably could use some time to make sense of what he had learned.

"What kind of break?"

"We'll get off at the Ercolano stop," she said, clearly excited. "I have an idea. Come on, Thomas, my retreat starts tomorrow and then I won't be able to leave the house. One last excursion for a couple of hours, and then you can see Pietro, okay?"

For once she let him just sit and think, and as the train sped along the seawall with its patches of black sand beach, she produced a silver cell phone from a pocket in the sleeve of her habit. Thomas raised his eyebrows at the phone.

"Oh," she said, with a playfully dismissive wave, "we're all very modern these days."

Thomas smirked.

"*Pronto,*" she said into the phone, then mouthed "Father Giovanni." She introduced herself in faltering but competent Italian and asked a series of questions. The answers seemed to satisfy her.

"What was all that about?" asked Thomas.

"Wait and see," she grinned, girlish.

The surprise was waiting for them in the street by the Ercolano station: a white, two-door Fiat rental car.

"We have to drop it off at seven, so that gives us two and a half hours," she said, pleased with her scheme. "I've been wanting to do this since we got here."

"Do what?"

"Visit the cause of all the trouble," she said, as if this were obvious.

For a moment Thomas's heart skipped. What was she talking about? What did she know.

"Vesuvius!" she said into his baffled face, "the volcano."

"Oh," he said. "*That* trouble."

She fumbled with the keys, shaking her head at his slowness, chuckling to herself.

She was a surprisingly good driver, which was just as well, because the road across town was narrow and hazardous, and the moment they began to ascend the mountain itself, things deteriorated. Roberta clearly enjoyed the hairpin turns, the blaring of horns at every bend, the skirting of the precipices on the passenger side, but Thomas quickly wearied of it all, and after ten minutes, he was getting nauseated. Twice they had to inch past great lumbering coaches descending from the summit, and other cars were constantly rocketing by at wholly unreasonable speeds.

"Wow!" said Roberta, as a tiny white van shot around the corner toward them, missed by inches in a blaze of horn, and headed down toward the town without slowing one iota. "He was moving!"

She seemed quite delighted by the whole thing. Thomas stared out at the purplish cone of the volcano above the tree line, and tried to ignore their zigzagging ascent.

When they finally stopped in a parking lot of pinkish-brown gravel, he took several minutes gazing down over the trees to the gleaming sea for his stomach to calm.

"Come on," said Sister Roberta, as if she were leading a Girl Scout hike.

Thomas looked bleakly around and up. They were still a long way from the crater.

"Now we walk," said the nun, as if this were a special treat.

She marched away in the lowering afternoon sun, her crucifix swinging with each pounding stride of her sandals so that their buckles jingled faintly with each step.

There was a gate at the entrance to the trail. Most of the tourists were on their way down. The thin, long-haired woman at the turnstile checked her watch.

"Straight up and down. No more than fifteen minutes at the crater," she said, tearing off tickets from a spool without looking at them.

A few yards beyond the gate the path began to climb steeply, cutting back on itself and then slanting hard up the mountain.

This will be no picnic, thought Thomas, wearily. His feet already ached after the day's walking.

Maybe he shouldn't have come. But a part of him did want to see the volcano. As Roberta had suggested, it was the heart of the story of Pompeii and Herculaneum, towns that would otherwise have evolved normally, their first-century glories forgotten.

The rock and cinder path was straight, fenced on one side with wooden beams, cut away from the slope up to the summit on the other. Up here there were no trees, and the mountaintop rose smooth and featureless save where stray boulders of the same porous rock jutted out of the cone. He had expected the stone to be gray, but the base colors were browns, pinks, and violets, the rock grainy like pellets and pitted with air pockets. Here and there were straggling grasses and lichens, but for all the fertility of the lower slopes, there wasn't much growing up here. The summit was a dead landscape, barren, but with a savage beauty of its own.

Everyone was going home. A party of Italian teenagers jogged jauntily past, but a lot of the others—many of them in their fifties and sixties, none of them locals—looked exhausted. As Thomas trudged wearily up, letting Roberta get ahead, he checked behind him a couple of times. They might have been the last people admitted.

It took them twenty minutes to reach the top, and when
they did the little stall selling drinks and postcards was closing for the day and the summit was all but deserted. On the inside of the path the jagged crags that marked the crater's rim
were broken by stretches where only a single looping chain
separated the visitor from the hollow below. Thomas peered
down, not certain what to expect, and found a vast conical depression of tiny stones. The sides showed blasted and splintered rock, scorched black and white, stone that looked as
hard as flint but had been shattered by the force from below.
Smoke drifted up in lazy gusts from spots all around the crater
walls, but the center of the depression looked still and tran-
quil. There was no heat, and only the merest tang of sulfur in
the air.

"This way," said Roberta, leading away from the edge toward a narrower path than the one they had ascended. The trail
slotted down the outer slope of the cone and out of sight.

"Where does that go?" Thomas asked, with a sour look.

"Around the crater," she said, cheerily. "Got to go around
the top. Got to do the thing properly. Come on, Thomas."

He trudged in her dusty wake as the sun began to set and
the last of the tourists began their descent.

"On the other side," she shouted over her shoulder, "we'll
be able to look across the crater to the bay."

"I can hardly wait," muttered Thomas.

"And we can say a prayer."

Better and better.

Thomas's feet hurt.

"Slow down," he called. "I think I'm getting the Stigmata."

"The what?" she said, turning, looking quizzical.

"The Stigmata," Thomas replied. "You know, when your
hands and feet bleed. Feet, in this case."

"Oh, the Stigmata," she said. "I misheard."

She still looked a little confused, maybe even offended.

"Sorry," he said. "Bad joke."

"That's okay," she replied. "I'm used to people not understanding miracles."

"And you believe in things like that?" he said. It was a sincere question and there was no mockery in his voice. "Manifesting the wounds of Christ?"

"Of course," she said. "The Lord works in mysterious ways, his wonders to perform," she intoned, seriously.

"But Stigmata," Thomas pressed. "I mean, what's the point? Why would God inflict open wounds on people? I don't get it."

"Well, I've never actually encountered it," she said. "Though I'm sure it happens. The world is full of sin, and sometimes the Lord sees fit to punish sin miraculously."

Thomas stared at her, but she kept walking and did not meet his eyes.

"Look," she said. "We're almost at the other side."

"Yes," said Thomas.

"I think we should pray for the repose of the soul of that man who was killed. This place is full of the grandeur of God."

She climbed the shifting shingle to the rim and looked out across the volcano's great mouth to the sea. The sun was low and amber now, so that the inside of the crater was slashed in half, part in deep shade, part seeming to burn with an orange light vibrant as flame. There was no one else around.

"Kneel with me," she said, dropping, her face lit by the same glow so that she seemed passionate, radiant in her conviction.

Thomas climbed up beside her, but he did not kneel, and his brain was racing.

"What did you say his name was? The dead man?" said Roberta, her eyes closed, her hands joined in front of her, fingers pointed skyward like a statue of the Virgin.

"Satoh," said Thomas, absently.

"We thank the Lord for this bountiful day, and pray for the souls of Mister Satoh and for Father Edward Knight," she began. "May they rest in peace. Our Father, who art in Heaven . . ."

She intoned the words slowly, so that Thomas could join in. He did, but awkwardly, his cracked voice barely more than a whisper. He had expected something more appropriate: *Eternal rest give unto him, O Lord . . .* Something like that. But she had chosen the Lord's Prayer.

". . . give us this day our daily bread . . . ," she continued.

Thomas was staring out over the great smoking hollow. The climb weighed heavily on him, and there was something surreal about this place, about praying—for the first time in years—for his dead brother, with this woman he didn't know.

". . . as we forgive those who trespass against us . . ."

The whole thing felt dreamlike, as if all his doubts and sadness had drifted unexpectedly to the surface, but other things were nagging at him. Pietro had given a sermon on the Immaculate Conception, he recalled, as if hearing the account of it through an echoing tunnel . . .

"I didn't understand most of it, of course—my Italian is not good enough—but it was a beautiful sermon, full of devotion and piety. At the end he was close to tears at the thought of Our Lord being conceived without sin, then entering this dreadful world . . ."

He had been irritated at the time, but it had been turning over at the back of his mind ever since. Surely the Immaculate Conception wasn't about the birth of Christ at all? He barely remembered such things anymore, but he was almost sure it was about the birth of the Virgin Mary, the only person since Adam and Eve to enter the world without the stain of original sin. Frowning, Thomas stopped mouthing the old familiar words, and Roberta's voice went on alone.

"For thine is the kingdom, the power, and the glory . . ."

Thomas's drowsiness, his drifting toward grief, left him instantly.

"Forever and ever. Amen."

Another phrase came back to him.

"Sometimes the Lord sees fit to punish sin miraculously."

Punish? With Stigmata?

Stigmata was a sign of piety, a manifestation of a saintly devotion to the crucified body of Christ.

"For thine is the kingdom . . ."

And while many Catholics wouldn't give much thought to it these days, surely you would expect a Franciscan to know . . .

"Forever and ever . . ."

Particularly since the most famous of all Stigmatics was . . .

"St. Francis," he whispered aloud.

As he did so, he became aware that Roberta was no longer kneeling beside him. She was behind him.

CHAPTER 43

Pestilence was moving before she finished the prayer. Knight was looking distracted, tired, and a little weepy, which had been the idea from the start. She rose silently, drawing the little Walther automatic from the pouch over her stomach, leveling it at the back of his head in the same motion in which she thumbed off the safety with casual expertise.

Just two shots, and then the shallow grave she would scoop out of the ash and pumice on the unvisited slope of the volcano. It might be years before anyone found him.

Catholics, Thomas thought, *don't say those last lines as part of the Lord's Prayer. In the mass they are part of the congregation's answer to the priest.*

"Deliver us, Lord, from every evil," said the priest in his memory, as Thomas flung himself over the edge, and the gun went off behind him. *"And grant us peace in our day . . ."*

Pestilence cursed as the shot went high over the man's diving form.

What the hell had just happened?

He had just dropped into the crater, as if he'd known she was about to spray his brains over the Goddamned mountain.

She scrambled forward, cursing the clumsy, jangling sandals, raising the gun and peering down its barrel as she neared the edge. There was nowhere for him to hide in there. It was inconvenient, and getting his body out to where she could bury it would be harder, but she'd still have the pathetic bastard, and maybe she'd make him pay for his dramatics.

Thomas fell into the crater and rolled, trying to stabilize himself so that he could at least look around. It was dark, but not dark enough to stop her from picking him off. He clawed at a promising outcrop, missed it, and tumbled another ten feet. For a split second he saw her standing on the rim, her habit lit by the last of the sun, face livid, gun raised and flashing.

The report came a moment later, and the volcanic dust inches from his head kicked up as the bullet slammed in.

Then he hit a spike of rock that reared out of the sandy funnel like a breaching whale, and he swiped at it, grabbing and holding on to stop his fall, only then wincing at the pain in his fingers. The stone was hot.

Pestilence had fired two hasty shots and hit nothing. Now she forced herself to breathe and aim, but in that moment Knight's flailing descent shuddered to a halt, and he was clawing onto a jagged hunk of rock. Her shot, which had been trained to his momentum, missed, pinging off stone a foot or so beneath him, and in that second, he squirmed around the rock and out of sight.

Her anger flared again. She checked the clip in her pistol and began walking carefully down into the crater.

The lower side of the rock was a fissure, or series of fissures, and though it wasn't clearly visible in the dusk and shadow, there was a steam vent belching thin wisps of hot vapor. As soon as he felt secure, Thomas took his hands off the rock and opened them to the air. They wouldn't blister, and apart from some tenderness, there was no serious harm. He fished for a loose rock and braced himself for Roberta's arrival.

There was no sound for perhaps a minute, but it was impossible to move on this surface without sending little streams of tiny stones trickling down into the cone, and he heard her when she got a foot or two above the crag.

If you were her, what would you do?

Pestilence paused, bare feet splayed. She had left the clumsy, noisy sandals on the crater's rim. She had the gun in both hands, swiveling carefully, sighting down the barrel as she had been trained. He could be still sheltering beneath the rock or trying to creep up one side or the other. Her best approach was over the top. She put one foot on the rock and stepped up.

It took a second for the burning sensation in the soles of her feet to reach her, then she was scrambling, leaping, and there was Knight, waiting for her, lunging into close quarters as she fired, off balance, missing.

Just don't lose the gun.

Thomas hit her with his full body weight, pushing the pistol wide, but she didn't let go, even as she fell back against the rock, and without so much as a beat, it was swinging back toward him. He fell on her then, pinning her arms, trying to make her drop the gun clutched in her right hand.

But she was strong. He was so used to her religious disguise that a part of him still couldn't believe what she really was, but the pressure on his wrist as she began to turn the pistol in toward his ribs dispelled any lingering sense of "Sister Roberta."

She's going to kill you. Now.

With his left hand still trying to control her gun hand, he released his right, grabbed at her face, and twisted her head as hard and fast as he could. If she had expected it, he would never have had the strength, but as it was she didn't see it coming, and he was able to turn and hold for just a second.

She had been lying right beside the smoking vent. The volcanic steam hit her face and she cried out, writhing in a pain that opened her other hand. The gun fell out. Thomas pounced on it.

He turned to find her up and coming for him, the left side of her face red from the scalding gas. Her eyes were full of fury, hatred, and something else, something smug and self-satisfied.

She knows you won't shoot.

Thomas hesitated, and then, just as she was almost upon him, switched his grip on the gun and slashed hard with it across her forehead.

She fell heavily on top of him, unconscious, and for a long bizarre moment, he lay in the crater and looked up at the sky, the coolness and tranquillity of the evening settling all about him.

CHAPTER 44

Thomas left her where she had fallen. She would probably be out for a while yet, and when she woke she'd be without transport. He took her gun and her phone, then made the long walk back to the parking lot, climbed over the gate, and took the rental car.

The fact that Roberta had been ready to kill him had stripped away all he thought he could rely on. Now he knew only three things: first, powerful people were prepared to kill to keep Ed's death unexamined. Second, he had to get whatever he could out of the old monsignor. Third, he had to get out of Italy as quickly and cleanly as possible. He didn't know where to go or how he was going to get there, but he had no doubt that Roberta—or whatever her real name was—was not working alone. If he spent another night at the Executive, he was sure, it would be his last.

He drove to the Ercolano station, abandoned the car, resisted the urge to grab a beer from a neighboring bar, and took the train to Garibaldi and a cab to the hotel. On the train he searched Roberta's phone for any dialed or received numbers, but all the directories had been wiped clean.

"Cops were looking for you, bro," remarked Brad with a broad grin. He was lounging at the Executive's bar with a glass of orange juice in his hand and flagged Thomas down before he even collected his key. "What you been up to?"

Thomas stiffened.

Roberta?

Not yet, surely. And she wouldn't go to the police. This had to be about Satoh.

Thomas smiled weakly and turned to the level gray eyes of the concierge.

"They want you to call them as soon as you return," the Italian said. "And if you don't, they want me to call them for you."

It was almost a question and Thomas thought fast.

"How about I step out," he began carefully, "to talk to the priest round the corner and *then* come back and *then* we have this conversation, you and I?"

The concierge looked at him for a long moment.

"Be quick," he said, at last.

It was nine o'clock. Giovanni answered the retreat house door and immediately shook his head.

"Pietro is not here," he said. "He's at his church. Santa Maria del Carmine."

"Do you have a phone number for him there?"

"Yes," said Giovanni, fishing in his pocket and producing the retreat house's business card. "The second number."

"Okay," said Thomas, walking away.

"He will not talk to you," said Giovanni.

"He has no choice," said Thomas, still walking. "And neither do I."

He walked quickly away from the hotel, dialing on Roberta's phone, scanning the dark but busy street for a cab.

Pietro answered on the third ring, giving the name of the church in a brusque mumble.

"This is Thomas Knight. Eduardo's brother. Don't hang up."

He had no idea how good Pietro's English was. He paused and, for a moment, there was silence.

"Yes," said the voice at the other end, sounding far away.

"I'm coming to see you," said Thomas with force. "Now. Someone just tried to kill me."

He didn't know how much of this the old priest was getting, and part of him didn't care.

"Okay," said the priest.

Thomas stopped in his tracks. No shouting? No threats? Then the voice came back, slow, careful.

"Tanaka is dead?" it said.

"Tanaka?" asked Thomas.

"The Japanese," said Pietro.

"He told me his name was Satoh."

"He is dead?"

"Yes."

Another long pause, and what might have been a sigh.

"Okay," he said.

"Okay what?" said Thomas.

"I will show you Eduardo's papers."

"You didn't burn them?"

"No."

Thomas's surging triumph was tempered by anger.

"But you deliberately made it look like you had, so that I wouldn't ask to see them again. Where are they? I want them now."

"I say *messa*."

"Mass?"

"Yes," said the priest. "You come?"

"Come to mass?" said Thomas, incredulous.

"Yes. Come. Pray for me."

"No," said Thomas, brushing away the invitation irritably. He was in no mood for an olive branch, particularly after "Roberta's" use of the same ruse on Vesuvius.

"Half hour only," said the priest.

Either the priest was using a short form of the liturgy, or he motored through it. But there would be nobody there and there would be no singing. That would keep it short. This was no scheduled mass he was being invited to. This would be just the two of them.

You could go. Sit at the back, listen, like you used to.

No.

"You go ahead," said Thomas. "I'll be there by the time you're done."

"Okay," said the priest, giving in, and then the phone went dead.

Thomas took a cab up past the museum and through a labyrinth of increasingly chaotic streets. Here as elsewhere in the city the churches were joined to the neighboring buildings, and since they lacked spires, they were identifiable only by their ornate doors and the invariably sooty inscriptions above them. Thomas peered out of the window looking for Santa Maria del Carmine as the streets got narrower and poorer, though the buildings themselves had clearly once been opulent. The traffic got heavier, more dominated by tiny cars and scooters, often overburdened with multiple children, all laughing and shouting to each other.

The cobbled roads of the Sanita thronged with foot traffic too, and there were the ends of makeshift markets at intersections where people were clearing away trays of submerged clams, crabs, and mussels. Twice the driver stopped and leaned out the window to ask directions. A young woman in a pink T-shirt and designer sunglasses pointed up the street without speaking and then eased off between the honking cars as if she couldn't see them or—more likely—as if they were beneath her consideration. They parted before her like the Red Sea and she strode down a street where washing hung like a triumphal arch.

Thomas paid the driver ten euros and he pulled away, apparently glad to head back to more familiar neighborhoods. Thomas couldn't blame him. He hadn't felt so out of place since arriving in Italy, maybe for many years before.

Since Japan.

There were no tourists here. He had stepped into the heart of a community where he was a curiosity. He had seen nothing of Naples's much-touted street crime, but at night in a place like this he felt as if he were wearing a sign around his neck. He felt the frank, interested, and mildly amused eyes of people on him as he strolled through the place where they worked and played and lived, and he felt like apologizing. All he needed was for Pietro to kick him out into the street and he might need more than apologies to get out of the place in one piece.

It was completely dark here now, the streets unlit.

Perfect.

He felt the weight of the gun in his jacket pocket.

"Hi," said a shirtless kid on a bike. "Hi, American."

He was perhaps eight. His buddies roared with laughter and echoed his greeting. Someone shouted "Coca-Cola," and they laughed some more before running off into the night.

Santa Maria del Carmine was pale yellow, trimmed with gray stone, well maintained, but old without being monumental. The road, he noticed with a little chill, was Via Fontanelle alla Sanita. He approached the church door, grasped the ring, and twisted it. The door swung softly open.

CHAPTER 45

The church was cool and dim, its pale, uncluttered nave brightened only by the lights of a few votive candles in front of a statue and the gleam of brass on the altar. The ranked wooden pews were empty. There was no sound, no sign of anyone there.

Thomas inched forward, aware of the way his footsteps echoed. He felt the old mixture of awe and anxiety that churches had always produced in him, heightened this time by anticipation. He couldn't begin to guess what the strange old priest would tell him. He inhaled, tasting the trace of incense and candle wax, and then began to walk down the side aisle toward the front. At the altar rail he paused, repressed an impulse to genuflect, and went through a door in the wall.

The door gave onto a passage leading to a tiny sacristy that was as empty as the church.

"Hello?" he called. "Monsignor Pietro?"

Nothing.

In the corner he saw and climbed a cramped staircase up to the priest's equally cramped living quarters: a single room with a hot plate and a sink. The toilet was off the sacristy passageway. The bedroom had no central light and the desk lamp was meager indeed, so that the room was bathed in a dull copper glow.

He looked around the bare room.

"Father McKenzie, darning his socks in the night when there's nobody there . . ."

His eye fell on a book. *Hymn of the Universe* by Pierre Teilhard de Chardin. The name was familiar and the book was in English. One of Ed's.

He flipped it open at random, found a passage marked by a vertical pencil line, and read.

Blessed be you, harsh matter, barren soil, stubborn rock: you who yield only to violence, you who force us to work if we would eat.

Blessed be you, perilous matter, violent sea, untameable passion: you who unless we fetter you will devour us.

Blessed be you, mighty matter, irresistible march of evolution, reality ever newborn; you who, by constantly shattering our mental categories, force us to go ever further and further in pursuit of truth.

Thomas turned to the frontispiece and read about the author: an early-twentieth-century French Jesuit.

Weird, he thought. *And unsettling, that conviction, that strange, intense mysticism, particularly in service of so concrete a subject. Matter? What brand of Catholicism sung hymns to matter?*

Thomas brooded, listening to the silence, his mind wandering back to what Pietro had said. He had known Satoh, apparently, though he had called him Tanaka, and his death seemed to have changed things. Why?

The cry that tore the silence—a long, trailing wail that snaked up the stairs from somewhere far away—snapped Thomas to his feet, carried him toward the stairs on a wave of horror and despair.

CHAPTER 46

Thomas descended without hope, driven only by a mad need to know. He ran, his heart thumping, stumbling down the stairs, into the sacristy, back through the lightless passage. He burst into the church.

It was quite empty. The rear doors were still closed. The pews were deserted. Thomas stepped up onto the elevated part of the sanctuary, his back to the altar, and gazed down the length of the nave: nothing.

And then he heard a slight pattering like rain behind him.

He turned slowly, the trepidation he had felt cooling, hardening like stone in his gut. Behind the altar the stone floor was half covered by a gleaming irregular pool, and though the light was low it was clear that the liquid was a dark, terrible scarlet. Another drop fell into the pool, then another. Thomas forced himself to look up.

Against the rear wall of the apse was a high altar with a golden tabernacle, six tall candles, and, above it all, a framed icon of the Madonna and Child with a triangular pediment. Suspended in front of this from the gallery of the dome above, hanging by a length of heavy chain, was the monsignor.

No. Not this. Not now.

His torn cassock was black and glistening with blood so that it was hard to see what had been done to him, but it seemed that the chain that bore his weight had been laced through his chest, so that he hung by his breastbone in the air of the chancel.

For a long moment Thomas could not move, and then he caught the merest whisper of sound and looked up. The priest's eyes had opened. He was still alive.

Thomas looked wildly around, the spell broken. He couldn't climb up the altar to him. He had to get up to the gallery in the dome.

Where are the damned stairs?

He leaped down the steps of the sanctuary and threw open the door to the sacristy. There in the wall was a doorway, behind it a flight of stone steps. He ran up them two at a time and cannoned out into the emptiness of the dome so fast that he almost went right over the rail.

The gallery was narrow, the rail a single wrought-iron rod circling the dome at waist height. He forced himself to slow down, inching to where the chain had been lashed to the slender fence, leaving twenty or thirty feet coiled untidily. It would take an age to untangle the knotted chain that kept him suspended there, so there was nothing to do but drag the old priest up. Thomas grasped the chain, slick in places with blood, and began to pull.

Pietro was a big man. Thomas strained, but he just couldn't move him. He tried to gather the chain over his shoulder, but the dome gave him nowhere to go and the more he pulled, the more it felt like the weight would drag him over the rail. He relaxed and took a breath. Below him, the old priest groaned. He wouldn't last much longer.

Thomas braced his feet against the iron bases of the rail, leaned back as far as he could, and began to haul using only his arms and chest. He worked hand over hand, six inches of chain at a time, head back, teeth clenched, his shoulder blades squared, and sweat breaking out all over his torso. He pulled with one hand till his fist reached his shoulder, then did the same with the other. Each pull was harder than the one before it, each one strained his muscle and sinew till he thought something would pop, and twice he felt his grip slide a link or two down the chain, so that he had to just hold it tight until the energy to pull farther came back to him. At last, with a cry of determined fury, he hauled the priest to the top.

Thomas seized Pietro under the arms, dragging, shunting, levering him up and over the rail. As he did so, the pistol slipped from his pocket, hit the gallery floor, and bounced through the railings and down, clattering hollowly in the church below.

He's dead already, Thomas thought, panting, and for a long moment the priest made no sound or movement, and his blood-spattered face was still as earth.

Then the eyes flickered and opened halfway, and the mouth parted.

"Thomas," he said, slowly, struggling to get the words out. "I am sorry."

"It's okay," said Thomas, biting back his horror, staring into the man's face to avoid seeing the rest of him. "It's okay."

"*Mea culpa, mea culpa, mea maxima culpa,*" he whispered.

My fault, my fault, my grievous fault . . .

"What did you do?"

"Tanaka," he said.

"The Japanese guy? What about him?"

"Took him inside."

"Inside where?"

But Pietro closed his eyes again and tears squeezed out, though whether they were from pain or memory, Thomas couldn't tell. The priest was dying. He had only seconds left.

"Ed's papers," Thomas breathed, forcing himself to ask, feeling callous for doing so, but knowing this was his last chance.

The priest smiled softly. He was already slipping away, fading.

"*Il Capitano,*" he said.

"What?" Thomas gasped. The priest's eyes had closed. "*Capitano?* What do you mean? Pietro? PIETRO!"

And then the eyes opened again, like a fish using the last of its strength to turn against the current, and one hand grasped Thomas's wrist with sudden and surprising power. His mouth opened, but though the eyes seemed to strain and the muscles of his throat constricted, the words didn't come.

"What?" asked Thomas, begging, coaxing. "Tell me."

The grasp on his wrist tightened still further, pulling him close, and the monsignor's mouth whispered into his ear, each urgent, terrible word forced out with the last of his strength.

"*Il mostro,*" he gasped. "The monster. He. Is. Still. Here."

And then he was gone.

The silence that followed his last breath was broken by a sibilant, hissing snarl, and Thomas turned to see the creature he had glimpsed in Paestum, nestled at the top of the stairs not ten yards from where he stood.

CHAPTER 47

It was a man. Just. He was naked to the waist, pale and spindly with large splayed hands, broad shoulders, and a crumpled baby face with small pale eyes. When he snarled, Thomas could see that his teeth had been filed to V-shaped points. He was hairless and blood-streaked and he exuded malice. In one hand he held a long, curved blade, light and honed to what promised to be surgical sharpness, but broad and hooked like a sickle.

Thomas didn't need to see the man move to know how deadly that weapon would be in his hands. There was no other doorway, no other staircase save the one in which the goblin man was crouching. Without a second's thought, Thomas grabbed the trailing end of the chain in both hands, tossed the length of it over the iron railing, and vaulted into the air above the chancel.

The chain kicked and slid in his hands as his weight came to rest, and then he was loosening his grasp and sliding the rest of the way. He was on the sanctuary floor before Pietro's killer had scurried to the railing.

He expected his would-be attacker to descend by the stairs, so there was something doubly alarming about the way the man leaped froglike out to the chain, following him down with easy precision. Thomas moved fast, making for the sacristy door.

He tried it just as the other completed his descent: locked. He ran to the back of the church and the main entrance that would put him back into the street where there were people, but this too was locked. For a moment he shook the handle and cursed, and then he turned and saw the man with the bat face skulking slowly up the left-hand aisle, loping, almost on all fours, and Thomas could see only one other door that looked as if it might get him out.

He ran down the right aisle, scanning for the fallen gun. There was no sign of it. He neared the door.

Be open. Please God, be open.

It was. It put him in a passage like that on the opposite wall that led to the sacristy, and Thomas ran down it, relief turning to panic as he saw that the passage ended in another door. If this was locked he'd be trapped . . .

He tried it. The latch clicked but the door did not move. He pulled and pushed, conscious of the hissing snarl of the killer in the church behind him, and only then did he see the black key in the lock. He turned it, hands fumbling, and then shoved. Too soon. He felt the lock stick and had to take his shoulder from the door while he turned the key all the way. He could hear the killer getting closer.

The latch clicked. Thomas pushed, eyes wide, heart hammering, and tore through it. He slammed the door behind him, realizing too late that he could have taken the key and tried to lock it from this side.

For a second, feeling the cool night air on his face, he thought he was free. Then he saw how the ten-foot concrete walls rose up on each side of the path, how the path led to a rock wall only yards ahead. Overhead, the night sky was half shielded by tree limbs that stretched out over the open-topped tunnel. But the door at his back was starting to open again, the snarling suddenly louder.

Thomas stumbled forward, his eyes wild, looking up and around for a way out of the blind alley. Nothing. Not, at least, till he looked down.

There was an opening in the rock, human-made, round like the mouth of a well, and inside it was a long wooden ladder, down into the dark earth. On a hook in the rock above the hole was a black rubber flashlight.

Thomas looked back once, saw the door open, and began to climb.

Five feet, ten, twenty, thirty feet down into increasing blackness, and then the pale, moonlike face of the killer appeared at the top, with his hard little eyes and terrible teeth, and Thomas was jumping the rest of the way, dragging at the ladder, pulling it away like Jack hacking down the beanstalk before the giant could follow.

The ladder fell with a resounding crack that boomed all around him, echoing through the stone caves and passages. The killer could not come that way, but he might use the chain to climb down, might even be able to do it unaided. Thomas was not safe yet, and even if he had been sure of his escape, he would have felt little better, because he knew beyond any doubt where he was.

He was in the Fontanelle.

And may God have mercy on my soul, he thought.

CHAPTER 48

He didn't want to see, but he couldn't move around without light, not with that monster up there. He clicked the flashlight on and it produced a soft, yellowish beam. Thomas turned it up the shaft and saw nothing but stone and the distant fronds of green leaves against the sky. No goblin face, no wiry frame creeping down the wall . . .

He rotated the light around him, expecting a tight, dank tunnel like that made by the archaeologists in Herculaneum, but the cave was large and square, evenly carved and massive to the point of airiness. The ceiling was a good twenty or thirty feet above him, the walls angled up slightly so that you might imagine that the outer form was pyramidal. He breathed in. No foul odors; no musty, stagnant air; no claustrophobic sense of being entombed. Not yet.

It's not so bad, he thought, starting to walk.

The relief, after the horrors he had feared and those he had just experienced, made him want to laugh aloud.

Just find another exit. It's not bad. Could be much worse.

It was.

His flashlight had fallen on a low wall, perhaps a couple of feet high that ran the length of the passage on both sides. In fact it was a kind of shelf and on it were stacked strange-looking objects, pale and regular, vaguely familiar even at a distance but somehow unclear until he got a little closer.

They were bones. Heaps of them. Human bones. Long thigh bones placed end to end and stacked like logs. Then a row of skulls facing forward. Then more femurs. More skulls, working up the wall in a regular pattern. In this part alone were the remains of several hundred people, just lying there, arranged like bricks, each one once part of a living human being.

Thomas had seen human bones before, but this was different. For one thing, there were just so many of them, just sitting there so that he could reach over and touch them.

He stared as if stricken, as if he had never confronted death before, his eyes wide, gooseflesh breaking out on his arms and down his back.

There were just so many of them . . .

He walked forward till he came to an intersection in the great vaulted corridor, and the passages seemed to extend all around him, receding into darkness, all lined with the same stacks of bones. The patterns of the arrangement varied, but that only made them less easy to get used to, as did the occasional inclusion of other parts: a pair of shoulders, an intact rib cage.

In places some of the skulls had been placed in glass-fronted boxes, one, two, or three at a time. Many were labeled with names, but they were, Thomas thought, the names of those who had adopted the bones, not of the dead themselves. The eyeless skulls that watched him from the shadows were all completely anonymous. It was like stumbling into a mass grave behind a death camp, and though these people were largely the victims of disease rather than murder, he felt their presence keenly so that the hairs on the back of his neck stood upright and a deep chill settled into his own bones.

The place was huge. He turned down one of the broad passages, trying not to look too closely at the ranked remains, and found he was looking at three virtually life-sized crosses, the middle one slightly taller than the other two. He panned his flashlight beam down and saw that each cross rose out of a pile of human skulls.

Golgotha, he thought, with a shudder. What the Gospels called "the place of the skull."

It was no wonder Giovanni hated the place, no wonder the Church had closed it. It wasn't merely macabre, it was redolent with superstition and something deeper and more unsettling still: the arranging of the bones hinted at ritual, at a close, even habitual relationship with the dead, with the very idea of mortality.

Thomas recalled images of a chapel in Rome where the bones of the monks had been incorporated into the decoration. That was bizarre, but its pious aesthetic had nothing of the power of this place, whose order and simplicity was so much more ambiguous. The Roman chapel showed death as a portal for the believer, inevitable, but easily transcended by the orthodox Christian. This was just death laid out in its grimmest and least gilded might, and Thomas felt like Hamlet in the graveyard, finally getting something everyone knew but somehow managed to ignore.

Thomas checked Roberta's phone, but there was no signal, not that he had expected any under all these tons of tuff. He began walking again, flashlight fixed forward on the path so that he did not see those countless, long-dead faces.

You mean, so they don't see you.

That too.

But then he was in a new cavern, and here a kind of massive structure had been built, like the front of a church, perhaps thirty feet high, divided into niches surrounding a central statue of the Sacred Heart. Each niche was full of bones, more bundled femurs, more watchful skulls, stacked in their hundreds to the cavern roof, so that for a moment Thomas felt overwhelmed by the insistent presence of the dead massed at the limit of his flashlight beam, and gathered rank upon rank in the darkness beyond.

He had to find a way out.

He stood there staring, and was ready to walk away when he turned and for a brief second saw tiny pinpricks of light high in the darkness to his left. He took a few paces that way, raising the flashlight, but that didn't help, so he turned it down. He stopped, recoiling from the sight of a large glass pane set into the stone floor, beneath it a jumble of brownish skeletons, scraps of ancient clothing, maybe even some desiccated ribbons of flesh. This was how the bodies were found, he thought, before they were gathered up into the Fontanelle's strange, nurturing embrace. He went around the glass panel, still looking up, and suddenly there it was again: tiny spots of light like . . .

Stars.

He was looking at the night sky.

He moved forward faster, scanning with the flashlight, and found that the passage narrowed as the vaulted ceiling became limitless. The walls were no longer the sheer and sloping rock face from which the caverns had been carved, but stone blocks some fifteen feet high. He began to run, elated, sure of his exit, but then the darkness in front of him changed, solidified. He was looking at a solid wall of wood and metal, black and substantial, topped with spikes.

There was a door in it. Thomas tried it, pushed it, rattled the handle, but it did not move, did not make a sound.

He stepped back to consider it. It was painted and slick, without ledges or handholds. It had been designed to keep people out.

And will do just as well to keep them in.

He considered the walls of the passage, but they looked no more promising. Then he remembered the ladder down which he had come. If he could find his way back . . .

He shivered. Going back meant meandering back through that ghastly mausoleum, back to where the killer had seen him enter. By now the creature—it was still hard to think of him as merely a man—might have used the same length of chain he had threaded through Pietro's torso to clamber down into the cemetery after him. He could be waiting in the shadows, nestled in some pile of eyeless heads, whetting that sickle-shaped blade . . .

But here Thomas was trapped. If the killer emerged from the cavern proper, caught him here in the confines of what must surely be the main entrance, being close to the door would avail him nothing. He was better off in the caves with the bones. Thomas closed his eyes for a second, set his teeth, and breathed out. He had no choice but to go back in.

He took three reluctant steps, paused to find some semblance of determination, and walked back into the great stone vault. He edged around the glass floor, moving left into a tunnel, keeping the beam of his light low so as not to disturb the bones.

But then something stirred in his memory and he stopped. When asked what had happened to Ed's papers after the fireplace ruse, the priest had said "*Il Capitano.*"

Pietro's dying words lingered in his mind like ghosts. At the time they had meant nothing to him, but now, quite suddenly, he was sure he understood. *Somewhere in here,* Thomas thought, *somewhere piled amid the thousands of others, is a single skull, one bound to an old ghost story about a captain who left the grave to attend the wedding he had orchestrated for a young woman who had tended his bones.* And under that skull were his brother's papers.

Okay, thought Thomas, panning his flashlight over the fleshless faces. *But which one?*

CHAPTER 49

Walking faster now, he tried to remember what Giovanni had told him about the legend of the Captain. For a moment he could think of nothing except the outline of the story, the woman who wanted a husband, the marriage celebration, and the good-looking stranger who had offended her new spouse.

What about the skull?

It was shiny, he recalled, polished so that no dust clung to it.

That smacked of a legend that had been given an anchor in reality. Somewhere in the Fontanelle was a glossy, polished skull, one forever tied to the old tale of the Captain. The story was well known, so the skull wouldn't be buried in a pile somewhere, indistinguishable from those around it. It would be by itself, marked out from the rest. Pietro had hidden the notes where they would be safe, but he had also made them recoverable.

Thomas approached the closest waist-high ledge on which the skulls were stacked in blocks of eight, and began to scan them for one that might look different. They were all different, he thought, if not in the ways he wanted. That was what made them so unsettling. He thought all skulls would look the same, but they didn't. Some of it was just about the way they had been positioned: staring blankly forward, looking off to the side, or rocking back in what looked unnervingly like laughter. Some of the difference was in the state of decay: some more complete, teeth intact, eye sockets sharply formed, nasal cavity clean. Others were rotted, broken, or marked by violence Thomas could only hope had happened after death: the skulls split, cheeks broken, septums collapsed. Some even looked as if their tops had been surgically sawn off. Some were evenly pale as alabaster; some gray and mottled; some brown, stained, and hung with a fibrous filth Thomas dared not name. And among them were smaller skulls: children, babies.

Christ, what a place.

He stared at the smallest skull he had seen, riveted to it, fighting to suppress the images, the memories that were rising within him. Thomas blinked and turned away deliberately—

Not that. Not now.

—but found that the nagging dread he had felt since he arrived in the cemetery had turned into a deep, penetrating sadness. Maybe that was what kept people away, he thought as he walked, forcing himself to look again, to study the remains. It wasn't the Gothic horrors of ghostly apparitions and silly stories that clung to these bones that was so unsettling; it was the way they each tried to tell you who they were, each dead face once loved by someone, now nameless and forgotten. And there were so many of them, so that in his head Thomas began to feel their presence swelling, like voices lost in a crowd.

Was one of them Ed's?

It was a curious thought, nonsensical, and he shrugged it away, but its implication registered in some deep recess of his mind.

You never even saw his body.

He pushed the self-pity away, striding forward with even more deliberation as he scanned the bones around him.

And then he saw it.

In a glass box marked with the year 1948 was a skull brighter, slicker than the rest. It was ivory-colored, toothless, but otherwise large and well-preserved. Someone had placed a red glass votive lamp in front of it, though the candle inside had burned out long ago. It sat prominently on a corner ledge. Thomas set down his flashlight and carefully picked up the glass box and set it on the floor.

Beneath it was a folder stuffed with papers.

Thomas tucked them under his arm and replaced the box with the gleaming skull.

"Thanks, Captain," he said, and then, struck by something like reverence, touched the top of the box with his fingers, as if completing some kind of ritual.

He had taken no more than a couple of steps, however, when something stopped him, something as much instinct as actual sight or hearing. He turned to stare down the long gallery. Something else was here. Something alive.

Thomas kept quite still and now he heard it, down at the end of the corridor, something moving, skulking. He closed

his eyes and strained for more, at once catching the sound he
had least wanted to hear: a rasping, hissing snarl through unnaturally pointed teeth. He was coming.

CHAPTER 50

He wasn't afraid, not this time, not as he had been before
when the killer had come creeping up the stairs into the dome
where Pietro was dying in his arms like some hellish Pietà. He
had been scared then, as he knew he was meant to be. That
was what this ghoul did, what he fed on: fear.

But Thomas had been walking the halls of the dead for the
last half hour, and while he did not want to be carved like
Satoh, or strung up like the monsignor, he was not afraid of
the killer's ghoulish theatrics, and that was a kind of victory.
If he had still had Roberta's gun, he would have faced the gargoyle down, shot him if he'd had to. But he was unarmed.

He shut off the flashlight and crouched in the darkness,
thinking and listening, trying to home in on the ghoul's snuffling, on the animal noises he had cultivated to scare his victims.
A disdainful anger flared in Thomas, and he suddenly didn't
want to hide anymore. He inched back to the wall as silently as
he could and reached out with his left hand, fingers spread. He
moved it cautiously through space, felt a hard ridge of bone and
moved back another foot, carefully so as not to dislodge any of
the skulls. The snuffling and hissing was getting closer.

Then there was light at the end of the passage, a flickering,
yellow light that cast leaping irregular shadows on the walls.
The ghoul had taken a candle from the church, Thomas thought,
and the idea pleased him a little, made the ghoul more human.
The ghoul didn't like the dark.

Thomas's left hand found the edge of the glass box. He

traced his fingers lightly over its surface till he found the simple latch. He opened it and blindly raised the lid. He reached in with both hands and lifted the shining skull of the Captain out. Still crouching, he cradled the skull in his lap, then raised the glass box and balanced it on his left hand, like a waiter with a tray of drinks. His right strayed back to the skull, grasping it by the back. Then he squatted there among the bones, his face among the piled skulls, and waited for the ghoulish candle bearer, quite calm, quite uncannily calm.

The killer's pale, bald head came into view, the candle held aloft, the sputtering flame showing more of him than he could possibly see himself. The ghoul twisted his head suddenly and Thomas saw it again, the batlike face, the filed, jagged teeth. And the curved knife. Thomas saw that too, and his muscles began to tauten like those of a sprinter in the blocks.

The killer took three more paces toward him down the broad passage, and Thomas saw the hungry malevolence in his tiny eyes. A part of him wanted to leap to his feet and run as far and as fast as he could, but the smoldering, bullish anger had taken control now, stifling the urge to flee. The candlelight made the hollows of the ghoul's cheeks look as deep as those of the skulls around him, and the bones of his naked chest and shoulders showed tight under pale, blood-splashed skin as he came closer: five yards, three yards. Another step and the ghoul would see Thomas crouching in the shadows at the end of the gallery.

And then the bald man froze, candle held high, blade outstretched: he was listening, and something came over his features that changed him utterly. The calculated wickedness faltered and he looked unsure of himself, a transformation that made him smaller, more human.

Thomas could hear it too. It began with the groan of a great door opening, then voices, men's voices speaking in hushed tones. Thomas couldn't catch the words, but the music of them was certainly Italian. They had come in through the main door.

Who the hell would come in here at night, letting themselves in as if they owned the place?

The police? Could they have found Pietro already? If so, suspect or no suspect, Thomas's best chance was with them.

Without pausing to consider further, he leaped to his feet, took one long stride toward the ghoul, and thrust the skull of the Captain into his face with his left hand. The ghoul flinched away in surprise—perhaps even in horror—and as he did so Thomas brought the glass box around hard, smashing it over his head with his other hand. The ghoul crumpled, hissing, dropping the sickle, clawing at his eyes as the blood ran down his face. Thomas kicked once and he dropped entirely, moaning in pain as the blade skittered away into the darkness.

Thomas snapped on the flashlight to see where it had fallen, and in the sudden leap of shadows, the ghoul rolled into a loping retreat. Thomas hesitated, cursing himself, but his moment of advantage was past and pursuit would likely get him killed. This was no time for justice of any stripe, and he wasn't the person to administer it. Right now, it was more important that he get out in one piece.

Thomas walked quickly toward the entrance, to where the men had come in, though they were now silent. As soon as he rounded the corner, half blinded by their flashlights, he knew they weren't police. Quite the contrary, in fact. The clothes, the body language were all wrong. One of them had a gun. He had stumbled into the local Mafia who—as Giovanni had warned him—met from time to time in the Fontanelle.

CHAPTER 51

Thomas considered his options and, in a second, chose graceful bravado.

Very Italian, he thought, as he put the folder of notes back under his arm and began to walk. He was still holding the skull of the Captain.

He turned the corner at an even pace. Five men in long coats were silhouetted against the door. All had flashlights turned on him; two had guns. Thomas didn't hesitate, didn't raise his hands. He saw the gray rectangle of space where the door was, and he made for it, walking with long determined strides—but not overly quick—as if nothing were more normal.

Somebody spoke to him in Italian and, when he kept coming, repeated what was clearly a question in a higher, more insistent register. Another gun came out and was trained on him. Someone whispered.

Thomas kept walking. One of the men stepped closer to the wall, and then another on the other side did the same. They were parting before him, and beyond them the massive door was still ajar.

"*Buona sera,*" said Thomas, nodding formally, not making eye contact, not slowing down, but thrusting the skull into the hands of one of the nearest men. The man took it before he realized what it was, and then began sputtering his outrage.

God alone knew what they had expected when they had come in here, but it wasn't this. In the caves behind him he could hear the snarling rage of the ghoul. The Mafiosi—if that's what they were—could hear it too, and their attention was leaving Thomas and gravitating to the darkness behind him. Another gun came out.

Then Thomas was walking between them, and though they watched him, no one spoke. He kept going, stepped through the door without looking back, and turned right into the street by the church. He was out before he realized what their flashlights must have made glaringly obvious. His shirt and trousers were stiff with the unmistakable rust of Pietro's blood.

CHAPTER 52

His composure was feigned. It was what he guessed would serve him best with those particular men, but he didn't feel anything like as collected as he had seemed, and once out in the night air, he found his pulse beginning to race as the day's accumulated horrors registered fully for the first time. His brain had managed to push back the enormity of Roberta's deception, the attempt on his life, the death of Pietro, and the episode in the Fontanelle, but now it was all massing above him like a dam threatening to burst. He also ached from his various exertions, the fighting and the running, but he knew that he had to somehow keep it together, now more than ever.

He found a side window into the presbytery and broke it as quietly as he could with his elbow. He allowed himself no more than three minutes inside, time enough to wash, dump his clothes, and grab a pair of ill-fitting trousers and a cotton shirt, both gray, from Pietro's wardrobe. They smelled musty, as if the priest had grown out of them long ago and they had merely hung there ignored ever since. He let himself out of the side door, walking in a manner that he hoped looked both casual and businesslike.

He wanted to call the police, tell them about Pietro and the ghoul in the Fontanelle, but he knew that he was a suspect in the death of Satoh and that he was the obvious link to Pietro. He also knew that he was no longer being merely threatened and spied upon: someone wanted him dead. Pietro's body would probably remain undiscovered till morning, when a flower arranger or pious parishioner who stopped in to light a candle on her way to work would find him there. Thomas winced at the thought.

"Sorry," he said aloud, to both the dead priest and whoever would be scarred by finding him.

But if they wouldn't find Pietro till morning he had the rest of the night to go underground. He dared not go back to his hotel, but he had his passport and wallet with him. Roberta would be waking, maybe was already hitching a ride back into town, relying once more on the way her Franciscan habit made her respectable and safe.

But what did "going underground" mean in a city he didn't know, where he didn't speak the language beyond ordering a glass of wine and a pizza? He had two allies remaining in the area, he thought. Deborah Miller, whom he barely knew and who would be leaving the country in a matter of days, and Father Giovanni, whose friendship and trust would take a significant hit when the death of Pietro came out.

You have to get out of Naples.

And go where?

He hailed a cab and mimed tapping on a computer keyboard.

"Internet?" said the driver, checking his watch. It was after ten. *"Si."*

Thomas got in.

The Internet point he was driven to wasn't a café so much as an alcove in the corner of a sparsely populated bar. The computer was an ancient, bone-colored machine that seemed incapable of running anything produced in the last twenty-five years, the mouse a built-in orange tracking device the size of a billiard ball, the keyboard surrounded by large green lighted keys. It looked less like a computer than the representation of one from some sixties sci-fi show.

Astonishingly, it not only worked, it was fast and Thomas was soon online.

He was surprised to find a message from Deborah. It read simply, "Check this out. Intriguing, huh?" With it was a link to a *New York Times* story dated two days ago. Thomas read the headline, EVIDENCE OF EARLY CHRISTIANITY ROCKS JAPAN," and then stared openmouthed at the picture below it. It showed a beaming Japanese man holding a silver cross, studded with precious stones, the center marked by a now-familiar fish with leglike fins. For a long moment he just looked, then he read:

> *Japanese anthropological science was today sent into astonished confusion by celebrity archaeologist Michihiro Watanabe, who revealed the discovery of a Christian burial site in a seventh-century Japanese tomb. If authentic, it would not only demonstrate a previously unknown Christian evangelism to East Asia, but would antedate the first known presence of any Europeans in Japan by many centuries. "It's a breathtaking discovery," said Robert Levine of the Center for Asian Studies at Stanford University. "It will necessitate the complete rethinking of Japanese-European relations in the medieval period." The burial site in landlocked Yamanashi prefecture is structured in traditional Kofun style but contains what has been preliminarily identified as an early Italian crucifix amid what seem to be the bones of European travelers . . .*

Thomas sat back and blew out a long sigh. Not just Japan: Yamanashi, the very place where he and Kumi had met.

Thomas read the text again. He knew his brother had been to Japan. Was this what took him there? Was this the Herculaneum cross Ed was alleged to have possessed?

You knew it would come to this.

He pulled up a series of travel websites and began looking at flights to Japan. Then he wrote to Deborah, to Jim, and—on impulse—to Senator Devlin. All three messages contained the same text.

"In danger. Going after Ed. Will be in touch."

He needed another safety net. He stared at the three addresses that would receive the e-mail, then separated them out and attached his complete itinerary to the message that would go to Jim.

CHAPTER 53

The Seal-breaker contained his rage with difficulty.

"How can you not know where he is?" he demanded.

"I was monitoring the hotel," said War. "He was initially with Pestilence, and then he was picked up by Famine."

"And he evaded them both," said the Seal-breaker.

"Yes, sir. A tracking device was planted in his luggage," said War, "but he appears to have abandoned everything at the Executive."

"Not very professional, is it," said the Seal-breaker, "your monitoring of this high school teacher."

"No, sir. Sorry, sir."

The Seal-breaker rubbed his forehead and scrunched his eyes shut. *Three of them on site, and Knight still walks away.*

"And you think he may have left Naples?"

"Yes, sir."

"And there is reason to assume he knows?"

"Famine could not confirm what he got from the old priest, but his presence in the Fontanelle suggests that he was looking for something. We think it at least possible that the papers the priest destroyed were decoys designed to throw Knight off the scent."

"It's all a bit moot now, isn't it?" said the Seal-breaker. War had never heard him sound so irritated. "And Pestilence's cover is blown. What sort of shape is Famine in?"

"Cuts and bruises, nothing worse."

"I meant, mentally speaking."

War hesitated. How was anybody supposed to put the mental state of that lunatic into words?

"He's angry, sir," he said. "Vengeful."

"Good," said the Seal-breaker. "The moment you find Knight, let Famine off the leash. Pestilence too. I'm sure she's itching to prove her worth."

"Yes, sir," said War.

"And you?"

"Of course, sir."

"Is your team ready?"

War hesitated. "Isn't it a bit premature to bring them in, sir?"

"Not from where I'm sitting," said the Seal-breaker. "Just make sure they are ready."

"Yes, sir."

"So how do you plan to locate Knight?"

"We can continue to monitor his recent haunts," said War, "but if he has left the area we may have to take our lead from the Italian police. We are monitoring radio traffic and staking out the local railway station and airport."

"These all sound a little desperate," said the Seal-breaker. "And if the Italian police get to him first, that would be very bad indeed for us, would it not?"

"Yes, sir," said War. "There is one other option, though, sir."

"Which is?"

"Knight took Pestilence's cell phone."

"Is there anything he could learn from it?"

"No, it was clean."

"Is the GPS working?"

"Yes, sir. But he doesn't have it switched on right now. The moment he does, we'll have him."

"Make sure you do," said the Seal-breaker. "I don't need to explain to you—you of all people—the importance of ending this right away. Silencing Knight earlier would have attracted too much attention. But the decision to let him poke around at his own pace has proved . . . unsound. I don't care which of you does it, or how, but he must be terminated immediately. Clear?"

"Clear, sir."

So all they needed now was for Knight to make a call: any call to anyone, and they would have him. The Seal-breaker smiled to himself. It had a certain . . . what? Irony? No. Symmetry. That was it. He recalled as clearly as if it had been yesterday putting the very same model cell phone into Father Edward Knight's hand.

"You'll need that, where you're going," he had said to the priest, grinning.

And he had, in a manner of speaking. Without the phone, they would never have gotten his coordinates so precisely, would never have gotten him at all. And now his brother . . .

Cell phones, he thought, smiling wistfully. *What would we do without them?*

CHAPTER 54

There was nothing direct from Naples, and nothing that would get him to Milan in time for the next day's Tokyo flights. Thomas didn't want to spend two more days in Italy. It was no longer safe. His best option was a flight from Frankfurt. It was no faster than the Milan flights, but it would allow him to get out of Italy a day sooner. He looked at options to Frankfurt and found that the cut-price carrier Ryan Air flew from Bari to Frankfurt Hahn for the absurdly low price of thirty-five dollars U.S. Bari was on the eastern coast, almost directly across from Naples. There were trains that could get him there in about five hours. He confirmed the booking, hoping that no one was watching activity on his credit card too closely right now.

The cabdriver had waited as asked, and in another ten minutes Thomas was getting out at the Garibaldi railway station. He hadn't been there after dark and the place lived up to its checkered reputation, but he found an information counter and was pointed to a magazine shop where, for reasons he couldn't decipher, tickets for the Bari line were sold. He took a local train to Caserta and then killed forty-five minutes waiting for the overnight express.

While he was waiting he found the station's restaurant, a grim and smoky affair buzzing with fat flies, and ordered a plate of pasta with mussels from a big man who seemed much put out by the presence of a customer. The waiter or cook, he might have been both, offered him wine, which Thomas considered for a second, then declined. He needed a level head.

The food was remarkably good—given the place, unreasonably so—and it could have absorbed all of Thomas's attention if he hadn't taken this moment to finally look through the papers he had retrieved from the Fontanelle.

They consisted, for the most part, of a single dog-eared journal, supplemented by maps and charts of the coast around Naples, photographs, museum guides, and a sheaf of stapled pages torn from a stained yellow legal pad. The journal provided a kind of narrative written in daily extracts dated through two weeks of Ed's stay in the Naples area, stopping abruptly on the twentieth of February: a month before he died. They enacted a version of Thomas's own visit, featuring many of the same locations, documenting the same oddities and half-discoveries, raising the same questions, so that it was unnervingly like reading about himself. There was more detail, more clutter, more abandoned leads than Thomas had found, but the basic trajectory seemed the same: Ed had been researching the curious legged-fish symbol, a feature of almost a thousand years of the religious iconography of the Naples area, in its pagan and Christian forms.

Ed had clearly visited places as far afield as Rome, Florence, Bologna, Milan, and various towns in Sicily, but his notes made one point quite clear. Though the Christian fish (and its pagan forebears) appeared throughout Italy and the surrounding region, the legged variant had never been found more than seventy miles from Naples. Like the Hera/Mary pomegranate, the legged fish was a peculiar local variant, and it was this that had apparently excited his brother. Ed had included countless biblical references to fish and water, reserving special annotation for those that might be read allegorically, suggesting a passage beyond death.

Christ's walking on water, Thomas read, *is not merely a miracle of power. It shows His control over the natural world and all that is in it, including death. Walking on water affirms His corporeality and transcends it."*

Other passages applied the fish image as much to Christians as to Christ himself. One read:

> *But we little fish, according to our IKTHUS Jesus Christ, are born in water, and we are saved in no other manner than by remaining in the water.* Tertullian, AD 200.

Another was labeled "on the agape or sacred meal which became the Eucharist," and read:

> *I see the congregated people so arranged in order on the couches and all so filled with abundant food, that before my eyes arises the richness of the evangelical benediction and the image of the people whom Christ fed with five loaves and two fishes, Himself the true bread and fish of the living water.* Paulinus of Nola, AD 396.

Thomas remembered the Paestum tomb paintings, the young men feasting, the legged fish emerging from the red water.

He paid for his meal and reached the platform as the train, the sleekest he had seen so far, pulled into the station and the PA system came to life in Italian and English. Thomas, luggage-less, climbed aboard and took a seat by the window, though it was too dark to see much of anything outside.

He was deeply tired, and as the train pulled out of the station and picked up speed, he felt himself relax for the first time since his visit to Paestum.

But sleep wouldn't come, so for the first hour of the journey he stared out the window determined to see something in the darkness. The carriages cast a bluish light in window-shaped stripes so that between the tunnels he could glimpse rugged grasslands, trees, and a meandering river that constantly reappeared beside the track. From time to time he returned to Ed's notes, unfolding the charts with their detailed mapping of the undersea contours of the bays of Naples and Salerno.

Thomas rubbed his eyes and fished for Roberta's phone. Giovanni weighed on his conscience. He wanted to call the priest, explain what had happened, at the very least break the news of Pietro's death gently, offer sympathy that—he hoped—would also be taken as proof of his innocence. But it was very late, and he should probably let the man sleep. Tomorrow would be a rough day.

His desire to call Deborah was less easy to pinpoint, but no less easy to squash. He liked her, *admired* her, was perhaps a better way of putting it, he decided, and he didn't want her to think badly of him. But she would also be sleeping, and his explanations could wait till morning.

Actually they can wait longer. You've done nothing but get her into trouble, so she'll probably be glad to see the back of you.

He frowned, wondering what part of him was wary of his interest in her, and why. Unbidden, the image of Kumi came to mind.

Not still carrying that torch, I hope.

He stared out the window and tried to think of nothing.

He slept shallowly for two hours, waking when the train came to rest in Foggia. The delay began to unsettle him, and when the train began moving in the opposite direction he panicked. Were they being rerouted? He gathered his papers together and stood up, but no one else on the train seemed concerned.

Not everything is about you, Thomas. It was Kumi's voice in his head, the old reproof. *For all your causes, Thomas, you're an arrogant son of a bitch. Always have been.*

Not always.

They pulled out of the train yards, past the backs of balconied houses, through an industrial landscape of sidings and cement works sprouting shoots and silos. It was dawn, and in a few more minutes he could see flat meadows with yellow, daisylike flowers and clumps of poppies, vibrant in the half light. Then swallows and magpies, and fields with hedgerows, the rugged wildness left behind, this landscape tamer, more tropical and sprinkled with palms.

It was six o'clock when the train pulled into the Bari station, and the air was cool and scented with the sea. He found a taxi and asked for a hotel: any hotel. He didn't care if the driver's brother ran it. He just wanted a place to rest for a few hours.

He registered at the Vittoria Parc Hotel under his own name because he hadn't thought to try to do otherwise, and because now such deception—and its attendant difficulties of passports and credit cards—seemed utterly beyond him.

In his dark and spacious room, he sat on the edge of the bed, checked his watch and called Giovanni first, Deborah second. To both he said simply that he had not killed Pietro, that he was sorry for the trouble he had caused them, and that they should try to believe that he had not abused their trust. Before either of them could say whether they believed him, he hung up, promising to call again when things were clearer.

Clearer to whom? he wondered. *Him? Them? The police?*

The alarm set, Thomas lay down in the curtained room and finally let his mind go blank. In minutes he was asleep, Roberta's forgotten cell phone, still switched on, resting on the nightstand.

And as he slept, War, Pestilence, and Famine came for him.

CHAPTER 55

When Thomas opened his eyes four hours later it took him more than a minute to remember where he was. The heavy drapes shut out the light so completely that it might have been night, though his stomach told him it was lunchtime. He showered, ate in the hotel restaurant and wondered how he would spend the afternoon. His plane for Frankfurt didn't leave till ten, one of the ways the airline kept its costs down. There was no point sitting in the airport for hours where he could easily be recognized if security had been alerted, and he didn't want to loiter in the hotel lobby either. If nothing else, he needed a change of clothes.

He checked out and ordered a hotel shuttle into the old town, arranging that it would pick him up after he'd had time to wander, get an early dinner, and take him to the airport. The woman at the desk was dressed like a flight attendant in the hotel's red and blue colors, wore horn-rimmed glasses, and spoke excellent English. She responded to his gratitude as if nothing could be less worthy of notice; Thomas wondered if he was being patronizing. He apologized for not speaking Italian, and she shrugged this off too, barely looking at him, smiling only when the account was finally settled and she could hand him off to the driver.

The driver, who introduced himself in Italian as Claudio, wore a black suit and tie with an immaculately laundered white shirt, so that Thomas felt conspicuous in Pietro's castoffs. Claudio showed him to one of the hotel's identical navy-blue minivans with heavily tinted windows, and he took a seat in the back. They drove along a coast road lined with palms and elegant beachfront property facing a marina.

"Old town, yes?" said Claudio.

"That's right."

"*Castello?*"

Thomas didn't even know there was a castle. He had read nothing about Bari.

"Sure," he said.

"I pick up you at seven o'clock, *vabbene* okay?"

"Yes."

"You have no bags?"

"No," said Thomas. "We can go directly to the airport."

"Okay," said Claudio, shrugging at this clearly eccentric behavior. "You go see church in old town?"

"I guess."

"Streets very . . ." he took both hands off the wheel to gesture *narrow,* "small. Very hard to attack. When Saracens came, they could not win here. Small streets. People shoot from windows. Shoot . . . ?"

"Arrows?"

"*Si.* Arrows."

"Is there much to see at the castle?"

"Not much. It police house now. But has art made here."

Thomas nodded to show he understood: a craft center.

The castle was certainly impressive from the outside, a broad, low design with massive square turrets on the corners of the outer walls and a stone bridge over a drained moat. Inside the towers of the keep rose up, pale ocher with touches of rose.

"Beware of pickpockets," said Claudio, pulling the cab over in front of a streetfront café, "and call if you want to leave."

Thomas took the offered card and thanked him.

"You still have the signal?" said War.

"Yes," said Pestilence, still in her nun's habit. "He's down near the castle. Park here and we'll intercept."

"I think that's my call, don't you?" said War.

"Fine," said Pestilence, returning her gaze to the map she had picked up at the car rental office. "Wait. The signal is on the blink. Maybe he's gone inside somewhere."

"Great."

"No, it's back," she said. "There must be interference. If

the streets are narrow or there are a lot of tall buildings it could mess with the GPS transmission. So, fearless leader, what's the plan?"

"We'll split up."

"Brilliant," she muttered. "No wonder you're the general."

"Do I have to remind you what happened when you had him . . . ?"

"No," she interrupted, touching the tender side of her face where the volcanic steam had hit her.

"Okay," said War. "I'll keep the car and take it down to the coast road between the castle and the old town. You work your way down there from this side."

"What about him?"

She nodded to the backseat without turning around. She never looked at Famine when she could avoid it. Now he was crouched low in the seat, sharpening his knife with a leather strap.

"Keep an eye on the GPS," said War, over his shoulder, his eyes on the mirror. "If the target enters any buildings, follow him in and try to maintain visual contact till a kill opportunity presents itself. Got that?"

Famine showed his triangular teeth in a grimace.

"I asked if you got that?" said War.

"Yes," hissed Famine.

"He's a Goddamned liability," muttered Pestilence. "Especially now. He attracts attention and we're no longer in the business of trying to frighten people. You got a real weapon as well as that damned knife?"

In answer Famine leaned forward, his pale bald head craning around so that he was almost cheek to cheek with Pestilence. As she flinched away to the right, she found herself looking into the barrel of a large, black automatic that Famine was holding in his right hand. She pushed it away, and he snarled his pleasure, mouth open, tongue lolling.

"Save it for the fucking tourists," she said, turning away.

"Mind your language," snapped War.

CHAPTER 56

Thomas had bought jeans, a couple of shirts, a light jacket, and a few other essentials. He had changed in the store and dropped his castoffs in the Dumpster behind a restaurant before wandering into the old town proper. In moments he was lost.

The Bari streets seemed to have been made in miniature. Often they were only eight feet wide, the houses rising up three or four stories high in a continual wall on each side. Buildings connected across the street with arches. There were no sidewalks and room for only the smallest cars. The streets wound unpredictably, turning sharply without warning, running into junctions where four or five nearly identical streets slanted off at irregular angles, their destinations impossible to guess. Some of the buildings sprouted square towers so that even the skyline was too cluttered to reveal a sense of direction. Washing billowed across the road, strung from windows over flower-decked shrines to saints. Trays of homemade gnocchi dried in the sun, and women with babies sat in doorways, watching the world go by.

He passed under the sheer white walls of the imposing cathedral, but the only door was locked. He wandered along a street and found himself—surprisingly—back where he had started, on the road with the castle and the bay beyond. He was turning to walk away when he saw Brad Iverson getting out of a white Alfa Romeo parked only yards from where Claudio had dropped him off.

The impulse to call to him, remark on the coincidence, ask if he was there on business, lasted less than a second. Thomas ducked back into the shadows of the Strada Attolini and thought fast.

He's one of them. They've followed you here.

But how?

He peered carefully around the corner. Iverson was holding a phone, studying it, but not dialing.

Thomas snatched the phone from his pocket, fumbled with it, and hit the off button. When he looked around the corner again, Iverson was moving about, eyes on the phone, as if trying to get a signal. Thomas ducked back into the street and started running into the heart of the old city as if a thousand Saracens were after him.

There were three of them, if the ghoul was one of them. There might be more, but three of them he would recognize. He could try to find a policeman, but that would get him into hot water of a different kind. He had to get to the airport. Unseen.

He kept running down the Strada S. Chiara, just trying to put some distance between himself and the man who had called himself Brad as he had chatted affably about nothing at the Executive's breakfast buffet. But even as he maintained his lumbering rhinoceros run, he knew that he was losing his sense of direction, and he might well be rushing right into the arms of Roberta or—worse—her ghoulish colleague. He slowed to a breathless halt, looked around, and moved down a street toward what looked like a large open space where the white of the flagstone was set startlingly against the deep blue of the sky.

The piazza was the forecourt to another great pale church, the Basilica of St. Nicola, and one of its great wooden doors was ajar. Thomas crossed the open square and ducked inside.

The church was clearly Norman, high-gabled and square without spire or dome, and had only a squat tower over the entrance. It was cool inside, the nave largely the color of its stone, save for the dark columns and the high roof whose painted panels were framed with gilt. Thomas looked for somewhere unobtrusive to collect his thoughts and found a stairway down by the high altar signposted *ALLA TOMBA DEL SANTO*.

To the tomb of the saint.

He descended hurriedly.

He found himself in a long shallow chamber that stretched

beneath the sanctuary of the church above and was lined with pews. There was a pair of ornate side chapels and, in the center, a railed screen behind which lay a long stone sarcophagus lit by candles that sparkled on the gold ornamentation of the tomb. An elderly woman knelt at one of the chapels, but the place was otherwise deserted. Thomas edged into one of the pews and slid along, feeling the sweat he had not noticed before, listening to the hammering of his heart. He needed a strategy, and quickly.

"I've lost his signal," said War into his phone. "He could be anywhere."

"Before it was intermittent," said Pestilence. "Now it's gone completely, which means either he's shut it off or he is inside something very solid."

"Like a church," War concluded. "Send Famine into each church he can find. Let him hunt."

"You sure?"

"Just let him do what he does."

"And if he starts taking out civilians?"

"There's a greater good here," said War. "From here on, Famine is off the leash."

CHAPTER 57

Famine didn't like moving around in daylight. He felt conspicuous, vulnerable. He had built his identity as an assassin around darkness, because when it came right down to it, everyone was afraid of the dark, and when he was in it, they were right to be. The shaved head, the filed teeth, the overlong fingernails had all been extensions of a certain physical oddness that had always been there.

And it wasn't just physical. He had embraced his strangeness when the world had decided it didn't like what it saw, but what the world had seen wasn't ultimately about what he looked like. It was about the blankness in his eyes, the hollowness, the inability to care. It wasn't an animal lack of humanity the world saw in those pale irises; quite the contrary, it was extremely human. It was an impulse to casual cruelty.

He lived to make others afraid. He fed off their panic, their terror when they saw him coming, when they sensed what he might do to them. He lived for that. Needed it. It slaked his famine, an appetite no amount of blood could truly quench.

This was not his kind of mission, this running about in the sun, armed with pistols, looking for the quick kill. But success in such things brought him more satisfying meals, longer, slower banquets of the macabre and the horrific. So for now he would do as he was asked, let them give him the orders as they always did, reliant as he was on their protection for his various indiscretions . . .

The phone bleeped once. Knight was signaling again. He wasn't far, right outside the Basilica of St. Nicola. The signal lasted no more than thirty seconds, flickered for almost as long, and then vanished again. He'd gone inside, and Famine, ever hungry, rejoiced in silence as he felt for the haft of the knife in his pocket.

"Did you see that?" War demanded into his phone.

"Yes," said Pestilence. "Famine is on the scene and closing. He's in the basilica."

"Get there. Cover the exit. If the target emerges, shoot him down. Worry about witnesses later."

"If I can get away, no one will identify me," she said with a grim smile. "All they'll see is the habit."

Famine scanned the interior of the great church. There were a handful of tourists, a few solitary worshippers, but no services, no crowds. He kept to the shadows on the edge of the nave, moving deftly, keeping the hood of his coat up so that no one noticed him at all. He liked that. He liked the idea of cornering Knight somewhere and getting good and close before showing himself. He'd be paralyzed with fear. He might even scream. Famine felt a rush of pleasure expand from his loins.

He had almost completed a circuit of the nave. There was no sign of Knight, but somehow Famine felt his presence like a scent in the cool, still air of the ancient church where the dust turned in the colored light from the high windows.

He began his descent into the crypt.

"Tomba del santo," he read silently to himself.

Indeed.

CHAPTER 58

It had been a gamble, but one Thomas had thought worth taking. He had left the basilica to call Claudio at the Vittoria Parc, and then shut the phone off again. If they were tracking him through it, they'd come here, thinking he was inside. In fact he was hastily moving through the narrow streets, wending his way back to the road where Claudio was to collect him. But he had to kill fifteen minutes, and the castle across the road seemed the most secure place to do that.

He rounded a corner at speed. At the end of the street ahead he could see the sky and the edge of the castle wall. He could also see Brad Iverson coming toward him. As Thomas skittered to a halt, Iverson's surprise evaporated and he dropped to one knee, the oversized pistol sliding from under his jacket, extending and firing in a single, smooth movement.

Thomas flung himself down and rolled as shot after shot cannoned toward him. A planter under someone's window exploded in a shower of dirt. Smoke kicked up from the cobbles as another bullet ricocheted whining away. Then Thomas was scrambling back and Iverson got purposefully to his feet and came forward.

Thomas ran blind, ducking down an alley, barely keeping his feet as he broke into a sprint, hurling himself through a laundry line of tablecloths, all conscious thought shut down. He saw a half-open door, considered it for the briefest of moments, and then ran on, taking care to slam it hard as he passed.

War was in pursuit. Up ahead he heard the clang of a door and, when he turned the corner, was just in time to see it juddering on its hinges.

"Clever," he thought, running past it.

Thomas knew he couldn't outrun Iverson. He'd seen him up close and the guy was clearly an athlete who worked hard to stay in shape. Thomas had only guile and the peculiarities of the town on his side.

Here come the Saracens, he thought, weaving right and taking the first intersection to the left. He had no idea where he was now, no idea how close Iverson was behind him.

Two more intersections. He was slowing. A third. Then he was out, back in the main street, and finding a surge of speed to take him across the bridge to the castle.

"He's in there," shouted War.

Famine had joined him, his eyes burning with anger at the way Knight had slipped away from him in the church.

"What happened to the signal?" said Pestilence, over the phone.

"It's the streets and the buildings," said War. "There's too much interference."

"Either that or he knows."

"No," said Famine suddenly, brandishing his own phone as if it were a knife. "It's back."

"Okay," said War, gazing over to the castle. "You go in first. I'll back you up. Pestilence, monitor the signal and respond to its movements. It's going to cut in and out in there, but when it's clear I want you close and tracking. Move."

Another gamble. Thomas had bolted into the castle, shut the phone off, and taken a moment to get a sense of the place. The gatehouse was at the western corner of the perimeter wall. Inside was a keep with two carved entrances and cars parked along the front-facing wall. The keep was hollow, containing a flagged courtyard, its walls the inner side of rooms, offices, and exhibit halls. It was completely self-contained. Standing in the middle of the courtyard beneath four palm trees, Thomas flicked the phone on for one more moment.

It rang.

He hesitated, then answered.

"You can't hope to get out of this alive," said a familiar voice.

"Sister Roberta," he answered. "Calling about my spiritual welfare?"

"You should have killed me when you had the chance," she said.

"That was probably a mistake, yes," said Thomas, thinking fast. He knew they were coming, trying to pinpoint his location. For all he knew, they had a sniper somewhere . . . He moved to the nearest ground-level door and stepped inside a dim hall, its walls hung with vivid and outlandish masks: the local craft show. "Hello?" he said. "I'm afraid I'm losing your signal . . ."

There was a crackle, a descending series of electronic notes, and then silence. He hung up, and ran back to the courtyard and out, back the way he had come. Beside the gatehouse was a stone arch and a flight of stairs with a sign prohibiting entrance. He brushed past it and climbed up onto an open roof with access to the castle walls. He was on the corner tower overlooking the bridge.

He flung himself down. He was on a roof rather than in a turret, and the rim of stone was only a couple of feet high. He crawled to the wall and looked down. Running across the bridge toward him was Brad Iverson. Twenty yards behind him was a Fransiscan nun.

So where's . . . ?

He rolled onto his back as the ghoul sprang from the staircase, knife in hand.

CHAPTER 59

Thomas wasn't truly conscious of it, had not processed the awareness fully, but he had heard the ghoul's trademark snarl a fraction before he rolled. He had heard it in the same instant he had wondered where the ghoul was, and as he rolled over he raised one knee to protect himself from the attack.

Thomas saw the ghoul's dive, saw the blade flash white in the sun, saw the smug hatred in his eyes falter as Thomas's raised knee caught him hard in the chest. The knife went wide as the other collapsed on top of him, and for a moment the two men looked into each other's eyes, their faces almost touching. The ghoul bared his filed teeth, extended his long, pink tongue.

Revolted, Thomas reacted as he had when he had felt the bat in his hair in the Herculaneum tunnel, flinching away. He tore one hand free and jabbed hard at his attacker's face with the heel of his palm. The ghoul writhed with unnatural speed, shaking off the thrust and snapping at it with those awful teeth. Thomas snatched his hand away and then, knowing he might have only seconds to live, and seeing as through a red haze Pietro's dying face, kicked hard upward, extending his bent knee so that his attacker was thrown backward.

The ghoul flailed on the ground, but with a rush of power from his sinewy arms he sprang to his feet, before Thomas could even sit up. He bounded over to where Thomas still lay, arms spread wide like a crucifix, steadied himself with one foot on the lip of the wall, and reversed his grip on the knife. He raised it for one exhilarating and ceremonial plunge into Thomas's heart.

Hissing with the satisfaction of total victory, the ghoul brought the knife scything down. In the same instant, Thomas snapped his left arm down to his side, sweeping the ghoul's foot from under him.

For a second the bald man seemed nothing more than that. As the surprise and panic coalesced in his pale eyes, he fought to regain his balance, the drop over the low wall yawning suddenly toward him. He swung a hand out, almost in supplication, but there was nothing anyone could have done to stop him.

It all seemed so slow, a movie effect or a memory, the way the ghoul wavered, hung there in space for a second, and then fell heavily over the turret wall to the rock below.

For a long, slow beat, Thomas lay there and breathed, and then hunched into a crouch and looked down.

The ghoul lay bleeding on the stone bridge, his body twisted and still. And there was Brad, reaching back into his jacket for his pistol, looking up at him.

But then he heard shouting. Some of it came from Roberta, who was calling to Brad, warning, it seemed, telling him to get away from the body. Some of it, however, came from someone else, a man, yelling in Italian. Then there were more voices, and as Brad moved hastily back across the bridge toward the old city, Thomas saw policemen in uniform coming out of the gatehouse below and gathering around the body.

"It police house now," Claudio had said of the castle.

Thomas jerked back out of sight. The police had momentarily scared Brad and Roberta off, but he still had to get out of here. He checked his watch. Claudio would be parking across the street in less than five minutes. If Thomas was to leave the castle now, Brad would shoot him down, police or no police. There was, after all, only one way out of the castle.

Thomas was fairly sure that the police had not seen he was up here, but sooner or later one of them would come up to see if they could tell why the ghoul fell. He had to move. If he went back down the stairs he would walk right into them and would not be able to avoid interrogation and, probably, arrest. The frontal wall extended all the way to the far turret, which was covered in scaffolding, the ramparts themselves blocked with more makeshift barricades and orange tape. Keeping as low as he could, Thomas began edging along the crumbling wall. As he did so, he turned the phone back on and dialed.

CHAPTER 60

"Sit down," said Pestilence, still watching the castle gate. They were at the streetfront café across the road.

"I nearly had him," said War.

"He can't stay there all day. We'll get him as soon as he moves. He's still outside and the signal is strong."

"Unless the cops pick him up," said War, darkly.

"He doesn't want that any more than we do, especially now. If the police spot Knight up there they'll take him in for questioning, and in no time he'll be a suspect in all three deaths."

"He had better *not* get caught," said War. "This is bad enough as it is."

Pestilence said nothing. Neither of them wanted to discuss how the Seal-breaker would respond to the loss of Famine, psychopathic loose cannon though he obviously had been.

They watched as an ambulance arrived, picked up the body, and left briskly, lights and siren on.

"What is Knight doing?" said War, checking his GPS. "He's moved all the way to the other end of the wall, where that construction work is."

"You sure there's no other way out?" asked Pestilence.

"Sure."

"Is that the same kind of certain knowledge that didn't figure the castle would be a police station?"

"Shut up," said War.

For a moment, she did. Then she got to her feet.

"He's coming down, moving back toward the gate," she said. "He's going to make a run for it."

"No," said War. "He's not. Get the car."

He was staring up the road out of town. She followed his gaze and saw the navy-blue minivan with the name of the Vittoria Parc stenciled onto the side as it turned onto the bridge and up to the castle.

"Get the car!" he repeated. "Quick!"

She moved fast, snatching the spare key from inside her pouched sleeve and hurrying the twenty-five yards to where they had parked. She got in, started the engine, and turned the car around in a squeal of tires, knocking over a bicycle that had been propped by the curb.

War was watching the GPS, motionless.

"He's moving," he said, as Pestilence pulled the rented Alfa Romeo to the café and pushed the passenger door open. He clambered in, barely taking his gaze from the phone's display, looking up to confirm what it was telling him. "Yes," he said. "Perfect."

The blue van emerged from the gatehouse, crossed the bridge, and pulled out into traffic.

"Stay a couple of cars back," said War. "He's heading for the railway station. This time, he's ours."

CHAPTER 61

Thomas sat in the castle gatehouse and checked his watch. One of the policemen who had been loitering since the ghoul's body had been taken away seemed to be watching him. It was time to go. If Brad and Roberta—

the absurdity of those names! They sounded like they should be hosting a subdivision barbecue

—hadn't taken the bait by now, they never would.

He left the gatehouse and crossed the bridge back into the old town. There was no sign of his pursuers or the white Alfa Romeo they had been driving. There was, on the other hand, Claudio, pulling over the hotel's second minivan.

"You know you have to pay for both shuttles," he said, rolling the window down.

"Cheap at twice the price," said Thomas getting in.

"The other driver call me," said Claudio, watching him warily, as if his passenger had turned out to be a little crazy. "You okay?"

"Yes."

"And you want me to go . . . ?"

"Airport," said Thomas. "At last."

"I'll do it," said Pestilence.

They had followed the blue van to the railway station, where it had just pulled over.

"Here?" said War.

"I'll do it before he gets out. Kill the driver too. If I'm fast, no one will see, and if anyone remembers me later . . ." She gestured toward the habit. Then she stretched out her hand and War, nodding, slapped his automatic into it. "Besides," she added with a hard smile, "I deserve this."

She got out and walked briskly. The van hadn't moved, though the engine was still running.

Taking your time to pay your fare, Thomas? she thought. *You smug, stupid, self-involved . . .*

She glanced around once, then lowered her head, swept the pistol from her sleeve, and yanked the door open.

The back of the van was empty, with only a cell phone sitting on the rear seat. As she stared at it, the driver gunned the engine and pulled away, leaving the side door flapping and Pestilence gazing stupidly after it.

PART III

THE BONE MOSAIC

CHAPTER 62

Ryan Air's flight to Frankfurt was a cheerful confusion, an efficient no-frills operation that felt a little like a traveling holiday camp. When it touched down, the passengers broke into spontaneous applause. A bizarre response, thought Thomas, wondering if they did things like that before 9/11. Not in America. But here? Probably. And looking around him he thought that the applause wasn't relief so much as appreciation for the pilot expressed by a short-lived community for whom the journey was a bit of an adventure.

No one stopped him in Frankfurt. If an alarm had been raised about his departure, it was slow in spreading, and as the Japan Airlines flight to Tokyo tucked its wheels up, Thomas finally began to relax. The flight was thinly populated and he could stretch out and get some sleep. It was all behind him, at last, and for a few hours he would not think about what had happened or what he would find when he touched down.

Such willful oblivion lasted no more than five minutes, shattered by a voice beside him, a low, ironically conversational tone that he knew at once.

"If it isn't the globe-trotting, atheist archaeologist!"

Thomas, who had been staring blankly out the window, turned in disbelief.

It was Jim. He was wearing an olive-colored woolen sweater and jeans without dog collar or crucifix, but the priest's wry smile was the same as ever.

"What the hell are you doing here?" said Thomas.

"Language, my son," said Jim with mock horror, as he dropped into the seat beside him.

"Seriously," said Thomas. "What on earth . . . ?"

"Never been to Japan," said the priest, plucking the in-flight magazine from the seat pouch and thumbing through it as if nothing could be more ordinary. "Been saving my meager

wages for years waiting for something exciting and expensive
to come along. But like most priests, your brother notwithstand-
ing, adventure on the high seas isn't exactly part of the daily
routine. So, 'Jim,' I says to myself. 'If you want excitement or—
for that matter—just a change from sick visits to the environs of
Chicagoland, you have to make it happen yourself, take the bull
by the horns and . . . '"

"Enough," said Thomas.

"You sent me your itinerary," the priest answered. "I took it
as an invitation."

"It wasn't."

"Apparently," said Jim. "But like I said, I'd never been to
Japan. And it sounded like you could use some company.
Maybe some help too." Jim didn't look at him, his eyes still on
the glossy pages of some article about beaches in Tahiti.

"Why didn't you fly direct from O'Hare?" said Thomas.
"Why fly to Frankfurt?"

"Cheaper," said Jim. "I counted out the dusty shekels I kept
in a jar under the bed and found that the private plane serving
champagne all the way was a bit rich for my clerical blood.
Hopping from airport to airport saves a pile, and allows us to
get reacquainted along the way. With your itinerary in hand,
and thanks to the beneficence of the good people at Japan Airlines, I was able to book a seat beside you all the way. Can't
say fairer than that, can you now?"

"I guess not," said Thomas, smiling, trying to keep the
wariness from his face.

"Brilliant," said Jim. "Drink? Normally it would be a bit
early, but I really have no idea what time it is anymore. In fact,
I couldn't swear to what day it is. Ironic, eh? It's like I've had
a few already."

Thomas smiled again, trying not to like him too much. He
couldn't afford to lower his guard. Vesuvius had taught him
that. But there could be no harm in a little drink. He flagged
down a flight attendant and requested a couple of miniature
whiskys: Jack Daniels, as it turned out.

"So, you going to fill me in or what?" said Jim.

Thomas hesitated only a second and then started telling him what had happened in Italy. Part of him was cautious and watchful throughout, looking for a telltale response from the priest, and that same part sifted the material as it came to mind, prepared to hold back anything that seemed too revelatory. But in the end, he told Jim everything, because either he really was an innocent looking to help and knew nothing, or he already knew. In either case Thomas found, somewhat depressingly, that he had discovered little that might truly unsettle his enemies.

The Irish priest was a good audience, asked appropriate questions, responded with shock at the right points, and fell into a puzzled silence at the end.

"I don't know if Ed died because of his research into this 'new' symbol," said Thomas, "though I can't imagine that anyone would think that worth killing for. But there are these other goons trying to stop me from asking questions. There are the planted weapons in my home in Chicago, and there are the deaths of Satoh and Pietro. Ed died for a reason, and someone is spending a lot of time and money to see that I don't find out what that reason was."

"And you think you'll find the answer in Japan?" said Jim.

"It's where he went after Italy," Thomas said with a shrug, "and there's the story of the Herculaneum cross and this weird tomb find that suggests that Italian missionaries went to eighth-century Japan. My gut says it's all connected, but how . . ."

He opened his hands in a gesture of casual bafflement, as if he were releasing a bird.

"You're going to see your wife?"

"Ex."

"Right," said Jim.

"Maybe." Thomas shrugged. "I'm not sure yet. I'm making this up as I go."

"Might be a good opportunity to—you know—reconnect. Bury the hatchet."

"Ah," Thomas replied, "the Catholic priest as marriage counselor. I always got a real kick out of that; after all, who better than the celibate clergy who deny women a place in their world to advise couples on how to keep their marriages strong? Classic."

"Who says the church has no sense of humor?" said Jim, grinning.

"Is there anything new on the weapons they found at my place?"

"Nothing in the press except a few speculations that the trail has gone cold," said Jim. "I spoke to the DHS agent again, Kaplan, and he said that tests were moving unusually slowly."

"I don't understand why they haven't tried to reach me," said Thomas.

"Assuming they haven't," said Jim.

"What do you mean?"

"These guys who have been after you seem to have a lot of information, a lot of resources. You don't think they could be . . . ?"

"Government?" said Thomas, incredulous. "No."

"Why not?"

"Because if they are . . ." said Thomas, pausing, trying to find the words.

"Then we're one step from a primal anarchy without law or justice or apple pie?" said Jim.

"Something like that."

"Welcome to the world, mate," said Jim.

"You have Ed's subversive edge," said Thomas. "I still can't get used to that in a priest."

"Because we're supposed to be so . . . orthodox? Religion being the opiate of the masses and all that?"

"I guess."

"Some of us believe in a socially activist church," said Jim.

"That's how you get involved in evictions?"

Jim flinched. "Who told you about that?"

"Why don't you tell me about it yourself?" said Thomas.

Jim blinked, and then said, with careful emphasis, "I've never been to Japan. I wonder what it will be like."

He went back to his magazine.

CHAPTER 63

It didn't start till they were out of the airport. Airports, after all, tend to have little character, little that marks them out as different from each other. So Thomas felt nothing as he wandered Narita airport's cramped and cluttered environs, except perhaps when he heard the pattering announcements in Japanese, and even those were too predictable to really do it. But once they were on the bus into the city, it started, that sense of the familiar and the strange crowding in on him like déjà vu, as if he knew this place, as if a part of him had never left, and—at the same time—that he didn't belong and never had. By the time the bus was idling at the station in Shinjuku, Thomas's hands had begun to shake slightly. Twenty minutes later, as they dragged their luggage into a down-market noodle house for a bite of what Ed called "local color" before looking for Kumi, Thomas—now ashen pale and taking hurried, shallow breaths—was seriously considering taking the next bus back to the airport.

He concealed it from Jim, whose face had been pressed to the tinted window ever since they left the airport, marveling with a tourist's awe at the landscape, at the road signs, at Tokyo Disneyland flashing past pale and tawdry, at the clustered skyscrapers, the sea of black-haired people moving through the streets, the splashes of neon and the colossal video screens. Jim talked constantly, exclamations mainly, but punctuated with questions no one answered, and all the time he gazed around him, his eyes like saucers, a man transported to a planet he had never truly believed in. It was hardly surprising that he was oblivious to the fact that his traveling companion was experiencing something like posttraumatic stress. Thomas was buoyed on steadily building waves of panic and anxiety bizarrely underwritten by the insistent sense that he had never left this place, that he still lived here with a girl called Kumi whom he one day hoped to marry. . . .

He had known it would be like this or, more accurately, had known it would be something like this, some pained and bewildered sense of stepping back into the past. He had never experienced anything quite like it in the States, even when returning to the streets where he'd been raised, pacing the rooms of the house where his parents had lived and, eventually, died. All that felt lost and immediate at the same time, but it also felt real because he had never doubted that it would be basically the same as when he played stickball on the corner with Ed and Jimmy Collins from two doors down. But this, this was different. Japan was different.

Thomas had known nothing about Japan before he had gone to work there. For him it had been exotic, foreign, and however much he grew used to being there in the two years he had taught high school in the little town southwest of Tokyo, it had never stopped being exotic and foreign. When he left, he took a piece of it with him in Kumi, but when she left him, it had all gone away, shut out of his life, his reality. In a few years it became hard to imagine that such a place really existed, that he had been there, that it had shaped who he was. Even on those rare drunken occasions when he could bring himself to look at pictures taken there, his experiences in Japan increasingly felt as if they had happened to someone else. He could stare at those photographs baffled for hours, gazing at himself, trying to remember what it had been like, that life on the other

(planet)

side of the world, trying to believe in it. But it was too strange, too alien, too utterly lost to any notion of who he was now.

And now he was back and it was all still here. The faces. The voices. The traffic. The climate. The immaculate gardens.

The tiled roofs and timbered houses. The glimpses of ancient wooden shrines clanging in the mind like temple bells. Then the model food in the restaurant windows. The cries of "*irrashaimasse*!" from the staff as they came inside. The red and black paper lanterns splashed with calligraphy. The new-wood smell of the building, almost smothered by the rich but simple aroma of the food itself. The picture menus with their bowls of thick, steaming noodles . . . There was nowhere he could look that didn't somehow insist that the world had wobbled on its axis and reality had changed.

You don't belong here. Never did. Never will.

But it was inside him too, dyed indelibly in his sense of self.

Ay, there's the rub.

Because however much he had tried to shut Japan out of his life forever, it had shaped him, had even—he dreaded to think it—given him his best years. Since then everything had unraveled. Being back here again was like stepping back a dozen years to when he had been young and cocksure, when the world and all that was in it had been spread out before him, when life had been so full of promise, of purpose, of fulfillment.

"I think I'm going to be sick," he muttered suddenly. And as Jim snapped out of his reverie for a moment to stare at him, Thomas looked for a place to throw up.

CHAPTER 64

Thomas stood with his hands on the ancient wooden rail and watched the ceremony inside, the bride in an iridescent kimono, her face white and still, hair piled and artfully pinned with lacquered chopsticks, the groom in black, watchful and a little nervous. The Buddhist priest wearing a broad, circular hat chanted over the dull clanging of occasional bells as incense spiraled from the stone votary. The temple was open to the air on two sides, the central podium draped with red and gold fabric. From his vantage, the couple, the priest, the structure itself and the manicured pines that stood in the background, were a window on a world perhaps a thousand years old. Only the groom's stainless steel watchband suggested they were anywhere close to the twenty-first century.

He kept his eyes on the ceremony that was unfolding only yards away. He had sensed Kumi's silent approach, Jim standing off to the side, but had not turned or moved away, and she had had no choice but to stand wordless beside him. That was why he had called her at the Agricultural Trade Office and told her to meet him here where there could be no scene, no shouting or ugliness that would disrupt the serene formality of the rites being performed before the small, silent crowd of onlookers.

"You shouldn't have come," she said.

Thomas didn't look at her. Instead he spoke in a whisper, glad of something his eyes could follow that wasn't her.

"We nearly did this. Remember? A second ceremony to be held in Japan . . ."

There was a long silence. The priest smiled at the couple who responded nervously and took sips of what was probably sake in wooden cups.

"Go back to the States, Tom," she said. "Don't contact me again, okay?"

He started to say something, but she just shook her head, and there was something sad and weary in her voice.

"Go home, Tom. And get some rest," she added. "You look old."

She leaned into him, kissed him on his cheek, her lips cool, her touch so light he barely felt it, and then she was walking away.

Thomas stared ahead, gripping the rail harder now, just as the bride broke her stillness just long enough to sweep her hand into her husband's for the briefest of moments before becoming once more a part of the ceremonial tableau.

CHAPTER 65

"Should we find a hotel?" said Jim. "I can stay by myself if you'd rather, but it would save money. I don't snore. I think. Actually, I don't have a lot of good evidence on that."

He smiled sheepishly, his faint humor part of an awkwardness that had hung over him since Kumi's brief appearance. Thomas was not sure about Jim, but this at least seemed genuine, and he felt something like pity for the man. There's nothing worse than being the third wheel, he thought, though I imagine priests wind up feeling like that a lot.

"Darning his socks in the night when there's nobody there . . . "

"Sure," said Thomas. "I could stand to save some money. God knows how I'm going to pay these credit card bills."

"Right," said Jim, smiling with what might have been gratitude, then looking quickly away. "Know anywhere reasonable?"

"In Tokyo? Good luck. But that's okay. We're not staying here anyway."

"We're not?"

"We're heading west into the mountains of Yamanashi," said Thomas. "There's something I need to see."

"But what about . . . ?"

"There's nothing for me here," said Thomas. He swung his gaze around deliberately looking for a subway station or a cab, avoiding Jim's eyes, and found himself looking at the glossies on the corner newsstand. His eyes slid over the impenetrable kanji as they always had so that the few words he could read popped out of the background like neon. He took two hurried steps and picked up a copy of the English-language edition of the *Daily Yomiuri*. Two men were smiling and shaking hands from an inset cover picture, one Japanese, the other Caucasian.

What the hell?

It was Devlin.

CHAPTER 66

The senator, according to the paper, was part of a goodwill trade delegation involving representatives from states most likely to benefit from a deal lowering tariffs on imported fish from the Pacific Northwest and non–genetically modified grain from Illinois. He was due to give a press conference following a series of meetings at the Keio Plaza Hotel in Shinjuku. If he was quick, Thomas thought, he could catch the end of it.

"That's a coincidence," said Jim.

"Maybe," said Thomas.

They looked at each other for a moment, like poker players watching for signs of a bluff.

"You don't completely trust me, do you?" Jim said.

"Not completely, no."

"So why are you taking me with you?"

Thomas laughed, a short, mirthless bark, and said, "Call it a leap of faith." They didn't speak again till they reached the hotel.

"The average U.S. tariff on imported soybeans, corn, and wheat is twelve percent," said Devlin, stretching his large frame in a barrel-backed chair of the hotel bar. "You know what the Japanese equivalent is?"

Thomas shook his head.

"Fifty percent," said Devlin. "And that's just the standard tax. There are seventy-two so-called 'megatariffs' of one hundred percent or more on foreign imports. Can you believe that? Rice imports are kept to seven hundred seventy thousand tons, which is less than ten percent of the country's needs. We talk about free market, but this is a joke, or it would be if it weren't criminally protective of their own crippled agricultural system. Anyway, that's why I'm here."

"Just that?" said Thomas, watching Hayes, who was, as ever, ghosting the senator, absorbing his every word, his face blank.

"Just that," said Devlin. "And I hoped, after your last message, that I would run into you," he added as a concession, smiling quickly so that his bright, chisel-like teeth flashed in his square jaw.

"You knew I was coming to Japan?"

"I knew Father Ed had been here and that you were following him," said Devlin.

"What else do you know, Senator?" said Thomas.

Jim shifted in his seat.

Devlin looked around the bar, deciding what to say, and then he leaned forward.

"Details are sketchy," he said, "but your brother died during a counterterrorist operation. That is why no one is talking. A number of hard-line militant Islamic separatist groups are based in the Philippines and in the surrounding area. One of them seems to have been the target. Now, what I can't find out is whether the DHS thinks Father Ed was involved with them somehow or whether he was in the wrong place at the wrong time and got caught in the crossfire. Either way they would see the situation as delicate. If he was a homegrown terrorist, they'll want to find out all they can about him before they go public."

"And if he wasn't?" said Thomas.

"Then they screwed up," said Devlin. "They killed not only a civilian, but an American and a priest. Imagine how that would play, for God's sake."

"Bad press?" scoffed Thomas. "That's what they're worried about?"

"It's what everyone in Washington worries about," said Devlin with a bitter laugh.

"And just how hard would they work to keep it quiet?"

"If you mean would they attempt to take you out to keep the story under wraps," said Devlin, "forget it. No way. This is America we're talking about."

Thomas looked down and said nothing.

Thomas sank his hands into his jacket pockets as they walked toward the railway station with their meager luggage.

"So?" said Jim. "What did you make of that?"

"Not sure," said Thomas. "You?"

"Politicians!" Jim shrugged. "Who the hell knows what they really think about anything?"

"You thought he was lying?"

"I thought he was holding something back," said Jim.

Thomas nodded, then stopped.

"What?" said Jim.

Thomas looked confused. He had drawn a square of paper no larger than a stamp out of his pocket, catching himself as he was about to throw it away. Now he was staring at it.

"He slipped you a message?" said Jim, incredulous.

"Not him," said Thomas, almost as disbelieving. "Kumi."

CHAPTER 67

Thomas and Jim rode the Chuo line from Shinjuku to Kofu, arriving in a little over three hours. Tokyo's urban sprawl turned slowly into the wooded mountains of Yamanashi and the Japan of the great nineteenth-century woodblock print-makers: rice paddies; steep-sided irregular hills, their tops lost in mist and cloud; and tiny, remote shrines. And, of course, Mount Fuji, a snow-crested, symmetrical echo of Vesuvius.

In the course of the journey the sense of déjà vu with

which Thomas had been struggling since they touched down
returned with greater force than ever as they neared the town
in which he had spent the two years before graduate school.
He fell into himself, drawn by the gravity of memory, relieved
that Jim was asleep and would need no commentary. He
reread Kumi's note, considering the appointment at what had
been one of their favorite places, and it was impossible not to
see it as promising harmony, so that the train seemed to be
taking him into his past.

They took a cab from the station, the driver in white felt
gloves opening the rear doors automatically, and as Jim remarked on this Thomas found his brain articulating the same
"Yes, that's how it was" that it had been doing since they arrived. In ten minutes they were at the entrance to the Zenko-ji
Temple, pacing the long avenue through the sculpted black
pines to the faded red structure, and every step was, for
Thomas, uncannily familiar.

An old man on a set of steps was wiring a long bamboo
pole to the long, straight limb of a pine. He glanced at them
from under his broad-brimmed straw hat and bobbed his head
in greeting. To the left was the great bronze Buddha surmount-
ing the ornamental garden Thomas had seen in rain and snow,
and to the right was the cemetery of stone figures and square
wooden staffs carved with kanji. He saw Kumi before she saw
him. She was standing in front of a row of squat stone figurines
that looked like diminutive Buddhas shaped like babies in various poses. *Jido,* they were called, he remembered. Many wore
red biblike aprons called *yodarekake,* one of which Kumi was
adjusting.

She turned when she sensed them there, moving quickly
toward them. Thomas was surprised to find her embracing
him, muttering relief that he had made it and apologies for
their last meeting.

"You've cut your hair short," said Thomas.

"Shorter, yes," said Kumi. "It's been like this about three
years."

"I liked it long."

"I know," she said.

It was shoulder length now. It used to reach almost to her waist.

"It looks . . . professional," said Thomas.

"Thanks," she said, with a knowing, sideways smile that was so familiar, so absolutely *her,* that Thomas flinched and looked away.

"I'm Jim Gornall," said Jim. "I work at the parish Ed was serving when he died."

Kumi shook his hand and bowed fractionally, a habit she had acquired since being back, thought Thomas.

"I'm being watched," she said, straight to business. "A guy was in my office the day I called you. An American. I'd seen him before on Sotobori Dori. There's a golf store next to my office building and he goes in there."

"Maybe he just likes golf," said Thomas.

"Americans give up golf when they come to Japan, Tom," she said. "They can't afford it."

"You think he's Homeland Security?"

She shook her head.

"Homeland Security already questioned me about you," she said. "If this guy's government he's going through some fairly covert channels. My office is only a block from the embassy so it's sort of a magnet for U.S. businessmen looking to make a killing, but this guy didn't look official."

"How so?"

"He had a goatee. Hardly normal for anyone dealing with corporate or political Japan."

Parks?

Thomas nodded and told her about his dealings with Parks.

"I don't know where he fits in," he admitted, "but he's involved and he's dangerous. If it was him you saw in your office, then he went there pretty much directly after leaving St. Anthony's in Chicago, and he must have gone from there to Italy."

"Whoever it was," said Kumi, "I had no idea what the state of my phones were so I had to make it sound like I wasn't really talking to you."

"I'm kind of surprised you are," said Thomas.

He said it lightly, but he meant it and her smile was an evasion.

"DHS knows you are in the country," she said. "I'm not sure why they aren't talking to you or having the Japanese police pick you up. They probably figure they can learn more by watching."

"Or they are hoping I suffer some sort of tragic accident so that all this stuff just goes away," said Thomas.

"Thomas is developing a very bleak view of our nation's government," said Jim.

"What do you mean 'developing'?" she said. "Thomas has prided himself on his skepticism about the U.S. government for as long as I've known him."

"Let's just say I'm getting more cynical in my old age," Thomas answered.

"Shame," she said, deadpan. "You were such the wide-eyed innocent before."

"Did you come here to help or just catch up on your insults?" said Thomas.

"A bit of both," she said. "I can't stay long. I'm supposed to be pouring soothing oil on the minister for agriculture, forestry, and fisheries in . . ." she checked her watch, "three hours. This trade delegation from the States has people jumpy."

"Devlin?"

"Among others, yes. You know him?"

Thomas told her of his meetings with the senator and his link to Ed.

"You think it's a coincidence that he's here now?" she asked.

"I don't know," Thomas said. "Were you in contact with Ed when he was here?"

She hesitated.

"He stayed with me for a couple of days, but all our energy went into not talking about you," she said. "In fact we talked about very little. I think he was relieved to go."

She sounded wistful.

"But you think he came here?" said Thomas, strictly business.

"I know he came in this direction," she said, "because I helped him with the train schedule, but he didn't say where he was going and I heard nothing from him after he left Tokyo."

"That's unlike him," said Thomas.

"Yes. He seemed anxious, troubled, even," said Kumi. "When I asked him about it he said he'd tell me later, when things were clearer to him. He didn't talk about his work or why he had come. I let him be, because I suspected some of it was about us. I hadn't seen him for five years, remember, not since . . ."

"You left me," said Thomas. "Yes."

Kumi looked away, chewing the inside of her cheek as she did when restraining herself.

"So unless it really was all about *us,*" he said, using that last word as if it were a kind of in-joke, "then something happened between his decision to leave Italy and his arrival in Japan. He seemed quite happy according to the people who met him in Naples. What made him so 'troubled'?"

"It would help if we knew exactly where he went when he left Tokyo," said Jim, who had been staying on the conversation's perimeter in case it became too personal.

"I think I know," said Thomas, "though I don't understand why."

CHAPTER 68

Outside the NHK studio in Kofu, Thomas joined a huddle of foreign journalists clambering off a bus, held up his passport and an old library card as the throng moved through security, and took a seat at the back. They were shown a five-minute video showing the layout of the site and listened to an elderly local archaeologist who explained the significance of the find. The translator was poor and clearly made no attempt to pass along the more technical details, but the archaeologist was clearly excited, and that set the tone for the afternoon.

When the foreign journalists—mainly Australian, Dutch, and German—were shown into the press conference proper, the place was already packed with locals, and the podium was surrounded by microphone stands and halogen lamps. Some of the major papers—*The Yomiuri* and *Asahi Shimbun* in particular—had at least five people in their teams, poised with recorders and cameras of all kinds, and every staff member of the TV station seemed to have abandoned their other duties to see Watanabe.

"Are the Beatles back in town?" said Thomas to a reporter with a toothbrush mustache who wore a *New Zealand Herald* badge on a cord round his neck.

"This guy's bigger," he said. "Or he will be soon. Or he wants to be."

He smiled wryly at his final modification and then started taking pictures. Michihiro Watanabe had just walked in.

The room virtually exploded, flashbulbs going off so frequently that the brilliance was almost constant. A wave of applause swelled around the room, and all but a handful of the journalists—mostly foreigners—were beaming and cheering. It was a sportsman's reception, a rock star's.

For an archaeologist, Thomas thought, he looked like one too. He was thin, but well muscled, his arms roped with vein and sinew. He was perhaps fifty, but looked ten years younger, and his black hair was spiked with gel. He wore gray-lensed shades with a hint of blue, and a close-fitting designer T-shirt with a metallic sheen. His manner was understated, but comfortable, and he smiled easily at the cameras.

"Michihiro Watanabe, the thinking Japanese woman's crumpet," whispered the New Zealander.

Thomas watched the way the station's women grinned girlishly and needed no translation of *crumpet*.

Watanabe took control of the proceedings, chatting amiably, making the occasional self-deprecating joke, and nodded to an assistant at the back who showed PowerPoint slides of the dig on a screen behind him: a few charts and diagrams, but mainly stills of the tomb, its contents, the neighboring—as yet unexcavated—tomb, and, of course, the great man himself, peering at the ground, pointing things out to his team, and generally looking casual, clever, and in control. The translator added a running commentary, stumbling over dates and—Thomas suspected—editorializing freely as the core elements of the find were laid out.

"Contrary to previous belief," he said, "this demonstrates the presence of non-Asian foreigners in Japan in the middle Kofun period—about AD 600—and strongly suggests that they were early Christian missionaries."

Everyone in the room knew this already, but it still caused a ripple of excitement, as if they had needed to hear it live to make sure, or that they had half-expected Watanabe to retract the outlandish claim. For the last four days, the site had been the source of the best stories of a scientific nature to hit Japan in years. Information had been carefully regulated, trickling out in teasing sound bites, the site and Watanabe's lab facility close by kept under tight security. This was understandable given the scale of the find, but it also smacked of carefully orchestrated marketing.

Finally, with the air of a conjurer who had saved his best trick for last, Watanabe produced a Perspex box from under the podium containing a partial skull with the lower jawbone separate but intact and an ornamented silver crucifix. The crowd pressed forward and the wall of camera flash began again.

"The Japanese skull has very rounded eye sockets," said the translator, as Watanabe showed comparative diagrams. Even to Thomas's untrained eye, some distinction was clear. ". . . as did its Kofun forbear. The eye sockets of a European skull are clearly oblong, identical to those of the remains from our site. The long bones from the burial also supply evidence that the bodies originated in Europe, though these bones are considerably more fragmentary. A Japanese Kofun femur is noticeably straighter along its length than the European. As you can see, the examples from the grave are quite curved."

Questions followed, mainly in Japanese, mainly softballs that Watanabe took some pleasure in stroking out of the park. Yes, there is evidence of Eurasian connections during the first and second centuries between Rome and Han China via the silk road. Yes, the Great Wall of China was—after all—built to keep out the Hsiung-nu—the same Huns who were besieging Rome. Recent DNA evidence suggests that a skeleton in Sian, China, that is more than two thousand years old is almost certainly European. The great ecumene between China and Europe was the realm of militant nomads who surely affected both cultures, and there may have been express contact with Japan via the Siberian kurgan. When all came to all, the lack of prior evidence was not a good enough reason to assert that there could not have been contact between East and West, between Europe and the farthest shores of Asia. There are also the famous blond mummies of western China . . .

It went on for some time and gradually deteriorated into "human interest" questions about how he stayed motivated, his work ethic, his "genius" for the shocking speculation that no one else was prepared to make but which was the only one to truly fit the facts. By the end, it was clear that this was less an inquiry into his finds than it was a canonization of the finder. The only sour note came from the New Zealander.

"Is it not true that the Jomon predecessors of the Yayoi-Kofun Japanese have misled people before into speculating on a Caucasoid background?"

The audience turned to the foreign press corps and murmured among themselves as the question was translated into Japanese. Only Watanabe remained unflappable.

"We are confident," he said in English, smiling at the surprise that this strategy produced in his audience, "that these bones show clear European origin in ways absolutely different from Kofun Japanese bones."

"Even though the survival of Kofun bones is comparatively rare?" the reporter shot back.

"Not so rare that there can be any dispute about what they look like," said Watanabe. "But to be absolutely sure, we are subjecting the bones to every available test, including small-scale measurement of the craniofacial details, which will then be run through a computerized data-evaluation system based on known examples. The data will be processed by an independent analyst."

His smile never wavered, but his gaze drifted to the graduate student beside him, and Thomas felt sure that something passed between them. The student lowered his eyes as if in reverence.

The applause at the end was more than polite, more than enthusiastic. It was, again, slightly frenzied as only receptions of celebrities are.

"Get used to it," said the New Zealander, leaning in to Thomas. "He's not going away any time soon."

In a profession generally known for its dustiness, Watanabe was clearly a star, one who had always had a flair for dealing with the media. Now he had a real find to match the pizzazz of his personality.

"Why is it such a big deal?" said Thomas.

"Every Japanese kids' textbook will tell you that Europeans didn't come here till 1543 when a Portuguese boat ran aground on the southern tip of Kyushu. Francis Xavier—or *Saint* Francis Xavier, depending on your persuasion—arrived, Bible in hand, six years later. If Watanabe is right, all that goes out the window. You have Christian evangelists deep in the Japanese heartland seven hundred years earlier than anyone suspected. It's big news, all right. Certainly big enough to keep Watanabe's highly polished smile on our TVs for a long time to come."

"I don't think I get it," said Thomas. "I mean, I understand, but I don't get the hoopla."

"It's partly him," said the New Zealander, zipping up his camera bag and nodding toward the platform party. "He could find a Coke bottle in his yard and make it sound exciting. But it's also them."

"Them?"

"The Japanese. They don't like being late arrivals at the important events. For the most part they take from whatever religion they want when they want. Buddhists worship at Shinto shrines on certain festival days, and have Christian-style weddings like they see in the movies. But Christianity is where it's at, and the Japanese like to be at the heart of whatever is cool. Jesus is cool, apparently. And if they can rewrite history to discover that Christianity has actually been around here about as long as it has in the rest of the world—and a lot longer than it has in America—so much the better."

He smirked, mirthlessly, and Thomas saw in him a familiar type of disgruntled ex-pat, himself a minor celebrity by sheer virtue of his foreignness but always a little on the outside of the culture in which he had chosen to live.

"See you at the next one," said the journalist with mock jauntiness.

As he walked away, Thomas looked back to the platform party, where Watanabe was still being photographed and fawned over by the local NHK anchorwoman. She nodded and smiled in vociferous agreement, and Thomas felt a stirring in himself of the New Zealander's bitterness, a stirring rather like memory. He watched them, Watanabe in his designer shades and all other eyes on him. Except one.

It was Watanabe's assistant, a young, sallow-faced Japanese man in his early twenties, a graduate student, formally dressed, his hair was parted on the side. He was darker skinned than most of those around him and could have passed for Korean or even Malaysian. His gaze was fixed on Thomas, his expression unreadable, though there was a hint of something behind the studied blankness, and when his attention finally strayed back to Watanabe, Thomas thought he saw a hint of unease.

Thomas took a couple of steps forward and something very strange happened. Watanabe was in full flow, delighting all with his homey, quirky brand of academia, when he suddenly stopped midsentence. His audience waited politely, and someone giggled, thinking this was part of his performance; he tipped his sunglasses down his nose till he was peering directly out at Thomas. Then he became quite still, and Thomas, feeling the oddness of the moment, did the same.

The rare glimpse of Watanabe's eyes prompted a flash of someone's camera, and in that brilliant splash of light, the archaeologist looked cautious, even wary. The audience looked from him to each other, still smiling awkwardly, and then, slowly, like a theater audience that realizes that the show is going on in the house behind them and not on the stage, they turned to Thomas.

There was a moment of complete silence, and then the sallow-faced graduate student was talking again, pulling attention toward himself, so that finally even Watanabe turned, and the smiles that had grown strained and fixed broadened again. Almost immediately, a security guard appeared at Thomas's shoulder with the translator who was asking to see Thomas's credentials, using his body as a screen to block out the platform party, and begin shepherding him toward the door and out.

CHAPTER 69

"They knew me," said Thomas. "How do you explain that? Watanabe and the other guy, the graduate student, they recognized me the moment they saw me."

Kumi was back from her Tokyo meeting, back, she said, without further explanation, for the weekend. They had rented three rooms in a traditional hotel or *ryokan* in Shimobe, a village beside a river a few miles outside Kofu. It was quiet and just picturesque enough to make the idea of three tourists staying there plausible, but small enough that any strangers asking about them would stand out as much as they did. A local train could have them in Kofu in a matter of minutes or take them up to the mountain shrines of Minobu.

"How did they react to you?" Kumi asked.

"That was the weird thing," said Thomas. "Watanabe looked uneasy, even scared."

"It can't be because of what you've learned," said Kumi with a casualness that brought color to Thomas's cheeks. "We don't really know much of anything."

"You're working on that, are you?" said Thomas, his voice a little strident in the tiny, six-mat room, with its sliding paper-covered *shoji*.

"I have someone asking questions at the Philippine embassy, for what that's worth," she said, apparently missing his irritation. "They should be calling any time now, but I don't expect much given the way we've been stonewalled so far."

"Are you sure it was you they recognized?" said Jim. He was squatting shoeless on the floor, looking distant, monkish. "I mean, what if they thought you were someone else?"

"Like?" said Kumi, her eyes thoughtful.

"Ed," said Jim, his voice quiet, almost apologetic. "It wouldn't be the first time you'd been taken for him."

"But how would they have known Ed?" said Thomas.

"Satoh said Ed knew about a cross," said Jim. "You came here because something like that cross just appeared here. Is it possible that Ed somehow made the same connection?"

"But the find wasn't made till after his death," said Kumi.

But Thomas was watching the priest, his eyes hard.

"What he means," he said, "is that the cross is a fraud, that it was planted here, and that my brother was somehow involved. That's right, isn't it?"

"I'm just speculating," said Jim.

"Maybe you shouldn't."

"Maybe I should go back to Chicago," said Jim, levelly.

"Maybe you should."

"Oh, please," Kumi inserted. "Will you two grow up? He's

trying to help," she added to Thomas. "Gratitude might be the better way to go. And we won't get anywhere by dodging unpleasant possibilities."

"Do you think Ed would have been involved in anything like that?" Thomas demanded. Kumi sighed petulantly, irritated. "Do you?" he pressed.

"No," she conceded. "But he *was* in Japan. If he came out here he never said so to me, but I'm increasingly convinced he was keeping his cards pretty close to his chest. There was a lot he didn't tell me."

She studied the mat floor, suddenly disconsolate, and Thomas felt that the admission had cost her something, though he wasn't sure what.

"I should be able to find out," said Jim. "If Ed was here and was not being particularly secretive, the local clergy would know. He would have made contact. Or if a strange foreigner appeared in their church, they would remember."

"What if he skipped church?" said Thomas, dryly.

"Not something priests usually do," Jim responded in kind. "Certainly not priests like Ed. The Catholic congregations here are minute and all the priests are foreigners, mainly Xaverians from Italy but some Js too. There's no way he wouldn't have spoken to them unless he was completely undercover. Let me talk to the priests in Kofu."

"And I'll talk to Watanabe," said Kumi, abruptly rejoining the conversation as by an act of will.

"What makes you think you'll get anything out of him?" said Thomas.

"Well, for one thing, because he won't know I have any connection to you," she said. "I can play the native pretty well now. He won't even know I'm American."

"And for another thing?" Thomas prompted.

"Have you ever seen Watanabe without a demure and attentive starlet on his arm?"

"You're suggesting a honey trap?" said Thomas, incredulous. "No way."

Kumi smirked, amused both by his response and the idea that he could stop her.

"I just don't want you to get into trouble," said Thomas.

"Really?" she said. "Sure you wouldn't love to charge to my rescue on a white stallion? I'll fight my own battles, Tom. Always have."

Her phone rang. She answered it in Japanese and stepped into the corner, putting her hand over one ear to block out the sound of the room. Not that there was much. Jim was brooding to himself and Thomas, struck by the scent of the tatami, the familiar strangeness of rooms like this, was floating through memory to when he and Kumi had first met. They had spent months discovering precisely this kind of time-capsule hotel, wholly disconnected from the modern world outside. Everything within it had felt unique and magical, precious and irrelevant to the rest of their lives, like insects trapped in amber, like love.

Kumi's tone had become clipped and she was pacing as she tried to find a way back into the phone conversation. She pressed, beseeched even, within the polite constraints of formal Japanese, but it was clearly a lost cause, and when she hung up, she cursed. But there was more than frustration in her eyes, though few people besides Thomas would see it. She was unsettled, scared even.

"What?" said Thomas.

"My embassy contact," she said. She was very still after the pacing, as if deliberately reining in something powerful and chaotic. Thomas found his heart was beginning to race.

"And?" he said.

"No one is talking," she said, "and I've been told in no uncertain terms not to contact them again."

"So we've learned nothing new," Thomas sighed.

"One thing," she said, and she was quite pale now. "Nothing solid, only rumors. But the word is that Ed did not die in a car crash."

"I never believed that anyway, and Devlin said . . ."

"Tom," she said, cutting him off. "Listen. He wasn't the only one to die. There were maybe twenty or thirty local people killed at the same time, in the same place. None of them were terrorists. It was a bomb. A big one."

CHAPTER 70

Thomas woke the moment he hit the chill water, panic opening his eyes. His legs were drawn up to his chest and strapped in place with silver duct tape, his wrists lashed together behind him.

It took a moment for it to all come back to him.

He had been out for a walk to think, to get a little space. He had returned to the *ryokan,* letting himself in because Jim and Kumi were out. The woman who ran the place said there had been a *gaijin*—a foreigner—snooping about. Thomas had gone to his room, but someone had been already inside, waiting. He had been hit from behind, hard enough to plunge him into unconsciousness . . .

The shock and cold of the water made him cry out, a wordless gasp of terror as he fought to understand what was happening.

He was inside, in a tiled room with a sink and a central floor drain, and he had been dumped fully clothed into an *o-furo,* the square tub common to traditional Japanese bathrooms. He writhed and splashed as best he could, but he was secured with the duct tape and could barely move, let alone get out.

Standing over him, drenched and breathless from the exertion of getting him into the bath, was Parks. He was pointing that replica short sword squarely at Thomas's chest.

"Hi," he said. "You've been out for a while. Don't know my own strength."

He sounded chatty, even friendly, but there was an edge to

the remarks, as if he were only just resisting to the urge to slash the sword across his face.

"What the hell is this?" said Thomas. "Get me out of here."

"The Japanese have lots to teach us about personal hygiene, don't you think?"

"This is absurd," said Thomas, sitting on the bottom of the tub like an Egyptian cube statue while his captor loomed over him. He felt stupid and powerless. He blinked and swallowed. His mouth was dry, his stomach empty to the point of nausea, and his vision blurry. The blinking helped. He tried, stupidly, to rub his eyes, and Parks chuckled.

"Come on," said Thomas, his voice echoing flatly in the tiled room. "You have the weapon. Get me out of here."

"Right," said Parks, not moving. "Good idea. Especially since I'm so very stupid."

He leaned forward and Thomas flinched back, sure Parks would stab him with that purposeful blade, but he only chuckled again.

"The sword," Parks said, as if just noticing it in his hand. "It has a certain style, don't you think? And firearms are so hard to get in Japan, you know. Satoh had a gun. You wanna see it?"

He reached behind him and produced a small black automatic, casually pointing it at Thomas's face.

"Neat, isn't it?" he said. "Heavier than it looks. He didn't take it to Italy because it would be difficult to get it through airport security, and he didn't know that the paranoid loser brother of another paranoid loser would try to gut him like a fish."

The core accusation took a moment to register in Thomas's mind, and another moment for the extent of his danger to strike home.

"You think *I* killed Satoh?" he said.

"I gotta say, I was surprised," said Parks. "Didn't think you had it in you. Didn't think old Satoh would give you the option. The man had skills, you know?"

"This is a mistake," said Thomas. "I didn't kill him."

"Italian police think you did," said Parks.

"They are wrong," said Thomas, more urgently. "The man who killed Satoh died in Bari. He had tracked me there. We fought on the walls of the castle and he fell."

"Another victim, huh?" said Parks, mock impressed. "Quite the serial killer, aren't you. And let's not forget old Monsignor Pietro. Wouldn't tell you what you wanted to know, huh?"

"This is crazy," said Thomas. "I found Satoh dead. I found Pietro dying. The killer was still around both times. The second time he tried to kill me too."

"But you survived where a black belt martial artist didn't," said Parks. "Sounds plausible, English teachers being famed for their survival skills. And then you killed the guy who did it on some castle in . . . ?"

"Bari," said Thomas. His mouth was dry. He tried flexing his wrists, but the tape wouldn't budge and the slightest movement made giveaway ripples. He thought the water was warmer than it had been.

"Bari," said Parks. "Right."

He stood up and walked away for a moment, turning his back, confident Thomas couldn't move.

"So here's what we do now," he announced. "We talk, or rather, you do."

"About what?"

"You can start by talking about this."

Carefully he laid something down on the tabletop, stood up, and watched Thomas's eyes. It was the silver votive shaped like a fish.

"What am I supposed to say about that?" said Thomas.

"Where did you get it? Where did it come from?"

"I didn't get it," said Thomas, irritated. "As you well know. It was in Ed's room in Chicago. I had barely noticed it before you came in and stole it. The next time I saw it was when the police showed it to me in Italy, among Satoh's things. How did you get it back?"

"This is a different one," he said. "You will have noticed by now that the water you are sitting in is getting warmer. Marvelous things, *o-furo,* don't you think? It has a heater built right into the bath, gas in this case. Leave it on long enough and the water will boil. The controls are, of course, well outside your reach. So, tell me about Ed's silver fish. Where did it come from? Originally. Where was it made and when?"

"How the hell should I know?" said Thomas. He could hear the gas heater now, feel the water warming quickly all around him. "You aren't listening to me. I know nothing about that thing. NOTHING. All I know is that Ed was interested in religious images of fish with oversized fins. I heard there was supposed to be a silver cross with one of those fish on it. Satoh told me about it, but I was skeptical. Now there's talk of a similar cross here in a grave about eight hundred years too early. Does it sound like an odd coincidence? Sure, but that's about as far as my insight goes. Okay? I don't know anything about it. Now how about you take this Goddamned tape off my wrists?"

He was playing up the righteous indignation a little, watching Parks's response, but his panic was showing through. The water was already hand hot and getting warmer by the moment.

"This one was bought in Bilbao, Spain," Parks said suddenly, looking at the fish. "It is silver."

"So why are you asking, if you already know where they come from?" Thomas demanded, shifting, trying to stir the water so that the heat that was building at the bottom would dissipate. He was starting to sweat.

"I didn't say where it came from. I said where it was *bought.* It's old and it's not from Spain. I think it was made in Mexico about three hundred years ago, and that it traveled to Spain as a lot of silver did in trade. What do you think of that?"

He was probing, trying to trigger a response. Thomas was getting desperate.

"I don't think anything of it," he said. "It means nothing to me. It came from Mexico? Oh. How interesting. Can I go now?"

The water was starting to steam.

"You know that the Smithsonian was sent a strange fish scale found in Florida in 1949? Like a coelacanth scale?"

Thomas had the fleeting idea that Parks was insane.

"No," he said. "I didn't know about that."

"Your brother did," said Parks, leaning in close, the pistol lolling casually from his hand. "Where did he die?"

"The Philippines," said Thomas. It was only later that he realized he had finally given Parks something he didn't already know. The man's eyes widened and his jaw dropped a little.

"*The Philippines,*" he repeated in an awed whisper. "Where in the Philippines?"

"I don't know," said Thomas.

Parks reached forward and dunked him hard so that his feet rocked up in front of him. His head tipped back under the scalding water, and through the pain came the sudden surety that if Parks didn't right him soon, he would drown.

He was dragged back into a sitting position and gasped the cool air. His skin was bright pink. A few more minutes and he would start to burn.

"That's all they told me," said Thomas. "Leave me in here as long as you like. That's all you'll get: the Philippines. For God's sake, get me out . . ."

But Parks was lost in thought, whispering *"The Philippines"* to himself like some odd, quizzical mantra. He seemed to have forgotten Thomas entirely, and when he did finally remember his presence Thomas found himself wishing to be ignored.

"You really don't know anything, do you?" Parks said with something like wonder. "All that poking around in Italy, and you still know nothing. Satoh said you would be useful, but . . ."

He shook his head, like a parent whose child has disappointed him one time too many. Then he raised the pistol again and aimed at Thomas's face.

CHAPTER 71

For a moment Thomas saw right into the gun's barrel and he felt only weakness and defeat. As he closed his eyes, the first lines of the old prayer came to him: "Out of the depths I cry to you, O Lord, Lord, hear my voice . . ." Then the deafening report of the gun . . .

Except that it wasn't the gun. The bang was made by the door behind him, clanging shut. Parks had gone.

The relief came out unbidden.

"Thank God," he said to the empty room, unsure whether that too was a prayer, or merely an expletive. But the soft hiss of the gas heater killed his relief before it could flower. The water was approaching boiling. Parks had left him to die.

He fought against his bonds, hoping that the hot water had loosened them, dissolved the glue on the tape . . . something. But nothing gave. He could barely see through the steam. He didn't know how much longer he could stay conscious. He fought to stand up, but the tape bound him too securely.

He rolled as best he could and got his head under the faucet above the tub. If he could use his teeth to turn the cold-water faucet on, he might buy himself some time. As he got into position he began shouting for help in English and Japanese. His shrill cries bounced around the tiled room, making him recoil, but he kept shouting.

Then the door burst open.

For a moment he thought it would be Parks, come to finish the job, but it was Kumi, followed by Jim. Without hesitating she plunged her hands into the scalding water and hauled him as far out as she could. Jim got his arms underneath him and between them they dragged him out.

"Parks." Thomas gasped.

Kumi, silent and focused as always in crisis mode, turned the cold tap onto him, while Jim used a penknife to slit the duct tape apart. Thomas sprawled on the blessedly cool tiles, barely able to speak.

Jim considered the steaming tub.

"I admire your desire to go native, Thomas," he said. "But in future, I'd stick to showers."

"On behalf of the Japanese people," said Kumi, who had sunk exhausted onto the wet floor, "I'd like to point out that the duct tape is not traditional."

CHAPTER 72

Security was tight at the excavation, and journalists were being admitted only in small, guided groups and then not into the chamber proper, which was considered too fragile for non-professionals to be traipsing through. When all evidence had been gleaned from the inside of the tomb it would be opened to the public, but that could take months.

Thomas was still wearing his faked credentials, and since the guards seemed intimidated by non-Japanese documents, he was admitted to the tour without undue scrutiny. There was no sign of the New Zealander.

In fact, there was little to see outside the tomb itself, and the briefing was clearly being handled by junior staff. The burial mound had, apparently, been known for some time and had been duly fenced off. The first discovery that Watanabe and his team had made, however, when they had begun the excavation three weeks ago, was that the tomb was considerably larger than had been suspected. The visible mound had turned out to be only the top of the tomb, whose actual perimeter extended far beyond the fence inside which the assembled journalists now stood.

The tomb, said their guide—a slight, earnest woman who introduced herself as Miss Iwamoto—had eight sides.

"As you can see," she said, "it is quite large. Each side is almost thirty meters long, though they were largely buried under the earth with only the top of the mound visible. Most of the Kofun tombs are distinctly keyhole-shaped, so the eight-sided variety are quite rare. In the early Kofun period the body was usually buried at the top of the mound, but in later tombs like this—which date from the seventh century AD—the body was buried in a stone-lined chamber under the mound. The chamber was accessible via a passage over here," she pointed, "called *yokoana* chambers. If you step this way you can see that the *yokoana* was once painted, though it is difficult to make out the subject of the painting. Watanabe-*sensei* will try to determine its content in the course of his analysis."

They moved silently with her to the stone-lined opening. Work lights had been set up inside, but they were dark and only the mouth of the tomb's inner chamber was visible.

"In this case," she said, gesturing to a glass-topped display box that had been set up beside the roped-off passage, "you can see some of the ceramics that were buried with the dead man. Also found inside were mirrors, beads, a sword, and some horse equipment. These are being analyzed and are not on display. You can see some of the *haniwa* which were often found on Kofun burials, though their purpose is unclear."

The objects she pointed to were clay cylinders propped up against the walls.

"About two hundred were found on the tomb, mostly plain, but some were figures of animals and men."

"Is it true that there were animals living inside?" asked one of the journalists who had been looking thoroughly bored by all the archaeology.

Thomas expected Miss Iwamoto to be disparaging of what was obviously an attempt to Disney-fy the story, but she seemed to brighten and grow considerably younger as she replied.

"A family of *tanuki*—a Japanese animal a little like the raccoon—had been living in the main chamber," she said.

They are so cute. But very mischievous animals. Watanabe-*sensei*'s team are hoping they have not damaged the remains."

"Where is the cross?" asked Thomas. He was losing patience.

"It is being studied at Watanabe-*sensei*'s laboratory. It will be put on display when tests are completed."

So what the hell am I doing here? Thomas wondered. He turned to leave but found that the previously apathetic security guard had become very focused. On him. At his elbow was the blank-faced graduate student from the press conference. They were both coming toward him.

After the scares of Italy, Thomas was ready for anything. The worst they would do was ask him to leave. He braced himself.

"Excuse me, sir?" said the student. "Can I get your name, please?"

"Jenkins," said Thomas. "Peter Jenkins."

"What news agency are you with?" said the student, ostentatiously scanning a clipboard of names. His English was good, his gaze level, his tone neutral.

"I'm with the *New Zealand Herald*," said Thomas. "I left my card in the van."

Watanabe's assistant—his nametag read TETSUYA MATSUHASHI—watched him unblinkingly for a second and Thomas was sure he didn't buy it.

"You don't appear to be on the list," he said. He was calm, even pleasant, but Thomas had no idea what he was thinking. "All credentialed reporters must carry their paperwork on them at all times. I'm afraid I must ask you to leave."

Thomas shrugged. He wasn't learning anything here anyway. As he walked away from the huddled journalists and the great burial mound, the student called after him.

"And, Mr. Jenkins, the security perimeter will be more carefully restricted in future. This is a very valuable site and we don't want things going astray. I'm sure you understand."

"Sure," said Thomas. "Where is Mr. Watanabe?"

"At his laboratory in the city," said Matsuhashi, but his eyes flickered toward the trailer parked beside the edge of the site. "Archaeology is not all glamour in the field. There is a lot of time spent on tedious tests."

"Tests on materials from this site?"

"Mainly," said the student, "but he is a very busy man and this is not the only site he is studying."

"Anything from overseas?" said Thomas.

Matsuhashi's face shaded. "Not usually," he said. He seemed uncertain, hesitant.

"But recently?"

"A couple of crates arrived for him some weeks ago," said Matsuhashi briskly. "For his expert opinion."

"From?"

"I don't know. Is there something on your mind, Mr . . . ?"

"Jenkins," said Thomas, smiling. "No. Just curious. Have you seen inside the crates?"

"I expect it's Kofun pottery," said Matsuhashi, his eyes steady.

"My name isn't Jenkins," Thomas blurted suddenly. "It's Knight. My brother was a priest. Did you know him?"

"Knight?" said Matsuhashi, his face glazed like a ceramic mask. "No, I did not know him. Now, if you don't mind . . ."

Thomas nodded, smiled, and walked away, sure the other man was watching him all the way out, sure also that he was lying.

When he got back to the *ryokan* he heard Jim muttering in his room and slid the paneled screen aside. The priest was squatting on the tatami beside a low table, on the other side of which Kumi knelt, her weight on her calves in formal Japanese fashion. There was a bottle of local wine beside the table and a plate of crusty bread.

"I leave you peace, my peace I give you," he was saying. "Look not on our sins but on the faith of your church and in your mercy keep us free from sin and protect us from all anxiety . . ."

He looked up at Thomas.

"Mass," he said. "You're welcome to join us if . . ."

But Thomas was already shaking his head and sliding the door closed.

CHAPTER 73

The name on his passport was Harvey Erickson, and it identified him as blind. He wore large sunglasses with heavily tinted and slightly mirrored lenses, a long copious overcoat, and equally copious facial hair. His teeth were bright and even, his hands gloved with fawn calfskin that relinquished their hold on his red-tipped white cane only when he was sitting.

He had passed the flight and subsequent train ride in almost complete stillness, ignoring flight attendants as if they were not there, speaking barely a dozen words in the last twenty-four hours, proffering tickets and identification when requested in silence. He sensed that people avoided him even with their eyes, but he liked his solitude so that was all to the good.

He didn't like Japan with its strange smells and noises, but he tapped his way along the sidewalk, listening to the way the crosswalks sang their cheery electronic prompts anchored in old melodies, until he found his way to a cheap hotel in a corner of the town cluttered with bars, pool halls, and timbered *yakitori* houses. By nightfall the streets were quiet except where dubious women lured drunken, red-faced "salarymen" inside for the kinds of pleasures he would never experience.

That was okay too. He had other sources of amusement.

He stood in front of the bathroom mirror, minus the coat and gloves, and removed the heavy glasses with his long pale fingers, catching the way his irises contracted in the low but sudden light. Playing blind had been no great hardship, and as well as granting him a particular kind of anonymity, it had allowed him the darkness he preferred. He slid the wig from his bald skull and peeled away the beard, rubbing the spirit gum away as his familiar features took shape again. The cut across his scalp had closed, and most of the bruising had faded to a slightly metallic shadow.

Lastly he grimaced into the mirror, his lips pulled back from his teeth like a snarling dog, and dislodged the molded dentures, revealing the filed points of his own teeth beneath them. He flicked a pink, wet tongue and hissed at his reflection with something like pleasure.

Famine was back.

CHAPTER 74

Jim was waiting in a white Toyota sedan on the road outside the dig. The press had largely drifted away, and only a few starstruck groupies remained.

"Is Watanabe here?" said Thomas.

"The girls think so," said Jim. "I suspect they would know best."

"His assistant—Matsuhashi—said he was at the lab in Kofu. Didn't want me to see him."

"I might have some idea as to why," said Jim.

"Ed came to Kofu? Oh, my prophetic soul."

"For at least two days," said Jim. "About ten days before he died. He introduced himself at the local church, ate with them, said mass at least once, stayed overnight."

"So not exactly an undercover visit," said Thomas. "What on earth was he doing?"

"He must have come to the site."

"It seems so," said Thomas, "but there was no site then. The find wasn't made till after he died. What brought him here?"

"Got me," said Jim. "So what do we do now?"

"We wait," said Thomas. "Keep an eye open for the esteemed archaeologist."

There was a long silence.

"Back in Chicago you said you were a missionary," said Thomas.

"So?"

"Why does America need a missionary?"

"American Catholics put too much faith in faith."

Thomas frowned.

"It's not just about what you believe," said Jim. "It's about how you act, how you live the gospel, and I don't mean in the way you police other people's morality. Ed understood that. Some priests can be great blokes while you're watching the game, but as soon as religion comes up they put their holy hats on. All they have to offer are rules and sanctimonious platitudes. Not Ed. He got it."

"Got what?"

Jim thought for a moment. "Being a Christian means being one with the poor and the oppressed. We share their bodies as Christ shared his. We participate in their lives, in their social conditions, their political and economic environment."

Thomas looked at him. He remembered what Hayes had said about an eviction and wondered if Jim's principles had recently been put to the test. He wanted to ask about it, but more immediate concerns were pressing.

"Look," said Jim.

It was beginning to get dark outside. The last of the journalists had been bussed out, and the translator, Miss Iwamoto, was opening the door of her own white car, casting a blank look at the three women who still lingered hopefully outside the hastily erected chain-link fence. Matsuhashi had emerged from the trailer and was talking to the night-duty security guard, who nodded, as if receiving orders. Then the girls were being shepherded out of the compound toward the road, looking disconsolate. All but one.

"I guess someone is going to get lucky after all," Thomas muttered with weary distaste.

Matsuhashi opened the trailer door and the remaining girl, a willowy Japanese woman in a black cocktail dress, her hair down, gave him a minuscule bow and stepped into the rectangle of light from the doorway. Matsuhashi, his final duty of the day performed, nodded his farewell to the security guard and walked down to the lone car left on the gravel drive. The woman went in, turning outward only to close the door behind her.

It was Kumi.

Thomas put his shoulder to the car door in a flurry of expletives, but Jim reached over to restrain him.

"You knew?" Thomas spat. "You knew that was her? What she was doing?"

"She told me not to tell you," said Jim.

"Yes, I can see how that would ethically trump any other moral concerns," roared Thomas. "That's my wife!"

"Ex," said Jim.

"Oh, well that makes it all right, doesn't it, *Father?*"

"She's doing it for you," said Jim. "And, as she said, she can look after herself. She won't do anything . . . unsavory."

"Unsavory?" Thomas shouted back. "The whole thing is unsavory."

"She's going to see if she can get him to reveal anything . . ."

"I think that's a given, don't you?" snarled Thomas.

"Information," said Jim. "And while she's in there, he is conveniently occupied. So I'm going to drive you to the lab in Kofu and give you a chance to poke around there. I'll come back here. Kumi got us a couple of those card-operated cell phones. Here. It's already programmed. She can call us if she needs us."

"And you'll charge in like the cavalry in a Goddamned dog collar, will you?"

"Hopefully not damned," said Jim. He started the engine. "Okay?"

Thomas sighed. "Just get back here fast," he said.

Kumi had done her research. The girls outside had been younger than her, but too obvious and tawdry in their dress and manner to have had a chance. She had spent an hour or two poring over the online sketches of her celebrity target in *Shukan Shincho*, *Shukan Bunshun*, and other tabloid weeklies. Watanabe liked a touch of class, or the appearance of it, and he liked a challenge, if only because his inevitable conquest appealed to his vanity. There was no whisper that he forced the agenda if he didn't get what he wanted, though she suspected that rarely happened.

He was wearing tight black jeans with a large silver belt buckle modeled on a Navajo design, alligator boots, and a collarless white silk shirt open at the neck, sleeves folded loosely at the cuffs and pushed up to the elbows. He wore blue-tinted glasses and smoked with a studied coolness as he acknowledged her entrance. He didn't need to look at her too closely right now. Matsuhashi had made the invitation, but Watanabe had made the choice.

Kumi entered carefully, opting for smaller, more graceful movements than was her norm, letting her eyes bounce around the surprisingly luxuriant trailer with a carefully judged blend of shyness and coquetry. It was all out of her character, but she was used to playing roles in her line of work, albeit not usually this grotesque, as foreigners—female foreigners in particular—were bound to if they were to succeed among Tokyo's "*salary*men."

Watanabe made a bobbing bow and babbled his *dozos* and welcomes and slick compliments with a clumsiness that was almost endearing. For all his stardom, he wooed like most of the Japanese men she had known, with a boyish awkwardness that tempted her to lower her guard. He offered cigarettes, which she declined, and champagne, which she accepted.

They spoke in Japanese. She had no intention of revealing her background and had the language facility to mask it. She could not convincingly embrace a Japanese regional dialect, but the woman she was playing would do everything in her power to suppress such limiting ordinariness, so she figured that would pose no problem. She was the slick Tokyoite visiting a college friend who worked for NHK. She had seen him at the press conference and had been . . . intrigued. He smiled, gratified, and said he didn't recall seeing her there.

"I didn't want you to see me until I had decided what I was going to do," she lied easily.

"And what are you going to do?" he said, enjoying the game.

"Have a drink," she said, cool, giving nothing away, but doing so with a frank look right into his shaded eyes.

Delighted, he clinked his glass against hers and sipped.

For ten minutes she made small talk, let him make his incremental flirtations while keeping her distance physically, maintaining a very Japanese reserve without shutting him down. Then she led the conversation around to the dig, emphasizing how interested she was, how impressive it all made him. Her persona wouldn't praise him directly, but praising his work did the job nicely. He didn't want to get off track, but seemed to recognize that this was the route to greater intimacy, and began to talk about the site, how he came upon the first artifacts, what struck him as unique about the bones . . . Carefully, discreetly, without shedding her restrained calculation, Kumi grew keen and wide-eyed, rewarding his casual preening with a brush of his hand with hers.

"What about the rest of your team?" she said. "Do they work too, or do they just schedule your groupies?"

He laughed at her frankness.

"Matsuhashi is a student of mine," he said. "Not a great archaeologist, but very loyal. Scientists don't have bodyguards, but he does the job well enough."

"He is very imposing," said Kumi.

"You don't know the half of it," Watanabe confided, refilling her glass. "He's a ninth-degree black belt in *tae kwon do* and *shim soo do*. That's Korean sword stuff. Did some prison time before embracing archaeology."

He waved his arms suddenly, half imitation, half parody, and squawked like Bruce Lee before lapsing into helpless giggles.

"Does he protect you?" Kumi pressed. "Make sure no one gets in your way?"

"I don't need him for that," said Watanabe, dismissively. He was getting more obvious as the alcohol took hold. "I can look after myself. And I have other friends. Powerful people."

"I'm sure," she said.

"That's right," he said, removing his shades and leaning into her, staring into her eyes with desire and a hint of menace.

CHAPTER 75

Watanabe's office was in the Yamanashi Archaeological Institute, a low-slung concrete affair with a brown pebble-dash finish and a slab roof that might have passed for architecturally intriguing in the sixties but now looked merely shabby and a little squat: a blockish toad crouched on the edge of the town as if unwelcome. He had university-loaned spaces in Tokyo and Osaka for when he was doing fieldwork close by, but this was where he spent most of his time, in easy striking distance of the Kofun sites that had become the center of his career.

Thomas got out of the car a couple of blocks before the facility and walked the rest of the way, a baseball cap pulled low. Yamanashi was no Tokyo, and foreigners still stood out.

"Get back to Kumi," he said to Jim. "If anything happens to her . . ."

"Go," said Jim, handing him a flashlight from the glove

compartment. "Classes will be finishing up. It's the perfect time for you to get in."

He walked through a park where the cherry blossoms were just opening and waited there for three long minutes before students began to emerge from the building. He pushed through the glass doors, head lowered, walking fast.

There were no more than eight faculty on staff judging by the office listings, two of whom were part time. Two of the other six were away on digs, one was on sabbatical, one more away at a conference. Watanabe, the school's celebrity, was elsewhere, which meant that only one full-time teacher was working at the moment. He located the classroom on the second floor and waited.

Within a minute, the last of the students began filing out. Thomas got a look at the teacher—a small, middle-aged woman with a hawkish look and outlandish horn rims—and then stooped to his backpack so that she wouldn't notice him as she walked by en route to her office. Thomas tailed her carefully, slipping into a bathroom down the hallway from her room. When he heard the door open and close a second time he glanced out in time to see the teacher taking her coat and bag, fishing in her pocket for keys as she left for the day.

A janitor would be making the rounds at some point, and maybe a graduate student or two using the labs to complete research, but he hadn't seen sign of any so far, and was fairly sure he had the place to himself. So far as he could tell there were no security cameras or any surveillance devices except a motion-activated security lamp in the parking lot. It was clear.

Watanabe's office was on the same hall. He tried the handle, but the door didn't move. It was the only door in the building with two locks, one in the handle and a deadbolt above it. Thomas had no secret skill with such things, no knack with hairpins, no magical electronic devices that would send the deadbolt snapping back, but he knew what was studied in this building and, after a brief consideration of the door's strength, he started trying every other door he could find.

A janitor's closet was unlocked, but he found nothing useful there. Next was a disused office full of old furniture and over-stuffed filing cabinets. Then he found the storeroom he was looking for, made his selections, and returned to Watanabe's office.

Kumi pulled back, putting a single finger on his advancing lips and pushing him playfully away.

"Patience," she said. "Things are always better when you have to wait."

"Depends on how long you have to wait," said Watanabe. It was grudging, but he sat back, even managed a smile.

"You must travel a lot in your line of work," she said. "Tell me about it."

She offered the subject as another stage of the game, one that would seduce him still further.

"I spend a lot of time in Korea," he said.

She grunted dismissively.

"Nowhere more exotic?" she said. "Europe? France? Italy?"

His eyes narrowed, hardened, and he seemed to shed his drunken clumsiness. Kumi backpedaled.

"I've never been," she cooed. "Prague. I hear Prague is beautiful. I'd love to go there. Or Vienna."

"I've been to Italy," he said, relaxing. "It's dirty. Ugly. Naples especially."

Kumi tried to keep the flicker of excitement out of her face. He was watching closely.

It wasn't going to be subtle, and it wasn't going to be quiet, but Thomas was going to get in. He slid the bit of the mattock he had found in the closet into the crack of the doorjamb and used the long handle as a lever. The wood of the frame began to splinter immediately. He adjusted the position of the bit and tried the same movement again. The entire frame rippled and bucked, tearing half an inch away from the wall. With the flat edge of the mattock he pushed, prized, wrenched, until there was a pile of wooden fragments at his feet, and the door finally yielded to a jolt from his shoulder.

It juddered open, revealing a spacious, utilitarian office containing a metal desk with a computer, phone, fax, and a series of heavy steel filing cabinets. There was also a long table arrayed with boxes, tubs of chemicals, a pair of microscopes, and assorted other equipment that Thomas could not name.

The window blind was down. Thomas closed the slats, shut the door as best he could, and switched on first the flashlight, then the computer. While it warmed up he searched the room quickly, unsure what exactly he was looking for. The filing cabinets were all locked, and he doubted he would get into them with the mattock. A stack of packing cases stood in the corner behind the door, two of them large and wooden, containing only wood shavings, the shipping labels carefully stripped off.

One of the desk drawers was unlocked. It contained a series of folders each holding stacks of paper covered in numbers and formulas, and in Japanese far too technical for Thomas to decipher. One folder, however, contained numbers keyed, it seemed, to three different samples, identified by the number and letter combinations 4F, 12A, and 21A, the first page of each beginning with the equation:

$$D^2 i,j = (x_i-x_j)^2 \, Pw^{-1} \, (x_i-x_j)$$

x_i = vector of values for individual i,

x_j = mean vector for population j,

Pw = pooled within-sample covariance matrix

Thomas stared at the numbers and the formula, but could make nothing of them beyond the fact that the numbers looked like measurements in millimeters.

But measurements of what?

The next folder contained graphs, and numbers, apparently for a larger set of samples, only some of which reappeared in the other folder. With these there was a cover letter, in English, dated March 10, from a company called Beta Analytics in Miami, Florida. The pertinent information seemed to be a column of data keyed to sample numbers: 250±75 BP (BETA-895) [Sample 1A], 1000±75 BP (BETA-896) [Sample 1B], right through to 200±75 BP (BETA-909) [Sample 25D].

Thomas read over the numbers twice, looking for a pattern, or something, anything, that would make some kind of sense to him, but it was hopeless. The symbol in the middle of each data cluster resembled a cross, but it was surely a margin-of-error marker. 250 plus or minus 75. But 250 what?

Years?

Perhaps. But what did "BP" mean?

He just didn't have the knowledge or skills. For what seemed like the hundredth time since Ed died, he felt completely out of his depth.

CHAPTER 76

"What were you doing in Naples?" asked Kumi.

"Research," said Watanabe.

"Archaeology?"

"Not really," he said, losing interest in the subject. "Tourist stuff, mainly. Just looking around."

"Anything in particular? Renaissance? Ancient Roman?"

There was that look again, cagy, watchful. Kumi sipped her champagne.

"Just looking around," he repeated.

"Do you have your own collection?" she said, shifting tack. "Ancient artifacts?"

"Some," he said.

"Valuable?" she asked, feigning an almost erotic excitement.

"Some," he said again, smiling. "Very."

"Where do you keep them?"

"At home. I could drive you over if you like . . . ?"

The question hung in the air for a moment as Kumi thought. In answer, she drained her glass and stood up.

Something was bothering Matsuhashi. Not that there was anything new about that. The last six months had planted more nagging anxieties in the back of his mind than he had experienced in the first twenty-four years of his life. But this was different. It was tugging at him, just out of earshot, like a voice over a badly tuned radio that faded in and out before you could grasp the words.

Like a memory.

It was something to do with Knight, with both the Knights, in fact: the dead priest, and his brother who was pretending to be a journalist.

He turned the TV off, snapped open a can of Kirin, and flipped open his laptop. He typed in the URL for Edward Knight's church, hoping it hadn't been updated yet. It had. The new guy was there now, Jim Gornall, and there was an obituary for Knight with requests for prayers. Some of the old images had been collected into a little tribute album, and Matsuhashi set it to slideshow as he sipped his beer. The pictures came up for five seconds at a time: Knight with a youth group in casual clothes, Knight with the bishop at a confirmation, Knight saying mass in vestments of green and gold, Knight with a hammer on a Habitat for Humanity building site, Knight presiding over a wedding . . .

Wait. Go back.

He stopped the slideshow and studied the image: Edward Knight, perhaps five years younger than when Matsuhashi had seen him last, and the happy couple, the groom looking oddly like him as only a brother can, and the bride . . .

He picked up the phone and dialed, his eyes straying back to the computer screen.

Watanabe closed the trailer door as the phone began to ring inside.

"You need to get that?" asked Kumi.

"Nah," he said, aiming the Mercedes key fob at the car till the alarm system chirped and the doors unlocked.

"Good," she said. "I don't like being upstaged."

He grinned and escorted her to the car, opening the passenger door with a bow of mock chivalry.

Kumi climbed in. Watanabe had just closed the door and was walking around to the other side when she heard his cell phone go off. Through the driver's side window she saw him hold it up and consider the incoming number. He sighed, mouthed "work" through the window and raised the phone to his ear.

The computer was, not surprisingly, password protected. Frustrated and antsy, Thomas logged on as a workstation user, went online, and pulled up his e-mail. As he did so, he fished in his pocket for a card, steeled himself, and picked up the phone, hoping he remembered the country code sequence. It rang three times before she answered.

"Deborah," he said, "this is Thomas Knight."

He thought he heard her draw in her breath, but she said nothing.

"I know this is unexpected, and you probably have heard all sorts of things about me, but I assure you . . ."

"I know you didn't kill those people," said Deborah. She sounded not so much sure as decisive, as if she had taken a dive from a high board and knew that any faltering now would lead only to disaster.

Another leap of faith.

"Thank you," he said. "Can you pull up that picture you sent me? The one from the article about the Japanese site?"

"Hold on," she said.

He opened the image and considered it.

"Could you date it?" said Thomas, staring at the glowing image of the silver cross with the legged fish in the center.

"Not reliably, not from a picture. Stylistically I would say it was medieval, European, possibly seventh or eighth century."

"And the fish?"

There was a pause.

"I see it," was all she said.

"And?"

"What are you asking me, Thomas?"

"I'm asking if this could have come from the grave site you've been excavating in Paestum. You said you thought it had been picked over before you got there. Could this have come from that grave?"

"I can't make that kind of assessment based on a picture, Thomas," she said, her voice rising. "Thomas, if you start saying that this cross came from my site in Italy, you are making a very serious accusation against the Japanese archaeologist who claims to have found the piece there. You just can't do that without real evidence. It's potentially slanderous."

"Could it have come from the Paestum grave?"

"You aren't listening . . ."

"I am, and I appreciate your caution on my behalf, but just tell me. The possibility must have occurred to you or you wouldn't have sent me the article! Could this cross have been looted from the Paestum site?"

"It matches the crosses painted on the tomb slabs. The fish is an unusual detail because of the oversized front fins. I haven't seen anything like it outside this region and nowhere else in Christian art. That still doesn't mean the Japanese site is a hoax. Maybe there was some kind of early evangelical movement we don't know about that originated in Italy but traveled to Japan . . ."

"No," said Thomas. "It's all wrong. There's something going on, something big. Ed found out about it. He must have."

"I thought the Japanese guy who was killed . . ."

"Satoh," said Thomas.

"I thought he said the cross was from Herculaneum?" she said.

"But that's too early, isn't it?" said Thomas. "I think he was lying, trying to feed me a line that would make me look for it harder, push me to learn what he had not been able to."

"Thomas, listen to me," said Deborah. "If you are getting close to what got Ed killed, they—whoever they are—will know. You need to get out of there before you get yourself killed."

"Maybe," said Thomas. "Not yet."

Jim was freaking out. When the trailer door had opened, he had breathed a sigh of relief. Kumi had got through the ordeal okay, maybe had learned something useful, and was now out and safe. Then Watanabe had followed her out and together they had gotten into his swanky Merc, but not before the archaeologist had taken a cell phone call.

Jim was parked across the street and the light was bad, but he had seen the look on Watanabe's face, the way he checked back to where Kumi was sitting in the car, waiting for him, the way he stepped away from the vehicle to finish his phone call. And then, when he had joined her inside, there was something about the way he spun his wheels as he pulled quickly away that seemed more than machismo.

She was in danger. He felt it in his bones. He didn't know how her cover had been blown, but it had, and now everything was falling apart.

He swung the rented Toyota out into the street and followed, fumbling in his pocket for the cell phone.

* * *

"What about the bones?" said Thomas to Deborah. "The Japanese site contains European bones that seem to date from the same period as the cross. Could they have come from the Paestum grave?"

"No," she said, and now she was definitive, the former gray, cautious note in her voice quite gone. "Bones don't survive in Paestum. The site has been too wet for too long. No human bones have survived from the occupied period."

"So he would have to have gotten them from somewhere else," said Thomas. The idea hit him immediately. "Pietro assumed that Satoh was the man he had called Tanaka, but what if he wasn't? What if the monsignor had met an entirely different Japanese man who was calling himself Tanaka?"

"Watanabe?" said Deborah, incredulous.

" '*Took him inside,*' " said Thomas, Pietro's words echoing through him. "That's what he said before he died. It was all his fault, he said. He took Tanaka inside."

"Inside where?"

"The Fontanelle," said Thomas. "And, knowingly or otherwise, Pietro gave Watanabe what he needed."

"Oh my God," said Deborah, revulsion and outrage audible over the telephone line's muffling distance.

"He had several crates arrive a few weeks before the Kofun find. His assistant hasn't seen inside them. I got the impression that was unusual."

"You think they contained . . . ?"

"Bones," said Thomas. "Yes."

There was a momentary silence, then Thomas said, "Can I describe some lab results to you: see if you can help me make sense of them?"

"Sure," she said.

Matsuhashi moved quietly across the darkening forecourt. The front doors of the Yamanashi lab were still open, as his teacher had feared. Anyone could be inside. Of course, they weren't concerned about anyone. They were concerned about Knight.

There had been no car parked outside but that meant nothing. The graduate student walked quickly, silently, along the ground-floor corridor to the stairs. All the lights were out, which was probably as well. He palmed the knife in his pocket and stalked softly down to where a crack of light showed through the splintered jamb of Watanabe's office door. He moved soundlessly, like an assassin.

CHAPTER 77

"Does the name Beta Analytics mean anything to you?" said Thomas.

"Yeah," said Deborah. "They're a testing lab in Florida. The museum used them once when CAIS in Athens was over capacity. They are fast."

"What kind of testing do they do?"

"Radiocarbon dating. Why?"

"So Watanabe was trying to determine the age of something. What does BP mean?"

"Before Present," said Deborah. "Though it really means 'before 1950.'"

So the numbers were years counted back from 1950, plus or minus 75.

"Okay," said Thomas, "listen to this." He looked at the column of data, but the cell phone in Thomas's pocket vibrated suddenly.

"Hold on," he said to Deborah, putting the phone on the desk. "Yes?" he said into the cell.

It was Jim.

"Watanabe has got Kumi in his car. He might know who she is."

Thomas leaped to his feet and started moving toward the fractured door at the exact moment that it cannoned in on him. It hit him square in the face, sending him sprawling backward as Matsuhashi burst in, launching himself directly at Thomas. The bluish light of the computer screen flashed briefly along the blade in his hand, and the cell phone flew from Thomas's palm as the two men connected.

Thomas was completely overwhelmed. The other man was younger, stronger, skilled, and prepared for the fight. Even without the knife he would have been too much for him. The student pinned him easily, straddling him, holding his arms in place with one hand and one knee so that his knife hand stayed free and controlled. Thomas had nothing left but his voice.

"It's too late, Matsuhashi," he said, unnecessarily loud.

The Japanese man glanced at the phone on the desk, saw it was off the hook, and clicked the phone cradle with one hand. Then he picked up the fallen cell phone, pocketed it, and returned to the desk phone, dialing without taking his eyes off Thomas.

"You are in a lot of trouble," he said, almost casually.

Thomas drew himself up into a sitting position, confused.

"You too," he said.

"I doubt that," the other smiled.

"I told you," said Thomas. "I know about the whole thing."

The student paused and let the phone click back into place. His expression was difficult to read, but something was there, beneath the surface amusement, that was . . . what?

Curious? Apprehensive?

Maybe.

"Your boss should lock all his files away better," said Thomas, testing his left wrist where the other man had knelt on it.

"What is it that you think you know?" said the student. "If it's interesting, maybe I won't hand you over to the police."

The police? In the circumstances, Thomas would be delighted to merely be arrested for breaking and entering. Something was odd. Maybe Matsuhashi really didn't know.

And maybe he just wants to learn whatever you have found out before he slits your throat.

"I already told my friend what I found out," he lied.

"No, you did not," said Matsuhashi. "I timed my entrance carefully."

"She knows enough to ask some very embarrassing questions," said Thomas.

"About what?" He was getting irritable now, thinking Thomas was just playing games.

Thomas nodded toward the files on the desk.

"Results from the radiocarbon tests," he said.

"So?" said Matsuhashi. "We do such tests all the time."

"On European bones?" said Thomas. He was taking a chance now. His throat felt tight, his mouth dry.

"Those tests have not yet been performed," said Matsuhashi. "The bones from the tomb are being prepared for testing. It takes time."

"I don't mean those tests, the ones he'll tell the press about. I mean the ones he has already done."

"What are you talking about?"

"See for yourself," said Thomas. "Performed, and the results delivered ten days before the Kofun burial 'find.' "

Matsuhashi stared at him. He took the documents off the desk slowly, one eye on Thomas, and pored over them. His face clouded, then froze. When he looked up again his whole body seemed jittery, flickering with nervous energy. He looked frantic, panicked, and when he spoke, it was defiant.

"These could be any sets of results. If you are suggesting some kind of fraud . . ."

"They aren't just any results, though, are they?" said Thomas. "They concern two crates of old bones imported—stolen in fact—from Italy, as was the silver cross. Watanabe brought the bones, but he didn't want to plant any that weren't old enough. The C-14 scan would reveal that too easily, and most of the bones in the Fontanelle were Renaissance and later. He had to sift through for the oldest fragments, ship them here, and then run the tests so he knew which bones were old enough to plant in a Kofun grave. It would be a sensational find! European bones a thousand years earlier than any discovered before? It would make his career."

Matsuhashi wasn't saying anything, wasn't looking at him. He was staring at the sheets of paper, his eyes wild.

"Only the bones that are dated around a thousand years before present would be old enough," said Thomas. "Those are the ones he planted in the Kofun tomb."

Matsuhashi didn't look up. He was checking and rechecking the numbers, flicking through the graphic readout, searching for a flaw.

"The other data," said Thomas, nodding at the pages with the formula and results in millimeters, "is a system for determining the racial origin of bones based on measurement. Yes?"

The other man nodded so fractionally that Thomas almost missed it.

"So Watanabe chose the bones that were old enough to fit the Kofun period," said Thomas, "then had their craniofacial features measured to be sure that they would be proven categorically European before he buried them."

"It is not possible," said Matsuhashi, still not looking up. "He is a great man. And this could not be done."

"Let me speak to my friend," said Thomas. "I think my wife is in danger."

But the other man didn't seem to hear him, and his grip on the knife did not slacken.

The car sped up.

"You live out here?" said Kumi, peering out the window to a grove of bamboo thick and tall as telegraph poles.

"Yes," said Watanabe simply.

She didn't believe it. Things had been going so well till the phone call, but since then she had felt him slide into himself. He didn't look at her, spoke only in monosyllables when she asked him something directly, and made no attempts at seduction.

Got to get out of the car . . .

CHAPTER 78

"If the site had been disturbed prior to the dig," said Matsuhashi, ignoring the way Thomas's eyes moved between the knife and the phone, "the team would be able to tell. The earth would not be properly compacted. It would look like filler."

"Maybe they did and decided to say nothing," said Thomas. "I'm going to speak to my friend on the cell phone now, okay?"

"NO," said Matsuhashi. "You don't know what you are talking about."

He began to shout in Japanese, raging, so that suddenly he was transformed and terrifying. His face locked into a widemouthed grimace. It took a second for Thomas to realize that he was crying.

"He is a great man," he whispered in English.

"Maybe so," said Thomas.

"Not maybe!" shouted Matsuhashi, and he looked young, his blustering anger quite empty.

"Okay," said Thomas, calming him. "But in this case, at least, he has not been honest."

He waited to see what defiance this would produce, but the young man looked merely surly and said nothing, though the tears ran down his cheeks. It was quite dark now and the Venetian blind glowed with a soft opalescence from the streetlamps outside. Thomas looked at the phone on the desk. He wondered where Jim was. Where Kumi was.

"Give me the knife," he said, "and let me talk to my friend."

Matsuhashi looked at the knife as if wondering how he came to be holding it. Carefully he set it on the desk.

"So," Thomas continued gently. "How did he get into the burial chamber without anyone realizing?"

There was a long silence, disturbed only by the student's trembling sobs.

"Maybe the *tanuki*," said Matsuhashi at last, sinking heavily onto the desk. He wiped his eyes and took a long uneven breath, suddenly quite calm so that Thomas felt the worst was past. But it still might be too late.

"What?" he asked, and there was a note of desperation in his own voice now.

"The site was penetrated by *tanuki*—a kind of animal. They opened a passage into the burial site. Entrance through there would perhaps go unnoticed . . ."

"Please let me call my friend," he said. "I need to make sure my wife is okay."

Matsuhashi turned to him and looked closely into his face. For a moment nothing happened.

"I will call," he said.

The car climbed out of the basin where Kofu sat, leaving the lights of the town behind them. Kumi and Watanabe had fallen silent, neither one bothering to maintain the charade, just driving, lost in their own thoughts as the tiny, terraced rice fields fell away and the land became rugged. When they pulled over, it was on the edge of what might have been a farm, the walls tumbled down, the concrete drainage ditches overgrown and singing with crickets. The moon hung low and full over the black pines.

"Here," he said, getting out, taking the keys.

She had no choice but to get out onto the deserted road. It could hardly be more dangerous than being inside the car . . .

The ringing of Watanabe's phone was startling in the oppressive silence, and he answered it with something like relief.

"It's not her," said Matsuhashi. "I checked the picture. It looks a little like her, but it's not her."

"You are sure?" said Watanabe.

"Yes. Is she okay?"

"She . . . yes. You're sure?"

"She's a journalist with a Tokyo weekly looking for a scoop. She has probably called in once already."

"A journalist?"

"Yes," said Matsuhashi. "Don't do anything you wouldn't like to read about on Sunday."

Watanabe hung up and took a long look at the woman who was standing by his car gazing at the moon, pretending not to be terrified.

"Thank you," said Thomas.

Matsuhashi looked utterly blank, drained of all emotion.

"What will you do now?" asked Thomas.

Matsuhashi shrugged. "There is nothing to do," he said. "In Japan we do not cross our teachers. We are . . ." he fought for the word, "apprentices. We don't 'bite the hand that feeds us.' "

He grinned sadly at the phrase.

"No," said Thomas. "I guess not. But there are things I still need to know. About my brother."

"I cannot help you."

"I know. I must speak to Watanabe-*sensei* myself."

It was the first time he had given the archaeologist his title, but he did it out of respect for his student, not for the man himself.

"He will tell you nothing," said Matsuhashi. "He is a good liar."

He grinned that sad, pained grin again.

"And you?" said Thomas. "You won't tell him that you know about the fraud? Even though it means that everything in the papers, everything in the academic journals, everything that will be taught in schools is wrong?"

Matsuhashi slumped further, his head down toward his belly, a picture of defeat and despair.

"I cannot stand against him," he whispered. "I have not the strength."

Whether he meant political or moral, Thomas couldn't say.

"Did you know my brother?" he asked.

"I did not travel to Italy," said Matsuhashi, frowning at the change in tack. "I saw him here but I did not know his business. He met with the *sensei* . . ." he caught himself, "with Watanabe-*san*. At first they seemed glad to see each other, but I think they argued, quietly."

"About what?"

"I don't know. They just changed. Became cold to each other."

"He was here two days?"

"Yes," said Matsuhashi, calmer now that the subject was less controversial. "He worked in the lab most of the time, had dinner with Watanabe-*san*. We were deciding which mounds to excavate and were using satellite images of locations all over Japan. He was very interested in the technology. Then they argued, and I took him to the station."

"Did he seem very angry or upset when he left?"

"No," said the student, frowning again as if this had seemed odd to him. "He seemed cheerful, even excited."

"Did you know a man called Satoh, or maybe Tanaka? A man who knew Ed in Italy?"

"No."

"He will do this again, you know," said Thomas, redirecting abruptly. "Watanabe, I mean. If you let him get away with it this time, he'll do it again. There are going to be a lot of questions about this find. Someone will poke holes in his ideas and he'll invent more evidence to cover his tracks. You could spend half your career manufacturing the same lie for him. Would you rather be a real archaeologist or a fake celebrity?"

The question hung in the air like smoke, and as the time passed and the student said nothing, Thomas thought it had dissipated. But then Matsuhashi began to move very gradually, straightening up, his back losing its arch one vertebra at a time. His eyes were shiny with more than tears, and they had a brittle light to them that seemed both determined and a little mad.

CHAPTER 79

It was midnight. Kumi had called Jim to say that Watanabe had left her on the side of a mountain road ten miles from the city edge. She was unharmed, but furious as only humiliation could make her. At the moment, for reasons Jim couldn't quite grasp, she seemed to blame Thomas.

Jim took the rental car and went looking for her, apprehensively studying road signs whose characters he couldn't read. Coming around a tight bend, he saw her. He braked hard and the tires skidded fractionally as the car came to a halt, so that Kumi, barefoot, her high heels dangling forgotten from one weary hand, flinched out of the way. She braced herself for whatever freak might be propositioning her this time, and her steely gaze softened not one iota when she realized it was Jim.

"Where the hell is Thomas?" she demanded.

"He's at the lab with Matsuhashi," said Jim.

"Yukking it up over beer and poker?"

"Hardly," said Jim, quietly.

"Just bonding with the guy who handed me over to whatever that creep wanted."

Jim nearly pointed out that Matsuhashi had, in fact, also gotten her out of the situation, and that she had insisted on meeting Watanabe against Thomas's wishes, but it wasn't his place. More to the point, he guessed that this was only the leading edge of an argument that went back years, rooted in the landscape of their relationship like Joshua trees.

* * *

"Ready?" said Thomas.

By way of answer, Matsuhashi pushed the buttons on his phone and waited for Watanabe to pick up. As soon as the conversation started, he turned away from Thomas, unwilling to show his face even in the darkness of the site.

Thomas's Japanese wasn't good enough to understand the technical nuance of the argument that followed, but Matsuhashi had planned his speech in advance and Thomas had the gist.

"There's a problem with the bones from the find," said Matsuhashi.

"What kind of problem?" said Watanabe. He sounded slurred with sleep or drink, probably both.

"The team has been preparing the samples for radiocarbon dating," said Matsuhashi, "and studying everything that came off the bones in the process."

"So?"

"There's pollen."

"You woke me after screwing up my evening to tell me there's pollen?" said Watanabe. "Of course there'll be pollen. So what?"

"It's the wrong pollen. It's *olea*. Olive."

Watanabe was silent for a moment, and when he spoke his voice was odd. "There are olives in Japan," he said.

"Yes, but they are a new cultivar. The olive did not come to Japan till the Bunkyu period in the 1860s."

"What are you saying?"

"The find is contaminated," said Matsuhashi. "The bones were not buried there. They were interred somewhere else, somewhere olives grow. They were moved later. The bones may be European, but the burial is not."

There was a long silence.

"Tell no one," said Watanabe. "Seal the remains until I get there. Don't let anyone see them or your results. Then go home. Got it?"

"Got it. Will you go to the lab directly?"

There was a momentary hesitation.

"I'll be there first thing in the morning," he said. "I need to get some sleep."

Matsuhashi hung up and, for a moment, just stood there, looking at the black hump of the burial mound.

"Well?" said Thomas.

"He's on his way."

CHAPTER 80

Thomas lay on his back on the far side of the trash mound where the filler dirt from the site had been dumped. When the excavators had carved the earth from around the burial mound, they had created a great sloped cone of rubble and sandy earth that was actually taller than the mound itself. From where he lay Thomas could look out over the entire site without being seen, though with no permanent lights in place, there was little to see in the dark. The night was still and calm, too early in the year for the metallic drone of the cicadas.

Watanabe arrived half an hour before dawn. He had parked at least a block away and entered the site silently, his movements furtive. He had brought a flashlight no larger than a pen, and most of the time he worked without switching it on. He took no more than five minutes to prepare, and then disappeared around the back of the mound. Thomas listened, but he could hear nothing, and for a full ten minutes it looked as if Watanabe had left.

"Where is he?" he whispered.

"Inside," said Matsuhashi, who had not moved at all for at least two hours.

"How did he get in? The entrance is right there."

"There must be another *tanuki* hole we didn't know about

on the other side," said Matsuhashi. "Clever. It must give him access to the unexcavated part of the mound."

Another silent five minutes passed, and, then they heard him moving around again outside the mound. Thomas risked a look. The darkness was graying fast and the archaeologist had stowed his flashlight. He was bent over the ground, barely moving except for his hands, rubbing, polishing one tiny object at a time, using what might have been a child's toothbrush, working with infinite care. He wore gloves and had spread some kind of tarp on the ground, but the meticulousness of the scene was belied by the feverish muttering that increased as time passed. He was desperate, panicking.

Thomas turned away, easing back down the slope, careful not to dislodge so much as a pebble.

"How long does pollen last?" he whispered.

"Tens of thousands of years," Matsuhashi said, still not moving. "The outer shell is almost indestructible. It can say much about conditions when an object went into the ground."

"If it's really there," said Thomas.

Matsuhashi didn't speak for a moment, then said, "He's going back in. It is almost time."

They waited till the sun was barely over the horizon, the chorus of birds winding down, before they made their move. It was simple enough, climbing over the top of the fill heap and down into the excavation site proper. They did not speak and still moved quietly, unwilling to reveal themselves.

Watanabe didn't see them at first. He emerged, looking grubby and distracted, and had already gathered his tools before he looked up and saw the pair of them standing there, waiting.

He became quite still, and then, as if he might yet ride this out on personality alone, snapped on his trademark grin. Without the shades he looked old, haggard.

"Early start?" he said in Japanese.

Matsuhashi stood silently, his back ramrod straight, his eyes on the ground, like a soldier at inspection.

"It's over," said Thomas. He felt no triumph, just weariness and a desire for it all to be done. But there was something he needed to know.

"Tell me about Ed," he said. "My brother. What exactly did you fight over?"

"I don't know what you are talking about," he said.

Thomas looked to Matsuhashi, but the student just stood there as if paralyzed, unable to look at his teacher.

"Tell him about the pollen," said Thomas.

"What pollen?" said Watanabe with an unconvincing shrug. He was going to brazen it out after all, convinced his student wouldn't turn on him. "Do you know anything about any pollen?" he asked his student, inching closer, looming.

"No, *sensei*," said Matsuhashi. "I know of no pollen."

Watanabe smiled, genuinely this time. His hands patted his breast pocket and located his trademark shades.

"Your brother," he said, "was a fool."

"He came for the cross?" said Thomas, persisting with an effort.

Watanabe looked at Matsuhashi, who seemed so still and powerless before him, and permitted himself another grin.

"You came here to make accusations against me that you cannot substantiate," he said. "Your brother did the same. Whining about giving a proper burial to certain . . . human remains." He shook his head and chuckled. "A strange quest for a priest, no? Wanting to return dead people—whose names he didn't even know—to some hole in the ground on the other side of the world?"

He rolled his eyes at the absurdity of the thing.

"That's all?" said Thomas, aghast. "He came to get the bones back to Naples because Pietro was eaten up with guilt for selling the dead down the river? That's all? What about the cross? The fish symbol? His research?"

"Research?" Watanabe sneered. "He was a priest. What could he be researching that would be of interest to a scientist? We didn't discuss it."

Watanabe shrugged again, pleased with Thomas's disappointment, and the shrug looked real. Ed's time in Japan had been a sidebar, a tangent, and Thomas's following him here was just so much wasted time. Anger welled up in Thomas and he turned to Matsuhashi.

"Finish this," he said.

But Matsuhashi, his cheeks tear-streaked again, seemed incapable of speech or movement.

"You see, Mr. Knight," said Watanabe, slipping his shades on, "we Japanese are very loyal to our *sempai*—our superiors. Matsuhashi-*san* is my student, my *kohai,* my inferior. His future is also mine. Without me he is nothing."

Thomas looked from him to the student, willing him to speak.

"There is no pollen," said Matsuhashi with great slowness, each word hauled out like a millstone.

"Yes," said Watanabe. "You must have made a mistake in the lab . . ."

"There never was any non-Japanese pollen on the bones," said Matsuhashi, and suddenly he straightened up and looked his teacher directly in the eye. It was such a surprising and defiant gesture, one Thomas was sure Watanabe had never seen from his student before, that the archaeologist took a step backward. "But," Matsuhashi continued, "you did not know that, which is why you just entered the tomb and cleaned off the artifacts you had planted earlier, artifacts that you hadn't planned to 'discover' for several days."

Watanabe flinched as if slapped.

"That's a lie," he said, very quiet.

"No, *sensei,*" said Matsuhashi, eyes lowered again, the soldier standing before his superior.

"Yes," said Watanabe, "it is."

"No," said Thomas, gesturing to the perimeter of the site. "And we have proof."

Curious, Watanabe peered out over the tops of his shades. People were emerging from cover close to the entrance, others on top of the fill heap. They had video cameras and long, foam-covered directional microphones. NHK had agreed to come only when Thomas had warned that a minor reporter with the *New Zealand Herald* would scoop the entire story and make Japanese archaeological science into a laughingstock unless they came. They hadn't believed his tale, but they would now. Everyone would.

"No!" shrieked Watanabe, hurling himself at Thomas. Flashbulbs fired, hardening the soft morning light like a blaze of gunfire.

CHAPTER 81

The pictures were everywhere by breakfast time. The TV news all showed the NHK footage every ten minutes and the newspaper headlines shrieked. It was a feeding frenzy, and if they had loved Watanabe's meteoric rise, that only made his graphic fall all the more sensational.

Parts of a third skeleton were recovered from the "unexcavated" area of the mound, including some apparently genuine Kofun ceramics and a contemporaneous terra-cotta statue of the Virgin Mary, probably Italian in origin. The Blessed Mother cradled a pomegranate in her right hand.

Watanabe was facing jail time for fraud of various kinds and Matsuhashi had become a reluctant celebrity in his own right, moving to the head of a short list to take over the Yamanashi Archaeological Institute on completion of his doctorate. That might change when the cameras averted their gaze, of course, but for now, Thomas had a resounding success on his hands, and though he dreamed of the ghoul in the Fontanelle, he woke with a sense of relief and a kind of closure.

So his depression after the news broke was not immediately easy to explain. He shunned the spotlight, letting Matsuhashi take the credit whenever possible, which seemed both politic and ethical. It was the student whose neck had been on the block, who had finally had to stand up to an archaic system of patronage, which could have utterly torpedoed his career.

But the ordeal had taught him nothing useable about Ed, except that he had been in Naples at the same time that Watanabe had been trawling for unnoticed bones and Christian artifacts, and that Ed had pursued him to Japan to demand their return. The crucial link that then took him to some obscure place in the Philippines, the link that had DHS creating a terrorism file with his name on it, was no closer now than before Thomas left Italy.

But at least you've completely alienated your ex-wife . . .

Kumi was still angry about the way he had left Jim to ensure her safety while he set about laying traps with Matsuhashi. The fact that she hadn't been hurt was irrelevant, she said. He argued that Jim couldn't have done what Matsuhashi needed, that only he could have closed the thing out the way he had.

"Of course," she snapped back. "Always the hero, the leader, aren't you, Thomas? Always hogging the limelight except when you are really needed, except when *I* really need you."

And it was clear then, as it should have been much earlier, that they weren't really fighting about the evening she had spent with Watanabe at all. They were fighting about what they always fought about, even if they never said so out loud.

Anne.

Don't say the name. Don't think it. Ever.

But he felt as he had felt all those years ago that it hadn't been his fault. He had run interference for Kumi. That was how he thought of it. He had protected her, dealing with their friends and family, keeping her out of it while she recovered. It never occurred to him that what she had really wanted was for him to stay in there with her, crying day after day. He worked better by keeping moving, getting past it.

For which she never forgave you.

It was ironic when he thought about it, because he never

had gotten past it. Not really. It had been the beginning of the end, and not just with Kumi. With lots of things. Marriage, work, God, and, by extension, his brother. And here it was again, ghosting their most recent squabble as it always did, always would.

"I need to get back to Tokyo," she said. "Devlin has some scheme that's raising eyebrows and they need me back there."

They were sitting in a quiet restaurant in Kofu on the main street up to the railway station where the statue of Takeda Shingen sat in full samurai armor.

"Excuse me," said Jim, getting to his feet and nodding in the direction of the restroom, fooling nobody.

It had been intended as a kind of victory dinner, but a pall had settled over them the moment they had sat down.

"Okay," said Thomas, staring at the vegetable tempura on his plate. They were out of shrimp, apparently. A national shortage had made them both scarce and expensive. Not that it mattered. His appetite was gone. "Okay," he said again.

His acceptance clearly irritated her, but she wasn't about to argue. He ordered another beer. That irritated her too, but she let it slide.

"I like Jim," she said. "Having him here is oddly like . . ."

"Being with Ed," Thomas completed for her. "I know."

"I'm sorry this hasn't worked out," she said. He didn't know what *this* meant exactly, and didn't know for sure that she did. "I think you have to let it go. Go back to the States. I don't know that you'll ever really know the truth about Ed. I hate it, but . . . You need to go back to the States. Get a job. Get on with your life."

His beer arrived.

"That's what I'm good at, right?" he said.

"I didn't say that," she said.

"I know."

He found himself hoping Jim would return so that neither of them would say any more, so that they could go back to their disconsolate dinner, make small talk, stay inside themselves, hollow though they might be. He took a long swallow of his beer, and she looked away.

"I'm sorry," he said, as soon as he put the glass down. "I have to go. I'll be back as soon as I can. Tell Jim . . . I don't know. Something."

Kumi did not speak and he could think of nothing else to say, so he left.

CHAPTER 82

Pestilence had abandoned her nun's habit. In her tailored business suit she looked younger, tougher, her arms and legs strong and tanned. It was still impossible for a *gaijin* to completely disappear in Tokyo, but her new attire at least bought some anonymity.

She was uncomfortable nonetheless. Between the two of them, she and War had surveyed as many major hotels as they could and had staked out Kumi's Tokyo office, but they had nothing new to report, and had come to dread the Seal-breaker's calls. Knight and his companions had dropped off the map.

They knew he was in the country and that he had contacted his ex-wife. They had a car but they were driving blind. Neither of them spoke Japanese and they had no idea where to start looking. The Seal-breaker's calls had become terse, threatening. He was talking about bringing Death out of cover. Pestilence had taken to wandering aimlessly around the pachinko parlors and tech stores of Shinjuku, hoping for a chance sighting. It was as desperate and pointless a search as she had ever conducted.

And then, quite suddenly, it wasn't.

She picked up her phone and called the Seal-breaker, something she had done only three times in her life.

She stared up at the JumboTron above the entrance to a TV store, waiting for him to pick up. They were showing footage of some archaeological sting in which a local celebrity scientist had been busted. She hadn't been paying attention before, and understood little of the details, but the case had been everywhere for the last twelve hours. It now seemed beyond belief that she had not noticed the white man who was talking to the archaeologist on the grainy blue-gray video.

"Yes?"

"I have him," she said.

"Finally," said the Seal-breaker. "I suspect you'll find one of your number is ahead of you."

Pestilence paused.

"I'm sorry?"

"The Italian papers have been buzzing with the story of an incident in Bari," he said.

"The death of Famine," she answered, bracing herself.

"Not exactly," said the Seal-breaker. "Apparently a man— and a strange one, by all accounts—was taken for dead after falling from the castle walls."

"Taken for?" Pestilence echoed, suddenly stricken with panic. "What do you mean, 'taken for'?"

"I mean that he woke up in the ambulance," said the Seal-breaker, his voice hard now.

"He's alive?"

It wasn't just shock, there was something else in Pestilence's voice, something between resignation and dread.

"Concussed and injured," said the Seal-breaker, "but, yes, very much alive, which is more than one can say for the ambulance driver and one of the EMTs."

"He got out," she said, her voice flat, without incredulity or hope. For all the Seal-breaker's disapproval she had been happier thinking Famine dead.

"And reached Japan without my help," said the Seal-breaker. "I think he knows something he didn't tell you, something he got from the old priest or from Satoh before they died. I think he knows where Knight is and has gone after him. He has a vengeful streak," he said, adding, "and I fear he can no longer be relied upon to tell friend from foe."

Pestilence hung up ashen faced, and it was almost a minute before she remembered that they had reacquired the target, that Knight was waiting for them in Yamanashi.

If Famine hasn't found him already, she thought, wondering what he would do to the man who threw him from the castle, what he might do to them too for abandoning him . . .

CHAPTER 83

Thomas caught Matsuhashi at the lab as he wrapped up another round of interviews and press conferences.

"Do you believe Watanabe's story, that Ed only came to get the bones returned?" he said.

"Yes," said Matsuhashi, clearly wishing he had something more satisfactory to offer. "He did not stay long. I gave him a ride to the station."

"What did you talk about?"

"Not much."

"He went back to Tokyo?" said Thomas.

"No. At least, not directly," said Matsuhashi. "I helped him buy his ticket. He did not speak Japanese."

"Where was he going?" asked Thomas, urgent.

"Kobe," said Matsuhashi.

"Kobe?" said Thomas. "Did he say why or if he knew someone there?"

Matsuhashi shook his head sadly. "I am sorry," he said.

"Is there a museum in Kobe," said Thomas, "or maybe a school or . . . some kind of archaeological institute?"

"Probably," said Matsuhashi, "but nothing famous. There's an aquarium. Supposed to be very good. If you are planning a visit . . ."

"I'm not," said Thomas, managing a smile. "Thanks."

He began to walk away.

"Wait," said Matsuhashi. Thomas turned back to find the Japanese man earnest, one hand raised, index finger extended. Thomas had never seen him look so spontaneous and animated. "He left a bag at the station. He probably came back for it, but . . ."

"Come with me?" said Thomas.

"It would be my pleasure."

They reached the station from the town side, parked in a lot dominated by bicycles, and emerged behind the statue of Takeda Shingen no more than a couple of blocks from where Kumi and Jim were finishing their dinner, talking about God knew what. Thomas pounded up the steps to the ticket offices in the graying evening light. Kofu was a regional station, connected to Tokyo by a reasonably direct line, and to Shizuoka by another, but there was no Shinkansen—bullet train—line here in the mountains. Thomas let Matsuhashi do the talking.

"Knight," he said. "Edward Knight. A foreigner who came through around March fifth."

The woman at the desk, in her fifties, her too-black hair piled up on her head, tapped computer keys and nodded. There was such a locker, as yet unopened, she said, but it was against company policy to open it unless requested to do so by the police.

"This is his brother," said Matsuhashi.

The woman smiled and bowed as Thomas thrust his passport in her face, but she cocked her head to one side, grimaced with a suitably pained sense of personal failure, and told them that nothing could be done.

Matsuhashi began to talk, explaining politely, but she kept shaking her head and smiling. There was nothing she could do. Matsuhashi rephrased his request, but she shook her head.

"*Watashi no kyodai ga, shinda,*" Thomas blurted out. "My brother is dead."

The woman became quite still. Then she looked to Matsuhashi, who nodded gravely. She hesitated, looking at him, and then opened a drawer and took out a ring of keys. She said something to Matsuhashi that Thomas didn't catch.

"What was that?" he said.

"She said her mother died two months ago," he said.

Thomas looked at the woman. Her eyes met his briefly and she nodded.

The locker contained a backpack in which were a change of clothes, some books and a clipping from the *New York Times*. It was dated April 4, 2006. The headline read Scientists Call Fish Fossil "The Missing Link."

There was a picture, a fossil skeleton dominated by a heavy brown skull, lying next to a lifelike model of the creature itself. It was greenish and scaly, stocky, with a stumpy tail and a broad, crocodile head, the eyes on top. The body was fishlike but the head was reptilian, and the front fins that began just below the massive jaws were clearly legs.

"What the hell is that?" Matsuhashi whispered.

"That," said Thomas, hastily scanning the article, "is *Tiktaalik roseae*. A nine-foot monster that swam in water and hunted on land at the end of the late Devonian era, three hundred sixty million years ago."

"Edward was interested in paleontology?"

"No," said Thomas, "not, at least, for its own sake."

"Then what?" said Matsuhashi.

But Thomas did not speak for a long moment in which the student, the railway station with its traffic and PA announcements, and everything that had been in his mind till that moment all vanished. In their place was a kind of slideshow in his head, mosaics of strange fish from Herculaneum, carvings of crocodile-headed sea creatures from the Temple of Isis in Pompeii, the bizarre legged fish crawling out of the red water in a Paestum tomb painting . . .

But that made no sense. This creature from the newspaper had been dead for three hundred fifty million years.

So what was it doing swimming through the art of Roman Italy?

CHAPTER 84

Thomas headed back to the restaurant elated, prepared to cut through all hostility and skepticism with the power of his conviction. He had it, at last. After all the wandering, the vagaries of his questioning, he had it. There were still a lot of holes, but it was as if he had been searching through a box of keys and suddenly found one that fit the lock perfectly. There were other doors beyond, but this first one was the most important. Now he would keep trying keys till the other doors opened as well.

Kumi will have waited, he told himself. She wouldn't just leave without saying good-bye. Now at least they would have something to talk about, something that might keep her with him a little longer.

It was dark outside the railway station and the restaurant was in one of those mazy, narrow back streets hung with dusty red paper lanterns splashed with Chinese characters in black. The air was thick with the steam from kitchen vents, heavy with the scent of *ramen* and *udon* noodles. High on a wall a Kirin beer sign glowed.

And there was something else.

Thomas had felt it when he parted from Matsuhashi outside the station—a momentary sense of something on the edge of his perception, something he had *almost* seen—and now it was back. He slowed, listening, trying to decide which sense had stirred, glancing over his shoulder.

Nothing. The alley was deserted.

He picked up speed again. The restaurant door was only twenty yards away. But there it was again, different this time, not behind him but ahead, something tugging at a primal alarm. He stopped, gazing through the steam that hung like mist over a swamp, and there, just beyond the metal door, was . . . something, a black space in the wall like a hole or . . .

A shrouded figure.

As he watched, spellbound, the quality of the darkness shifted, defined itself. It moved. Pale, long-fingered hands appeared, rose and pushed back the concealing cowl. The same terrible face.

"No," said Thomas, still frozen. "You're dead."

The ghoul hissed its familiar response, baring those awful teeth, reaching inside its robe and drawing out a long-bladed knife.

"No," said Thomas.

It was too much, after everything else. This at least he had thought was finally behind him, and the realization that it wasn't, that it had to be faced again, sapped all thought and energy from him, hollowed him out. He remembered the struggle on the castle walls, the fall, the ambulance . . .

With its lights and siren going, said a voice in his head. *They don't rush anywhere with corpses.*

Thomas could only stare as the truth sank in. He had survived, the bogeyman from his dreams, and he had come across the world to get him.

The ghoul emerged slowly, eyes flashing, jaws gaping, easing spiderlike into the empty street with infinite deliberation. Then, without warning, he sprang.

He was so quick, so improbably quick and strong, that Thomas could only react as the ghoul landed on him, grasping at his knife hand, falling backward under his weight. In Bari, Thomas had been ready for him, his senses honed and adrenaline pumping from the flight through the old city. Now he struggled to find the sharpness he would need to stay alive while the other snarled and hissed, pleased with the fight. Thomas flailed and kneed and wrestled, but there was an inevitability to the thing, and the more he fought, the more he knew he would lose. The ghoul was too strong, too poised, too determined. The knife hovered above Thomas's throat, but only for a moment, and though Thomas used all his force to hold it back, it began to descend, point first.

Thomas rocked and squirmed, but could not break free, and the blade came closer. He felt it connect with the skin below his Adam's apple, cool and sharp, and he put all his remaining energy into pushing it back, channeling every iota of the strength he had left. For a second the pressure seemed to lessen, and then it was back, the knife was starting to cut, and Thomas knew that he had nothing left.

The ghoul's eyes rolled back with satisfaction, like a shark tasting blood, and then he quivered and became quite still. The eyes met Thomas's and they looked perplexed. They widened, flickering, a stream of emotions rushing through them, all turning into fear.

And then he was crumpling and sagging, muscles spasming and relaxing, and Thomas was clawing his way out from under him, gaping, horrified. A short sword stuck out of the small of his back. Still holding its hilt was Ben Parks.

CHAPTER 85

This time he was dead.

"We have to call the police," said Thomas, crouching, steadying himself.

"After we've had a little chat," said Parks.

He had dragged the corpse into a refuse-strewn corner and piled it with empty boxes "to buy some time."

"We should call the police," said Thomas again.

"They know where you are, Thomas," said Parks. "Not the

police. The others. The people who want you dead. The people who killed your brother. You call the police now and you'll never stop them. You'll never know why Ed died or why they're going to kill you, cops or no cops."

"You left me to die," Thomas snarled.

"In a hot bath?" Parks sneered. "Please. I just forgot to turn it off. I knew you'd be okay. The place was full of people. All you had to do was yell."

"I'm telling you nothing," Thomas said.

"Nothing I don't already know, trust me," said Parks.

"Trust you?" Thomas snorted. "You're joking."

"I just saved your life," said Parks. "For which, I think, you owe me dinner."

He nodded toward the restaurant. "I believe you have company. Get them out and we'll go somewhere less . . ." he mused as if searching for the word, "less close to people I killed on your behalf. What do you say?"

Kumi and Jim had both still been inside, mulling their options, saying their farewells. Kumi had made more calls and now was planning to return to Tokyo and work. Jim had not decided whether he would stay with Thomas or strike out alone for a few days before returning to Chicago. They responded to the news of the fight in the alley with shock and panic, and they watched Parks—who was bragging about the way he had tailed Thomas—as if he might assault them at any moment.

Thomas did not know what to think about Parks's apparent change in attitude toward him, but his life had seemed over only moments before and Parks had saved him, however violently. What he felt as a result was less trust than relief, and though he was still steeped in doubt where Parks was concerned, he owed him at least the chance to talk.

"So," said Parks, taking his seat at a pine table in a bustling restaurant-cum-bar full of shouting, sweating waiters balancing trays of beer bottles and sake flasks. "You just made a big discovery. Let's think . . ." He placed one finger to his temple, closed his eyes, and hummed, an adolescent psychic gag. "You have just figured out—finally—that your brother wasn't just interested in ancient *pictures* of fish; he was interested in ancient fish, if you see the distinction. More particularly, something that was kind of a fish, and kind of not, and had been dead for a very long time."

"What is he talking about?" said Kumi. She still looked pale and wary.

Thomas said nothing and took a long swallow of beer. He was already on his second.

"His brother and I crossed paths the moment he strayed from his area of expertise—symbols, God, and associated hokum—into mine," said Parks. "Though not in person. We shared an alliance with a Japanese man called Satoh who wound up getting gutted by that vampire freak who got his just deserts in the alley back there."

"And your area is?" said Kumi. She was trying to focus, to get back on track, if only—Thomas thought—to keep her mind off what had just happened.

"Science. Biology: marine, to be precise and," Parks continued, pleased with himself, "if we are going to be really specific, evolution."

Kumi's eyes flashed questioningly to Thomas, and back to Parks.

"The very reverend Ed," Parks continued, "recognized certain oddities in the representation of a fish from a very limited geographical set grouped around Naples. The images were unlike anything he'd seen anywhere else and were confined to a span of about a thousand years, vanishing around the eighth century after the appearance of his Christ. He came to the conclusion—and this was the clever bit—that said images represented not just an abstract idea but an actual creature. It was fishlike, but with certain amphibian characteristics including a fully mobile head, lungs and—wait for it—legs, made up of shoulder, elbow, and wrist. It was what we wacky folks in the trade call a *fishapod*—a late Devonian transitional species between fish and landlubber tetrapods like *Ichthyostega*. Cool, huh?"

It was uncanny, thought Thomas, the way he just kept going, as if nothing had happened, as if he hadn't killed someone only an hour ago. It was also ironic. Parks couldn't have chosen a more perfect way to demonstrate that he was on Thomas's side, but the ease with which he seemed to have recovered from the incident made Thomas still more wary of him, though the nature of that wariness had changed. Before he had assumed Parks was an enemy. Now he was an ally, but somehow this did not make him any less dangerous, any more human than his murderous adversaries.

"Thomas," said Kumi, her eyes still fixed on Parks, "this is crazy, right? What is he talking about?"

"Ah, but Thomas doesn't think it is crazy, do you, old buddy, old pal?" Parks oozed, loving every second of it.

Thomas reached into his pocket, drew out the *New York Times* article, and spread it out on the table, carefully, as if it were immensely fragile.

"*Tiktaalik roseae*," said Parks. "You really did do your homework, didn't you? I'm proud of you, buddy."

Thomas ignored him, drank, and then said, "This was in Ed's luggage. I don't know, but I think Ed may have believed it."

"That there were prehistoric fish in Pompeii?" said Jim, speaking up for the first time. He looked more than baffled. He was watching Parks and looked hostile.

"Not just in Pompeii," said Thomas. He was mumbling, uncertain, even embarrassed by the strangeness of it all. "Ed thought they lived throughout the region. They weren't common," he said, "if they were there at all, I mean: rare enough to have mystical significance that made them suitable for use in religious iconography."

"Amen, brother," said Parks, lighting a cigarette.

"And they lived into the medieval period," Thomas said, with sudden conviction, adding as an afterthought, "or at least Ed thought so."

"He even thought he knew where the last one died, didn't he, Tommy boy?" said Parks.

Thomas thought for a second, and then nodded.

"The Castello Nuovo in Naples," he said, recalling what Giovanni had told him. "The legend was that it lived in the dungeons and occasionally took prisoners. Eventually it was hunted, killed, and hung over the castle entrance."

"You said it was a crocodile from Egypt," said Jim, doggedly.

"They wouldn't have known a crocodile if it bit them in the ass," said Parks, "as this one did. Several times. They also wouldn't have known that the Nile crocodile is a freshwater animal, while the thing that haunted the castle dungeons came in from the sea."

"Eduardo liked this story," Thomas muttered to himself, quoting Giovanni. His emotions were high and confused, delight at solving the core of the mystery battling with sadness and disappointment that his brother had pursued so ridiculous a grail. He flagged down a waitress and ordered another beer. Kumi was watching, but he avoided her eyes.

"But you can't actually *believe* this?" said Jim. "I mean, even if Ed did. This fish thing in the paper died out hundreds of millions of years ago, you said. It wasn't around two thousand years ago because it was extinct! You don't come back from extinct."

"Tell that to the coelacanth," said Parks.

"The what?" said Jim.

"Another Devonian lobe-finned fish that was supposed to have been dead for about as long as our friend here," Parks said, tapping the newspaper article. "Till they started showing up off the Comoros islands near Madagascar in the 1930s. Caused quite the stir, I can tell you."

"Just there?" said Kumi. "The Comoros islands?"

"Until 1997, when another one showed up in Indonesia," said Parks. "A coelacanth, but genetically different from the

African fish: a completely separate population that we just didn't know existed."

"But you don't think there are coelacanth in the Mediterranean?" said Kumi.

"No," Parks laughed. "There's nothing in the Med we don't know about."

"But there was when Vesuvius buried Pompeii?" inserted Jim, still skeptical, even defiant.

"No," said Parks. "The fish Ed identified is not a coelacanth. It's something much more interesting."

"More?" said Thomas.

"When coelacanths were first caught, scientists called them the missing link," said Parks, "living proof of the evolutionary step when fish crawled out onto the land. This had been speculated based on the fossil record alone because of those large, lobed fins that could have functioned as legs. When scientists got to see them alive underwater they found that those fins moved in diagonal pairs, front left coordinated with rear right, like walking. But they didn't walk and the fins, in the end, really were just fins. The coelacanth is an evolutionary cul-de-sac, not a step toward land animals."

"Not my great-grandfather then," said Jim, dryly.

"No," said Parks. "But this," he said, pushing the newspaper clipping toward the priest, "or something very like it, was. It seems that they survived in very small numbers into the medieval period, isolated, living in highly particular environments: dark undersea caves, often made by volcanic activity, incredibly secluded but giving access to land via shallow water for the animals' rare forays ashore. Coelacanths live in deep water. One to three hundred meters or more. So deep that no one has been able to get them to the surface and keep them alive for more than a few minutes. *Tiktaalik roseae* probably lived in shallow pools, moving over land between them. Our boy is somewhere between the two, I think."

"I don't believe a word of it," said Jim. "It's nuts."

"*De Profundis,*" said Thomas, half to himself. "Remember the postcard he sent you? What if it wasn't a joke about de-

spair in this exotic place so much as a joke about what he had
found?"

"What do you mean?" said Jim.

"Out of the depths," said Thomas. "Not the depths of despair, but the depths of the sea."

"Smart," said Parks.

"I don't see it," said Jim, stonewalling.

"You think that my brother died over this?" said Thomas,
slowly, purposefully, so that everyone—even Parks—stopped
and looked at him. The four of them sat there quite still, wary,
anxious. "Assuming he is dead, of course."

Kumi gave him a quick look at that, but the others were
preoccupied with the question.

"Yes," said Parks simply.

"Why?"

"The root of all evil," said Parks. "Money."

CHAPTER 86

"Why?" said Thomas. Parks's remark about Ed dying over
money had sharpened his beer-dulled senses. "Who would
give a rat's ass about a fish no one has bothered to notice for
thousands of years?"

"You know what happened when the first coelacanth were
discovered off the Comoros islands?" said Parks. "It sent massive shockwaves through the scientific community. Every museum wanted one. Every aquarium wanted one. Who knows
how many were killed trying to get them to the surface alive.
Islanders who made pennies a month collected rewards of
thousands of dollars. And that was just the legitimate interest.
Unscrupulous Chinese importers will pay millions for coelacanth spinal cord. Who knows what the hell they think it's
good for, but the life essence of a fossil fish has got to be worth

more than powdered rhino horn, right? What wouldn't that cure? Erectile dysfunction? Alzheimer's? Cancer? It's magic."

"Say this is all true," said Thomas, brushing it aside as irrelevant. "Why are you even talking to us? What do you want?"

"What I want," said Parks, "is an alliance."

Thomas snorted.

"You have got to be kidding!"

"Why do you want an alliance with us," said Kumi, "if you know everything we do and more?"

Thomas gave her a quick look at that "us." So she wasn't gone just yet. He felt himself relax, surprised at how tense his body had been.

"I need to know where your brother died," said Parks. "I have a boat—a large one—courtesy of the Kobe aquarium, by whom I have been employed. It is currently moored off the coast of Shizuoka. Help me find where Ed died and you can come with me. Or you can have a crate of beer, if you'd prefer it."

"We've been through this," said Thomas, ignoring the remark. "If you recall your attempt to poach me, you will remember me telling you in no uncertain terms that Ed died somewhere in the Philippines. That's all I know."

"Then we need to find out more," said Parks, waving a menu to the waitress and ordering sushi in competent Japanese.

The waitress apologized for the poor sushi selection. A national shortage, she said. Parks ordered the *tonkatsu* instead. Thomas just stared.

"I still don't get it," said Thomas. "You think people will pay big money for fossilized fish bones?"

"The fossils are valuable, sure," said Parks, "but that's not what we're looking for."

"He's not a paleontologist," said Kumi. "He's a biologist. He's not looking for fossils."

Jim and Thomas stared at him.

"Give the lady a prize," he said. "I'm a marine biologist and I'm looking for this."

He slid his free hand into his jacket and produced a photograph the size of a paperback, which he served onto the table like a card player laying down four aces.

The picture showed a gleaming fish of chocolate brown, except of course, that it wasn't a fish exactly, having the crocodilian features of the *Tiktaalik roseae*. But this was no model. It was wet, and heavy, and part of the tail was folded over on itself, and it was surrounded by other smaller, more conventional fish on a long wooden slab scattered with ice.

Thomas stared.

"What am I looking at?" he said.

"A nonfossilized, nonancient, very recently deceased fishapod," said Parks, grinning.

"You found one?" Thomas said.

"Not me," he said, a little rueful. "Ed."

"Ed found the thing from the pictures, the thing from the castle dungeon?"

"Not sure if it's the exact same animal," said Parks, "but it's pretty damn close."

"Where?" said Thomas. "How?"

"That's where I'm hoping you'll be able to help," said Parks. "From what you've said, I think it was taken in the Philippines. Which is also where this was made."

He reached into another pocket and put the silver fish votive on the table between them.

"But the Philippines," he said, "is more than seven thousand islands and I have no idea where to start."

"Nor do we," said Thomas.

"No," said Parks. "But Ed did. He didn't stumble onto this. He was here in Japan, he went to the Philippines, and in a matter of days he had found it. What did he know? What had he figured out that led him right to a creature no one else has ever knowingly found?"

"It looks like a fish market," said Kumi, still staring at the picture.

"Bingo," said Parks. "Which, incidentally, was how the Indonesian coelacanth was first discovered. Some random biologist on his honeymoon, wandering through a village market, spotted it on a stall. A local fisherman had pulled it in and didn't know what else to do with it. I'm guessing someone did the same with this."

"Where?" said Thomas again. "How did you get this?"

"Your brother sent it to Satoh two days before he died," said Parks. "E-mailed. We tried to track the location of the originating computer, but got nothing."

"Was there a message with it?" said Thomas, urgent now.

"Two words," said Parks. *"Found it."*

"It's amazing," said Kumi, studying the picture, unable to keep the awe out of her voice.

"You know what it looks like to me?" said Parks, his eyes aflame.

"What?" said Jim.

"The death of God," he said. "For real this time."

CHAPTER 87

Pestilence had taken only ten minutes to move from the Kofu railway station to the alley where Famine's body had been concealed. It was still dark, but she had moved as if she knew the city inside out, checking her GPS only when she came to a junction. Famine had turned his phone on as a precaution, it seemed, right before staging whatever Halloween treat he had planned for Knight. Obviously it hadn't gone so well. The phone, still switched on, was under a bundle of clothes he must have taken off in preparation for his theatrics. It sat behind an air-conditioning unit only yards from the Dumpster containing its owner's corpse and the weapon that had killed him.

Goddamned amateur-hour freak.

The sword was familiar. She weighed it in her hand thoughtfully.

She called War and gave him the short version: yes, he was

dead, for sure this time. No, no one had found the body. Yes, she
needed him there immediately with a van to help get rid of the
body. They didn't want the police involved. She could add stuff
to the Dumpster that would conceal the corpse for a little while.

"Any sign of Knight?" said War.

"No," she said. "But he was here only a few hours ago and
he can't have gotten far. I'll find him."

CHAPTER 88

"I really appreciate this," said Thomas.

"No problem," said Matsuhashi. He seemed more relaxed,
more assured since the Watanabe story had settled some. His
colleagues, even the faculty who were directing his work,
treated him with a certain deference, and though some of that
was surely just the political caution of people who had already
backed the wrong horse once, some of it was just as surely ad-
miration. He had bucked the system in daring and dramatic
fashion, and emerged not only unscathed, but looking like a
rising star whose work was rivaled only by his ethics.

But if he was on the path to celebrity, Thomas found he
was handling it quite differently from his former mentor. He
was more confident, more content, than he had been, certainly, but there was none of Watanabe's flash, his disingenu-
ous self-deprecation, or his love of the media's attention. He
had matured, it seemed, and though the press clearly admired
him and what he had done, they were losing interest in him as
an icon. That, Thomas thought, was probably for the best.

Still, at the Yamanashi Archaeological Insititute, doors
opened for Matsuhashi that would not have opened for other
graduate students, and the red tape that would ordinarily have
bound Thomas's requests to see any computer records of what
his brother had been working on during his stay were sharply

cut. Japanese organizations could have endless protocols that would hamstring any unconventional inquiry, particularly if it inconvenienced or embarrassed other people, but with Matsuhashi in his corner it seemed there was nothing that he would not be granted.

"He worked here for two days?" said Thomas.

"Apart from meals and a couple of meetings with Watanabe-*san,* he was here almost all the time. I should be able to pull up most of what he was looking at on the university's satellite-dedicated system unless he purged the cache completely."

"What makes you think he was using that?" said Thomas. "Couldn't he just have been surfing the web or writing documents?"

"He could have done that," said Matsuhashi, his fingers flashing over the keys with incredible speed, "but he got Watanabe-*san* to give him password clearance for accessing the satellite data."

"What do you use it for?"

"The equipment was set up for topographical scanning and detection of burial mounds throughout the country."

"Using satellite images?"

"Yes," said Matsuhashi. "As with the site we eventually excavated, the visible part of the mound was only a fraction of the actual burial site. We were attempting to use synthetic aperture radar—SAR—to detect shapes under the earth."

"That's possible?"

"Oh, yes. It is sensitive to linear and geometric features on the ground, particularly when different radar wavelengths and combinations of horizontal and vertical data are employed."

Thomas gave him a blank look.

"Sorry," Matsuhashi said, looking up from his typing. "The point is, it works. SAR beams energy waves to the ground and records the energy reflected. It's not even new technology now. In 1982 radar from the space shuttle revealed ancient water courses below the sand of the Sudanese desert. Airborne radar has been used to track prehistoric footpaths in Costa Rica."

He paused and frowned as a new page of data scrolled down the screen.

"What?" said Thomas.

"These coordinates are odd," said Matsuhashi. "They are not in Japan."

Thomas felt it again, that quickening of his pulse. "Where are they?"

The student pulled up one image after another and his frown deepened. The pictures showed what looked like irregular crenulations of coastlines, white against a black background, with large areas of each picture awash in vivid colors, green edging into yellow, into orange, into red, magenta, and brown. Each image was marked with a date and time, and the file was labeled "SeaWiFS chlorophyll produce and wind field from SAR."

"What the hell is that?" said Thomas.

"I have absolutely no idea," said Matsuhashi, "but it's not burial mounds."

The next set of images again seemed to show coastline marked in vivid green, blue water, and a scattering of iridescent magenta paling to white. The file was marked "AVHRR: visible, near and thermal infrared composite." Then there were charts of numbers, graphs, and clusters of coordinates.

"Could this be measuring underwater caves?" Thomas ventured.

Matsuhashi shook his head.

"This data seems largely surface focused," he said. "It may penetrate a few feet down, but no more. And measuring caves wouldn't necessitate these multiple passes. See? We have a series of images of the same locations taken over the space of several days. Caves don't alter unless there is massive seismic activity, so why the repeat imaging? And this set of images seems to be taking into account wind direction, which wouldn't be relevant for undersea structures."

"What about this reference to chlorophyll?" said Thomas. "That's plants, right?"

"It's what plants use for photosynthesis, yes."

"I don't get it," said Thomas.

"Me neither," said Matsuhashi, looking less sure of himself. "This is a long way from archaeology. Let me make a call. I'm very popular at NHK right now," he added with a rueful smile.

They printed a selection of the images and drove over to the TV station. Thomas hung in the background as the staff fawned over their local hero, but drifted back into range as they sat down with the station's chief meteorologist, a scholarly-looking man with salt-and-pepper hair and a neat mustache who, of all the people at the station, seemed ignorant of or unimpressed by Matsuhashi's celebrity status. He was, Matsuhashi assured Thomas, an expert on satellite imaging, particularly if they involved weather as these pictures seemed to.

He peered at the images, nodded gravely, and uttered his verdict in Japanese.

Thomas followed as best he could, but the man seemed to be complaining about what was on offer at his local restaurant.

"What is he saying?" he asked.

"He's saying that this is why he can't get sushi-grade fish for the second time this year," said Matsuhashi, simultaneously amused and bemused.

"Habzu," said the meteorologist to Thomas.

"I'm sorry?" said Thomas.

The weatherman took a pen from his desk and wrote on a notepad: *HABS.* He repeated the letters carefully.

"I don't know what that means," said Thomas.

The meteorologist spoke quickly, Matsuhashi rushing his translation to keep up. "Little plants in the water," he said, typing *HABS* into his computer search engine. "Dangerous. Poison all the fish." The meteorologist indicated the computer screen. *"Habzu,"* he said again, with a told-you-so air.

The picture showed a sunlit beach, idyllic except for something strange that made the brain retreat and adjust, something that skewed reality, made it dreamlike. The sea had turned to blood.

"HABS: Harmful algae blooms," Matsuhashi read. "Also known as . . ."

"*Akashio,*" said the meteorologist.

Thomas didn't need the translation.

"Red tide," he whispered.

It was as if turning the key he had been trying had not just worked, it had released a dozen other locks, and suddenly Thomas's head was filled with the booming clang of a dozen doors swinging open.

CHAPTER 89

Thomas was exhilarated. Even the tranquillity of the Minobu temple complex couldn't mute his enthusiasm.

"Some biblical scholars," he said, "have speculated that the plague of Egypt that turned the Nile to blood was the earliest documented instance of red tide, the massive blooming of microscopic algae or phytoplankton that can turn the water red. There are lots of different kinds. I think we're looking at something called *Alexandrium tamarense.*"

"Which does what?" said Kumi.

"It's a dinoflagellate that causes PSP," said Parks, pacing the gravel forecourt. "Paralytic shellfish poisoning. It affects mussels, scallops, clams, and so on. Eating contaminated shellfish can shut down your respiratory system completely in bad cases: death within twenty-four hours."

"Giovanni caught it the day before Ed left Italy," said Thomas. "A mild case, but enough to get Ed thinking."

He had called the Italian priest to confirm his hunch before rejoining the others. Giovanni had been surprised to hear from him, but not hostile, and he did not blame Thomas for Pietro's death. Thomas's relief had fed his current euphoria.

They had taken the train up to Minobu and climbed the two

hundred eighty-seven sheer, broad steps up to the temples. It had been Kumi's idea: a break, she said, a change. They needed to get out of Kofu, put some distance between them and the body of Thomas's attacker, a body to which there had been no reference in any of the local news media. Kumi seemed to find this silence disquieting. Murder, particularly so strange a murder, should dominate the news for days in a place like Kofu.

The Yoshino cherries were in flower, a pale, fragile pink against the stark tree limbs and deep blue of the sky. The trip was, more importantly, a reenactment of a visit she and Thomas had made together years before, and as such it represented a truce, albeit a cautious one, frail as the cherry blossoms.

Parks, who seemed curiously immune to the ageless beauty of the mountain retreat and its ancient wooden temples, had come up separately from wherever he was staying in Kofu.

"PSP doesn't just kill people," he said. "It affects the whole food chain. Anything that eats the dinoflagellate becomes toxic to whatever then eats it. It doesn't just shut down a few restaurants in Maine; it can wipe out whole fish populations."

"Unless the fish is unusually equipped to find a new food source," said Thomas.

Parks stared at him. "Oh, that's good," he said.

"What is?" said Kumi.

"Our fishapod," said Parks. "It spends almost its entire life in the water, probably in caves, swimming about, using its rudimentary legs to move around, catching fish. But if the environment changes suddenly and its usual food source disappears . . ."

"Wiped out by HABS," Thomas chimed in.

". . . then it has something the other fish don't have: legs, and a way of breathing air at least for a little while. It climbs out of the water and eats something else until the sea has returned to normal."

"It fits our Paestum painting," said Thomas, "which is the

only image we have of the fish actually coming out of the water. This is what Ed guessed. The red water in the painting isn't just apocryphal symbolism, as the fish isn't merely a Christological icon. It was a real fish. Real crimson water. The legged fish came ashore when the sea turned red."

"Life out of death," said Jim. "No wonder Ed thought he had hit the symbolic mother lode. It's the perfect image of Christ transcending the cross."

"Ed used the satellite imagery to track current outbreaks," said Parks, brushing the theology aside. "He was matching environmental data—water temperature, depth, subterranean topography—from what he knew of the Naples sites to other locations in the world that shared outbreaks of the *Alexandrium* dinoflagellate. Then he watched for repeat occurrences and went hunting."

"Do you know where?" asked Kumi. It was a cautious question, and her glance at Parks let Thomas know what she was really asking: *If you know, will you tell him? Do you trust this man who has attacked you twice before?*

Thomas met her gaze, then looked past her to the temples nestled in the rich green of the hills.

"If I try to leave the country by conventional means," he said, "I'll be stopped and turned over to either the Italians or some antiterrorist division in the U.S. I don't want to spend the rest of my days waiting for a trial at Guantanamo."

"What about going to Devlin?" said Jim.

Thomas opened his mouth to speak, but he caught something in Kumi's face, a shadow, maybe a memory or a realization. He looked at her, but she just shook her head fractionally. She wanted something kept to herself, for now.

Parks was watching Thomas, smirking with anticipation.

"Come on, Tommy boy," he said. "Share."

Kumi turned away, staring out across the wooded valley. Thomas slowly drew the papers from his jacket pocket and spread them out. He had plotted the satellite image coordinates onto a map of the Philippines.

"The day before Ed left Japan," he said, putting his finger

on a tiny island in the remote Sulu Archipelago, "a red tide bloom began here. It lasted almost a week. By the time the seas returned to normal, my brother was dead."

For a long moment they all stared at the map. Then Parks flexed his fingers back, one hand at a time, till the knuckles cracked, and grinned.

"Anchors away," he said. "All aboard that's going aboard."

"Not me," said Kumi. "You might have found something and you might not, but I think you should hand it off to the authorities before other people get killed. You should call the embassy, tell them what you know, and stay out of it."

"Oh," said Parks, "like we can trust *them*."

"Jim?" said Kumi.

"I came to help," said the priest. He shook his head, thoughtfully, wrestling with something. "I owe it to Ed. If there's something I can do . . ."

"Thomas?" she said, suddenly seeming very tired and small.

"Sorry," he said. "I have to. Till I know. Till it's over."

She nodded, resigned, but said nothing.

"Guys' trip!" said Parks. "All right! Get the beer and I'll see that we score some hookers. Except for Joe Celibate, here."

"Wait," said Thomas. "There's something else you might want to look at before you start volunteering for this particular cruise."

The others looked at him.

"Thanks to Matsuhashi and the NHK meterological office we got some other images, satellite photographs taken at thirty-six-hour intervals of about a half-mile stretch of beach in the center of the red tide outbreak."

He laid each picture out in turn.

"This is the first one," he said.

"Looks idyllic," said Kumi, scanning the pale sand of the palm-fringed beach viewed from above. "Apart from the red water, of course. What are these?"

"Fishing boats," said Thomas, "pulled up onto the shore. And here are the huts of the village just beyond the tree line. Now, here's the second image."

It was almost impossible to make out anything except the red water. The land was blotted out by a thick gray cloud.

"Is that a storm?" said Parks.

"I thought so, at first," said Thomas. "But the larger-scale images show no significant weather in the area."

"So it's . . . ?" Kumi faltered.

"Smoke," said Thomas.

"You can't be sure," said Parks, looking uneasy.

"Here is the third image," said Thomas.

The sea was blue and sparkling, the beach as idyllic as before, except for some dark smudges close to the trees.

"Where are the boats?" asked Kumi. The question had been casual, but when no one answered she followed it with another, and this time her voice was full of dread. "Where is the village?"

"Gone," said Thomas. "It's all gone."

CHAPTER 90

The sun had barely risen over Fuji's snow-capped symmetry when the helicopter from Narita slowed to a roaring hover just above the trees that lined the river bank. The door was already open, and in no more then fifteen seconds the three assault troops had slid down the nylon cord and onto the sandy shore. No one saw them come, and by the time early risers were gaping out of windows at the sound of the helicopter, it had already moved off, heading swiftly northeast toward the city.

The soldiers were clad in black battle dress uniform and class three flak vests, Eagle jackets, and Nomex hoods that left only the eyes uncovered. They moved with practiced speed, their Heckler and Koch MP-5-SD6 submachine guns with integrated silencers pivoting, scanning, like parts of their bodies. They had been ordered to be cautious, to use deadly force on any civilians who might derail the mission only when absolutely necessary, but they were taking no chances. The targets themselves, of course, would be given no such latitude. On that, their orders were perfectly clear. "Targets pose an immediate and credible threat and are to be eliminated by any available means."

Still, it was supposed to be a stealth mission, kills made silently, the bodies spirited out by helicopter in no more then fifteen minutes. The soldiers moved quickly up the river bank to the south side of the single-story *ryokan*. They had no specific information on which rooms the targets were occupying and there could well be other foreigners in the building, a building for which they had no specs, no blueprints, no real reconnaissance of any kind. The attack squad were also the information collectors, so target location needed to be doubly prompt.

The team leader nodded and the other two soldiers separated, staying low to the ground, moving almost on all fours, the long-barreled silencers of their guns' eyes searching for prey. He wished they had gotten here an hour earlier. This was a predawn mission if ever there was one. What minimal intel they had said that there were only five guest rooms and the living quarters of the woman who ran the place, but they couldn't be sure how many rooms the targets were using: could be as few as one or as many as three.

The team leader rose carefully and looked into the window four feet above the ground: a kitchen, no sign of life. He moved laterally, stopping behind a manicured yaupon holly. He was close to the front entrance and the building's most exposed side, which gave onto a gravel road into the village. He returned to the kitchen window, applied a suction pad to the window pane, and drew a brisk circle around it with a diamond-tipped glass cutter. With a little pressure on the suction pad the circle snapped neatly out and he was able to reach in and flip the latch. In less than thirty seconds, he was inside.

The kitchen was cramped and bursting with oversized blackened iron pots, one of which hung over the hearth from a

chain. The surfaces were of a graying wood, the floor slabs of
stone. Apart from the egg-shaped electric rice cooker, the
place might have been a thousand years old. Leading with the
muzzle of his weapon, he ducked into a squat low enough to
see beneath the navy cotton *noren* that hung from the door lin-
tel and moved through into the hallway, leaving dark boot
prints on the pristine floor. No sign of anyone.

A series of sliding doors extended down the matted hall.
With the exception of the kitchen, the whole building was basically a single room divided by paper covered *husuma* into
six-mat tatami rooms all branching off this central corridor. A
sneeze at one end would probably be heard in every bedroom.
He inched along the hallway, aware of deep, rhythmic snoring
coming from the nearest room. As he laid his hand to the
screen door, the second of the team appeared at the other end
of the hall. They had come in through the back door. He shook
his masked head once: nothing to report so far.

The team leader pushed the screen sideways and it slid in
its wooden grooves with only the smallest whisper. The room
was dark, but the sleeping form was an elderly Japanese female, curled up on a futon on the tatami floor: the proprietor.
He closed the door and moved down the hall as his second
leaned back out of the room he had checked: still nothing.
They were running out of rooms.

He tried the next door, then the next, weapon poised and
ready to fire. Both were deserted. A look at his second confirmed the same at his end. The targets had moved on.

He nodded back to his second, suddenly anxious to get out
of this strange wooden house with its air of foreignness and
antiquity, and gestured dismissively with one hand.

Move out.

Once a terror cell like this was flushed out into the open,
their advantage quickly diminished. He'd get them next time.

CHAPTER 91

They had gotten off the train at Zenko-ji, a couple of stops before the main Kofu station, because they didn't want to be standing around there waiting for their connection to Shizuoka. Kumi would leave Thomas and the others there, taking the train to Tokyo and the rest of her life. She sympathized, she said, but she had to walk away. They would say their farewells here at her request, in a place that had once been special to them, then walk the rest of the way to the main station and their respective trains.

But Kumi had one piece of news to offer, something she confessed she had been wary of telling Parks. Thomas, forcing himself to the decision, said she should tell them all what she knew. They needed to trust each other. She shrugged, unconvinced, but told them anyway.

"Devlin," said Kumi. "His visit isn't just about taxes. He's hammering out the details for a trade deal. Guess what he wants to import?"

"Fish?" said Jim.

"Yep," said Kumi. "Japan is the biggest importer of fish in the world and he wants in."

"From Illinois?" said Thomas, skeptical. "From where, Lake Michigan?"

"He's sponsored some semisecret farming program," said Kumi. "There are these greenhouses in southern Illinois growing tomatoes and such hydroponically . . ."

"Hydro what?"

"No soil," said Parks. "The plants grow in nutrient-rich water."

"And they are farming fish in that water," said Kumi. "Tilapia at the moment. And they are trying the same conditions for a specially cultivated hybrid striped bass. Could be a massive boon for the Illinois economy if Devlin can pull off an import deal here."

"He never mentioned it," said Thomas, looking to Jim for confirmation.

"Keeping it quiet," said Kumi. "Get an edge on the competition."

"Maybe," said Thomas.

Parks was looking thoughtful. Thomas could feel them all trying to make the connection in their minds, but either they didn't know enough, or it wasn't there, so they sat in silence.

In any case, Thomas had something else on his mind. The faded red temple where they had first met after Tokyo was private and secluded after the grandeur of those they had just visited. It was the perfect place to give voice to an idea that he had been holding on to like a man protecting a candle flame in a strong breeze.

"Listen, I've been thinking," said Thomas. "I know it sounds crazy, but has anyone considered the possibility . . . ?"

"What?" said Kumi. She looked wary.

"Now just hear me out," he said.

"Go on."

"Has anyone considered the possibility . . . ?"

"That Ed isn't dead," said Jim. "That's what you were thinking, isn't it?"

"I was just wondering," said Thomas.

For a long moment they all just stared at him, and the silence of the temple precinct seemed absolute.

"Your brother's dead, Tom," said Kumi, at last.

"So they say," said Thomas. "But we haven't seen a body. We don't have clear evidence where or how he died. Maybe he didn't, maybe he just went underground . . ."

"Tom," said Kumi, cutting him off like someone laying down a heavy burden as gently as possible. "We know there was some sort of explosion. A lot of people died. He was among them."

"We don't know that for sure," he said. "If there were lots of bodies, if they were . . . damaged, unrecognizable, who is to say someone didn't just assume he was among them because he'd been in the area or . . ."

"They were sure, Tom," said Kumi, weary again, and sad because she didn't want it to be true but couldn't make herself believe it wasn't.

"And how can we trust what we're being told anyway?" Thomas continued. "We're being given the runaround by everyone. Why should we believe anything they say? Why do we take it on trust that he's dead?"

"You can't let yourself believe this, Tom," said Kumi.

"I'm just saying . . ." Tom began.

"Let him go," said Jim.

"You too?" said Thomas, rounding on him. "I thought you were the man of faith, the man who could believe things?"

"Not this, Thomas," said Jim. "I believe he's dead."

"It's hard," said Kumi, "but you have to accept it."

He turned on her then, an old anger suddenly boiling up inside him as if a forgotten wound had split open.

"*You* tell *me* to accept it?" he snapped. "*You* are telling *me* to get over it? Oh, that's perfect."

Kumi flushed. "That's enough, Tom," she said, though there was the hint of a plea in her eyes. "Don't."

"Don't what, Kumi?" he shot back, the pain making him cruel. "Don't what? Don't mention the little stone babies over there?"

"Shut up, Tom," she said, tears starting to her eyes, her hands rising to her ears to block him out, silencing him as a child might.

But Thomas didn't stop. He got hold of her and spoke loudly into her face. "Don't mention the child-sized hole in your gut you've been carrying around for the last seven years? Are you getting over that any time soon, Kumi?"

She hit him then, a sudden stinging slap across his face that brought silence to the temple garden. Then she fled, stumbling a dozen yards away, sobbing into her hands. Jim went after her, but slowly and keeping his distance. Parks stood for a moment, frozen, his eyes wide, and then he drifted away by him-

self, leaving Thomas alone with his grief and his shame, as it
had always been. The shadows of the four people that had
blurred into an amorphous whole resolved and separated,
drew on the gravel their stark, negative images of loss and isolation.

"You lost a child?" said Parks, turning to Thomas. He was
whispering in a strange way and his eyes were still wide.

"No," said Thomas, hollow. "Yes. Anne. A late-term miscarriage."

"Does that make a difference?" said Parks, looking toward
Kumi. It was an accusation, bizarre coming from him, but an
accusation nonetheless. Thomas was also watching her, but he
was seeing only that day when they had sat in the parked car
outside the obstetrician's clinic, crying together but already
separate. Now he just shrugged like a man exhausted, and
spoke the question he had nursed as long as she had.

"How do you mourn the loss of what you never had?"

CHAPTER 92

The temples in Japan had always left Thomas with a sense of
calm and beauty, but if they were spiritual places it was a kind
of spirituality he didn't really understand. He resented the
church he had grown up in, but he understood it. Zenko-ji, Minobu, and places like them were fascinating to him because
they were otherworldly, exotic, but in them he always felt
alone. If there was one thing he had always understood about
Ed's religion it was the way it imagined a community, a living
social world spreading out from the altar. Other people—
Japanese people—probably felt something like that here, but
Thomas couldn't, and he was surprised to find that he wished
he were in church, a church he knew and recognized, not as a
tourist, but as someone born with it singing in his blood.

They left the temple with barely a word. Kumi's face was still red, but she had wiped her tears away in a brisk, decisive fashion that said the subject was now closed. For a moment Jim took her hand, but though she thanked him for the gesture she permitted it for only a few seconds before releasing him and insisting that they begin the walk to the station in Kofu.

Thomas drifted behind her, saying nothing, remembering the route past the net-covered vineyards, through the narrow, winding streets of garden walls, down to the old *onsen* baths, each curve in the road surprising him with its painful familiarity. Uniformed schoolkids cycled past as they always had, less interested in the foreigners than they once were, perhaps, but otherwise the same. He had lived here, even if he had never quite belonged here, and the way the place tugged at his memory now made him feel old and lost and irrelevant.

A more recent memory came back to him: Peter the Principal giving him his marching orders. *"You've gone from maverick to pariah, Thomas—and I'll be honest here—I don't really understand why."*

"I know," he had said. *"I'm sorry."*

And now he was back here, in his Japanese prehistory, wondering what the hell he was trying to achieve, these three mismatched people with him. Outside a corner store stood a pair of vending machines. One of them sold beer in oversized cans. Thomas walked toward it, fumbling in his pockets. An odd, rhythmic pounding drifted over the tiled roofs.

Drums?

It sounded like it. He paused, straining to hear, and then walked quickly after the others, but it wasn't till they came to the edge of some dusty high school playing fields that the extent of the thing became clear. He realized it in the same instant that Kumi turned to him, her eyes bright with the same knowledge, the same memory.

"It's the *Shingenko matsuri*," she said.

He nodded, his smile matching hers for its balance of joy and sadness.

"What the hell is that?" said Parks.

"More prehistory," Thomas said.

The field was packed with people clustered in groups of twenty or more, all marshaled under glorious banners, all dressed or in the process of being dressed in the armor of samurai or their foot soldiers armed with bows, pikes, and *katana*.

It was the annual celebration of Yamanashi's sixteenth-century warlord and folk hero, Takeda Shingen. Today thousands would march in battalions around the major streets of Kofu: schoolchildren, company men, office workers, civil servants, and half the population of the city—including a special regiment of foreigners—while the rest of the populace cheered them on. It was as interminable as it was spectacular and would go well into the night before Shingen's representative would dismount from his horse and preside over the closing ceremonies. Thomas and Kumi had walked in the procession twice before, had cherished the silliness and grandeur of the thing so much that even now, with all that had been lost between them in the intervening years, the sight of it worked like nostalgia on them.

"Can we stay and watch a while?" she said.

"Sure," said Thomas, drawing beside her.

"There isn't time," said Parks. "We have to get to the station and out of here."

"Just a few minutes," she said, and Thomas gave Parks a look so that he shrugged and walked away to wait for their moment to pass.

"It's pretty cool," said Jim, watching a samurai in black armor laced with red and gold cord lead his ranks of armored troops out and into the streets.

"Yeah," said Thomas. "It is."

For ninety seconds they just watched.

"You ready now?" said Parks, tapping his watch.

"Kumi?' said Jim, leaning into her with immense gentleness, pretending not to see her tears.

She nodded once, and they began to walk once more.

* * *

War thought the parade was a pain in the ass. The sleepy little town was suddenly teeming with people and the sidewalks were jammed with stalls selling all kinds of inedible shit. He had dispersed his team all over the major roads around the railway station because he was sure that was where Knight and the others would go, but it was a nightmare trying to make sure they didn't get past him in the crowds. He had to stop them here, and though he didn't especially want to start shooting with all these people around, the procession might distract long enough for a few bleeding foreigners to be bundled into a van.

He checked in with the team leader, a man War had personally recruited after his second tour with the Navy SEALs in Afghanistan.

"You in position?"

"Got the north side of the station covered, sir," he said.

"How are the crowds?"

"Not so bad up here. There's nothing to see."

"Keep your eyes open," said War. "And if you see them, call for the van before you start shooting unless it's absolutely necessary."

There was something odd about the man on the corner, odd enough to make Thomas stop in his tracks and press the others back into the alley. They were only a few blocks from the station now and the parade was close to its height in terms of noise and energy.

So why is that guy watching the crowd?

He was tall, athletic-looking, and vaguely Nordic, though the clothes were generic American and too warm by half for the mild weather. He looked serious, focused, dangerous.

"They're here," said Thomas, ducking back into the alley.

"Which one is it?" said Parks.

"Don't know," said Thomas. "Never seen him before."

"So how do you know . . . ?"

"I know," said Thomas. In the States the foreigner might

have been a security guard keeping an eye on the crowd. Not here.

"We can't get past him," said Jim. "And there'll be others."

"What if we took a cab right up to the station?" said Kumi.

"The streets are blocked off," said Thomas. "We can't get there without being spotted."

"What if it's *not* them?" said Parks. "Just because you see a stray foreigner doesn't mean it's them. You've seen them. I've seen them. If this is someone different, maybe it's not them." He sounded more than insistent. He was getting desperate. "I mean, how many can there be?"

"How the hell should I know?" said Thomas, not wanting to think about the scale of the organization that was bent on stopping or killing them.

"We've got to get on that train," said Parks.

"Wait," said Kumi, taking charge as she sometimes did when facing a crisis: her way of getting through it. "Come with me."

"You're sure they were on the train from Minobu?" said War into his headset. He was getting irritated now, because he was also getting anxious. He needed to call the Seal-breaker and tell him that all was in hand. That *they* were in hand. Or dead.

"Yes, sir," said the team leader. They were seen to get on, but my man on the platform in Kofu says they did not get off at this end."

"Could they have stayed on?"

"Unknown, sir."

"Unknown?" said War, petulance getting the better of him. "What kind of answer is that?"

"Sorry, sir. It's unlikely but we can't be sure."

"Make sure," War snapped. "Get on that train and search it."

"Yes sir."

War went back to scanning the crowd. This ludicrous parade was the problem; all these heathen idiots marching about in their golden-age crap. Any other day of the year the streets would have been deserted and a gaggle of foreigners would have stood out like sore thumbs.

Every face was turned toward the parade except his. He was therefore the only one who didn't see the four partially armored people, three foreign men and a Japanese woman, break from the parade line as it skirted the steps at the entrance to the station only feet from where he was standing, watching the crowd.

Kumi flagged down a schoolboy in the station, proffering a five-thousand-yen note and the bag of faux helmets that had been a good fifty percent of their disguise. By the time Thomas had collected their tickets, the kid was running back to the schoolyard's impromptu armory, grinning as if he had won the lottery.

CHAPTER 93

The Shizuoka train was faster than they had become used to, but it was still nothing like the Shinkansen. Parks complained constantly, sometimes even looking over his shoulder as if expecting their pursuers to come barreling down the largely deserted car. Thomas suspected he had other things on his mind, things as much concerned with where they were going as they were with where they had been.

"You think it's safe to use my cell phone?" Parks said. "I should really call ahead to make sure the boat is ready, but . . ."

He ended lamely and they all looked at each other. How easy was it to track a cell phone signal, or to listen in, and what kind of resources would their enemies need to be able to do such things? They had no idea.

"What do I look like," said Jim, "James Bond?"

Parks gave him a sharp look.

"You look like a priest," he said.

"Thank you," said Jim, choosing to read the gibe as a compliment. In response Parks, looking cocky as if he were spoiling for a fight, turned to Kumi.

"Thought you weren't coming?" he said.

"I called the *ryokan* in Shimobe," she said.

"And?" said Parks.

"They were raided during the night," she answered. "Early morning, actually. Someone cut through the windows. Nothing was taken. It seemed like they were looking for something or someone."

"They?" said Thomas, wanting to hold on to a more innocuous sense of the event. "How do you know it wasn't just a local thief?"

"Professional breaking and entering in a Japanese mountain village?" she said. "No. And local thieves rarely drop from helicopters."

Thomas just looked at her.

"Good thing we spent the night in Minobu, huh?" she said.

"But it raises an interesting question," said Parks. "Because if they tracked us to a little *ryokan* in the middle of nowhere, I'd say they had help."

"Not necessarily," said Kumi with a sigh. "Hiding foreigners in rural Yamanashi is like hiding a 747 in the desert. You can bury it, but if someone spots it, they are going to notice and remember. And besides, Thomas has been on national television. They didn't need an informant."

"Maybe," said Parks, "but I thought we might ask the Reverend Jim, here."

"What's that supposed to mean?" said Jim.

"I'm just thinking aloud," said Parks.

"What kind of an informant would I be if I told them where we had stayed the *previous* night?" said Jim. He turned away and muttered "Jackass" under his breath so that everyone heard.

Parks got up from his seat.

"Gotta pee," he said, looking at Jim.

Jim turned to stare fixedly out of the window, so that Kumi

and Thomas found themselves looking at each other directly for the first time since Zenko-ji. He gave her a quizzical look and nodded at the other two men, but she just shrugged and shook her head, half-closing her eyes.

"You're coming on the boat?" he asked.

"I need to call the office," she said. "I'll probably take the Shink up to Tokyo from Shizuoka."

"You didn't have to come," he said, resenting her still for sitting on the fence.

She sighed, glanced out the window, and turned back to him.

"I'm scared, Tom, okay?" she said. "I'd like to go back to my office and carry on like all this doesn't concern me or is over, but that's tough to believe. I want . . . I don't know, a conclusion. I want closure."

She wasn't just talking about Ed's death or their current predicament, and Thomas knew it. Their fight at the temple had not ended things between them so much as it had revealed how much had gone unsaid over the years. Thomas said nothing, but he felt it too, the sense that they were waiting for something to happen that would—at last—move them forward: separately, Thomas presumed, finally closing the door behind them, forever shutting off the part of their lives they had spent together.

"I don't know if I can come with you," she said. "I have some vacation time coming, but I don't know. I have to make some calls and do some thinking, okay?"

"Okay."

Thomas felt tired and confused. Parks and Jim were both being furtive in their different ways, and Kumi . . . He just didn't know about Kumi. Not for the first time, Thomas felt out of his depth, the shore long fallen away beneath him as he drifted into darker, deeper waters on unpredictable currents. For all he had learned over the past weeks he was still no nearer to figuring out who was commanding those who had pursued him across the world. Jim was right; he was no James Bond, and neither was Thomas. The idea that the people who wanted him dead, the people who had killed his brother, could manipulate government agencies or field trained killers in helicopters was frankly terrifying. He could only have survived so far out of the merest luck, and that was bound to change, and soon. Perhaps he should turn himself in to the authorities, let himself be taken to face the music at home or in Italy. He was innocent. That would count for something, right?

It should have been a rhetorical question, and for all his skepticism about authority, it normally would have been. But today, with his brother apparently dead and investigations into his own links to terrorism underway, there was nothing rhetorical about it.

God, he thought, *what I'd do for a drink.*

The four of them sat there in silence as the train rattled on around the base of Fuji and on to the coast. It was not an auspicious start, thought Thomas, to a voyage into the South China Sea and beyond. He didn't know how long it would take them to get there, but it was a journey on which trust would be in short supply.

Night had fallen on the Heiwa Dori, and the endless procession of faux samurai had finally come to an end with no sign of Knight and the others. War and his men still watched the railway station, but it was increasingly evident that their quarry had slipped through their fingers once more. He still watched, but his mind was otherwise occupied. He was waiting.

The inevitable call came half an hour later. The Sealbreaker's voice was calm and even, and while War delivered his professional assessment of their failure, the other man said nothing, so that when War finally stopped talking the silence unnerved him and he thought they had been cut off.

"Sir?" he said. "Did you get all that?"

"Yes," he said. "I would rather have heard something different, of course . . . but, yes."

"I'm sorry, sir," said War. "I don't know how they got by us, but it's chaos down here still . . ."

"Clearly," said the Seal-breaker, with such finality that War

fell silent as if struck. But then the voice came back and the irritation, the crispness had fallen away. "Well," he said, "I
would have preferred that it had not gone this far, but so be it."

"Should we monitor the station all night, sir?"

"No," said the Seal-breaker. "They are gone, but that's
okay."

"Sir?"

"It's not like we don't know where they are going," said the
Seal-breaker, as if he was musing to himself.

"Should we prepare to intercept?"

"No," said the Seal-breaker. "We've always known where
they would finish up if given the chance. Better hit them there
where another stack of corpses won't attract much attention.
Our best card is yet to be played, and there is a kind of symmetry to the thing, a fitting closure. I look forward to being on
hand to witness it all in person."

"You're going to come with us?" said War, aghast and a little excited. He had met the Seal-breaker only once in person.
Pestilence never had, a fact that War held as one of the clear-
est markings of rank between them.

"Certainly," said the Seal-breaker. "Regroup. Gather your
forces—all of them—and await deployment coordinates. I'll
be waiting for you when you get there. We'll end this together.
And War?"

"Sir?"

"Put this failure behind you."

"Yes, sir," said War, a rising panic overwhelming him at
the Seal-breaker's uncharacteristic compassion.

"The Lord works in mysterious ways his wonders to perform," said the Seal-breaker. As one door closes, another opens,
and through it is the way to glory."

"Yes, sir," said War, his suddenly cold skin prickling, the
hairs on his arms and neck standing upright, though whether
the sensation he was feeling was exhilaration or terror, he
couldn't say.

PART IV

THE JESUS FISH

We have reached a crossroads in human evolution where the only road which leads forward is towards a common passion . . . To continue to place our hopes in a social order achieved by external violence would simply amount to our giving up all hope of carrying the Spirit of the Earth to its limits.

—Pierre Teilhard de Chardin

CHAPTER 94

They had been at sea for almost two weeks. Thomas wasn't sure what he had expected when they reached Shizuoka, but the boat had surprised him. It was huge—more than a hundred feet long—stuffed with state-of-the-art marine research equipment including sonar and a two-man submersible, and run by a crew of twenty-two, not including scientists and guests. It was owned by the Kobe aquarium, and though Parks was nominally in charge of the expedition, the boat's staff structure rendered him little more than a passenger. Thomas had no idea what Parks had told them, but there had been a series of lengthy phone calls on the train and in the port before the expedition had been approved. God knew how he had overplayed their meager evidence, but they had eventually been welcomed aboard by Nakamura, the ship's captain, with typically Japanese politeness.

It was impossible to discern what the captain and his crew thought of their mission, and they kept pointedly to themselves. Nonetheless, Thomas suspected that they thought Parks a loose cannon, and that it wouldn't take much to turn the boat back to Japan. Whether the captain knew that the names of the foreigners on the passenger manifest had been falsified, he couldn't say, but Thomas spent the first two days on deck, watching for signs of the Japanese coast guard; however much they seemed to have escaped from the mainland, the boat would quickly feel little better than a floating prison cell if the authorities opted to pick them up.

Thomas hadn't learned that there was no alcohol on board till they set sail. At first he was merely disappointed that he couldn't have the beer he thought he had earned, but after two more days the subject made him irritable. Everyone but Jim stayed out of his way for almost a week: no mean feat on a boat. It was about then that Thomas began to reflect on the last time he had gone for more than two days without a drink, without several drinks, and his irritability turned into something darker and more private. The thirst had passed, for now, but he felt conspicuous, humiliated, and it was another two days before he began seeking out the company of the others.

"Welcome to our very own floating Betty Ford clinic," said Parks, with customary detachment. Jim winced, but Thomas shrugged it off.

The boat was called the *Nara,* though Parks had hung a hand-lettered sign over the side that read *Beagle II.* It cut through the blue water at what had first seemed like breakneck speed, till Thomas had taken to studying the charts with the captain at the end of the day, noting with dismay the way they were inching south. Two days ago they had gotten their first glimpse of the Philippines, easing down the western coast of northern Luzon, spending the night in sight of Manila, where the crew took on supplies. The foreigners had decided that passing through Philippine immigration wasn't worth the risk, so they had sat up half the night, jealously staring off toward the lights of the city. Now everyone was back aboard and pushing south once more, this time through the Sulu Sea towards the thousand-island archipelago of the same name that pointed a dotted and irregular arrow southwest to the Malaysian coast.

As they got closer, the crew grew quieter, more watchful. These waters had a bad reputation, as did the islands themselves, and not just for piracy. These were the stomping grounds of the Moro Islamic Liberation Front and the smaller but more radical Abu Sayyaf. The latter was the extremist and belligerent wing of a largely peaceful Muslim population whose home in the islands predated Spanish conquest but often found itself left out of the considerations of the Manila-centric government. Part of the disagreement between Parks and Captain Nakamura, it seemed, had concerned the safety of their destination, a place of bombings, assassinations, and kidnappings that most governments advised their people to avoid. Combine such facts with the occasional sighting of a ten-foot tiger shark streaking through the waters, and even the pale, palm-fringed beaches darkened, became—perhaps unfairly—places of menace.

"It's perfect, isn't it?" said Parks, appearing at Thomas's elbow.

"I guess," Thomas agreed.

"No," said Parks, "I mean it's a perfect habitat for the fish. Like Naples, all these islands are volcanic, the same undersea caves, the same warm waters. As soon as we get close to the island on the satellite images, we'll put the submersible down: a hundred meters or so should do it. See what's down there."

"You think we'll find them?" said Thomas.

"We'd better," said Parks. "It's what your brother died for."

"Maybe," said Thomas. "You think he died because someone wanted to keep the whereabouts of these fish secret?"

"Whereabouts or existence, yes," said Parks.

"Because they are worth money on the Chinese folk remedy market?"

"Maybe," said Parks, staring out over the water.

"But probably not," said Thomas, reading his tone.

"You want to know what I really think?" said Parks, rounding on him. "I think that it's not about money, or terrorism or science. Particularly not science. I think it's about antiscience."

"Which is what?" said Thomas.

"Religion," said Parks, like a man finally laying down his cards. "Specifically, Christianity. What I think is that your brother found swimming, walking proof of evolution, something he thought he could make some money off of, and they wanted him shut up."

"They?"

"The Church," he said. "His church, probably. What do you think the Reverend Jim is here for, Thomas? He's doing what he did when he was charged to watch over your brother. If we find the fish, you might want to toss him overboard before he brings the Catholic death squads down on us."

"You can't believe that," said Thomas.

"Really?" said Parks. "You want a list of what the Catholic

church has done to people who didn't agree with it? You want to hear about the Inquisition, or the Albigensian Crusade? Try this for size. It's July twenty-first, 1209, a town called Beziers in France. The armies of the papacy surround the town and demand the expulsion of about five hundred members of a heretic sect called the Cathars. Knowing what will happen to the Cathars if they are handed over, the town refuses. So what did the papal army do? They attacked. Ever heard the phrase 'Kill them all and let God sort them out'? That's where it comes from. More or less. It's what the papal legate or someone said when asked how they were supposed to separate the heretics from the rest. They sacked the town and slaughtered everyone they could find inside. Twenty thousand dead."

"That was a long time ago," said Thomas.

"Some things don't change," said Parks. "Religion doesn't tolerate dissent, doesn't debate truth. You are either with them or you are against them."

"But Ed was a priest."

"A priest who found evidence of evolution," said Parks. "That made him a target."

"I don't see why those two things are opposed to each other," said Thomas, "and I still don't see why this fishapod is such a big deal if all it does is confirm what you already know from fossils."

"It's not about scientific proof, because these people aren't interested in science except when they can use it to back up some half-witted tale about Noah's ark," said Parks with a sneer. "The fishapod wouldn't prove anything about evolution to the scientific community that they don't already know in general terms, but showing these things walking around might change a lot of minds that aren't in that community. The creationists and the intelligent-design crazies can point at holes in the fossil record all they like, but if you can then point right back to a living example of Darwinian evolution, it takes the wind out of their sails. It shouldn't, and if they were real scientists it wouldn't, but they aren't and it would. It will."

It was a credo, a statement of faith, and he reveled in it.

"Ed was a Christian who believed in evolution," said Thomas. "He can't be in that small a minority."

"Nonsense," said Parks. "He was a Christian who was prepared to dump his beliefs when the facts gave him an angle he could work for profit."

"You really don't know my brother at all, do you?" said Thomas.

"Didn't," Parks corrected. "He's dead, remember?"

"Christians can believe in evolution," said Thomas, ignoring him.

"America," Parks went on, "is the stupidest nation in the developed world. We cling to our ignorance. You don't think proof of evolution is a big deal? Tell the fifty-one percent of Americans who still don't believe in it. Tell the seventy-four percent of churchgoers who don't believe in evolution. Tell that to the Kansas board of education who were voted in solely to get evolution out of the curriculum, so that the schools could actually *train* their kids to be ignorant. You think I'm making this up? You can't make this shit up. We're living in the fucking Dark Ages and we're doing it by choice."

"I think Ed believed that the laws of science are the laws of God," said Thomas, thinking it through. "He thought that God made the world, but he did it by what you would call natural and scientific means over millions of years. God made man, but it took time because for God who resides in eternity, millions of years are but seconds."

Parks gave him a long strange look, and Thomas looked down at the water beneath their keel, embarrassed.

"And you agree with him?" said Parks.

"No," said Thomas. "I don't know. Does it matter?"

"It's Easter this weekend, did you know?" said Parks.

"I guess . . . No," said Thomas. "I'd forgotten."

"You know what's going to happen over there this weekend?" said Parks, nodding vaguely toward the coast.

"People will go to church," said Thomas, tiring of the conversation now.

"Sure," said Parks. "And then some of them will drive out to a field and will be nailed up on crosses for people to gawk at. Actual crucifixions in the twenty-first century, if you can believe that. People volunteer to show their holiness or to ask God for an extra loaf of bread or some damn thing."

"I've heard of that," said Thomas, noncommittal, jarred by Parks's scorn.

"And here's the best bit," said Parks. "They use stainless steel nails soaked in alcohol to avoid infection. Good, huh? They volunteer to be crucified, but they want to make sure that the nails they drive through their hands and feet won't *infect* them. Whack, whack, whack!" he said, miming the hammer strokes with a lopsided grin.

"So?" said Thomas.

"You can't have God and science," said Parks finally. "You have to choose one. If you don't, you're just swabbing for infection after you nailed yourself up."

Thomas said nothing. He wanted to respond, but even if he could guess what Ed would have said, he didn't know what he thought himself.

"Don't waver on me now," said Parks, slapping him on the shoulder as he walked away. "The battle lines are already drawn. You've been on the front lines for weeks."

A voice called to Parks from the helm. It was Captain Nakamura. Parks went to meet him.

"You okay?" said Kumi, sidling up to Thomas as he stared out over the water.

"Yes," he said, without thinking. "I guess. Parks . . ."

The sentence trailed off. He didn't know how to explain the leaden feeling the man's words left in him.

"He's a man on a mission," said Kumi. "A crusader."

Thomas smiled at the irony and nodded.

He hadn't expected Kumi to still be with him. Until the moment the boat actually left the dock, he had been waiting for her to leave.

Oddly enough, Parks had made the decision for her, albeit indirectly. She had phoned the Kobe aquarium, calling as a

State Department representative pretending to be looking into the unconventional hiring of an American citizen. She had, she confessed, been determined to uncover something about him or his story that would reveal the folly of their expedition. She had found nothing. Parks was in good standing with his employer, who clearly regarded him as eminently qualified—with a Stanford doctorate, no less—focused and cheap. The closest thing to a blot on his record was his failure to get tenure at Berkeley, where he had been an assistant professor right out of Stanford. Though Nakamura had final control of the *Nara*, the Kobe people clearly trusted Parks's judgment. The fact that he was obsessive to the point of irrationality didn't seem to matter much.

"I think they want to ride his wake," she had said. "They'll let him run his quest aground and then, when he finds what he's looking for, they'll hop out to grab all the publicity. If they can land a specimen—alive or dead—it will make them the single most prestigious outfit of their kind in the world."

"So you trust him?" Thomas had said.

"Not as far as I can throw him," she replied. "But if he's legit and on the verge of something important, I want to be there."

"As a representative of the American government," Thomas added with a wry smile.

"Close enough," she had said, before squeezing his arm and walking away in the way she used to, long ago, so that Thomas just stood on the deck for several minutes staring at the water.

That had been two days ago and he still didn't know what it had meant.

"How's Jim?" he said now.

"Distant," said his ex-wife. "He seems confused, even a little sad. Why don't you talk to him? You've barely exchanged words since we left Japan. Is it that he reminds you of Ed?"

"I don't know," said Thomas. "Maybe. You like him, don't you?"

"Yes," she said. It was a clear, definitive answer, but it was one she had chosen to make, a statement of faith and hope,

maybe even a little charity. It was less a description of her
feelings than a statement about the world she wished to live in.
Thomas nodded simply and said nothing.

Parks was coming back toward them, beaming.

"We'll be there in two hours," he announced. "Who's coming in the sub with me?"

"I am," said Thomas. He hadn't thought about it before, but
he knew that if anything was down there, he had to see it.

CHAPTER 95

Deborah Miller sat at her desk in the Druid Hills Museum in
Atlanta and frowned. Who was this Matsuhashi and why was
he e-mailing her these weird aerial images? He claimed, in
formal and very slightly strained English, that Thomas Knight
had asked him to forward them to her, though he said he didn't
know why. She cycled through them again: the village on the
beach, the scarlet water, the smoke, then nothing. It had to be
about his brother, but what she was supposed to do about it,
she had no idea.

When she last spoke to Thomas, he hadn't known where
his brother had died. This would seem to represent new information, then, though she couldn't imagine what could wipe a
village off the face of the earth like that. She fished an atlas
out of the bookshelves and searched for the coordinates, hom-
ing in on the Sulu Archipelago in the Philippines.

She did a series of Internet searches for recent news stories
concerning the region, but turned up only stern warnings
from various governments about visiting what was obviously
a deeply troubled region plagued by terrorism. A small but violent group was waging a secessionist war to create a separate
Muslim nation for the islands of Mindanao and the Sulu Archipelago. As part of the war on terrorism, six hundred fifty U.S.

troops, including one hundred fifty special forces, had been deployed to Basilan (the largest island in the archipelago) in 2002.

Was the smoking beach the result of a terrorist attack, or some kind of counterterrorist strike? In either case, Father Edward Knight may have merely been caught in the middle, though what he was doing there in the first place, she couldn't imagine.

There was a tap at her door and it opened, admitting Tonya, the museum's communication director.

"Just made a pot of coffee if you want to get yourself a cup," she said.

"Thanks," said Deborah. "Hey, look at this, will you."

She had already given Tonya a detailed account of the strange subplot of her time in Paestum, so she didn't need to say much now to bring her up to speed.

"Why did he have this sent to you?" said Tonya.

"Thomas trusts me, I think," said Deborah. "And I don't think he trusts many people right now, and with good reason."

"I guess being interrogated for the same murder creates a bond between folks," said Tonya.

"Quite," said Deborah. "So what do you think?"

"I've never even heard of this place before," said Tonya. "And if you're talking terrorists and military strikes and all, I think this is way out of our league."

"So you think I should do nothing?" said Deborah, standing up and stretching to her full—and considerable—height.

"Hell no," said Tonya. "But I think you need to get in touch with the kind of people who deal with this sort of thing."

"I don't want to break Thomas's trust or get him into hot water."

"I'd say he was already in hot water," said Tonya. "And besides, you could call someone with connections who—for you—would be discreet."

"For me?" said Deborah, turning puzzled on her. But Tonya was just smiling her knowing, sphinx smile and Deborah got it.

Ten minutes later, coffee in hand but still pacing the office like some distracted shore bird, Deborah made the call. It took only two minutes to make her way through the FBI switchboard, and the voice that answered caught her off guard, though not as off guard as she was about to get him.

"Hello?" he said. "This is Cerniga."

"Hi, Chris," she said, businesslike, as if they had spoken only days before. "This is Deborah Miller."

CHAPTER 96

The moment the submarine's hatch was sealed, Thomas regretted getting in. It was tiny, about ten feet long, eight feet wide, and almost as high, with a bulbous acrylic cockpit that made the whole thing look like a diving helmet. It was stocked with basic survival equipment including a knife, flare gun, and minimal food rations, and was equipped with a sonar system, life support, and remote-controlled arm. It was yellow.

Predictably, Parks met Thomas's claustrophobic unease with song.

"Sky of blue and sea of green," he sang, *"in our yellow submarine . . .* All together! *We all live . . ."*

Thomas did not join in.

"You sure this thing works?" he said.

"State of the art, my friend," said Parks, overly chipper. "State of the Goddamned art. Will take us six hundred meters down if we want it to."

"We don't, do we?"

"Shouldn't need to," said Parks. "I'd be surprised if these things live more than a couple of hundred meters down. If they get much deeper than that, I don't see how they would adjust to the surface. Too much of a change in pressure. You ready?"

He wasn't, but he nodded anyway and managed to smile at Kumi, who was watching them through the thick glass nose of the craft. One of the crew gave them a thumbs-up, and the submersible was winched up and out over the side on the *Nara*'s A-frame. Thomas felt cramped and out of control as the vessel turned slowly on the winch, but he said nothing. Parks had started to sing again, in his element and loving every second of it.

The two men were sitting next to each other surrounded by the clear acrylic bubble of the cockpit canopy. Visibility was excellent, with only the rear and ventral regions obscured by the rest of the craft, and Thomas found himself feeling oddly exposed as they broke the plane of the water and dipped into its shifting bluish depths. He gripped his armrest and stared at the fish that darted past, flashing in the filtered sunlight that rippled and shifted in columns from above. It took him almost a minute to realize that he was holding his breath. He sucked the air in as Parks disengaged the winch automatically and the vessel suddenly became weightless in the swell.

The *Nara* had moored a thousand yards from the rocky shore. Though the island was edged with idyllic sandy beaches, they were interspersed with piers and cliffs of dark volcanic rock that extended well out into the sea. Taking the boat in closer would be suicidal, so to explore the rocky outcrops underwater—searching for the caves Parks thought were the habitual lair of the fishapod—they had to make the journey in the sub, cruising at a leisurely two knots.

They were diving too, and as the light outside lowered slowly, Parks flicked on the sub's lamp array, which included two halogen-bright spots facing forward on a rectangular frame. They barely made a difference here, but if the sub kept going down, they would be invaluable. Parks snapped a switch.

"*Nara*," he said, speaking loud and clear. "Come in."

"This is *Nara*," said a Japanese crewman, his English heavily accented. "Is everything okay?"

"Hunky-dory," said Parks.

There was a moment of silence, presumably given over to one of the foreigners translating, and then the crewman was back.

"Very good," he said. "All is . . . er . . . hunky-dory here too."

"Well, isn't that just dandy," said Parks. "Sonar is picking up a steep rock face ahead. Slowing to half speed, continuing dive, and commencing search."

Thomas shifted in his seat.

"Watch out for the giant octopus," said Parks.

"There are giant octopuses round here?"

"Don't be ridiculous," Parks grinned. "And it's *octopi*. Didn't they teach you anything in school, or was that day given over to how God made the little fishies?"

"I'm pretty sure there was one day when they told me never to go underwater in a plastic bottle with a guy who has tried to kill me," said Thomas.

"Still harping on that?" said Parks. "And I thought we were buds. How's our depth?"

"Fifty meters and falling."

"Good," said Parks. "I figure we're still five hundred yards from the cliff. On the beach side there's a coral reef—if the locals haven't dynamited it to get at the tuna and mackerel—but over here it just drops all the way down to sand. The sonar says we can go down another seventy meters. Don't be surprised if the cabin starts making odd noises. She'll hold."

Thomas shifted again and stared out into the shifting darkness. He had expected teeming fish, brightly colored and curious, maybe even a shark or two sliding past, but nothing was down here at all. No plants, no coral, no fish, just vague blue light.

What if there's nothing down here after all? What if Ed got it wrong and the whole thing has been a wild-goose chase?

"I'm slowing us down some more," said Parks. "We're getting close. I don't want to spook anything."

"Or run headlong into the rock," suggested Thomas.

"That too."

He checked the cascading stream of green lines on the sonar monitor.

"Should be entering visual range soon," he said. "Keep your eyes open."

They sat in silence for several minutes, the soft whir of the sub's five hydraulic motors the only sound in the deep. Thomas was getting antsy.

"You sure this sonar system is working?" he said.

"Shh," said Parks. "Keep looking."

"I'm just saying . . ." Thomas began. "Wait. Look there."

The infinite blue expanse in front of them had darkened and hardened in the floodlights.

"That's it," said Parks, cutting their speed to nothing. The craft drifted on, slowing, still diving, till they could see the pale seabed and the foot of the cliff. Thomas looked up and saw the black rock rising up in a wall all the way to the surface, well beyond the reach of their lights.

"Now what?" he said.

"Now we get as close as we dare," said Parks, "and we look."

CHAPTER 97

"That's way outside my jurisdiction," said Cerniga. "It's spook territory. CIA. NSA. God knows what else."

"I'm just asking if you can make a few inquiries," said Deborah.

"For old times' sake?"

Deborah held her breath, gauging his tone. Last time they had spoken it had been at the end of a case where she had helped him out, but the way things had wound up hadn't been characteristic of the case itself. Before the end he had spent a good deal of the time thinking she was a pain in the ass, and he had probably been right. But by the end she had earned his respect, and that was what she was banking on now.

Old times' sake.

She couldn't tell if he was smiling, so it was a gamble to answer as she did: "Something like that, yeah."

There was a pause in which he might have blown out a long sigh, and she could tell she had won.

"Congrats on the promotion, by the way," she said.

"Yeah, yeah," said Cerniga, and now she could hear the smile. "I'll call you back."

As the submarine drew closer it was apparent that what had looked to be a sheer wall of rock was actually a corrugated mass of irregular stone outcrops stretching up like the bones of the island, and what had seemed solid was pocked with recesses and tubelike caverns made as hot lava belched into the sea. Where the molten rock had been in contact with the cooling water it had hardened, but the hot core had continued to flow, creating great stone pipes running down to the seabed.

"No wonder we don't know anything about what lives down here," said Parks. "Combine the intricacy of the cave network with the fact that the only way in is almost a hundred and fifty meters underwater at the ass end of the world, a place populated mainly by terrorists, and it's hardly surprising we never found them before."

Thomas had had plenty of reasons not to like Parks before getting into the submarine, most of which had had to do with their encounters before making this fairly unholy alliance. He had thought that as long as their pact seemed genuine, as long as their goals were the same, he would have no difficulty getting past their previous hostility, but this was not the case, and not merely because Thomas hadn't forgiven him for abandoning him in the *o-furo*. It was simpler than that. Though he sometimes found him funny and couldn't help admiring his self-possession, Thomas just didn't like Parks, and the more time he spent with him the more the man's brash confidence and arrogant dismissal of whatever didn't interest him had begun to rankle. Everything he said seemed calculated to irritate or offend, and the fact that it was *not* actually calculated at all because Parks never really considered what anybody else thought somehow made it worse.

"Finding the fishapod here is going to be so huge," he said, "that everyone will forget that what this jungle backwater was previously famous for was the Muslim and Christian idiots throwing coconuts at each other."

"You look forward to that, don't you?" said Thomas. "Being the one to enlighten the world. So what's it all about, this quest of yours?"

"What do you mean?"

"There must be some reason for your Captain Ahab routine."

"Some personal tragedy, you mean? Some unbearable loss that turned me against God?" said Parks. "Yeah, my puppy died when I was three. Never got over it. How could Jesus let that cute little guy . . ."

"Okay, okay," said Thomas. "I get it."

"You don't need to lose a baby to see that the universe has no controlling intelligence," said Parks, "that the world is run by the greedy, the cruel, and the stupid. If there's a God, He fell asleep at the wheel right after humans showed up."

"Is that what you taught the kids at Berkeley?" said Thomas. The man had a knack for pushing his buttons.

Parks gave him a sharp look. "Found out about that, did you?" he said, the flicker of irritation turning into a sneering amusement. "If you don't want to be in a science class you shouldn't register for one."

"But they didn't dismiss you for preaching evolution at a university," said Thomas, connecting the dots as he spoke. "There's no way."

"So, you *don't* know," said Parks, pleased with himself. Thomas waited. "Preaching evolution is what it amounted to," said Parks. "Well within what I thought was protected by academic freedom."

"They didn't?"

"There was this one kid," said Parks. "Jessica Bane. *Bane of my life,* I called her. Cute, though. Smiled and said 'please' and 'thank you, professor,' started coming by my office talking intelligent design. I told her what I thought, and made it something of a theme in my lectures for a couple of weeks. Next thing I know I'm being dragged in on charges of religious intolerance."

Thomas felt himself withdraw a little, wary.

"Surely you could have appealed?"

"And spend the rest of my life walking on the eggshells of political correctness and cultural sensitivity?" he snapped back. "Please. I have a real career to make. I can't do that in classes stuffed with morons who want their science teachers to stand at the podium with a Bible in their hands."

"Has anyone ever told you," said Thomas, "that for someone who has nothing but contempt for religion, you have one hell of a God complex?"

"Hey, at least I use my powers for good," he said, grinning and joining his hands, mock angelic.

"You remind me of Watanabe," said Thomas.

"That hack? He's not a scientist. He's a wannabe movie star who figured he could make up the rules as he went."

"That's the thing about God complexes, though, isn't it," said Thomas. "Eventually you figure you're above the law."

"Oh, that's rich," said Parks, "coming from Mr. Fox News."

Thomas opened his mouth to respond but had nothing to say, and was fractionally relieved when Parks snapped, "You want to shut up now? This has to be done delicately."

He was maneuvering the sub into the mouth of a cave only a couple of meters broader than the vessel itself. Their lights shone into the cavern but revealed nothing, because the stone pipe turned up and to the left.

"No way can we get in there," said Thomas. "It's too narrow."

"We're not going to see anything sitting out here," said Parks.

"So look for a wider cave."

Parks sighed, but he pulled the sub back. They adjusted, moved right, and then floated up a few meters, ignoring two other caverns that were no larger than the first. The third was broader, but not by much.

"I say we go in," said Parks. "The tunnels probably get wider inside, at least for a ways. Where the molten rock hit the water it will have cooled faster, so the opening will be the narrowest part."

"But if some of the rock turned solid inside the tube the passage will be blocked."

"Then we'll have to make sure we have room to turn around and get out," said Parks, adjusting the sub's attitude so that its bulbous translucent nose pointed straight into the rock passage. "You think we should have bought her dinner first?" said Parks, leering.

"Just go slowly," said Thomas.

The engines whirred and the yellow submersible eased carefully into the stone tube.

CHAPTER 98

Deborah had been surprised to hear back from Cerniga so quickly, doubly so because he sounded so uncharacteristically tense. Her surprise had changed to alarm when he had told her he was coming to the museum and would be there in less than a half hour.

It was strange to see him again, particularly back here in her office, but there was no time for reminiscence or catching up. He looked serious, even agitated.

"On March thirteenth there was a counterterrorist air strike on two sets of coordinates in the southwestern islands of the Philippines," he said. "It was orchestrated not by the military but by the CIA. One location was a known Abu Sayyaf base and training facility. The other, the beach in your satellite images, was a fishing village with, so far as I can tell, no terrorist links whatsoever prior to the strike."

"You think they had special intelligence about the village?" said Deborah.

"No," said Cerniga, his voice hushed. "That's why I came over. I think something went wrong."

"What do you mean?"

He laid out some hastily copied documents, much of which had been blacked out.

"The Abu Sayyaf strike had been scheduled a week in advance, but nothing had been said about the other location prior to takeoff. After launch, two of the aircraft separated from the formation to make an attack run on this island."

"So?"

"So," he said pointedly, "I can see no evidence of actual orders directing them to do so, and when they came back, all hell broke loose. The base was shut down and emergency crews were dispatched to the island to collect survivors and, it seems, to throw a media blanket over the area. The target zone is really out in the wilds, so I doubt that was so hard to do."

"What about the pilots of the aircraft?" said Deborah. "If you are suggesting that they acted on their own, they must have been interrogated or something, no?"

Cerniga smiled and produced another sheet showing a table of technical specifications and a photograph of an odd-looking plane: long, slim, bulbous-nosed, with one downward and two upward-slanting fins at the tail.

"Meet the MQ-9A Predator B," said Cerniga. "A drone spy plane."

"Drone?"

"Pilotless," said Cerniga. "It's controlled remotely from the ground."

Deborah gave a low whistle.

"Exactly," said Cerniga. "It can carry up to fourteen Hellfire missiles or other stores including GBU-12 laser-guided bombs. It's got a Lynx II SAR and an MTS twenty-inch gimbal . . ."

"English, please," said Deborah.

"Right. Sorry," said Cerniga. "It can find, track, fix, and target by itself in real time. It's a descendant of the RQ Predator 1, which has been used as a strike aircraft since 2002. In 2003 one of them flown by the CIA accidentally killed a man and nine children in Afghanistan while hunting Taliban supporters, and that was with a payload of only two Hellfire missiles. What we are dealing with is bigger, faster, and a hell of a lot scarier in terms of punch."

"So how the hell do two of these go off course and hit the wrong place?" she said.

"They don't," said Cerniga. "That Afghan strike wasn't an accident in the sense of it hitting the wrong target. It hit the right target but the intel was bad. This is a very sophisticated weapon system, and when it goes wrong, that's usually because someone did something dumb."

"Or malicious," said Deborah.

Cerniga frowned, reluctant to go there.

"Come on, Chris," she said. "You said so yourself."

"Someone could have made a mistake with the coordinates," he said, without conviction.

"Has there been an internal investigation?" she asked.

"Of course," said Cerniga, "but those findings are kept under wraps."

"But no one has been fired for incompetence, right?"

"Not yet."

"So someone has covered their tracks," said Deborah. "Which means . . ."

"They could do it again," said Cerniga, unwillingly completing her thought.

CHAPTER 99

The sub swam slowly into the tubular cavern, two, five, ten meters in. There the passage ballooned for a moment, and they were able to rotate and look around. Parks shot video from a built-in camera of the environment and the mollusks that clung to the walls in bunches. There was almost no current down here and the still, dark waters were unnervingly lifeless.

"There could be anything down here," said Parks, eagerly, as the sub pressed on into the dark.

"Or nothing," said Thomas, whose discomfort with their predicament increased with each foot the sub nosed into the base of the island.

As if on cue a large, heavy-bodied fish with wide, pale eyes that had been sitting unnoticed on a rock shelf roused itself with a flick of sand particles and eased out of their lights.

"You see that?" said Parks. "That's a deep-sea anglerfish. These caves probably have an ecosystem unlike anything we've seen before. It's a very precise and secluded environment. There might be species that exist nowhere else in the world."

A shoal of guppylike fish swam in and out of view, their tails flashing with a low-grade phosphorescence. After them sped an eel-like creature with a pelican gape almost as wide as its body was long.

"What the hell was that?" asked Thomas.

"*Eurypharynx pelecanoides*," said Parks, "the umbrella-mouth gulper, or something quite like it. But it shouldn't be here. We aren't anything like deep enough. The caves must simulate depth in terms of everything but pressure. This is amazing. Unheard of. It's going to make my career."

Thomas shot him a wary look. The scientist's eyes were bright, almost feverish.

The tunnel ended abruptly, the far wall of the cavern looming in the lights.

"We'll have to turn around," said Thomas, relieved.

"No," said Parks. "Look."

He was staring directly up through the bubble canopy. The tunnel continued vertically, but narrower.

"No way," said Thomas. "It's too tight and we can't see up. If we got stuck in the rock up there, we'd never get out."

"Let's just have a look, shall we?" said Parks, already angling the sub so that she drifted up into the crevice.

"We can't see up there!" said Thomas.

The sub's lights were forward facing, so they had no idea what the structure of the rocks above them would be. Thomas put his hand forcefully on Parks's, and the vessel bobbled as they wrestled momentarily for control.

"Okay, okay," said Parks. "We'll turn her nose up; that way we can see in and get a sonar read."

Thomas nodded and removed his hand. Parks reset the controls and the sub's attitude shifted, rocking the men back in their seats as they moved to the vertical.

The light showed the brownish rock only feet from their hull, and then a large blank space.

"It's big enough to get in," said Parks. "Look at the sonar. There's a huge hollow in the rock just up there, a space the size of a basketball court. Okay?"

It wasn't a real question, and he was moving the sub into the hole before Thomas made his cautious nod. Tipped back in his chair, Thomas felt like an astronaut on the launchpad, but around him was not blue sky but rock and deep, black water. And God alone knew what else.

Two feet from the mouth of the cavern, several things happened at once. The sonar beeped insistently and the screen that had shown only the cavern hollow now showed the movement of something large inside, something that then swam into their lights and across the cave mouth. It was dark, mottled yellow, big—at least as big as the sub itself—and it caught the vessel's cab first with one powerful footlike fin, then with the trailing, undulating tail, so that the submarine stalled in its motion and clanged heavily against the rock wall. Thomas glimpsed a crocodilian head full of overlapping teeth.

But then the radio was squawking and through the panicked voices coming from the *Nara* he heard the unmistakable sound of gunfire.

CHAPTER 100

Cerniga had played every card he had, but the fact remained that he was a field agent in the FBI's Atlanta office and had little sway in matters of international counterterrorism regardless of his personal reputation. Things were tense enough between the FBI and CIA these days without him stirring the hornet's nest, he was told, particularly if he was going to throw around accusations of incompetence or worse. In truth, he would have given the matter up after the first phone call, but Deborah Miller had a knack for the persuasive, and—he had to admit—she was often right.

So he made more calls, checked the security of the lines, and told anyone who would listen at headquarters about his fears. He called the CIA and the Air Force as well, but couldn't get past the sense that he was being dodged. When he could get anyone to actually talk about the March thirteenth attack, they took one look at the security clearance issues and shut him down. It was Deborah who pushed the angle that would crack the door open an inch, scribbling in pencil on the back of a museum flyer:

"Tell them it's going to happen again," she said. "Same location."

What had been an inconvenient investigation into past embarrassments was now something quite different.

"Here's what we know," he said, after finally hanging up.

"The Predator drone has to be launched by a ground crew relatively close to the strike area."

"How close?"

"Not sure," he said. "A few hundred miles, probably. If the attack on the village where your friend's brother was killed was indeed deliberate, whoever did it did not have the authority to actually schedule the launch. Their mission had to be piggybacked onto a legitimate flight that was already scheduled. Since the aircraft that stayed on course never fired a shot, the legitimate flight was probably strictly reconnaissance, though the aircraft would have been armed in case a target presented itself while it was up."

"So for it to happen again," said Deborah, "there would need to be another scheduled mission in the vicinity of the beach."

"Right," said Cerniga. "And here's the weird thing. It makes sense that the CIA would give any credible threat a serious listen, but their tone changed completely as soon as I suggested it might happen again and soon. They took the coordinates and they moved out of that 'thanks-for-your-interest' mode."

"You think another drone flight is scheduled in the Sulu Archipelago?"

"For all I know," said Cerniga, "they are already in the air."

CHAPTER 101

It was Kumi's voice on the radio and it lasted no more than three or four seconds. Thomas caught the words *helicopter* and *attack* and then there was only the rapid burst of automatic weapons fire followed by the static of dead air.

"Their radio is down," said Thomas. "They might be dead. We have to get to the surface."

"Wait," said Parks, who was struggling to right the sub

after it had been bumped into the rock wall by the creature in the cave. "If I can get some film of that . . ."

"They need us," said Thomas. "Turn the sub around."

"They are probably dead already," said Parks, gazing out into the water, "so it doesn't matter how long it takes us to get back to the surface."

Thomas stared at him, as if seeing the man's true face for the first time.

"If I can just push the nose back into the cave and set the cameras running . . . ," Parks began. He paused at the pressure against his temple and turned very slowly. Thomas was holding the flare gun to the side of his head.

"Turn the boat around," he said.

"You fire that thing in here," said Parks, "and you'll kill us both."

"Probably," Thomas shrugged. "But I'm not on the edge of a shattering discovery, am I? In fact, I'm not on the edge of much these days, and the world won't miss me."

Parks held his eyes, gauging the truth of the remark, and then he nodded fractionally and began to steer the boat down.

"Got a plan, chief?" said Parks, the perpetual sneer reappearing. "Or are we just going to surface next to the boat and let them shoot us full of holes?"

Thomas said nothing. He had no idea what to do. He had to assume that the *Nara* had been taken. He figured that their sonar would have picked up any substantial explosion, so the boat was probably still intact, but who was still alive and where they were he had no way of knowing. Kumi had said something about a helicopter, so they could have been taken off the boat, but surely the attackers didn't have the personnel to comfortably guard the twenty-odd crew? And if Kumi and Jim had been taken, they could be anywhere by now. The island was the logical place to set down if the attackers wanted to stay local, if they thought there were still loose ends to tie up.

Namely you.

Exactly.

To take the sub back to the boat would be to give themselves up, or worse. They had to find somewhere else to beach
the sub and get onto the island. That way at least they kept the
initiative.

"Let me see that chart of the island," he said to Parks. He
still hadn't laid down the flare gun.

Kumi recognized the guy from the Kofu railway station as one
of the soldiers, but he was not the one who seemed to be giving the orders. The woman was, presumably, the person who
had masqueraded as a nun in Italy, though in her elegant
makeup, tank top, and shorts, that was hard to imagine. The
muscle were three guys in combat gear and armed with machine guns. One of them was black, all of them were built like
soldiers, and good ones at that. They called the leader *sir*, and
unless she had misheard, the woman had called him *War*. It
was bizarre and might have been funny, except that Nakamura
was already dead and she had a feeling they would be too,
soon, unless the situation changed radically.

The helicopter had come out of nowhere, the men dropping onto the deck of the *Nara*, shooting before anyone had
realized they were even armed. There had been no battle per
se, and the captain had been killed merely to keep the rest of
them in line. The radio, GPS, and other equipment on the boat
had been shot up as she tried to warn Tom, so they were effectively marooned, cut off from the outside world. The only
good thing was that in riddling the boat's communication sys-
tems they had also disabled the sonar, so they had no idea
where the submersible was.

The crew had been locked belowdecks, while she and Jim
were bundled into a lifeboat at gunpoint and sent ashore. No
guards had been posted on the boat, but with no way to send a
message to anyone else, the crew wouldn't be able to do anything even if they broke free, and if they tried to get the boat
moving again the gunmen would hunt them down from the air.
The helicopter had landed on the beach and had become a

kind of base camp, though it was impossible to tell how long they expected to be here. There seemed to Kumi to be an air of expectation among their captors, and there was a lot of standing around, as if they were waiting for something to happen.

"Nice beach," said Jim as they got closer. "I hadn't planned a beach holiday but this is nice."

Kumi gave him an appreciative smile. He was trying to keep her cheerful, but unnecessarily. She didn't wilt under strain, merely withdrawing, tortoiselike, until she had a clear sense of the situation and how she would resolve it. She felt no panic, not yet at least, and the killing of the captain had only toughened her resolve to do whatever was necessary to see that these thugs did not win. She didn't know what they wanted, but she would do all in her power to see they didn't get it.

The boat ground hard into the sand.

"Out," said the black soldier, pointing casually with his gun.

She clambered out, losing her footing as the boat rocked, and staggered ashore. Jim followed, still smiling doggedly. His eyes had had a glazed, distant look ever since the shooting of Nakamura, as if his world had been jarred out of its orbit.

One of the other soldiers approached them from the helicopter, spun her around, and pulled her hands behind her back. In seconds she was cuffed with a thin but unyielding strand of plastic like a heavy-duty zip tie. Then she and Jim were pushed across the beach toward the palm trees and the blasted remains of a thatched hut, the wooden walls half burned away by some terrible heat.

"In there," said the soldier.

Inside, Jim sat in the sand. Kumi studied their makeshift prison. They could get out easily enough, but it was a good ten- or twelve-second sprint across the sand into the trees, twice that to the water. They'd be cut down long before they could lose themselves in the jungle. She would have to think of something else.

* * *

"How long can we stay under in this thing?" said Thomas.

"Six hours," said Parks. "Nine at a push. If we switch to survival mode, we can make it longer, but then we have no power for anything else, including movement."

"So we need to beach, but after the sun goes down," said Thomas.

"They may know where we are already," said Parks. "If they have access to the *Nara*'s sonar or they have a sonar buoy they can drop from the chopper, we're a sitting target."

"We have to assume they don't," said Thomas.

"Is that like believing that the poor get their cake after death?" said Parks, snide as ever. "A leap of faith?"

"Not sure what else we have," said Thomas. "Take her away from the boat and stay deep. We'll go around the back of the island and wait for dark before beaching."

"That will take hours," said Parks. "And once we beach the sub, it's useless. Without the *Nara* we can't get it back in the water."

"Right now I don't see where we'd be trying to go," said Thomas. "Bring her about."

Parks sighed and moved the sub away from the rock wall, staying close to the rippled sand of the seabed. He moved slowly, since they were in no rush and higher speeds increased the chance of being picked up by sonar. "Cavitating," he called it.

"If they have sonar," he said, "they'll probably find us anyway, but there's no point screaming to them."

"Still think that 'them' is the Catholic Church?" said Thomas. "Dropping out of helicopters with machine guns? Doesn't sound right to me."

"The power, ruthlessness, and ignorance of religion never surprises me," said Parks.

"And you think these are the people who have taken my wife?" said Thomas, only realizing after he said it that he didn't use the habitual "ex."

"Yes. And you should forget all that stuff about Christian mercy. If you aren't with them you are against them. Forget all your nuanced, gray-area arguments; these people are waging a war against you as fiercely as if you fought for the Devil himself. Don't expect her to live through this, Thomas. You'll only make it tougher on yourself when you find her body."

CHAPTER 102

The phones had started ringing at the George Bush Center for Intelligence in Langley, Virginia. Meetings were hastily convened and Agent Cerniga's voice bounced by secure satellite into a room full of serious-looking men and women whose eyes were fixed on a series of projected maps and satellite images. Among them were photographs taken the day after the March thirteenth attack by a pair of rogue Predator drones on a remote fishing village in the Philippines. Most of the serious conversation went on after Cerniga's call was politely concluded with a formal thank-you to him and his agency for their diligence.

"Well?" said the deputy director. "Anything to it?"

A black woman in glasses spoke up.

"If the incident was the result of computer malfeasance, it was cleverly concealed to look like a system failure," she said.

"Is it possible, Janice?"

"It's possible."

"And had that possibility occurred to you before . . ." he checked his watch, "about a half hour ago?"

"Of course," she answered, with a hint of defiance. "It's my job to consider such possibilities."

Someone gasped, and it was only then that she realized that she had said the wrong thing. The deputy director stared at her and she felt the tension in the room escalate, as if everyone were holding their breath. He held her eyes with his as he spoke:

"I was told it was a system malfunction," he said. "No question. No doubt. Mechanical error." He paused, but if there was a question there, no one answered it. He spelled it out. "So I'm hearing about this other possibility *now* because . . . ?"

Everyone shifted. The deputy director was not a man to be left out of the loop without all manner of stuff hitting the fan if said loop didn't close satisfactorily. Janice removed her glasses and looked him in the face, conscious that her career might be about to take a punch from which it would never recover.

"We thought we could deal with the matter internally until we had some definitive sense of the chain of events, sir," she said.

"But questions are already being raised external to the service, yes?" he said, his calm suspended by tightening steel cable.

"Apparently. Yes, sir."

He watched her for a second without blinking.

"When this all blows over, Janice, you and I are going to talk," he said, without malice or bluster.

"Yes, sir," she said.

"For now I need a list of possibilities as to how it could have been done, how many people would have been involved, and who those people would be," said the deputy director. "I want that within the hour. Till then, I want all Predator flights grounded."

"Sir," said a middle-aged man with nicotine-stained fingers, "that might not be possible . . ."

"Make it possible," said the deputy director. "Till the system gets a clean bill of health and we know it cannot be hacked, nothing goes up. Clear?"

CHAPTER 103

Night had fallen on the tiny Philippine island. Parks had brought the submarine into the sheltered cove with the lights off, relying solely on the cascading sonar screen for a sense of their surroundings. They had sat on the bottom, thirty meters down, for four agonizing hours, waiting for the sun to set, sitting silent in the dark. For Thomas, who loathed cramped spaces and immobility, it was a good approximation of Hell.

They moved inland slowly, still without lights, coasting ghostlike to the surface and in to the beach, their engines barely turning over so that they seemed to drift with the tide. Before the light had gone entirely the formerly clear water had seemed blurred, presumably because of sand from the beach, and their view from the sub's cab had become thick and unspecific. Once the sun went down, of course, the darkness was absolute, and Thomas started to feel that he had been relying on his other senses for days. The emergency kit contained a flashlight, but they didn't want to attract attention to themselves and kept it off. They brushed the sea floor before fully surfacing, making the sub turn, oscillating into the current before inching forward and settling completely.

Parks popped the hatch and the night air flooded in like relief. All around them were the sounds of the ocean and the piping of insects from the trees. Thomas clambered out, the diver's knife pushed into his belt, still clutching the flare pistol. He looked around. A thin filament of moon rode high over the forest, and in its light the beach glowed white. If anyone came down to the water they would see the submarine, but they had run aground close to some hunks of deep-set rock, and from farther up the beach the yellow submarine might remain invisible. He splashed onto the shore and looked about him. No one was there.

"Now what?" said Parks.

He was still exuding the jaundiced air that had thickened the longer they sat in the sub without searching for his precious fishapod.

"Now we get into the trees and make our way east, to the beach where the *Nara* was anchored," said Thomas.

He had had more than enough time to consider his plan, but its details were still imprecise. Even if Jim and Kumi were alive, even if he could save them, he had no idea how they would get off the island or where they might hide till that was possible. The entire place was only a couple of miles across. But maybe they wouldn't need to stay hidden for long. Maybe the coast guard or the Philippine military would be on hand, following up reports of unauthorized helicopter presence. Maybe the *Nara* had even managed to get off an SOS before they lost their radio . . .

And maybe your attackers have the kind of authority that can push unwanted foreign governments away if they get too inquisitive . . .

Maybe.

At the head of the beach was a mango tree, dark and fragrant. Thomas stood under it for a moment while Parks caught up, and then led the way into a screen of coconut palms and yucca. Something in the treetops—a monkey, perhaps—called out, a great booming whoop of alarm at their approach, and then fell silent.

"I guess we're not in Kansas anymore," said Parks.

"Just stay close and keep quiet," said Thomas, pushing through the undergrowth in search of something like a path.

"You were very close to Ed," said Jim into the darkness. "Do you mind if I ask how close?"

"We were good friends for all the time I was in the States after Japan," said Kumi, "but that's not what you mean, is it?"

"Not really. I'm sorry. It's none of my business."

It was too dark to see her face, so the sound of her chuckling caught him by surprise.

"Ed was just a friend," she said. "Nothing more."

"So why does Thomas say he broke up your marriage?"

"Because Thomas needs someone to blame," she said, and there was no trace of a laugh now. "We met in Japan, and though I was second generation, the place was strange to both of us. When we left it was like something had gone away that had been part of the glue that held us together, if that makes sense. Ex-pats cling to each other in strange places. Out of that context, they have nothing in common."

"And that's why you split up?"

She sighed. "It's part of it," she said. "We committed to each other, determined to build something together, holding on to the history we had made together. But we're not easy people to get along with, and we drifted apart. The baby just focused it all, made it seem unfixable."

"So it had nothing to do with Ed at all."

"Ed advised a trial separation," she answered. "I had been confiding in him for years. He knew Tom better than anyone, knew how distant he could be. After Anne—the miscarriage, I mean—Tom was no help at all. I guess we weren't much help to each other."

Jim could hear that that last remark was something she had not thought before, that it was a concession.

"Anyway," she concluded, "I was going into a downward spiral and Ed suggested that we take a break from each other. So I left and never went back. Tom never forgave him."

"I can see how that would work."

"I know Ed meant well."

"In my experience," said Jim, "he always did."

"Tom said he helped you out, that you'd had a rough year," said Kumi.

"You could say that," said Jim. His voice was soft and she couldn't get a clear sense of where he was in the dark, but he sounded nostalgic, even sad. "There was a family in my parish called Meers. Single mom and two teenaged kids. Poor, sort of screwed up, in and out of trouble. Every month they struggled to pay their rent, every month I tried to help out with some parish funds. Borrowed some from the bishop a couple of times. Anyway, it came to a head after one of the kids—a fifteen-year-old, DeMarcus, his name was—got picked up for shoplifting once too often and everything went to hell. I met with the landlord and the police but I couldn't stop it. They wound up being evicted just as the first snowstorm of the year came in. Chicago's a rough city to be homeless in. Anyway, they refused to leave, the cops came, and there was some trouble. Nothing too bad but . . ."

"You were there," said Kumi.

"I was there," he said. "Threw a punch I probably shouldn't have, and woke up in a cell. The bishop did what he could but it was a mess. I was 'on leave' for a while, and that was when Ed was sent over to take up the slack. I wouldn't have got through it without him, and not just because he took on a lot of my duties."

"Your faith?"

"Took a hit, yes," he said. "Such things make the universe feel random and vicious. It's tough to feel that no matter what you do there are some things you just can't fix."

"Yes," she said. *A child-sized hole in your gut.* "Yes." She waited, then said, "How's the family now?"

"Eileen and the younger boy are doing well," said Jim. "They have an apartment and she's working a couple of jobs."

"And DeMarcus?" said Kumi, not wanting to ask.

"DeMarcus died his third night on the street. Walked into a drug deal, or said the wrong thing to somebody . . . We never knew for sure."

"God, Jim," said Kumi. "I'm sorry."

"Yes," he said. "Me too. Funny, isn't it, the way death throws everything into perspective? It made me feel . . . lost. Useless. Ed got me through it, but part of me still feels that if I gave it all up tomorrow, no one would really notice. Not really."

"I'm sure they would," said Kumi.

Jim thanked her, but he didn't say he thought she was right.

* * *

Thomas pressed on through the dense vegetation, following thinly beaten sand tracks that were already being over-whelmed by stiff grass and vines. Not so long ago there had been a fishing village on the island, but after the bomb—or whatever it was that had killed his brother—the survivors seemed to have moved on. There was no trace of habitation now and only the movement of bats, tarsiers, and lemurs hunt-ing fruit and insects in the treetops. He kept the sea to his right as he moved, but the forest was disorienting and he dared not venture too close to the shore, so that after a half hour he was unsure whether they had bypassed the beach.

"We might be able to see the *Nara* if it's still where we left it," he said, gazing out toward the water. The moon was setting and the darkness had thickened.

"If the boat had moved off before we left the sub, our sonar would have picked it up," said Parks. "Nothing carries through water like boat propellers."

"So where the hell is it?"

"We can't see anything from here. One of us will have to go closer to the beach."

Thomas sighed, but Parks was right.

"Follow me," Thomas said, dropping to a half-crouch and edging through a mass of ferns toward the shore.

There was a heavy clump of palms arcing up into the night sky, then only sand. Beyond that he could hear the lapping of the sea but could glimpse no sign of the boat. Hugging the tree line, he began to move, tracing the slow curve of the beach, till he saw it, quite clear, a soft white shape a good way from shore, the decks dark, but a pinprick of light showing through what he took to be a distant porthole. It looked perfectly placid.

"You think they are all on board?" whispered Parks.

Thomas shrugged.

He walked another thirty paces and stopped. There was something big and dark on the sand ahead of him, something the size of a hut, but irregular and somehow ominous. It was what had blocked the *Nara* from view. He skulked back into the trees and watched for a moment, but could make no more sense of the thing in the darkness.

"What is that?" he mouthed.

Parks shook his head. Then, without warning, he stepped back out onto the beach and turned on the flashlight, directing it at the strange, dark hulk on the sand. It took only a second for the dread of the thing to register in both men's minds.

Helicopter.

Parks's eyes grew wide in the sudden lamplight and he fought to shut it off, fumbling and flashing the beam around. He backed away, as if he had stumbled onto a corpse, and Thomas could only watch from the trees as a figure—barely more than a silhouette—emerged, dropped into a crouch, and aimed a submachine gun. Ben Parks had time only to look up from the flashlight before the night was stabbed with suppressed muzzle flash and the muffled cough of the silenced weapon, and then he was crying out and dropping to his knees.

CHAPTER 104

Ron Dalton, the duty officer at the island station, read the message twice before starting to shout. The jungle camp was tiny, barely long enough for the runway, and all the crucial ground control equipment was packed into a thirty-foot trailer. The Predator drone aircraft had no hangar and were transported disassembled in crates known to the crew as coffins. Dalton burst out of the trailer and stared at the runway where the fourth plane was taxiing into position.

"Abort!" he screamed into the thick jungle air. "Shut it down!"

One of the ground crew stood up and stared at him, but clearly couldn't hear over the Predator's engine.

"Problem?" said a voice behind him.

Dalton turned. It was Harris, the weird kid who played with the computers all the time and never talked. He might be just the person he needed.

"We have to abort the mission," said Dalton. "The targeting system has been compromised."

"Yeah?" said the kid, his eyes blank as ever. Then something appeared, a little flicker of satisfaction that Dalton had never seen before in the kid's face. He didn't like it. "You don't know who I am, do you?" said the kid, still smiling that weird little smile.

"What are you talking about?" said Dalton. "This is serious . . ."

"I said, you don't know who I am," said the kid, the smile stiffening.

Dalton started to walk away. He didn't have time for adolescent games. He muttered as much to himself as he headed back to the trailer, his mind already moving on. So he wasn't even thinking about Harris when the knife went through his shoulder blade and into his heart.

"See?" said the kid, over Dalton's wheezing body. "I am Death."

CHAPTER 105

It had been only a warning shot, and Parks's fall had been a gesture of submission, but the shock of the gunfire set Thomas's nerves ringing. He dropped into a crouch as another man emerged from the helicopter, and another came from a farther dark shape twenty yards down the beach that might have been a hut. Slowly Thomas withdrew, easing backward and crawling into the underbrush as the sound of raised voices drifted through the night: Parks sputtering surrender and at least two other men, their voices too low to be audible.

The woods had come to life again at the sound of the gunfire, monkeys and night birds screeching and cawing their outrage, so Thomas's plunge back into the trees excited no further calls of protest from above. He moved quickly, running down to where he had glimpsed the ruined hut: the perfect location for Kumi and Jim if they had been brought ashore. Parks's imbecilic business with the flashlight might be just the diversion he needed.

He ran flat out, then cut right, barely pausing to survey the situation, before sprinting out onto the sand, making directly for the thatched wooden shell that loomed before him. He reached it, panting. The door was bolted on the outside but there was no padlock. He flung it aside and kicked the door in.

Kumi and Jim looked up at him, both startled out of their sleep.

"Let's go," he said.

They scrambled to their feet.

"Where to?" said Kumi, as Thomas brought the knife across the plastic ties around her wrists.

"Just follow me," he said, and ran, back out across the beach and into the trees.

They had just made it, nestling briefly by a palm that bent almost to the ground, when a cry went up. The hunt had begun.

CHAPTER 106

Enrique Rodriguez tried to figure out what he had just seen. He had been lounging in his tent under the mosquito netting, cursing the damn heat and the damn jungle and this whole damn assignment, when he had looked up from his comic

book across the runway. The fourth plane was about to go up
after a lot of messing about, after which he could finally get
on with preparing the site for their return. Dalton, the duty officer, had come running from the control trailer, waving his
arms like a fool and yelling, and then someone had followed
him out: the nerdy kid they called "Specs."

Rodriguez had gone back to his reading, but then he had
looked up again, and Dalton was gone and the kid was crouched
with his back to him, rolling something into the tangle of underbrush behind the trailer. Rodriguez had stayed low as the
kid looked around, furtive-like, heading back into the trailer,
wiping his hand on the back of his pants.

Rodriguez was torn. He was comfy where he was, and anything to do with the kid annoyed him. Dalton annoyed him
too, in truth, always prying into what he was doing, complaining about his jewelry, threatening blood tests and God knew
what else because he didn't walk around like he had a pole up
his butt. Still, it was weird. One or both of them were up to
something and that meant there was something worth getting,
even if it was only knowledge. In a place like this, a little
knowledge could go a long way. He crawled out of his tent
and into the subdued lights of the runway.

He raised one hand as he crossed in front of the plane, and
one of the launch crew—Piloski, probably—waved and yelled
at him to get out of the way. Rodriguez flipped him the bird
and sauntered across. It's not like they were really ready to go
anyway.

He figured he'd check the trailer before he started poking
around in the jungle: make sure the kid was occupied. It was
narrow and windowless, accessed by a railed ramp. Rodriguez
tried the door, but it was locked, and that sure as hell wasn't
regulation. He stood there in the dark for a moment, thinking,
and then he heard shots from inside. He started loping back to
the runway waving like that idiot Dalton.

CHAPTER 107

Gunfire raked the trees. Somewhere in the canopy above them a coconut exploded and a cockatoo rose shrieking into the sky.

"A plan would be good," said Kumi.

"Run," said Thomas.

For a split second she stared at him, and then they were shooting again, and Thomas was sprinting into the trees, pulling Kumi behind him, Jim at her heels.

Thomas thought as he ran, plunging headlong along the sandy trail down which he had come with Parks. He checked his watch. They could make it back to the cove in perhaps twenty minutes. That would give them another hour or so before the sun came up.

"They're coming," shouted Jim.

And not just on foot. Through the screaming of the birds and monkeys, through the wild shooting and the roar of the blood rushing through his ears, Thomas could hear the helicopter powering up.

"This way," he said.

"Where are we going?" Kumi demanded. Her face had been slashed by a vine, but she didn't seem to have noticed.

"Just stay with me," he said.

They moved off the path then and into the yucca and stumps of palm so as not to leave tracks for their pursuers, though it was not the men on foot that Thomas was worried about. They had been running for five minutes, and he was sure the helicopter was up. Two more minutes and he heard its first pass overhead. It was low and the rotors scattered the heads of the palm trees this way and that like grass in a hurricane. They huddled down against the force of the wind, and then the darkness shrank to nothing and they were cowering in a daylight white as lightning.

The helicopter had a searchlight slung underneath.

A soldier appeared in a side hatch, the chopper's multibar-reled minigun trained down. Jim raised his hands in surrender. With an astonishing eruption of noise and rapid fire, the weapon opened up. Jim dropped to the ground, but the gunfire kept coming.

CHAPTER 108

The fourth drone was powering up, its rotor turning, the engine building to a sharp whine.

"Shut it down!" Rodriguez yelled.

"Can't," said Piloski. "The kid has overridden the manual controls. It's going up whether we like it or not."

"Fuck that shit," said Rodriguez. "Give me the damn machine gun."

Piloski stared at him. "Have you any idea what these things cost?" he said, gesturing to the plane that was starting to inch its way down the strip.

"Give me the damn gun!" yelled Rodriguez.

"You're crazy, man," said Piloski, raising his hands as if in surrender.

The plane was picking up speed fast. It was already a hundred yards away. Rodriguez lunged, grabbed the weapon, and spun, cocking it as he moved. He was barely stationary before the gun started belching fire, the sound drowning out the plane, and then he was running after it, still firing, his jaw set as the weapon shook and kicked in his arms. Nearing the end of the runway, the plane tipped upward into its climb. It was airborne. Rodriguez kept after it, emptying the magazine.

For a moment nothing seemed to happen, and then a plume of flame leaped up from the aircraft's nose. The drone seemed to stall, then rolled slightly like a wounded bird. The engine exploded and it spiraled down into the palms that clung to the seashore.

"Holy shit!" said Piloski, watching as the big Mexican came strolling back, the gun smoking in his hands. His face was black as thunder and, for a second, Piloski thought he might turn the weapon on him.

"Get him on the line," said Rodriguez.

Piloski didn't hesitate. He hailed the trailer and waited.

"Yes?" said the kid. His voice was low, spookily calm. Piloski nodded and Rodriguez grabbed the mike.

"Open the damn door," he said.

"They are all dead," said the kid with slow glee. "There's no one in here but me. This is my kingdom. My realm of death."

"We're coming in," said Rodriguez. "Open the door or we'll blow our way in."

"You can't stop them," said the kid. "The drones, I mean. They are programmed and the system is locked down. Even if you blew up the trailer you couldn't stop them now."

"Yeah?" said Rodriguez. "Well I guess that's what we'll have to do."

He hung up.

"That was a bluff, right?" said Piloski.

"We got a rocket launcher in stores?" said Rodriguez.

CHAPTER 109

Thomas didn't think. He tore his eyes from where Jim had gone down, snatched the flare pistol from his belt, aimed at the searchlight under the helicopter, and fired.

The flare left the gun with a dull *whup* and the smoke trail of a bottle rocket, and for a moment nothing happened, so that Thomas thought he had missed or fired a dud. He was patting his pockets for another flare to jam into the gun when the helicopter burst into a red and white light. The shot had gone straight into the hold where the soldier was sitting, and its phosphorescent explosion was like a grenade. The helicopter jerked in the air, its rotors scything through space as it kicked sideways, and then something blew inside, and the flare light was eclipsed by a burst of orange that became a fireball. The helicopter seemed to stall in the air, losing its shape as part of the tail was flung aside, and then it was falling.

Thomas rolled, flinging himself as far as he could as the wreckage crashed through the trees toward him. Then there was another explosion and for a second he couldn't think or feel and didn't know if he was untouched or dying. Then he was up again, pulling Jim to his feet, screaming at Kumi to follow. She moved fast, apparently unhurt, but Jim had been hit twice and by the savage light of the burning helicopter, Thomas could see that his eyes were flickering.

"Stay with me," he shouted. "Stay awake. Try to walk."

And shouldering a good deal of the priest's weight, he pressed on into the brush.

They moved slowly and Thomas was sure that it was only the chaos of the helicopter crash that had slowed their pursuers down. Without the chopper, they might even have decided to wait till dawn before continuing the hunt. That suited him just fine.

At the edge of the cove they settled in a grassy hollow. Jim lay back. He was still conscious, but only just. One bullet had gone through his left arm just above the elbow. The arm was probably broken, but it was the other bullet, which had gone through his shoulder, that worried Thomas. The exit wound was low under his arm, and God knew what damage it had done inside. He was struggling for breath and had probably taken some damage to his lungs. For all Thomas knew, he was dying.

He ran to the sub and retrieved the emergency kit. Kumi, who had always been better at such things, took it, applied antiseptic to the wounds, and bound them tight to stop the bleeding.

"I don't know what else to do," she said.

"This is good," Jim managed. "Thanks."

Kumi gave Thomas a look and her eyes were brimming.

"Sorry," said Thomas. "I thought if I got you out . . ."

"They would have killed us anyway," said Jim. "It was the right thing to do. I'm grateful."

"Now what?" said Kumi.

"How many guards are on the *Nara*?" said Thomas.

"None," she answered. "The crew are locked belowdecks. The captain is dead."

Thomas exhaled.

"So?" said Kumi. "Your plan?"

"I figure we use the sub," said Thomas.

"We can't all get in it," she said.

"Then leave me here," said Jim.

"We can all get in if one of us gets *on*," said Thomas.

"What do you mean?" said Kumi.

"I get in with Jim," said Thomas, bracing himself. "You sit astride it and we make for the *Nara*."

"And I'm supposed to breathe how?" she hissed.

"We'll only submerge enough to stay out of sight. A foot or two at most. You'll have your head above water."

"How come I get to sit on the outside?" she demanded.

"I know how to pilot the thing," said Thomas. "And Jim's blood will attract sharks."

There was a moment of silence broken by a snort. Jim was laughing.

"Now there," he said, his Irish brogue thickening suddenly, "is a sentence you don't hear everyday."

Kumi looked from him to Thomas.

"Okay," she said. "But we'd better be fast. It will be light soon."

Thomas was getting up, but then stopped.

"What about Parks?" he said.

Jim blew out his breath. "We can't get him out by ourselves," he said. "If we can get aboard the *Nara* and reach port, we can send the authorities. Our getting out of here is his best shot."

He sank back, exhausted from the exertion of speaking. Thomas nodded.

"Let's go," he said.

CHAPTER 110

The trailer was a smoking wreck. The rocket had blown right through the door and detonated inside, tearing a hole through the far wall and kicking up part of the roof, as if some drunken giant had taken a can opener to it. Rodriguez had entered shooting, taking no chances, but no one was alive inside.

The technicians had been stabbed or shot at their stations before he ever took the rocket launcher to the door, so only the kid had died in his assault. His body was sitting placidly in one of the office chairs, miraculously still balanced in place though the blast had taken half of his head away. A couple of the computers were still up and running, but Rodriguez and Piloski had not been able to get past the grinning death's-head screensaver Specs had apparently installed. Most of the equipment was irreparable, but there was still power running and some of the comm unit might be stirred back into life.

"Can you fix it?" said Rodriguez.

Piloski tore his eyes away from the kid and studied the smoking hardware.

"You sure screwed this good," he said.

"Can you fix it?" said Rodriguez.

"It'll take time, but yeah, I think so. The radio is dead, but we can wire through the satellite dishes."

"Do it," said Rodriguez.

There was no difference in rank between the two men, and Piloski had the neater record, but Rodriguez was in charge.

It took half an hour, Piloski working the cables and checking readings from his laptop while Rodriguez held the flashlight and checked his watch. Neither spoke. When it was done, Piloski merely said, "Let's give it a try," and clapped the headphones to his head. It took a further five minutes to isolate the band and raise HQ.

"Okay," he said, passing the headset to Rodriguez. "You're up."

Rodriguez gave his name and rank brusquely, cutting through all queries about why someone of his standing was using the comm system.

"We just launched three Predators," he said. "They are going to make one hell of a hole in the wrong place unless you can get them down."

He said it twice and then there was a long silence.

The drones had been up fifty-two, seventy-seven, and eighty-four minutes respectively. With haste, a Navy FA-18 from the aircraft carrier *CV-63 Kitty Hawk,* currently deployed in the Philippine Sea, might intercept the second Predator exactly twelve minutes before its scheduled beach strike, and the third twelve easy minutes later.

But the first drone, which had left the airbase twenty-five minutes before the others, was already out of range. They couldn't stop it.

CHAPTER 111

It was still dark, but only just. The horizon was brushed with pale pink, and though it made little difference under the water, Thomas was sure that they had only minutes before they would be visible from the shore. Jim was slouched in his seat beside him, barely conscious, fading in and out, but not losing any more blood and not getting obviously worse. Kumi floated above them like a mermaid on a dolphin's back, her jeans discarded, her belt lashed to the sub's camera array, her long, slender legs trailing out behind them. Twice she had pounded on the plastic canopy when he had inadvertently taken her too deep, but so long as the engines held out, they might just make it.

Thomas had kept the lights off because they were so close to the surface, so they were relying on sonar and on Kumi, whose head was just above the water. Now she patted the front and gestured boldly ahead; she had seen the *Nara*'s lights, and the boat lay directly in front. Thomas pushed the sub as hard as it would go, feeling the painful slowness of the vessel as they chugged out to sea, but hope had begun to blossom again. It was frail yet, but it was hope nonetheless.

Then Kumi was banging on the top, a frantic and urgent tattoo that sent Thomas pulling the sub up so that the top broke completely clear of the water. Before the sea had stopped running down the bubble, she was working the hatch mechanism. She flung it open and moved aside so that Thomas could stand and stare out into the gray light. He started to ask what the fuss was, since the boat was still a couple of hundred yards away, but he stopped.

A plane was coming in low: a flying boat with Japanese markings and no sign of weaponry. Thomas reached inside the sub, grabbed the flare gun, and handed it to Kumi, who, dripping from head to foot and now sitting astride the vessel, grinned. She took it, sighted, and fired. The sky overhead burst like the Fourth of July as the flare hung in place.

The plane circled back around, dropping like a gull skimming for fish. Thomas climbed out and held Kumi, all forgotten in the joy of rescue. Jim managed to stand, look out, and smile.

And then the flying boat was coming in to land, the spray kicking up around its floats so that the sub bobbled on the wake and Thomas had to hold on to keep his footing.

The aircraft came to rest between them and the *Nara* and, a moment later, the side hatch opened and a figure appeared, just visible as the sun finally pushed into the sky. A rope was thrown, and Thomas fastened it to a cleat on the submersible's bow with a practiced bowline. In minutes the plane was towing them.

But it was towing them back to shore.

"No!" Thomas shouted to the plane, waving his arms. "Take us to the boat! The beach isn't safe. I'll explain later."

The plane did not alter course, however, and as they continued to move forward, Kumi's smile stalled completely and she looked at Thomas with something like desperation.

"What are they doing?" she asked.

"Not the beach!" Thomas shouted again. They were close enough to touch the plane now so his yells sounded wild, out of control.

"I'm afraid we have to, Thomas," said the man in the plane's hatchway. His voice carried. A strong and comforting voice. A familiar voice. "We have things to discuss."

Thomas leaned forward and stared at the figure as the morning light finally reached his face. It was Senator Zacharias Devlin.

CHAPTER 112

Thomas stood on the beach, feeling the sleeplessness of the night suddenly weighing on him, making him somehow heavy and light at the same time, sleepy but full of nervous energy that turned his stomach. It wasn't just exhaustion, of course. It was also the surreal nature of the situation.

Kumi was holding his hand, a connection without romance or promise, and Jim was sitting bandaged in the sand. Ben Parks, his eye black from some previous encounter, was standing with him doing his best to look surly. Senator Devlin, dapper in a light linen suit, carried off with the air of a man incapable of looking effete, stood in front of them, smiling his practiced politician's smile. The flying boat's pilot stood to the side, shading his eyes, the flap of his sidearm unbuttoned, and Rod Hayes hovered formally behind like a butler, some kind of cell phone looped round his wrist. It was all oddly civilized, and Thomas had to fight a sense of embarrassment, as if the last few days had been some *Lord of the Flies* dream evaporating into irrelevance as normality asserted itself once more. Except, of course, that it had been no dream. The jungle was still smoking where the chopper had come down, and the meeting on the beach was being watched closely by soldiers and spies and killers.

Brad—the man they called War—was standing to his right, submachine gun cradled loosely in his hands. The woman he had known as Sister Roberta, unrecognizable now in shorts and tank top, was sitting by the torched bungalow, smoking, watching through impenetrable shades, a large automatic pistol trailing from one well-manicured hand. The two surviving soldiers, a lithe and clever-looking black man and a hard-faced guy with a shaved head who seemed to be the squad leader, stood with the sea at their backs, their weapons ready. For a long time, no one spoke.

The sun was still rising, color filtering slowly into the landscape. The sky was already blue, the sand pinkish white and the palms a vibrant green, but the sea that lapped around the lifeboat still seemed muddy.

"So," said Devlin at last. "Time to get a few things cleared up, I think."

Parks spat into the sand and Thomas saw that there was blood in his mouth. Everyone waited.

"I gotta be honest," said the senator, looking directly at Thomas. "I'm not really clear why we're here. Perhaps you can fill me in."

"I found what my brother was looking for," said Thomas. "The reason you killed him as you will now kill us."

Kumi gave him a sharp look, and the two soldiers exchanged glances. Devlin only smiled and shook his head.

"Ed Knight was my friend," he said. "We didn't see eye to eye on some things, but I respected him. I certainly didn't kill him."

"I'm sure you didn't pull the trigger or toss the grenade or whatever it was," said Thomas, "but you killed him sure enough. You didn't see eye to eye with him? Isn't that something of an understatement?"

"I don't think so," said Devlin.

"But you didn't want him on the school board, did you?" said Thomas. "You thought he'd be in your corner, being a priest and all. And then you started finding out what he really thought . . ."

"The evolution thing?" said Devlin. "Yes, I admit I was surprised. Even disappointed, and you're right that that was why I didn't put him on the school board. It wasn't about that issue per se. That subject is dead, at least for now. But I didn't want him sideswiping me on other issues down the line. So we agreed to disagree and I removed his nomination from the school board."

Parks snorted. "You're all the same," he said. "Liars and fools."

One of the soldiers tensed, his weapon shifting, but Devlin gave him a look and he stood down.

"You think you can change my mind by talking?" said Thomas, genuinely surprised. "After all this?"

Devlin shrugged. "What else am I going to do, Thomas?"

Hayes stepped forward and muttered into Devlin's ear, checking his watch as he did so, but Devlin shook his head and waved him away. Hayes stepped back and looked at the ground.

"I told you before," Devlin said to Thomas, "that I didn't believe your brother was a terrorist and I still think that. I still believe that you aren't a terrorist either, but this is a strange place for a U.S. citizen to be. I happen to know that the CIA has a secret airbase not two hundred miles from here that they use for antiterrorist surveillance. Strange place to find a Chicago high school teacher, wouldn't you say?"

"Not all terrorists are foreigners," said Parks. "We grow a pretty good variety right in the good old U.S. of A."

"And where would they be?" said Devlin, smiling indulgently.

Thomas nodded to the soldiers on either side of them.

"Right here," he said. "You're looking at them."

"These are counterterrorist agents," said Devlin, "yes?"

"Sir, yes, sir!" barked the black man.

"And those two?" said Thomas, gesturing in the direction of War and the woman.

Devlin looked to Hayes.

"Also counterterrorism agents," said Hayes. "Undercover operatives."

"That's bullshit," said Thomas, suddenly irritated. "They're killers, plain and simple, and have followed me across the damn world. Now can we cut the pretense? I'm tired and I don't want to listen to any more crap. Take us to our boat, or finish us off here."

There was another long pause and Devlin's face tightened, though whether with decision or confusion Thomas couldn't say. It took a moment to realize that he was staring past Thomas to the ocean, his eyes focused, and when he spoke it was slowly and with baffled alarm.

"Why is the water red?" he said.

Thomas turned and saw that he was right. The sea, which had been cloudy last night before the sun went down and had looked odd at dawn, was—now that the sun was properly up—clearly red, a vibrant scarlet that pinked at the shore and darkened to the rusty color of old blood as it deepened.

Parks had gotten to his feet.

"They'll come ashore," he said, breathless with the realization.

"What will?" said Devlin.

Once more Hayes stepped up out of the background, whis-

pering and tapping his watch still more urgently, and once
more Devlin waved him away.

"The fish," said Thomas, watching Devlin carefully. "The
ones my brother was looking for. The fish with legs like the
fossils found in Alaska. The missing link."

Devlin stared. "He found it?" he said.

"You know he found it!" Parks shouted. "That's why you
and your right-wing goons killed him. That's why you are going to kill us."

But Devlin looked utterly confused. He kept looking to
those around him, whether they were speaking or not, and his
gaze kept straying back to the red water lapping on the sand.

"Sir," said Hayes. "I think we have to leave this matter to
counterterrorism. We need to be getting back."

"No," said Devlin. "Something about this isn't right."

Thomas considered the big old man's thoughtful, anxious
eyes, and at last, he knew. He looked at Hayes, and suddenly
he saw it, the last pieces of the mosaic clicking into place so
that the picture shifted one last time and he knew.

"It's you, isn't it?" he said. "You are the one who's been
pulling the strings from the start. The trust-fund Republican.
A bit holier-than-thou, you said, senator, right?"

Devlin had turned slowly to face Hayes, his expression uncertain, expectant.

"Sir," said Hayes, ignoring Thomas. "We really need to go."

"Why?" said Thomas, defiant and genuinely curious,
though it was a curiosity touched with dread. "What is going
to happen?"

The tension of the moment was broken by a phone ringing.
The pilot of the flying boat took out what looked like an old-
fashioned walkie-talkie and spoke into it. The answering
voice boomed and crackled but was too indistinct for Thomas
to catch the words.

"Say again?" said the pilot.

The voice boomed back and the pilot's face fell.

"When? . . . This is nuts. Can't it be stopped?"

Again the staticky response, urgent, even shrill.

"Hold on," said the pilot. He lowered the handset and turned to the senator. "Sir, I'm sorry, but I'm getting a report of an incoming CIA strike on our present location. A missile-equipped aircraft is in the air. It has our present coordinates."

"Tell them to recall it," said Devlin, something of the confusion slipping away as he took control.

"Negative, sir," said the pilot. "The aircraft is a pilotless drone. It has been programmed to attack us here and the system hacked so that it cannot be recalled."

"How many?" said Hayes.

"There were four," said the pilot. "They were supposed to be on recon, but have been programmed to come here. One was destroyed on the ground, another two shot down by an F-18, but the first was too far ahead. They can't stop it."

"Let me speak to them," he demanded, reaching for the handset. As the pilot extended it toward him, Hayes snatched it, reached back, and flung it as far as he could into the crimson waves.

"What the hell . . . ?" exclaimed the pilot.

Hayes looked momentarily down at his own phone, pushed a button, and then, while everyone watched, snatched the pistol from the holster under his jacket. He shot the pilot twice in the chest and the man fell like a stone.

"Rod?" Devlin gasped, staring at his private secretary with horror.

Thomas stepped forward, but War and the woman were already moving in, guns raised. The two special forces troops looked panicked and unsure.

"Sir?" said the team leader, looking from Devlin to War.

"You're with me," said War, striding in, submachine gun level. "Pestilence! Over here."

Pestilence? thought Thomas.

"What is this?" said Devlin, still staring at Hayes. "What did you do?"

"None of your concern, sir," said Hayes. "Just do as you're told and you can walk away from this."

"Rod," said Devlin, "what are you doing? Is he right?" he said, nodding toward Thomas. "Is this about the *fish?*"

For a second Hayes just glanced at the ocean, and then he spoke softly with something like sadness.

"Faith is weak," said Hayes. "It has to be protected."

"From the truth?" said Devlin.

Kumi looked at Thomas, and he knew she felt as he did, out of it, forgotten.

"It would only confuse people," said Hayes. "And in that confusion would countless souls be lost."

"But murder for a Christian cause?" said Devlin, incredulous. "How could you think that was acceptable?"

"Sometimes the ends justify . . ."

"Are you crazy?" Devlin cut in. "All this intrigue and bloodshed over whether or not the Jesus fish on your bumper sticker has legs? This is insane. Blasphemous."

"The blasphemy is that scientists are given more credence than the Word of God!" Hayes exclaimed, his composure melting fast. " 'In the beginning God created the heaven and the earth,' " he exclaimed suddenly, intoning the words like a prophet. " 'And God said, Let the waters bring forth abundantly the moving creature that hath life, and fowl *that* may fly above the earth in the open firmament of heaven. And God created great whales, and every living creature that moveth, which the waters brought forth abundantly, after their kind, and every winged fowl after his kind: and God saw that *it was* good. And God blessed them, saying, Be fruitful, and multiply, and fill the waters in the seas, and let fowl multiply in the earth. And the evening and the morning were the fifth day.' "

There was a moment of silence. War's eyes were wide and bright. Pestilence smirked. Parks gaped with disdain. Everyone else looked uncertain, rattled by Hayes's conviction.

"That's the way it was, is, and will be," Hayes concluded. "No debate, no analysis, no literary criticism, no historical contextualization, except for the damned. The Word of the Lord is Truth and there shall be no second-guessing of it."

He smiled at their shocked silence and, with the toe of his polished wingtip, drew the two interlocking waves of the *ikthus* symbol in the sand at his feet. Everyone stared at it.

"I am the Seal-breaker," he said, "And this is the only fish we need to talk about."

"No," said Devlin, and his earlier confusion was quite gone now. The situation was clear to him and he had chosen his side. "Now, I can lend you some protection, but this will all have to come out. Put down the gun, Rod. This ends here."

There was a stillness, a moment of decision.

"Very well," said Hayes. He nodded to War, a small, almost casual gesture.

War's weapon coughed twice and the senator fell into the sand, clutching his chest.

There was a horrified pause, and Kumi put her hands to her face in horror and desolation. Hayes saw her and shook his head.

"Sometimes even the faithful make bad choices," he remarked.

No one really heard, because the lean, black soldier had swung his weapon round and pointed it into War's face.

"Sir!" he yelled. "Drop your weapon! Drop it or I will fire."

War, his smoking gun still trained on the fallen senator, hesitated.

"I am your commanding officer, Edwards," said War.

"No, sir, I don't believe you are," said the soldier. "This is not an antiterrorist operation. I believe we have been misled, sir."

"Your job is to follow orders, Edwards," said Hayes, "not to question them."

"I don't believe you have a part in the legitimate chain of command, sir," said Edwards, still staring down the barrel of his weapon at War, gripping it so that the muscles of his arms flexed and tautened and sweat broke out on his face. "You are a civilian," he said to Hayes, his eyes still on War, "and have no authority here."

"Edwards?" said War carefully. "Lower your weapon."

"Sir, no, sir," said Edwards. "This is not a counterterrorist operation." Then, his voice lower, and his gaze flitting from War to the team leader, who had been watching in tense silence, he added. "Did you know? Sir? Did you know?"

The soldier hesitated, his hard face and harder eyes giving nothing away.

"You did," said Edwards. "You said this was counterterrorist Black Ops. It wasn't. It wasn't even national security. So what was it?"

"Hey," said the team leader, a crooked smiling snapping across his face. "We all have a living to make."

And then the gunfire started.

Thomas dropped to the sand, pulling Kumi down with him. The team leader went down first, hit twice in the head, but as Edwards brought his weapon around to War, he seemed to sag and his face aged suddenly, freezing in position for a moment before he fell face first into the sand. Behind him, Pestilence, the woman Thomas knew as Roberta, was on one knee, her pistol smoking. Then Parks was snatching the diver's knife from Thomas's belt and lunging at her with a roar of fury.

War aimed at Parks and Thomas swung one foot around, cutting his legs from under him. He fell as his machine gun rattled a handful of slugs wildly into the air and Thomas pounced, grabbing madly at the hot metal of the gun, fighting him for control.

For the next ten seconds Thomas knew only a haze of desperate fury and the sure knowledge that he would be dead in a matter of moments, as somehow he rolled onto his back with War on top of him. He heard Roberta scream with pain and anger, he heard more gunfire, and then the man who called himself War, the man who had tailed him from Naples and shot at him in Bari, had his gun across his throat. War pushed with both hands and Thomas felt his breath tightening to nothing. War and Pestilence. The absurdity of this hired thug masquerading as one of the horsemen of the apocalypse, the sheer, unironic, pompous stupidity of the thing filled him with a sudden rage that had been building since he first heard that his brother was dead. He kicked and punched and clawed with an animal fury, but War held on.

Thomas never saw Kumi's approach, and War realized she was there only a second before the kick. He turned into it and her foot broke his nose, snapping his head back and allowing Thomas to thrust him off, machine gun in hand. He rolled into a crouch and took a second to assess the situation.

Roberta lay face up in the sand, Parks's knife sticking out of her chest, her eyes open but sightless. Parks was slumped across her, two bullet holes in his back. War was down and holding his face, Devlin and the two soldiers were already dead, Jim was probably dying. Only Kumi and Hayes were still standing, and he had her in the sights of his revolver. She hadn't seen him . . .

"Stop!" shouted Thomas. "Kumi!"

She turned impossibly slowly and her eyes widened at the sight of the gun's dark eye, but Hayes didn't shoot.

"Kick the gun over to me," he said.

Thomas did so. Hayes picked it up without taking his eyes—or his gun—off Kumi. For a long moment, nothing happened. After the gunfire, the shouting, the fierceness of the struggle, it felt like being thrust into a vacuum.

"Okay," said Hayes, "now we wait patiently."

"For what?" said Thomas, his breath still coming in urgent gasps, his nerves singing with adrenaline despite the stillness.

"For the Wrath of God," said Hayes with a quick smile. "That's the name of the aircraft. A wonderful thing, technology."

"Hold it," said War, looking up, his face blood streaked. "We wait? Why don't we just take the plane and go? Leave them here."

"Come on now, Steve." Hayes smiled at War. "You know better than that. This was never going to be a round-trip mission. You ensured that by failing to get them before they left Japan. The moment we all had to come here was the moment it became clear that none of us would leave."

"Steve," said Thomas, liking the smallness of the name,

the ordinariness. "The rider on the red horse is called Steve. That's great."

"That's all you people have to offer, isn't it?" said Hayes. "Irony. Relativism. An anchorless moral universe without God or principle."

"How is silencing the truth and killing those who disagree with you principle?" said Thomas. Kumi gave him a warning look but it didn't matter. They were all going to die anyway. He would not die in silence.

"How convenient it must be," said Thomas, "to always assume you have the moral high ground. You're a terrorist, Hayes, you know that? Nothing more. And as with most terrorists, I'll put my morality over yours any day."

"Faith must be protected," said Hayes. "Faith is all."

"No," said Jim. His voice was low, struggling. "Love is all. Without that you are just . . ."

"A gong booming or a cymbal crashing?" said Hayes, bitterly amused, training his weapon on the priest. "You people have nothing to offer." He looked hard at Thomas. "You believe in nothing so you have no strength to stand against those who do."

"Sir," said War, insistent, "I still think we can get out of here. I mean, I have a family, a son . . ."

Hayes aimed and fired once. The bullet went through the other man's head just above the right eye. War, or Brad, or—most pathetically perhaps—Steve, was dead before his body hit the ground.

"I thought you were with me all the way," said Hayes to the corpse. "I have no room for the self-interested."

"You're a crusader," said Jim quietly.

"That's right," said Hayes. "I am."

"Some sort of history lesson seems in order," said Jim, with a wry smile. "The Crusades were, after all, exercises in military barbarism and their goals had no place in religion."

"More watered-down relativism masquerading as Christianity," said Hayes with abject scorn. "You are as bad as Knight was."

"Thank you," said Jim, wearily. "Ed lived for truth and justice. I'm honored to be compared to him. So, you want to tell us about this plane that is going to take us all off to the fires of Hell reserved for liberals and relativists?"

Hayes blinked, apparently confused by Jim's composure, and then his former smile returned.

"See this?" he said, raising his left hand and showing the phonelike device dangling from his wrist. "It's a GPS navigation system that the drone uses as a targeting beacon. But here's the neat part. It's attached to a pulse monitor. If the drone loses my pulse, the Wrath of God is programmed to relock on the coordinates of your boat over there. How many crew are still on board? Twenty? More? I would have gotten them all if all four aircraft had made it, but someone has obviously meddled and now my one strike aircraft will have to make a choice of target. It's unfortunate, but one is more than enough."

Kumi shifted, her eyes lowered.

"So if I die before the Wrath of God arrives," Hayes continued, "so do the crew of the *Nara*. It's a moot point, of course, but I thought I'd mention it in case you had any more tricks up your sleeve. I have to say, you've been most tiresome, but it's nice to know that you'll die before me. Now, who first?"

And so saying, he holstered the pistol and swung the machine gun around to fire.

CHAPTER 113

Thomas and Kumi huddled together beside Jim, as Hayes prowled around toward the shore, his eyes on them, a lion selecting a young or wounded gazelle from the pack.

"God," Jim whispered.

Thomas took it for a prayer, but something in the tension of Kumi's grip opened his eyes. The water, the eerily red water that Thomas had first seen on the Paestum grave painting, was stirring, but not with waves. There were creatures in the surf behind Hayes, and they were coming ashore.

It's the red tide. They've come to feed.

Instinctively he took a step backward, and Kumi moved with him. Jim struggled to his feet and followed suit.

"Where do you think you're going?" said Hayes, and his coolness was now underscored by a certain pleasure that might have been righteousness. He cocked the machine gun and aimed.

"You say I believe in nothing," said Thomas suddenly, his eyes meeting Hayes's and holding them. "But that isn't true. I believe in complexity and intellect, in reason and tolerance. I believe in the spirit and in matter, and I believe that all these things are the gifts of a God who does not want faith over thought, or moralism over compassion. I believe, as my brother did, that God's creation is ongoing, evolving, according to the laws of a universe He devised."

Hayes stared at him, the weapon level, arrested by what he had heard, somehow unaware of the way they shrank away from him and from the shore at his back. Then he sneered, and his finger began to tighten on the trigger till something in their faces stopped him and he half turned.

The first creature out of the waves was eight feet long and a quarter of that was jaws. The second was bigger. It was the third that took him down.

Hayes sensed the movement and swung the gun behind him, opening fire, but they were all around him, and by the time one of them was whipping back and forth in its death agony, another had already lunged with its great crocodile maw, a surprisingly high and powerful strike driven by the tail, that brought it up as high as Hayes's chest. It seized him around the middle and slammed him into the sand. The second then grabbed his foot as he writhed and screamed and kicked, dragging him back into the bloody water. A fourth went for his throat, and with one last gurgling cry, he went quiet.

"The GPS marker!" shouted Kumi.

Thomas started forward, snatching for the gun as the fishapods lashed around his ankles.

One of the creatures had clamped hold of Hayes's left arm. With a lurching stride and swish of its muscular tail, the beast pushed back into the water and began to spin. The arm tore from its socket. Then another of the fish lurched into the fray, tugging at the severed limb. The first attacker adjusted its grip and pulled, and the hand came away with part of the forearm. Thomas reached into the scarlet foam, grabbed the freed GPS unit, and hopped away as one of the creatures wheeled and snapped at him, getting enough height to seize him by the shoulder.

Thomas fell back, clutching the transmitter, scrambling crablike up the beach.

"Now what?" he said.

"The drone will hit the *Nara*," said Kumi, "and we have no way of warning them."

"Give me that," said Jim, seizing the GPS unit with its pulse monitor. "How long do you think it has to be off before the plane recalculates its target?"

"I would have thought it was instantaneous," said Thomas, still watching the swirling mass of primitive creatures as they tore at Hayes's corpse.

"No," said Kumi. "Pulse is erratic. The system must accommodate irregularity and momentary disconnection. Why?"

Jim looked up and grinned, waggling one hand. He had fastened the pulse monitor to his own wrist.

"Even if that works," said Thomas. "How does it help? It just means that we are the target again instead of the boat."

"Me," said Jim. "You can still go. Take the lifeboat and make for the *Nara*. Now."

Thomas stared at him. "You're kidding," he said. "I'm not leaving you now."

"I probably wouldn't make it anyway," said Jim, considering his bandages. "This way at least I die with purpose."

Thomas just looked at him. Around them the wind pulsed and the trees beyond the beach swayed, sighing.

"No way," said Thomas. "Kumi. Say something . . . Kumi?"

But Kumi was crying, stooping to Jim, embracing him, clinging to him.

"See," said Jim to Thomas. "She gets it. Why are you always the last to figure things out?"

"This is crazy," Thomas roared.

"No," said Jim. "It's self-sacrifice. Not the same thing. Greater love hath no man than to lay down his life for his friends. Remember?"

"No," said Thomas, defiant still. "That's nuts. I won't let you."

"Are you my friends?" said Jim.

Kumi sobbed and hugged him tighter. Thomas stood quite still for a second and then nodded once.

"Well, then," said Jim, smiling, "you'd better go. And Thomas?"

"Yes, Jim?"

"Did you believe what you said to Hayes just now, about spirit and matter and compassion? Did you believe that or was it just a way of keeping his attention off the sea?"

For a moment Thomas just stood there, barely able to remember what had just happened, what he had just said.

"Both," he said. "I think."

Jim smiled and nodded thoughtfully. "Good enough," he said.

Thomas was still rooted to the spot. "I . . . I'm sorry I doubted you," he said, his voice binding in his throat.

"Doubt is integral to faith," said Jim. "Without it . . ."

He shrugged and opened his hands.

Nothing.

But . . ." Thomas tried.

"Go," said Jim, more urgent this time. "Now. Or it's all a waste."

Thomas reached a hand for Kumi's shoulder, but she shrugged him off, sobbing louder than ever.

"It's okay," said Jim, whispering into her ear. "Better this way. Clear, you know?"

And finally, she released him. Thomas led her away, half-blinded by his own tears as they ran across the beach to the lifeboat.

Jim watched them all the way to the boat and then looked back to the GPS unit on his wrist. There was a green blinking light that, he hoped, meant that the switch had not been detected. He was tired and in pain, but he couldn't quite shake the sadness of leaving the world. He recalled Christ in Gethsamane, waiting to be arrested, and praying, *"Father, if this cup might pass from me . . . But Your will be done."*

He considered the beach, the palms, the soft, refreshing morning breeze that had carried the voice of God to Elijah.

There were worse places to die.

Amazingly, the *ikthus* fish that Hayes had drawn in the sand had survived the chaos of the final battle. Jim reached over and, watching the beasts at the shoreline, drew two sets of legs beneath it. He considered the image, thinking of Ed, and added a cross for an eye.

Jim watched Thomas and Kumi driving the rowboat away from the shore, unmolested by the strange creatures on the beach, and raised his eyes to the horizon. Almost beyond the range of sight a slender aircraft with a bulbous nose and long, fragile wings was descending. It closed fast, and he watched its course, bearing in mind the *Nara* with its crew and the rowboat with his friends, holding his breath, waiting for the switch in approach that never came. It flew with purpose, gracefully, less like a hawk than a dove, swooping.

He gathered himself to his knees, wincing at the pain in his side and prayed in the words of the *De Profundis:* "Out of the depths I cry to you, O Lord, Lord, hear my voice. O let your ears be attentive to the voice of my pleading . . ."

The plane seemed to accelerate as it closed, dropping still further. Then came a flare of light from the pylons beneath its wings, and smoke billowed from the rockets as they sped toward him.

". . . Because with the Lord there is mercy and fullness of redemption," said Jim, eyes closed, as the missiles rained down around him.

EPILOGUE: *DE PROFUNDIS*

1. Two days later

Thomas gazed out over Manila Bay from his room on Roxas Boulevard and waited for a voice on the other end of the line. He was tired, despite fourteen hours of sleep, but he was clean and a good deal of what had been weighing on him since they reached the *Nara* had lifted.

"The Druid Hills Museum, can I help you?"

"Deborah?" said Thomas.

"This is Tonya, can I help you?"

"I was hoping to speak to Miss Miller," said Thomas. "This is Thomas Knight. I'm phoning from the American embassy in the Philippines . . ."

"Hold on."

Deborah was on the line in less than thirty seconds.

"Thomas?" she said.

"Yes," he said.

"I saw it all on the news," she said. "I'm so sorry. I tried but . . ."

"You saved my life," said Thomas, "and a lot of other people as well."

"If we'd been faster," said Deborah "we might have stopped the planes."

"And if you had failed to stop any, I would be dead and so would everyone on the *Nara.*"

"But your friend . . ."

"Died with dignity and purpose," said Thomas with force.

She was silent then, and for a moment he did not know what to say.

"There's a lot of interest in the fish," she said, grasping for something. "They said none survived the bombing, but there are scientists already demanding the release of the remains."

"It would be ironic if they were the last of their kind," said Thomas. "But who knows? Maybe there are other populations in the area, or elsewhere."

"The papers say Devlin's wife will take his seat until his term expires."

"I should write to her," said Thomas. "Or try to visit her in Chicago. Her husband and I agreed on almost nothing, but I think he was a man of principle and integrity. I wish I had realized that before he died."

"Death is like that," she said. "It changes the way you see life."

He nodded and smiled, knowing she couldn't see, knowing she understood.

"They have Ed's remains here," he said. "Just bones, of course, but I'm glad they have them."

"When do you come back to the States?" she asked.

"Soon. A couple more things to do before I get back."

"I hear your school is offering to rehire you," said Deborah. "You're quite the hero."

"Well," said Thomas, "we'll see about that. I have a gift for falling off pedestals. But, I don't know . . ." His smile stalled. He caught a fleeting recollection of Jim on the beach. "Maybe this time will be different," he said. He drained his glass of Bushmills, savoring it, and did not pour a second.

2. One week later

Tetsuya Matsuhashi sealed the package and handed it to the customs clerk, who smiled and bobbed her head in that pleased and embarrassed way that said his celebrity status hadn't completely faded. He took the train into Tokyo, thinking vaguely about visiting Watanabe before his trial, wondering what he would say to his former mentor. He reread Thomas's letter of thanks for his sending the satellite data to

Deborah and for his recent dealings with the American and Japanese officials who had been falling over themselves to figure out what in the name of God had been going on. And, of course, for his standing up to his *sensei:* an act that could have cost him his career.

Thomas had wished him well for his upcoming doctoral defense, but in truth it seemed unlikely that his school would deny him even if they were skeptical of his work. Great things were being planned for him. All he had to do now was be worthy of them. It was a significant pressure, but he had learned a great deal about himself in the wake of the Watanabe business, and he felt quietly confident in ways he never would have done before. Matsuhashi felt that he should be thanking Thomas, not the other way around.

Perhaps that was what he would tell Watanabe. He might understand. He might even respect him for it. Matsuhashi stared out the window and into the rain, and he smiled a little, for the first time in what felt like a very long time.

3. Two weeks later

It was cool in the Fontanelle, and though still dim there were ventilation shafts—like the one Thomas had entered that night so long ago—that allowed a green and dusty light to filter softly through the corridors of stacked bones.

"Here?" said Father Giovanni.

Thomas nodded and laid the box on the stone floor. It had arrived from Japan that morning, covered in official tape. He opened it carefully, reverentially, sitting back to reveal the contents. Giovanni lit a candle and set it on the low shelf as Thomas took the skulls from the box and carefully set each of them on the stack.

"This is all of them?" said Giovanni.

"All we could find," said Thomas. "These are the oldest, the ones Watanabe buried in the site. These others," he added, "are the more recent ones he couldn't use."

There was one skull left in the box. By comparison it looked bright, clean: new.

Giovanni looked at it. "You are sure you want to do this?" he said.

"No," said Thomas, honestly. "But I think it's what Ed would have wanted."

The two men looked in silence at the skull.

"I used to be afraid of this place," said Giovanni. "It seemed to me morbid. Horrific. Then when I first came here after Pietro's death it felt merely sad. But after a time . . . I don't know. I started to feel that the dead here were like family, that I was to look after them as I would an old aunt whom I didn't know well but who was too sick to take care of herself. Is that crazy?"

"Probably," said Thomas, smiling. "But I think I understand."

"Anyway," said Giovanni. "Now I am not afraid of the place and it does not make me sad. There is a purity to it, a clarity. It helps to keep things . . . what? The right size?"

"In perspective," said Thomas. "Yes."

"You don't mind that Eduardo will have no gravestone?"

"I do, but he spent most of his life working with the poor, the people whose names no one remembers. I think he would prefer to lie with them in death."

"And this is not him," said Giovanni. "Only the remains of his earthly body. Eduardo is long gone."

"Yes," said Thomas, his eyes prickling at the thought, and of the thought of Jim, his friend, who had given his life that Thomas might live.

A good man, he thought, remembering what Jim had said about Ed.

Yes. Both of them.

"Are you ready?" said Giovanni.

Thomas wanted to speak, but the words would not come. Kumi stepped forward, took his hand, and said, for both of them, "Yes."

Then Giovanni crossed himself and, in the words of the

Italian mass that he knew so well and so dearly, he began the funeral service for Ed, for Jim, for Senator Zacharias Devlin, for Ben Parks, even for Hayes, for those misguided souls who followed him, and for the nameless dead who lay around them.

AFTERWORD
AND ACKNOWLEDGMENTS

On the Fifth Day is, of course, a work of fiction, though elements of the story are rooted in fact, and I thought it might be of interest to readers to know what some of those elements are.

The fish at the core of the story is my own invention, but the story's use of the "living fossil" fish, the coelacanth, and the details of the recently discovered *Tiktaalik roseae* are all as factually accurate as I could make them. I stand indebted to Peter Forey (formerly of the Natural History Museum, London) and to Susan Jewett (of the Smithsonian Institution), and feel obligated to point out that the much discussed "Florida scale" supposedly sent to the Smithsonian in 1949 is almost certainly a myth. Silver votive fish like the one in the novel do exist, however, and their origin continues to be debated.

The locations in which the story takes place and the artifacts associated with them are all real, with a few small exceptions. Pompeii does indeed contain a "magic square" of disputed significance, and Herculaneum's House of the Bicentenary does have a shadow "crucifix" on the wall of an upper room. No cross matching that shadow has ever been discovered, and most archaeologists of early Christianity would agree with Deborah that the crucifix did not become a core element of Christianity until considerably later. The strange fish images found throughout the ancient sites I present in the book are all real (and you can see some of them on my website), though the idea that they refer to some hitherto unknown species is purely my own imaginative whimsy. The description of Paestum is accurate with the exception of the second diver grave, which I invented.

The Fontanelle cemetery is real, and though it is currently closed to the public, there are plans to reopen it soon. I am especially grateful to Claudio Savarese and Fulvio Salvi of Naples Underground for showing me around during a recent visit, and to Larry Ray for fielding some questions thereafter. Again, I will be posting images from the Fontanelle and other locations from the book on my website. The Captain legend does come from Fontanelle lore, as does the belief that the cemetery has housed local Mafia meetings. The legend of the crocodile in the passages beneath the Castello Nuovo is also authentic, though such stories accrue around lots of places.

Having lived a couple of years in Japan and visited several times since, much of the data on which I based those parts of the book came from memory, though I'm grateful to Masako Osako for her willingness to supply information where I was either forgetful or just wrong.

I am indebted to C. Loring Brace of the University of Michigan's Museum of Anthropology for his advice on dating and the racial classification of bones; to Janet Levy of the University of North Carolina, Charlotte, for her help on the archaeological uses of pollen; and to C. T. Keally for all manner of help concerning Japanese archaeology, recent scandals therein, and how I might perpetrate a fictional one of my own. Thanks also to my brother, Chris, for his help on issues of satellite monitoring.

My sense of Catholicism is derived largely from my own experience, though I have been fortunate enough to speak candidly to several priests in preparing the book. My thanks especially to my old friend Father Edward Gannon and to Reverend Philip Shano, S.J. Another old friend, Jonathan Mulrooney, introduced me to the extraordinary writings of Father Teilhard de Chardin, for which I am deeply grateful.

I intend to post images, links, and other information relevant to these subjects on my website (www.ajhartley.net), through which I can also be reached, if readers have comments or questions.

As ever, a book like this gets a lot of input along the way, and I would like to especially acknowledge those who saw early drafts and assisted in making the book what it is, particularly my wife, Finie; my parents, Frank and Annette; my brother, Chris; and my friends Edward Hurst, Ruth Morse, and Bob Croghan. Special thanks also to my agent, Stacey Glick, and my editor, Natalee Rosenstein, without whom none of this would be possible.

—A. J. Hartley (November 2006)

A RIVETING THRILLER FROM

A. J. HARTLEY

THE MASK OF ATREUS

"An exhilarating thriller
rooted in the dark side of history."
—Jeff Long, bestselling author of *The Wall*

"Move over Michael Crichton—
A. J. Hartley is right at your heels."
—J. A. Konrath, author of *Whiskey Sour*

Available wherever books are sold or at penguin.com

Don't miss the page-turning suspense, intriguing characters, and unstoppable action that keep readers coming back for more from these bestselling authors...

Tom Clancy
Robin Cook
Patricia Cornwell
Clive Cussler
Dean Koontz
J.D. Robb
John Sandford

Your favorite thrillers and suspense novels come from Berkley.